**Under the northernmost of Oldgate's four bridges,
a girl sits, listening to the water.**

She has a round face, gently curling hair, and a knife held in her fist. She is waiting for a meeting that she dreads as much as she longs for it.

Her name is Alys.

AGE
OF
ASH

AGE
OF
ASH

BOOK ONE OF
THE KITHAMAR TRILOGY

DANIEL
ABRAHAM

orbitbooks.net

Copyright © 2022 by Daniel Abraham
Excerpt from *Blade of Dream* copyright © 2023 by Daniel Abraham
Excerpt from *The Lost War* copyright © 2019 by King Lot Publishing Ltd.

Cover design by Lauren Panepinto
Cover illustration by Daniel Dociu
Cover copyright © 2022 by Hachette Book Group, Inc.
Map by Jayné Franck
Author photograph by Kyle Zimmerman

Hachette Book Group supports the right to free expression and the value of copyright. The purpose of copyright is to encourage writers and artists to produce the creative works that enrich our culture.

The scanning, uploading, and distribution of this book without permission is a theft of the author's intellectual property. If you would like permission to use material from the book (other than for review purposes), please contact permissions@hbgusa.com. Thank you for your support of the author's rights.

Orbit
Hachette Book Group
1290 Avenue of the Americas
New York, NY 10104
orbitbooks.net

First Paperback Edition: February 2023
Originally published in hardcover and ebook by Orbit in February 2022

Orbit is an imprint of Hachette Book Group.
The Orbit name and logo are trademarks of Little, Brown Book Group Limited.

The publisher is not responsible for websites (or their content) that are not owned by the publisher.

The Hachette Speakers Bureau provides a wide range of authors for speaking events. To find out more, go to hachettespeakersbureau.com or email HachetteSpeakers@hbgusa.com.

Orbit books may be purchased in bulk for business, educational, or promotional use. For information, please contact your local bookseller or the Hachette Book Group Special Markets Department at special.markets@hbgusa.com.

The Library of Congress has cataloged the hardcover edition as follows:
Names: Abraham, Daniel, author.
Title: Age of ash / Daniel Abraham.
Description: First edition. | New York : Orbit, 2022. | Series: The Kithamar trilogy book 1
Identifiers: LCCN 2021030651 | ISBN 9780316421843 (hardcover) | ISBN 9780316421874 (ebook) | ISBN 9780316591683
Subjects: GSAFD: Fantasy fiction.
Classification: LCC PS3601.B677 A72 2022 | DDC 813/. 6—dc23
LC record available at https://lccn.loc.gov/2021030651

ISBNs: 9780316421850 (trade paperback), 9780316421874 (ebook)

Printed in the United States of America

LSC-C

Printing 1, 2022

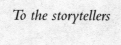

To the storytellers

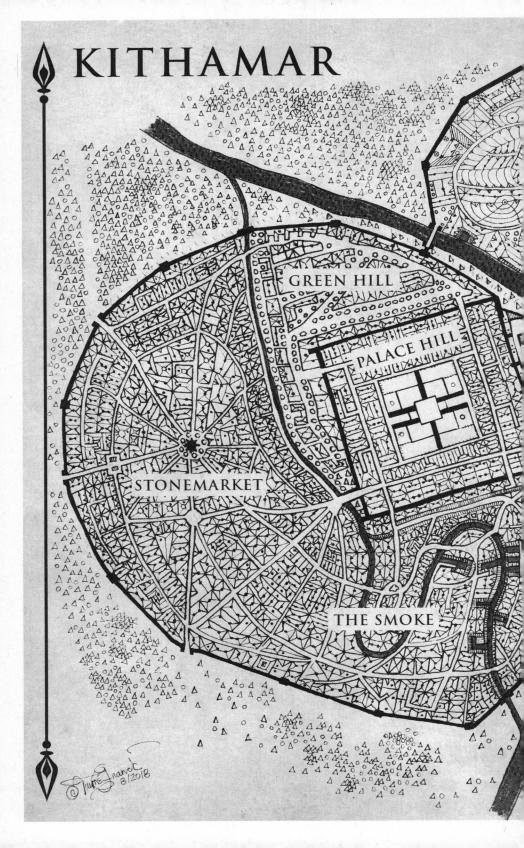

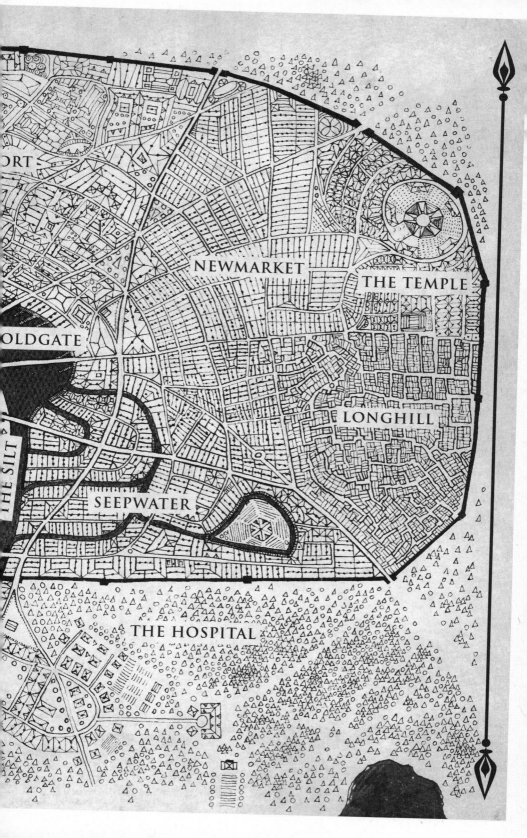

AGE
OF
ASH

In the course of a single life, a man can be many things: a beloved child in a brightly embroidered gown, a street tough with a band of knifemen walking at his side, lover to a beautiful girl, husband to an honest woman, father to a child, grain sweeper in a brewery, widower, musician, and mendicant coughing his lungs up outside the city walls. The only thing they have in common is that they are the same man.

These are the mysteries, and there is a beauty in them. In this way, Kithamar is a beautiful city.

All through its streets, Kithamar shows the signs and remnants of the cities that the city has been. Walls that defended the border of a younger town stand a dumbfounded, useless guard between the noble compounds of Green Hill and the fountain square at Stonemarket. The great battlements of Oldgate glower out over the river, its arrow-slits and murder holes used for candle niches now, and the enemy races who stormed or manned it sleep side by side in its armories because the rents are cheap. The six-bridged Khahon was the border between a great

Hansch kingdom and savage near-nomad Inlisc to hear it one way, or the first place that the frightened, violent, sharp-faced Hansch had come from the west if you told the story from the other bank. Now the river is the heart of the city, dividing and uniting it.

The ancient races killed one another and swore eternal hatred, only to bury their enmity and pretend to be a single people, citizens of one city. Kithamar has declared itself the subject of the one true god. Or the three. Or the numberless. For three hundred years and longer, it has been a free city, independent and proud and ruled by princes of its own rather than any distant king.

Only today, its prince is dead.

The reign of Byrn a Sal had been brief.

Less than a year before, the streets had filled with revelers and wine, music and joy, and more than a little imprudent sex to celebrate the great man's coronation. The months between then and now were turbulent, marked by ill omens and violence. A winter of troubled sleep.

Now, as the first light of the coming dawn touches the highest reaches of the palace towering at the top of its hill, the red gates open on his funeral procession. Two old women dressed in rags step out and strike drums. Black, blindered horses follow, their steps echoing against the stone. And all along the route, the men and women and children who are Kithamar wait.

They have been there since nightfall, some of them. They love the spectacle of death and the performance of grief. And, though few of them say the words aloud, they hope that the season of darkness will end and something new begin. Only a few of them ask their questions aloud: How did it happen? Was it illness or accident, murder or the vengeance of God?

How did Byrn a Sal die?

The black lacquered cart passes among the gardens and mansions of Green Hill. The heads of the high families stand at their entrances as if ready to make the dead man welcome if he should stand up. Servants and children and ill-dignified cousins gawk from the bushes and corners. Only the burned-out shell of the Daris Brotherhood ignores the funeral. And then the body passes into the city proper, heading first for Stonemarket and then south through the soot-dark streets of the Smoke.

Those lucky enough to have buildings along the route have rented space at their windows and on their roofs. As the death cart shifts and judders across the cobblestones, people jockey to look at the corpse: a little less than six feet of iron-stinking clay that had been a man. Behind the cart follow the highest dignified of the city.

The dead man's daughter—soon prince herself—Elaine a Sal, rides behind her father in a dark litter. She wears rags, but also a silver torc. Her chin is lifted, and her face is expressionless. The eyes of the city drink her in, trying to find some sign in the angle of her spine or the dryness of her eyes to tell whether she's a girl hardly old enough to be called woman drowning in shock and despair, or else a murderess and patricide struggling to contain her triumph.

Either way, she will rule the city tomorrow, and all these same people will dance at her coronation.

Behind her, the favored of the old prince walk. Mikah Ell, the palace historian, in an ash-streaked robe. Old Karsen's son, Halev, who had been Byrn a Sal's confidant and advisor. Samal Kint, the head of the palace guard, carrying a blunted sword. Then more, all wearing grey, all with ashes on their hands. When they reach the bridge at the edge of the Smoke—yellow stone and black mortar—they stop. A priest walks out to meet them, chanting and shaking a censer of sweet incense. They perform the rites of protection to keep the river from washing away the dead man's soul. Everyone knows that water is hungry.

The rite complete, the funeral procession passes through the wider streets of Seepwater, past the brewers' houses and canals where the flatboats stand bow to stern, so thick that a girl could have walked from one side of the canal to the other and not gotten her hem wet. Midday comes, the early summer sun making its arc more slowly than it did a few weeks before, and the cart is only just turning northeast to make its way along the dividing line between Riverport and Newmarket. Flies as fat as thumbnails buzz around the cart, and the horses slap at them with their tails. Wherever the funeral procession is, the crowd thickens, only to evaporate when it has passed. Once the last of the honor guard rounds the corner, leaving Seepwater behind, the brewers' houses reopen, the iron grates on their sides start accepting wagers again. Delivery men spin barrels down the streets on their edges with the practiced skill of jugglers.

It is almost sunset before the funeral procession reaches the Temple. The bloody western skyline is interrupted by the black hill of the palace. The colored windows of the Temple glow. Full dark takes the streets like spilling ink before the last song echoes in the heights above the great altar and the body of Byrn a Sal, purified by the mourning of his subjects and the prayers of his priesthood, comes out to the pyre. His daughter should light the oil-stinking wood, but she stays still until young Karsen, her father's friend, comes and takes the torch from her hand.

The term for the night between the funeral of the old prince and the coronation of the new one is *gautanna*. It is an ancient Inlisc word that means, roughly, the pause at the top of a breath when the lungs are most full. Literally, it translates as *the moment of hollowness.*

For one night, Kithamar is a city between worlds and between ages. It falls out of its own history, at once the end of something and the beginning of something else. The skeptical among the citizens—and Kithamar has more than its share of the amiably godless—call it tradition and merely a story that says something about the character of the city, its hopes and aspirations, the fears and uncertainties that come in moments of change. That may be true, but there is something profound and eerie about the streets. The rush of the river seems to have words in it. The small magics of Kithamar go as quiet as mice scenting a cat. The clatter of horseshoes against stone echoes differently. The city guard in their blue cloaks make their rounds quietly, or decide that for one night they might as well not make them at all.

Outside the city, the southern track where by daylight teams of oxen haul boats against the current is quiet and deserted apart from one lone, bearded man. He sits at the base of a white birch, his back against the bark. The small glass bead in his hand would be red if there were light enough to see it.

In a thin-walled bedroom above a tailor's shop in Riverport, a young man lies alone on a mattress. His right hand is bandaged, and the wound beneath the cloth throbs. He watches the moon rise over the rooftops, listening with his heart in his throat for footsteps on the creaking floorboards outside his door.

Under the northernmost of Oldgate's four bridges, a girl sits, listening to the water. She has a round face, gently curling hair, and a knife held in her fist. She is waiting for a meeting that she dreads as much as she longs for it.

Her name is Alys.

PART ONE

HARVEST

Kithamar is an unforgiving city. The common wisdom states that it was founded on hatred, but this is a misunderstanding. In truth, it was founded on hunger, and there are many kinds of hunger at its heart.

—From the secret journal of
Ulris Kaon, court historian of
Prince Daos a Sal

Years ago, before Prince Byrn a Sal's rise to the city throne and all that came after, Alys had been a young child and her older and only brother Darro left their mother's house for the last time and in anger.

Mother had discovered that Darro and some of his friends had been robbing warehouses in Seepwater, hauling whatever they found up to a trader in Riverport, and spending the silver and bronze they got on wine. Alys wasn't sure whether it was the theft that enraged their mother or that he hadn't brought a share of the money home. Maybe her mother didn't know either.

Alys had tried to stay small enough to go unnoticed while they shouted at each other. She remembered Darro screaming *I don't eat anyone's shit* and her mother yelling back *They will kill you if you don't.*

In the end, Darro took a satchel and a club and the pair of good boots that he and their mother usually traded off using depending on who'd be walking farthest, and he left. Mother threw herself on the cot, scowling and weeping. When her attention finally wandered to Alys, she shook her head.

"Your brother has a good heart, but he's drunk on himself. Don't be like him," she said, and pointed at Alys with crossed fingers like the street-corner blessing men did to ward off evil. "Don't you be like him."

Alys nodded her little head and swore she wouldn't. She even meant it for a while.

It was the coronation day of Byrn a Sal, the new prince of the city, and the beginning, though no one knew it yet, of his death.

The pull that Alys's little crew had going was one of the oldest. Usually it took four: a flea, a cutter, a fish, and a walk-away. It could be done without a fish, and even the walk-away wasn't necessary, though going without raised the risk of being caught. The only ones that couldn't be done without were the flea and the cutter, and the cutter called the go.

Or usually did.

Orrel was cutter that day because he had a light hand and a sharp knife. Sammish was the walk-away, because she had the kind of face that people forgot as soon as they looked away from her. They didn't have a fish. Alys was the flea.

The girl Orrel had pointed at was Inlisc in a brightly embroidered blouse, and she was an easy mark. Her smile was drunken, her steps unsteady. The necklace she wore was gold and pearl, and probably worth more than the girl herself. And Alys knew her.

Her name was Kana. She worked for a merchant family in Riverport, and the gold she wore wasn't hers. If Orrel stole it, the best the girl could hope for was being sent back to Longhill. Whipping was more likely. The bluecloaks of the city guard sewing stones in her skirt and dropping her off a bridge wasn't out of the question. It was why Orrel chose her. He was the kind that hated anyone who'd done better than himself. Kana was a traitor to Longhill, pretentious and holier-than-thou, lickspittle to the Hansch of Riverport, and he was ready to punish her for her good fortune.

Alys wasn't.

She said *No* with her fingers, and Orrel, across the road from her, frowned. He called the go again. He'd keep doing it until she agreed.

Alys walked to the girl. If it ended the day's pull, it did. Kana's eyes swam when Alys took her arm, confused but not alarmed. Alys grinned and kissed her on the cheek. With her lips near the girl's ear, she whispered over the noise of the crowd.

"There are thieves here. They have eyes on that necklace. I don't know what you were thinking to wear that here, but get out. Now."

She released Kana, laughed as though they were old friends, and walked away. The last she saw Kana, she had a protective fist around the pearls and alarm in her eyes.

Orrel scowled at her but moved on.

The crowd filled the little plaza where six streets converged. The merchants and porters and boat hands of Riverport mixed with the weavers and leatherworkers and shoemakers of New-market. Most of the faces were Hansch, but there were enough Inlisc that Alys and Orrel didn't stand out. Sammish never stood out anywhere. That was her gift.

Voices rose in song, one melody washing over the other until no one seemed quite sure what notes or words were supposed to come next. A red-cheeked old man, plump as a pig, had a cask of wine at the side of one street, and he was filling any mug or skin that was passed to him. Late summer heat thickened the air. Girls in gaudy dresses thrown together for the occasion or borrowed from some other celebration danced and spun and tried to stay out of the arms of the boys. They didn't always try very hard.

Orrel was tall and not bad to look at. He danced through the streets with his shirt off, his hands waving along with the rhythm of whatever song seemed loudest. His anger wasn't gone, but it was hidden. His grin was wide and innocent and considerably more drunken than he actually was. Alys was wearing a loose blouse and a skirt with slits up the sides that looked celebratory, but also left her legs free. She passed through the crowd ahead of Orrel, glancing back every few paces to see if he'd chosen another bird for them to pluck.

The next touch was a Hansch girl who was a little older than Alys, with ruddy cheeks that showed how much wine she'd swallowed. She was spinning in a circle with half a dozen others, their legs weaving a dance as they sang. She wore an armband of leather and silver with an amethyst the size of Alys's thumbnail at its center. The child of some moneyed family, Alys guessed, not noble but wealthy enough to be careless. Orrel called the go and started moving in without giving Alys time to object. They began their own dance with steps no one saw.

The trick was for the flea and the cutter to seem as though they were borne by the tides of the crowd but still reach their target in the same moment. If they moved too quickly or too straight, someone might notice, and there were guards in the streets. Alys slipped and slid through the press, grinning as though she were having the best day ever. It wasn't a lie. She loved this part. Orrel swirled and circled, and seemed almost to be veering off toward the east until a knot of young men blocked his way. He made an apology to no one in particular and turned back toward the girl. The knife was small enough to hide with his finger, and only sharp along one edge. Alys didn't even see it glint.

The flea's job was to distract, the cutter's job to take, and the walk-away's to vanish. Alys reached out and tapped the girl's right breast sharply. The uninvited and unexpected touch was more immediate than the tug at her arm as Orrel sliced through the armband's ties. The girl's lips were caught between confusion and affront. Orrel passed the cut-string armband to the inconspicuous shadow that was Sammish.

The change of hands was smooth and fast, and, most important, none of them looked at each other while it happened. Alys moved on in her previous path, Orrel in his, and Sammish—head down like she was late for something—in a third. It all took less than a heartbeat. They were that good.

If the girl raised an alarm, Orrel would drop his knife and claim innocence. Her lost band wasn't with him. Alys had done nothing beyond be too familiar, swept up as she was by the spirit of the day. Sammish was already elsewhere, lost in the city. That was the beauty of the pull.

When it was over, there was a moment when the touch realized something precious was gone. They grabbed at their pockets, feeling for the pouch that had been there, or looked around on the stones in case it had only fallen, thinking that whatever was lost might still be recovered. Sometimes they would flush with rage. Sometimes their faces would twist in disbelief. A rare few laughed. Whatever they did, it felt honest, and that honesty fascinated Alys.

She looked back, hoping to see the moment, but the girl only stood still in the crowd, her hand lifted protectively to her breast. Alys willed the Hansch girl to know, but she only looked dazed for a moment before turning back to her friends, and Alys felt a snap of disappointment. The bareness of her arm went unnoticed. She might not realize for hours.

Guards shouted, as unmistakable as angry dogs, and for a panicked breath, Alys thought that someone had seen them. They were caught. But the armed men pushing through the crowd wore red cloaks, not the blue and white of the city. The badges of office at their belts were silver and gold, not bronze.

The palace guard was clearing a path through the crowd. The new prince was passing by.

Byrn a Sal was here.

Ausai a Sal—his uncle—had been prince for all of Alys's life, but now he had been put in the past like a leaf on the river. The new prince wasn't a young man, but he wasn't old. It wasn't outlandish to expect decades under his leadership. If he was wise and lucky, Byrn a Sal might be prince for as long as Alys lived.

The horse he rode was pale and magnificent. Its mane and tail were plaited with silver and gold, and its coat shone like the surface of the river. Prince Byrn a Sal had a square face with a straight nose almost utterly unlike his dead uncle's. Dark hair rose a little up his forehead, and his trim beard had touches of white in it. He was so open and his smile so ready that he could have passed for a much younger man. Alys felt the press of bodies against her as the crowd surged closer, pushing her forward against the palace guard; a little chaos of bodies that churned around her. Byrn a Sal sailed through it and above it.

Another man rode behind him. He seemed to be the same age, more or less, with ash-brown straight hair. Alys had no particular interest in the Hansch nobility, but there was something familiar about this one. If not in his features then in his expression and the way he carried himself.

She turned to a woman who had been thrown beside her: older and in a linen dress that marked her as a servant belonging in the wealthier parts of Riverport. "Who's that?" she shouted over the voice of the crowd as she pointed.

"Young Karsen? He'll be running half the city by spring, you can count on it. God smiled on that one."

Alys stared at him, trying to see a man who God had smiled on. She couldn't make the thought match what she saw. His eyes met hers. A shock flowed through her, and a sense of being exposed.

Karsen nodded to her as if he recognized her as well, or maybe it was only that he'd met her eyes and was being polite. The prince and his friend moved on and their retinue followed them, men and women and horses. Alys watched them go with her heart slowing. She told herself her unease was only because being noticed when they were on a pull usually meant disaster. She told herself that was all, and that there was nothing eerie about the prince's companion.

The last to go were the redcloaks, turning to run forward to the head of the prince's train and open the way on the next street, moving with a practiced coordination that matched the best thieves of Longhill.

"You done?" Sammish had come unnoticed and was at her elbow, considering her with mild, muddy eyes.

"I was waiting for you, yeah?" Alys said. "Where's Orrel?"

"South," Sammish said, and they both turned and started walking, shifting through the crowd like fish swimming through weeds. "Says we make our way toward Seepwater, end it by the theater. University types will all be drunk and happy."

"They've got less money than we do."

"I'm just saying what he said."

"Fine, then." She'd crossed Orrel once already today. She should probably be grateful he was still working the pull at all.

"Why didn't you?" Sammish asked, pulling Alys back to herself.

"Why didn't I what?"

"The necklace girl. Kara. Why'd you sour the pull?"

Alys shrugged as they walked. "There are enough of them we don't need to take down our own."

"She's not us anymore, though. She's not Longhill."

"Longhill's always Longhill."

Sammish seemed to weigh the thought for a moment, then nodded. Longhill was always Longhill.

The street traffic thinned as they reached the canals of Seepwater. On other days, stevedores and customs men and mule-drawn carts would have filled the square. The singular moment in the city's life had emptied it, closed the port, and locked the warehouses. Tomorrow, a more familiar Kithamar would come back. It might have been her tiredness that left her longing for that normalcy. It might have been a premonition.

The people celebrating here were different from the ones they'd been hunting. The brewers and bettors and pawnbrokers who made the canals home were rougher than the merchants of Riverport or the artisans of Newmarket. A handful of disreputable students slouched and pushed each other, though they were long blocks away from the city's southern wall where the lectures were held. A young city guardsman with rosy pimples on his cheeks strutted through the crowd, surveying the people like a warehouseman considering his bales. An old man in a green vest so gaudy that Alys didn't at first notice the streaks of filth on it played a reed organ.

And Orrel swayed to the music, smiling beatifically among a dozen or more other revelers. Alys moved through his field of vision, not greeting him, but letting him see that she was there. He lifted his hands, but there were no words in his fingers now. This close to Longhill, there would be too many people who knew to look for them. Instead, he shifted his hips and his shoulders, spinning in the little group of dancers. She watched him, waiting for him to choose. His false drunkenness seemed less false to her now.

When the signal came, she thought he was joking.

The strutting, acne-faced guard was moving down the street, smiling at girls. Many of the girls smiled back. It meant something to wear the blue cloak. It meant, among other things, that if he chose to beat someone or steal from them or worse, he wouldn't be punished. Some girls liked that. They thought being the special one of a man like that would make them safe, and they were wrong. At best, it would mean that they were safe from people besides him.

Orrel started a swooping approach, smiling and tilting his face up toward the sun. His finger curved to hide the knife. Alys frowned and said *No* with her hands, but he pretended not to notice her. It was punishment for Kana and the necklace.

Alys didn't know if the tightness in her throat was anger or fear.

For the pull to work, all three had to reach the mark in the same moment. If Alys didn't start walking now, she'd have to rush at the end. It would call attention to her. If she refused, Orrel might turn aside, or he might not. If he trusted her to be where she was supposed to be and do what she was supposed to do, and she failed him, he'd be caught.

If he were caught, he'd be killed. The guard might take him to the magistrate first, or it might end here. He was forcing her to choose between letting him die or doing what he said.

She stepped forward. The guard paused at a little stand where a boy was selling honey cakes at two for a bronze coin. Orrel shifted his trajectory through the crowd, and Alys matched him. Sammish, her eyes wide and her lips thin, knelt in a doorway and pretended to dig a pebble out of her boot. Alys tried to take comfort that she wasn't the only one who thought this was a mistake.

Close up, the guard seemed young. His beard was thin fuzz, and his skin had the oily look of an adolescence not quite outgrown. Orrel strode casually toward the man's back. Alys had three steps before she reached him. Two. With another man, she might have brushed a hand against his crotch. A gentle squeeze of his sex to confuse and capture his attention. Instead, she yipped and stumbled forward like she'd tripped on her own toe. The guard almost didn't react quickly enough to catch her, and she had to really take his arm to keep herself from falling. She felt Orrel's tap only because she knew to expect it. For all his faults, Orrel's fingers were light.

"Sorry," she said to the guardsman as they stood back up together. "I'm sorry."

"Be more careful," he said, and Orrel was already past. Sammish's grey-brown back disappeared down the street. Alys nodded and made some stupid attempt at a curtsey the way she thought a guard-smitten girl might before she turned and walked away. She hoped the warmth in her cheeks would seem like a blush. The guard snickered as she went. She put her head down and headed east, into the crowd.

The thing to avoid was looking back.

She looked back.

The guardsman was still standing by the boy with the honey cakes, but his haughtiness had vanished. His tunic hung loose under the cloak because the belt that had held it was gone. His eyes were wide with alarm, his arms out from his sides as if amazed by some miracle. His lips quivered, and his chest worked like a bellows as he gasped.

Suddenly vulnerable, he reminded Alys of a child discovering that a beloved toy was broken. She wouldn't have been surprised if he'd sobbed. She felt neither triumph nor regret, but he held her attention. If she'd seen him bathing, he wouldn't have been as naked as he was at that moment. She would have understood him less.

He turned half around as if his belt might be behind him and teasing him like a puppy. He lifted his anguished gaze to the crowd.

When his eyes found hers, she knew she'd made a mistake. His jaw slid forward, and his lips pulled back. By habit, he reached for the whistle at his belt. She turned, walking away more quickly, telling herself he might doubt himself. Then, fast-hearted, she broke into a trot.

"Grab her! In the name of the prince, someone stop that bitch!"

All around her, people shifted in alarm and uncertainty. It would be seconds before they understood who he meant. The shape of her life rested on the edge of the moment.

The slap of boots against paving stones came from behind her. She muttered *Fuck*, scooped up her skirt, and with the guard close at her back, sprinted for Longhill.

Of the twelve districts of Kithamar, Longhill was the oldest. And the newest.

An Inlisc camp had been on that same ground when the Inlisc had been nomads and herders. The camp called Longhill had been built of wood then, and it was now.

The long-vanished buildings had been placed to shelter each other from the vicious winds of spring, and that same logic held as the camp became a village and the village became a war post: narrow, undulating streets that broke the fury of the weather kept the air calm even when storms raged overhead.

After the conquering Hansch crossed the river, burning the Inlisc homes to the ground and founding the city called Kithamar, Longhill was rebuilt from the same kinds of trees and in the same style. All that changed was its meaning.

As the long centuries passed, Longhill slept, but its sleep wasn't easy. It could never forget that it had once been free and unbound, and that it wasn't anymore. And it changed. Buildings decayed and rotted and were replaced, and the district grew into something both the same and new.

The little red temple to the old Inlisc gods, infested with dry rot and centipedes, was set afire and a road made over the ash pit. The wide square where Inlisc grandmothers had bought and sold worked leather and hand-woven cloth calcified as market stalls added roofs and posts and walls. Eventually, there wasn't even a free street to pass through.

The quarter remade itself. Street maps drawn just a generation before were worse than useless. There were stories that old Inlisc priests still held the ancient rites somewhere deep in the shadows and narrow streets, but no one seemed quite sure what those rites were. Round Inlisc faces and curled Inlisc hair were normal here. The food that old men sold door-to-door from greasy sacks used more hot peppers and pickled fish than they ate near the Temple or in Stonemarket. The hard, percussive accent of the people who lived in Longhill was a remnant of the language that they had once shared and now shared in forgetting. A city within the city, Longhill clung to its pride like a man with only one good shirt.

At its western edge, Alys's brother Darro sat on the third floor of a building that had been cut into shelter for fifty people or more. The shuttered room had a pair of benches, a waxed cloth with clean-picked chicken bones from his breakfast, and a blackwood table. The pale woman sat across from him. Her voice was usually half-dream, but today she was agitated. Shaken, even. He'd never seen her care about anything, and it was eerie.

"We *have* to get the knife. That's what I need from you. It will be fine, if we can get the knife back." She was trying to convince herself.

Everyone wanted that knife, it seemed. Magic and politics and the gods alone knew what else was involved, but what mattered to Darro was the money. And the sense, deep in his bones, that if he played this right, he'd be able to buy himself any life he chose. He tried to act like he was only what she thought he was.

"I have someplace to look. If it can be had for you, I'll have it," Darro said, and the woman nodded, trying to believe him. A finch tapped at the shutters, its yellow feathers nothing more than a bright shadow, and sped away. "I have your back."

She managed a smile.

"You do, don't you, little wolf," she said as she took a worn leather wallet from her belt and slid it across the table. Darro opened it with an affected calm. Ten pieces of untarnished silver glimmered as he counted them out. It was enough to let him pay Kennat Water for the use of the room and keep himself fed besides through the first frost if he was careful with it. "When can you have it?"

"Soon," Darro said, which was true. "Days, not weeks."

"Someone else is looking for it. Not a friend."

Darro tried to look as if he didn't already know that. "Someone else?"

"A woman from the Bronze Coast," she began, and a shriek came from the street. Someone was screaming Darro's name. There were other words in the cry, but the only one Darro could make out was *sister*.

He moved by instinct built from long years of worry. The shutters opened, and the light came in. Below him in the street, Young Caval was waving up to him. The woman's coronation-day costume of greasy yellow and watery blue was made forlorn by the distress in her expression.

"Darro! Darro! They're coming for your sister! A guardsman! They're in the little sac by Ibdish's. He's going to kill her!"

The stairway from his room to the street was dark as a chimney. The summer heat drew up it like he was running down into an invisible fire. Darro didn't remember grabbing his club, but it was in his hand: hard oak with the knobbed end dipped in lead. He reached the street and sprinted along the narrow roads. Speed-blurred faces turned to watch him with mild interest, as if he were part of the day's show. He knew each of them by name and expected no help. If the positions were reversed, he would have been leaning out the window, curious to see whether the drama below played out as comedy or something tragic. He ignored them and ran.

At the turn toward Ibdish's house, Darro's heel slid on a turd some man or dog had left on the cobbles, and he almost fell. Voices raised in threat and anger echoed down the closed street. One of the voices was Alys's.

The street widened a little where it ended, making a circle hardly wider than a stage with wooden buildings four stories high crowding in around it. There wasn't so much as an alleyway between them. The street and the doors to Ibdish's house were the only ways in or out, and Ibdish's wife had pulled her iron gate closed to keep Alys's troubles outside. Alys stood on the warped wooden steps, her face dark with rage or effort, her hands in fists at her side. A doughy bluecloak had his foot on the first step and a naked sword in his hand. Men and children looked down from the windows and roofs at the impromptu fighting pit.

"What the *fuck* is this?" Darro shouted, trying to pull the swordsman's focus away from his sister. "You step back from her!"

The guard turned. Three long, bloody scratches on his neck said that Alys had fought back already. Even as the man stepped forward, Darro's awareness spread past him, waiting for the sounds of feet or hooves. One man might be stopped. A full patrol couldn't.

"This isn't your concern," the guardsman said, but there was something off about the cut of his tunic. It was loose and blousy.

"I am Tannen Gehart of the city *fucking* guard. I'm taking this cunt for thieving or I'm cutting her throat right here, and I don't much care which. I'll put you in too if you don't shut your fish-lipped mouth!"

The guard's belt was gone. That was why he looked wrong. Darro stepped forward on the angle, watching how his enemy's blade shifted. "You're a guardsman, where's your whistle?"

"Not your fucking problem."

Darro shifted the angle of his approach. "You're a guardsman, where's your badge of office?"

"This one stole it," the guard said, gesturing back with his off hand. Darro didn't shift to look at Alys. He didn't want her in the boy's mind. It would take two fast steps to get close enough to strike and be struck. A blade was the better weapon, but Alys was at the guard's back. As if he'd heard Darro's thoughts, the guard brought his sword to the ready.

"All I see," Darro said, "is a fat boy in a cheap costume assaulting a girl half his size. Doesn't seem right, does it?"

The guard licked his lips. His gaze flickered. Darro expected him to turn or back away, but he'd judged the man poorly. The rush came with no more warning than a shift at the man's ankle. The sword curved in a tight arc toward Darro's neck, the guard's full weight behind it, and Darro pulled his club up to block before he knew he'd done it. The metal cut a bright notch into the wood.

The guard pushed past him, then turned. Alys and the steps up to Ibdish's gate were behind Darro now, and the guard stood between him and the free streets. It might seem like the attack had failed, but Darro knew he'd been outmaneuvered.

The guard knew it too.

"I don't give half a fuck about you, friend," the guard said, spit blowing from his lips. "But *that* bitch is—"

Whatever words he'd meant to say were interrupted by a wet splat. A stain as brown as mud drew itself down the guard's side, and he reared back from the stink. Someone had emptied a night pot into the street. Someone with good aim.

"Who did that?" the guard shouted up at the windows. A single tittering laugh set off a cascade of others. Darro kept his club ready. His knuckles were bleeding and raw. He didn't know how that had happened. The man shouted again, "Who insults the city guard?"

A long, amber arc of liquid came from a high window, splashing down near the guard without hitting him. Another followed from a different angle.

After that, the street became the wrong side of a turd pit. Alys and Darro pulled back against the iron bars at the top of the stairs while faceless Longhill showed the lone guard what it thought of him and the men he served. Driven back, the guard looked at Darro one last time, then turned and strode away before the impulse to rain filth on him could spread past the cul-de-sac. The stench was terrible, but Darro couldn't help laughing as he gagged. As Ibdish's rolling howl began behind them, crying out to know which of the half-dead bastards was going to wash his street, Darro turned to his only living sister.

"What was that about?" he asked.

She paused as if searching for words, then started bawling.

He daubed stinging ointment on his knuckles and leaned out his window, watching for trouble that hadn't come. Not yet. In the back of his mind, he was planning out how they'd escape if the city guard came around the corner with blades and flame. But maybe they wouldn't.

"I can't believe I *cried*," Alys said. She was sitting at the blackwood table, batting at the wallet the pale woman had left like a cat playing with a dead insect. "Right out where everyone was watching."

"Nothing to be ashamed of," Darro said. "You could have bled out on the stones. Would have, if someone hadn't thought of something funnier. Anyone would be shaken."

"I was fine once you came. You'd have beaten him."

"Maybe."

"You would have," Alys said. She'd been like this from the day she was born. Ready to assert that the world was the way she wished it could be, and then insist she was right until the gods relented. It frightened Darro to his bones, because she hadn't grown out of it. The day she did would be painful.

"At the very least, will you stop working with Orrel?" he asked.

"He's a good cutter."

"He's a *skilled* cutter. A good one wouldn't have gone cocky and put his flea across the city guard."

"It was my mistake. I'll carry it."

"Then you're smarter than he is already. Tell me you're not rubbing on him."

Her flash of disgust was more reassuring than a denial would have been.

"Good," Darro said. "You're too young."

"You don't get to say that."

"I'm your brother."

"You're not me. I'm the only one that gets to say."

"I'm the one rushing out to the street to keep you from being gutted like a trout."

"No one made you."

Darro closed the bowl of ointment and considered his wounds in the light of the coming sunset. The red of the sky and his angered flesh blended together. As long as the pus didn't bring heat with it, he'd be healed and the scabs forgotten by the week's end. He balled his hands into a fist to judge the pain, and then put it aside. "That's true. But I'll do the same again next time, and I'd rather not die."

She shifted, coming to sit next to him. Her eyes were solemn. They'd been that way since she was born, but in the last year, they'd gained a depth. She'd be a grown woman soon. He hoped she'd be a wise one, but he didn't expect it. "I'll try harder."

"No. Will is less than wind," Darro said. "You can't just decide to do the same thing as always, only better. It doesn't mean anything. Find what you did wrong, then make a rule to keep it from happening again. Something you can *do*. Like this: When you've made a pull, you keep your eyes down and forward for fifty steps. Just that, and you won't have to struggle to keep from looking back."

"All right."

"Count fifty," Darro said.

"Fifty steps," Alys agreed.

He wondered whether she would actually do it. If she did, it would help. It might save her life one day. But the more he said it now, the less she'd hear.

Outside his window, a thin sliver far to the north showed where the river entered the city. The water glowed gold with the falling light. Darro had meant to find food somewhere. The bakers would be selling their stale bread right now at two bronze a loaf. There would still be festival tents up all through River-port and Green Hill. The priests at the Temple might even be doling out little sacks of wheat and rye from the granary. He had some dried meat in his safe cache, though, and there were other things that needed doing.

Alys leaned back, tracing a flock of starlings with her fingers as they whirled over the water, preparing to settle until the next day's dawn. When she spoke, her voice was low. "It won't be safe for me at the common house tonight."

It was good that she knew it. "Go to Mother's."

"They'll look for me there. Let me stay here. No one knows where your room is. You change it all the time."

"I don't change this one, and you can't stay here."

"Please."

His sister, who he'd carried on his back when she was too young to walk, took his bruised hand. The heaviness in Darro's chest could have been impatience or love or both. He took the wallet from her.

"Go to Aunt Thorn," he said. "She'll keep you hidden until this all goes downstream."

Alys coughed out a laugh. "Why would she do that?"

He counted out his ten pieces of silver and put half of them in Alys's hand. "I'm keeping the rest. I have to eat too."

She started to ask how he'd come by so much, and he shook his head before she could. He thought he saw shame in her expression, and he wanted to smooth it away with his thumbs. He wanted her to be the laughing child she'd been when he was her age. He wanted the world to corrupt everything, only not her.

"I'm sorry," she said.

"Be careful," he said instead of farewell.

He sat alone for a time after she'd gone. The building popped and shifted as the daylight went from gold to grey. The summer heat loosened its grip on Kithamar, and a soft breeze from the north brought the smell of distant pine trees to cut the stink of horseshit and dogshit and manshit. Below him, an old woman who rode a beggar's bowl at the river came home, muttering to herself the way she always did. Above him, the two girls who'd bought the right to sleep on the open roof for a bronze a week climbed into their places. His ceiling creaked under their weight. Voices rose from the streets. Some were laughing, some were shouting. Anything softer didn't reach as far as his window. His hand only hurt a little.

This was all he had. All he could hope for, so long as he played by other people's rules. The pale woman and the scarred man, the actor with the spider on his hand, the bluecloaks and the red: all any of them would see when they looked at him was a hired knife from the guts of Longhill lucky and strong enough to keep himself and his family alive. Until he caught a bad bounce or lived long enough for age to weaken him. Any path besides that, he'd have to cut for himself.

Reluctantly, he went back to his safe cache. He plucked up a stub of black, rotten-looking candle and went back to his little table. He closed the shutters against the glittering of torchlight below him and the glittering of stars above.

It took him a few strikes at the flint before a spark struck the black wick. Whatever the string was made from, it burned easily. The tiny yellow flame stretched up, then bounced down, going round as an eyeball. The stinking smoke thickened into ribbons, and the ribbons swirled, one into the other, riding draughts of something besides air. Slowly, the darkness congealed. It wasn't the pale woman this time; this time it was the scarred man.

For a moment, they were silent. The scarred man smiled without pleasure. "You dismissed her."

"I apologize for that. There was an emergency. Family."

"We have other concerns than you. We have a hundred people in our compound as we speak, and each of them is more important than you are. We don't simply come whenever you summon us."

For a moment, Darro thought he would be turned away for the impertinence of going to Alys or for lighting the candle. That would make things interesting. He halfway hoped that it would go that way.

"I'm sorry," Darro said, as if he wasn't betraying anybody. "I wouldn't bother you now, except we had open business when I was called away. She said something about a Bronze Coast woman who was also looking for this knife, yeah?"

The scarred man narrowed his eyes, and Darro waited, his heart picking up speed. He wondered if he'd already been caught out in his almost-lie.

After a moment, the scarred man said, "That's right. And she's dangerous."

Aren't we all? Darro thought, but didn't say.

Aunt Thorn was a children's story first. In the old version, her mother was a woman from when the Inlisc had been a rootless people following the herds, and her father was the god of mischief. There were a hundred stories about her. How Aunt Thorn stole fire from the sun. The time Aunt Thorn turned into a horsefly and killed the son of a rival tribe. How Aunt Thorn hid Baroth's hunting dogs behind the moon. Alys had heard them all in one version or another, seen them turned into short and comic plays at the stage near the university in Seepwater, sung them herself sometimes when she'd been little.

No one knew the real name of the woman who'd taken the name for herself and her web of thugs. No one needed to. Aunt Thorn was the secret mayor of Longhill. If you were desperate, there was a door at the back of a particular alley that any Inlisc of Longhill could go to. Knock there, ask what you need, and pass money through the crack between door and stone. Sometimes a man would arrive with what you needed. Sometimes he'd bring you back your coin and tell you not to come to Aunt Thorn again. Sometimes something else would happen. Longhill could ask help from Aunt Thorn, so long as the one doing the asking was willing to risk being answered. Aunt Thorn might champion Longhill against the Hansch, but she was unpredictable. Having her attention was a throw of the dice, and anyone who crossed her ended ugly.

Once she'd explained her situation to the closed door, Alys pushed one of Darro's silver coins under it with a twig she found in the street, then stood waiting. For a long moment, she thought nothing would happen. She was trying to think where she could go to stay safe until Aunt Thorn's men came to find her when a deep scraping sound came, and the door swung open.

The man who waved her in was almost shorter than she was, but broad as a horse across the shoulders. A scar snaked across his neck and vanished under his collar.

"Come with me," he said. Alys looked down the street, not sure what she was hoping to see, then followed him. The stairs were dark, the steps old stone worn smooth by use. With Longhill above them, they passed through a maze of brick halls. Twice, the small man greeted others—empty-faced men who Alys would have turned back from if she'd seen them in the streets. Here, she nodded at them. It seemed wise to be polite.

The short man came to a hall with an iron chain strung across its mouth. He took down the chain, motioned Alys through, and put it back up behind them. There were voices ahead—women's voices in conversation. The short man scooted past Alys, opened a door she hadn't seen, and led her into a long, low room. Half a dozen girls only a few years older than her and three women considerably older sat or lay on wooden bunks. Three candles in tin holders were the only light.

The short man put a hand on Alys's shoulder.

"She's a guest, not a worker," he said. "Treat her like one of yours, but no clients."

One of the older women nodded. The short man patted Alys like she was a friendly enough dog.

"You'll be safe here," he said to her. "Safer than outside, yeah? There are gods in the streets these days."

Somewhere between her second night and her third day in the secret maze under the city, the bloodied man came. She'd lost track of sunset and sunrise, much less the more changeable aspects of the weather—rain or wind or the haze that sometimes rose from the river. The other girls and women talked and slept, coming and going on a schedule that Alys couldn't fathom and didn't inquire about. They didn't call each other by name, not even the pet names that anyone would have for the people they spent time with. Alys had to think it was because she was there, and petty intimacies like that weren't something that belonged in front of strangers. She respected the message they were giving her and kept herself to herself. No one asked about her, and she learned nothing about them until he came in.

She was on a bunk, braiding and unbraiding a length of her hair for something to do, when his voice came. It was low and masculine and raw with distress. At first, she couldn't make out what he was saying, and she assumed that whatever was going on was Aunt Thorn's business and none of her own. But he kept getting louder and closer. He was shouting something like *Arja* or *Erja*, and one of the other younger girls spat out an obscenity and ran out of the room. Alys sat up.

He was a stone wall of a man, broad across the shoulders and thick with muscle. His hair was black and greasy, and his shirt and trousers were dark with blood. He fumbled with the chain until it dropped and he staggered in, a wineskin in one meaty fist, and looked around. When his gaze landed on her, Alys realized she was the only other person in the room.

"Erja," he said. "Where's Erja?"

"I don't know who that is."

A look of vast annoyance narrowed his mouth just as the younger girl came back, one of the older women close behind her.

"Fuck's sake, Gosling," the older woman said, and the man smiled.

"Erja!" he said. "I knew you'd be here."

"Lie back," the older woman—Erja, apparently—said, then gestured to the girl. Together, they stripped the man of his shirt and cut his trousers free with a small knife. Alys sat, stunned by the vision of this vast, utterly naked man, sitting on the floor and drinking like it was all perfectly normal. There was a long cut along his chest and two more deep in his left arm. Every breath seemed to push a fresh stream of blood out. His gaze never left Erja.

The younger girl brought a green lacquered box from some-place deep in the brick halls and set it by Erja's knees.

"What were you thinking?" the older woman said as she pulled a spool of black thread and a hooked bone needle from the box. "You should have gone to the hospital. Not brought this here."

"They'd look for me there," the bloodied man said with a grin. "It's bad luck going outside the city walls anyway. You know that."

"It's bad luck bleeding on my fucking floor," she said, but a hint of friendliness had crept into her voice. She took out a stone bowl filled with a thick grey paste. "This is going to sting."

"You'd never hurt me," the man said. Still, he hissed when

she rubbed it into his wounds and cried out when she took the bone needle and started sewing him closed.

"Tell me what happened," she said. "It'll take your mind off the pain."

"Was getting the load from Witter, only he was holding out. Had the cart right there on the bridge and said he wouldn't let it go unless we paid him double. Mirril was backing him too."

Erja made a little encouraging sound in the back of her throat. Alys shifted forward on her bunk to get a better look. The gaping cut was almost half closed already, the older woman's hands weaving thread and skin with the speed of long practice. The grey paste, whatever it was, had stopped the bleeding. The man grinned and closed his eyes. Alys had never seen a man so clearly fashioned for violence and also so utterly vulnerable. He was magnificent in a frightening way.

"So," he said, "I told him 'Here's a counter-offer. I throw it in the river, everyone starts killing everyone else, and nobody gets paid for any of it.'"

Erja laughed, and Alys found herself smiling too. The young woman came back with a bucket of water and a clean rag. Alys hadn't noticed her leaving.

"Oh, Gosling."

"It's what my mother did when my brothers started fighting over something. Take it away from all of us, yeah?"

"So Mirril and Witter did this?"

"Them? No. But we were shouting, and the bluecloaks noticed us."

"The guard cut you?" The bloodied man nodded, and the older woman shook her head. "Maybe it's best you didn't go to the hospital after all."

"I knew you'd see to me. I just need a little rest," the bloodied man said, and squeezed the dregs out from his wineskin. The younger woman cleaned the blood off him as his gaze moved back to Alys.

"Who's this one?" he asked with a leer.

"Guest of the house," Erja said, and the big man scowled, disappointed. When he was clean, he stood and walked, still naked, back out into the brick tunnels. The younger woman put the iron chain up behind him after he left. When Alys looked up, the older woman locked eyes with her.

"You didn't see any of that, now, did you?"

"Nothing," Alys said.

Erja closed her lacquered box with a snap. "Good choice."

The broken woman came to the river at night.

She walked unsteadily through the thin young trees, pulling herself forward with every step. The pain in her shoulder and side had gone from sharp to a deep ache as the injured muscles tightened and set. Her wounds hurt less than the betrayal. The betrayal hurt less than the guttering of her hopes. She fought to breathe, and knew that she was losing the fight.

Above her, beyond the trees, the vast wall of a hillside they called Oldgate glimmered. At its top, her enemy's house. If she died here, the beast might never know that her bones rested at its feet. How odd to be so vast that your victories went unnoticed.

She chanted as she went, the rhythm of the words complicated by her hitching breath and the rushing of the river. They echoed in her mind, the syllables growing deeper, calling forth a space that was not space. The spiritual flesh of the city was not as thin as it had been on the night after Ausai died, but it wasn't as thick as when he had lived. That was a sign in itself, and she tried to take comfort in it.

Moonlight flickered from between a hundred thousand late summer leaves. Her feet sank into the thin, spongy litter of old rot. The day's heat was gone, and the cold that seemed to run through Kithamar's veins caressed her. She swallowed to loosen her throat and returned to her chanting and her walk.

She didn't hear him approach. He was simply there, looking like an old man with wiry hair sitting on a wide, wild stone. She nodded her respect, and thought she saw amusement in his eyes.

"Looks like you're having a shitty day," the old man said. "What happened to you?"

"I seek shelter," she gasped. The words hurt deep in her chest.

The old man tilted his head like a dog hearing a distant whistle. "Your accent's...Endil? Or, nah. Bronze Coast."

"I am priest of the six, and sworn of the spirit house."

"Long way from home, you."

"I know what you are, lord. Will you grant me this?"

The old man spread his hands, palms open. There were calluses on his fingers, and his nails were thick and poorly trimmed. "I'm just some asshole out enjoying the moonlight. Same as you."

"We have the same enemies. Will you grant me this?"

He sobered and went silent. She waited until she was sure he was not going to speak, and then she waited longer. She had no place else she could go.

At last, he shook his head. "No. This city is on fire, except nobody sees it. Risks are too high. There's no good reason for me to put my head out of my shell now, and a hundred good reasons not to."

"Help me, bury me, or watch me rot; I don't have the strength to leave here."

He narrowed his eyes. "You don't, do you?"

"Will you grant me this?"

It was the third time. The one that commanded an answer. The thing that looked like an old man chuckled, and then sighed. "Fine. Come with me. We'll see what we can do."

He turned and began to walk. When she tried to follow, her legs failed and she sank to the earth. The forest floor smelled of rot and new growth. It ticked with the movement of insects. Discovering that her eyes had closed, she tried to open them. Then tried again.

Strong arms reached under her knees and across her shoulders. When the thing that looked like an old man lifted her, pain shrieked across her body, but as it walked—its rolling gait like the shifting of a horse or a boat on choppy water—she leaned her head against its shoulder and the discomfort faded to something bearable.

"My thanks, Lord—"

"Yeah, don't use that name here," he said. "Call me Goro."

Eight long days after the coronation of Byrn a Sal, Grey Linnet woke before dawn. She had been Harld's Linnet when her husband had been alive, and Little Linnet and Red Linnet and Linnet Maganschild before that. Longhill had seen every incarnation of her from girl to woman to elder of the street.

When she rose from her small cot, she shooed out the rats with no great violence. She'd known rats her whole life. They held no terror for her. She ate a little of yesterday's bread, took her sack over her shoulder, and started her morning rounds gathering up the children: Dark Aman whose mother was Danna, Averith's girl; Big Salla and Little Salla, who lived across the street from each other and liked to hold hands when they walked; Elbrith Thin-as-a-Reed with his shock of white hair like an old man's though he was only seven. Some days, Grey Linnet got better than a dozen of Longhill's young. Other times, she might only find three or four.

She took them to the little wilderness in the center of

Kithamar where the living river put down sand and soil carved away from under the docks and port. The river had too many moods for making a home on the Silt to be anything but foolish, but things washed up there that had value. Even if the hunt brought her nothing, their parents would give her a bronze now and then for keeping the little ones out from underfoot.

In the rose-and-grey before dawn, Linnet passed by Aunt Thorn's door and saw Linly's girl Alys coming out. It didn't seem so long since the girl had been one of her little ones. Now, here she was with a face and body more like a woman than a girl. Linnet cooed the way she did with the children, clapped her hands together, and felt her own death a little closer than before.

"Look at you! My little Alys Woodmouse, all changed. You look so lovely, child. So lovely."

"You haven't changed at all," Alys said, and suffered Linnet to take her arm and pull her a little way along the street.

"Working for Aunt Thorn now? I would never have guessed it."

"I'm not," Alys said. "I had some trouble. I've been buying safety."

Linnet nodded, tugging the girl along. "Good, and good. Pay them like Aunt Thorn what they're owed, but never give them power over you. I've seen so many go that way, you know. So many. You were always a good, honest child."

"I should let you go," Alys said. She didn't quite keep the pity out of her voice, but she kissed Grey Linnet's cheek before she turned and walked away. She hadn't had to do that. Linnet watched her go, thinking about who she'd been when her hips had moved like Alys's.

It proved a good day. She had a half dozen pairs of small, willing hands and sharp, childish eyes to add to her own before the sun rose up as high as the Temple's crown. They went through Seepwater with the morning sun on their backs, skipping together and singing the song about the little dog that bit off her own tail.

Linnet's eyes weren't what they had been, and her feet and hands ached at the end of the day. If the children ever stopped coming with her, she'd starve, so she danced and capered and kept them happy, no matter how she felt. There were worse ways for a woman her age to live.

At the trade bridge between Seepwater and the Smoke— yellow brick and black mortar—a pole stood with bits of cloth nailed to it: a little blue dress, a little yellow blouse, and a soft white cap that might have fit a child of five or six years. They'd been taken from a drowned body and put here for the parents to identify.

Elbrith Thin-as-a-Reed tugged her sleeve. "What are you thinking, Grandmother?"

I am thinking that children are like elm seeds on the river: some manage to set roots, but most rot in the flow.

"I am wondering what treasures the good river brought us today," she said, then rubbed her hands together. "And I am just gid-gid-giddy as a pony to find out!"

The children shrieked and ran across the wide bridge. Grey Linnet laughed because she always laughed and followed as if she didn't dread the clamber down the stones.

If she had known then what she would find, she'd have turned back.

"What was it like?" Sammish asked.

Alys shrugged. "They put me in a tunnel, took my money, and gave me food and water and places to sleep and shit, and a half dozen whores to play cards with when they weren't sleeping or working. It was fine."

"You're back, then?" Sammish asked.

"I am," Alys said. "I have to be. I'm out of money, no thanks to Orrel. Need to talk to him."

It wasn't entirely true, but it was nearly so. She still had one of Darro's silver coins. It would have bought her another day or two, but after a week underground, she'd been hungry for sunlight.

"Haven't seen Orrel since the day," Sammish said, and her tone made it commiseration.

"He owes you too?"

Sammish shrugged. Alys sat next to her on the thin wooden bench, plucked up a clod of maybe-mud, maybe-manure, and tossed it at a flock of pigeons that rose into the air: black bodies against the white haze.

"Your brother was looking for him," Sammish said.

"If Darro found him, that may be where our money is. What have I missed while I was gone?"

Sammish leaned back, laced her hands behind her head, and recounted the gossip. The prince had called a council of the high families—"everyone of noble blood," they said—and then canceled it before they could meet. There had been a fight in Riverport and a bluecloak had been killed, but no one was sure who exactly had been involved, and no one from Longhill seemed to have had a blade in it. Someone had stolen a bolt of Gaddivan silk from a house in Newmarket, and Sammish had taken work from a pawnbroker trying to find who'd taken it and offer prices. So far, it hadn't turned up.

Sammish warmed as she spoke, and the color in her cheeks almost made her pretty. When she shrugged to say that was all she could think of, Alys pulled the last silver coin from her belt. Sammish looked hopeful, and Alys wondered how long it had been since the other girl had eaten.

"Pay me back when Orrel shows his face?" Alys asked.

Sammish grinned.

At the south gate, street traffic was thicker than usual with carts and mules hauling in crops from the farmlands: beets piled up as high as a standing man, smelling of fresh dirt and bruised leaves; peas and beans by the sackful, bouncing against the shoulders of haulers; even a few green-black melons, skins shining like they'd been polished, in the bed of a rough wooden cart.

The greater crop would come soon, and Kithamar would celebrate with pies and cakes and the slaughter of animals. Everyone would try to get fat enough to live through spring.

The wide lands outside the city tempted Alys, but guards stood by the gates, counting the carts and charging the tax. They wore blue, and while she didn't recognize any of them as the man who'd chased her to Ibdish's doorway, she wasn't sure enough to risk it. They went to Seepwater and the university instead.

Tuns of beer cooled and bumped against each other in the sluggish water of the canal. Strips of spiced meat cooked on a street kitchen's iron grate, the fat sizzling and calling up little bursts of flame. They sat at the canal and listened to young men with clipped, affected accents argue about whether nature could intend anything. None of the words meant much to Alys, but the boys who spoke them were pretty.

Alys had meant to keep back half the coin's value, but the sun hadn't touched the top of Palace Hill when the money ran out.

"Glad you're back," Sammish said with a slightly boozy, slightly overfed grin.

"Where else would I go?" Alys said with a smile only a little soured by the money she'd let herself waste.

"Good," Sammish said, leaned forward, and hugged her like they were sisters, then tottered back north, vanishing into the street before she had gone a dozen steps. Alys sat alone at the canal for a time, trying to enjoy it by herself, but without someone to look up to her and be grateful for her brother's money, the afternoon lost its salt.

Early as it was, her mind turned to where she'd be sleeping when the night came. She'd been gone long enough that her place at the common house would have gone to someone else, and it was late in the day to put her name in the queue. She couldn't go back to Darro without him asking why she wasn't still with Aunt Thorn. It was warm enough that she could pick a corner and sleep in the open, but if rain didn't soak her, dew would. Her mother's room meant Alys would have to put up with her mother's musky tea and her sometime-lovers. It seemed the least unpleasant of her options.

Since last winter, her mother's place was in a canyon of buildings, each sharing walls with those at its side. A rat could run across the street from corner to corner and never come closer than twelve feet from the ground. She walked there with the slow step of someone lost in her own daydreams and speculations.

Where the narrow street made its last curve, her mother was standing outside the thin, red-washed door, her mouth as slack and dismayed as a fish. Grey Linnet stood beside her, eyes red from crying. Alys felt her footsteps slow. Her mother saw her, and Linnet turned, pressed a palm to her old, worm-lipped mouth, and cried out.

"Alys! Oh, Woodmouse. I'm so sorry. We found him by the water. I'm so, so sorry, child. I am."

In death, Darro didn't look like he was sleeping. He didn't even look like Darro.

His skin was paler than it should have been; his lips and his skin were the same shade of colorless, like they'd been carved from a single block of wax. His arms and legs, water-swollen, were thick and less defined than the ones she remembered. Only his hair looked right, even if it grew from the wrong head. Like a child's clay doll, the corpse only resembled her brother.

The river did that.

His wounds were only little changes in texture. There was no blood. A few pale ovals marked where fish had bitten him. The cut that had killed him was easy to overlook, even though it was on his chest. A thin line where the skin had pulled back and not as long as the first knuckle of her thumb just to the left of his breastbone. Alys had seen sword wounds before, but they had been live ones, with blood still spilling out or mangled by clots and bandaging. This one looked too clean to be real and

too small to let a man's life out. She had the perverse urge to put
her finger into it and see how deep it went.

They killed him, she thought, but with a distance, as if she
were only trying the idea on for fit. She didn't have a *they*, but
that was small. Hardly an annoyance. *Killed him* was the part
that was too wide, too airy, too empty somehow to fit inside
her. It was like *They unmade the color green*, or *They murdered shoe-
strings*. It was nonsense.

They killed Darro.

The priests had laid him out in a small temple near the river.
The doors were red cloth stretched over frames of thin pine.
Incense by the handful tried to cover the smell of death. The
clove-and-rose smoke was so thick it was a taste. Candles and
butter lamps filled the room with a soft yellow light and a pressing heat. The icons of the gods were all bronze or carved wood,
and they came from every tradition: the Three Mothers, the
blind god Adrohin, Lord Kauth and Lady Er, a dozen more.
The priests had arranged them to look toward the altar, as if the
great powers of this world and the worlds beyond were all sharing in the grief. Only Shau, the two-bodied Hansch god who
guarded the gate between justice and mercy, looked away out
the window as if to say *What you are seeking is not here.*

A trickle of sweat ran down Alys's face and stung her eye.
Even with that, she didn't weep. She only looked at the body in
the soft, steady light. She began to understand that something
precious was gone. She waited to see how she would react.

"I'm very sorry," the priest said. "Death is a great mystery."

Darro didn't breathe. His eyes didn't move. They had killed
him.

"Your mother said he kept the Mattin rites?"

"If she says so. I don't know."

The priest lowered his head. For a moment, neither of them

spoke. When he did, his tone was an apology. "She asked for the partial rite. I understand if that's—"

"Full rites," Alys said.

"Yes. Yes, that would be better, but it would require—"

"I'll find a way to pay for it. Full rites. Everyone knows the river's hungry. His soul's not safe unless it's full rites."

"As you say, little sister."

He stepped back. The candle flames bowed as one, pulled by the same breeze. She moved closer to the altar. A sudden storm woke in her belly—rage or grief or something else—and she wondered whether she was getting ill. She thought about vomiting, but it seemed childish and overdramatic. Darro, who had sung her songs when their mother was too drunk to care for them, looked up at nothing from half-closed eyes. She took his hand, and it felt cold. She wanted to say something. She didn't know what.

In the twilight, Kithamar seemed like a place she'd never been before. Like she'd woken from a dream into a city that was too real to bear.

The stars were coming out, just a few at first with more appearing with every minute. Summer ivy traced its way up the mortar in the low stone walls. The flatboats floated on the canals with men calling to each other as they negotiated their ways across the water and into the warehouses and boathouses for the night. A small flock of finches, bright as festival kerchiefs, sped past her, fleeing some enemy she couldn't see. The stink of temple slowly left her nose, and the stink of the canal took its place. The storm in her grew wider, louder, more viciously angry as she walked.

The mourning group milling in the street outside her mother's house were mostly older men and women, but she recognized some of Darro's friends among them. Little Coop, who worked as a cutter some days, stood at the edge of the group, neither with it nor apart from it. Lurrie, who'd had eyes for Darro when they were both Alys's age, wept quietly. A grey-haired man sat with his back against the raw wood wall and played a mournful song on a reed flute.

Someone had set up a pot on the street and started a little fire under it, held in place by stones, with a jug of water beside it in case it had to be quenched quickly. Aunt Daidan sat beside it while Grey Linnet served out watery stew to all who came. There would be music and crying and stories tonight. Her mother would be fed on beer and sympathy. And when the morning came, there would be a soot mark on the street where the cookfire had been. It might stay there until the next hard rain.

Alys's rage glowed brighter than the flames.

Alys stepped into the circle of light. Linnet rose, opening her arms as if for an embrace. "Oh, Woodmouse!" Alys recoiled.

"Where is she?" Alys asked. "Where's my *fucking* mother?"

"Linly?" Grey Linnet said as she pulled back and glanced over her shoulder to the darkness of the thin house. Alys heard someone calling her name like the echo across the river.

Her mother sat in the darkness by her little cot: grey, greasy hair, permanently reddened eyes, and a bottle of beer in one hand. She looked up as Alys stepped in, and her gaze swam a little trying to find focus. She was drunk.

In the corner, an old man sat shaking his head at nothing. One of her mother's sometimes men. Alys didn't know him and didn't care about him.

"Daughter." Her voice was slurred. "We're all that's left, you and I. Come here. Come to your ma."

"*Partial* rites?" Alys said, and her mother's bloodshot eyes snapped closed. Her lips pressed thin, and she turned away. The rage in Alys's chest redoubled. "They found him in the water. He died in the *river!*"

The voices from the street went quiet, listening. The reed flute wheezed and lost its song.

"He was dead before they put him in," her mother said. "A strike like that one, and my boy was gone before he touched the ground. You could see that by looking."

"Do you know that? Were you there?"

"I don't want to talk about this."

Her mother's lover rose, his wide, greyish fingers fluttering in distress like moths. Alys ignored him. "Were you there?"

"No, I wasn't. Nobody was."

"Then you don't know!" Alys shouted.

"The rites are a pull," her mother's lover said. His voice was as dusty and insubstantial as the rest of him. "I was a priest for a few years down on the river towns. Anyone lost to the water, we'd charge double. It was just part of the pull."

A thin tear sheeted down her mother's cheek, and it felt like an insult.

"It's because you don't have the money, isn't it?" Alys said. "You drank away everything you had, and now you can't pay for his rites?" The lover tried to step in, and Alys prodded his thin, chicken-ribbed chest. "If you come between us, I will break you. Do you understand?"

Fear bloomed in the old man's face, but he stood his ground. A hand took Alys's shoulder. Grey Linnet. The woman's soft-featured face was red at the eyes and nose. Her mouth made a tiny "o" as she shook her head. "It's the grief, Woodmouse. Don't let the grief talk."

Alys pulled herself away, but Linnet stepped toward her, still talking. *No no no. It's all right. Pain makes us bite. You don't have to bite.* Alys made a fist, placed her knuckles between Linnet's breasts, and shoved her back.

"Do not *ever* fucking touch me," she said. To her horror, there was a thickness in her voice. She turned back to her mother. "If you can't take care of Darro, *I* will, and—"

Sobs choked off whatever else she would have said. She turned, wiping her streaming eyes with a sleeve, and stalked out into the darkness, trembling like the city was shaking with her.

The night was warm, even with the sun gone. The sound of the mourning party faded away behind her. Only her hitching, hurt breath stayed with her, tenacious as a dog. She walked west, toward the river, head down and jaw clenched. At first, she didn't know where she was going.

Then she did.

The edge of Longhill by moonlight was a darkness with greater darknesses folded in it. Even the fullest moon had to fight down to the narrow, curving streets. Other parts of Kithamar might have public lanterns or bluecloak guards patrolling with torchbearers. The wooden buildings of Longhill left little appetite for open flame, and if the guard came here after sunset, it was with violence in mind.

The echoes of her footsteps told her how open the street was. The texture of the cobbles in the road gave her some sense of where she was. A dog ran past her, its nails ticking against the stone. A man called out, but not so close that he was a threat.

If, as the builders said, houses learned by how they were used, the one where Darro kept his private room had learned to keep secrets: black under the stars and mazy within. For a moment, looking up at the looming shadow and the stars behind it, she almost changed her mind. There would be other places she could sleep tonight. She'd bite her own hand off before she went to her mother, but one of her friends would take pity. The only reason to go to Darro's room was that it was still Darro's, and nothing else was.

A narrow arch led to tightly winding, steep, lightless stairs. The scratching in the walls as she passed might have been rats or insects or the other tenants. She knew the trick of opening his lock, and slid into his room as quietly as she could. From the roof above her, a girl's voice muttered. When Alys opened the shutters, moonlight spilled into the room like milk water. She sat at Darro's blackwood table. The last place she had seen him. Her breath was calm now, but shallow. And it hurt.

She was empty. The small, dark rooms were empty. All the wide sky was empty. Sitting alone here, where no one would see her, she could feel the hollowness in her body. The anger was gone. And the grief. She'd fallen into a kind of numbness.

"Darro?" she whispered, and for a moment she could almost convince herself that there was someone there to answer back. The silence seemed to offer comfort or promise, but then it went on, and the silence was empty too.

She rose and went toward his pallet. She didn't see the opened cache drawer under the slats until her ankle hit it. The pain was like being bitten. She jumped back, cursing, and then, when the sting began to fade, moved forward on her knees, feeling ahead of her in the dark.

The safe cache was a board made to fit into a section of wall. The latch was cunning. If it hadn't stood open, she wouldn't have found it. The moonlight barely came back this far. Alys pulled out Darro's last, secret things: a cloth wallet, a lump of something black and waxy, a dagger in a leather sheath. She took them to the table and the light.

The wax stump was just a bit of candle with a prickly, dark wick. The blade was something more. The leather of the sheath was well made, with thick thongs to tie it to a belt, and an oval showed where a stone had been set in it and then pried off. When she drew it, the knife seemed to grab the light. The workmanship was good, and letters and symbols she couldn't read had been worked into the flat. The cloth wallet was soiled. She saw hundreds like it folded over belts every day. It rang when she weighed it in her hands. The coins that spilled out on the table were smaller than she was used to seeing. Some had the crest and likeness of Ausai a Sal. Others were marked with the flowing script of the Bronze Coast and images of a mountain she didn't know. But even the coins stamped in Kithamar were uncanny. Unfamiliar. Alys's mind rebelled. They were too dark for silver, too bright for bronze.

Fingers trembling, she counted gold coins: one dozen, and then another. Enough money to buy every building on the street three times over. It was more pure wealth than she had ever seen in her life. Her heartbeat went fast, like she'd been running.

They killed him. As shocked and hurt as she'd been, she hadn't asked herself until now who *they* were or why they'd done it. This was why. This had to be why. Her heart had ached. Now fear filled it like dark water.

She looked out the window at the street. Were there shapes in the shadows? Was someone there? If they weren't yet, they would be.

Darro, she thought, *what were you caught in?*

She made a little pocket of her shirt's hem, put it all—bag, blade, and candle—into the fold. Holding it closed, she went down into the night, vanishing before anybody could find her.

Orrel was missing, and apart from some lost money, Sammish didn't care. Alys was missing, and about that, Sammish cared very much.

She understood in a vague, abstract way that there had been a time she hadn't been in love with Alys. That she hadn't dreamed about her and gone to the taprooms Alys liked and worked any pull Alys would have her on. After all, Sammish had been born a baby like anyone else, and on that day she hadn't known the dark-haired girl with the sly smile and the broad shoulders. It stood to reason that Sammish had learned about Alys along with every other unchanging thing: the sky was blue, the river was cold, and she would lay her heart on Alys's altar if the older girl only gave her a sign. Alys didn't know because Sammish never said it, and because she was good at not being seen.

So while Orrel could live or die on his own schedule and not mean much to Sammish, Alys hadn't been seen in Longhill since the day they'd found Darro's corpse, and that mattered to her deeply.

○   ○   ○

"Any knives for me this week?" Sammish asked.

The alley was behind a row of stalls in Newmarket. The thin stretched-cloth door of the butcher's stood open before her. A pile of cracked bones and gristle seethed with flies, and blood was soaking up into her shoes, but the old butcher's smile was kindly.

"Is everything all right?" he asked. And when she didn't answer, "You seem anxious."

Today, the priest was saying the final rites for Darro, and if Alys wasn't there, Sammish didn't know where she would ever find her. But Sammish smiled the way she thought he'd find charming and shook her head. If he didn't believe her, he didn't press.

"Wait there," he said, then trundled back into the cool and dark of his shop. Sammish shifted her weight from one leg to the other, keeping her mouth closed and waving away the insects that tried to drink from her eyes. The leather sack at her hip wasn't hers. It belonged to a whetstone man who lent it to her once each week. For every five knives she brought him to sharpen, he paid her enough to buy a meal or a night's shelter. Other days, she did other work: sweeping the street outside a merchant's stall in Seepwater, wrapping twine for a weaver east by the Temple, hunting rats for the magistrate at a bronze coin for a dozen.

No one of her jobs would keep her from being streetbound, but all of them together were enough to eke out rent on a little room by a baker's kiln and enough food to live on. She liked the knife work best, even if it meant the most running. The merchant family couldn't hide their contempt and sometimes forgot to pay, the twine left her fingers raw, and she felt sorry for the rats. The money was just to keep her alive until she could reap the greater harvest later.

The whetstone man—Arnal his name was—had a brother who managed a brewery in Seepwater. He didn't own it—some rich family in Riverport did that—but he had the day-to-day running of it, including the choice of who sat behind the iron grates and marked wagers. Sammish was learning the numbers and letters they used there.

A few months of showing up for Arnal and his knives to prove she was reliable, and also teaching herself how to run the wagers, and then she planned to push for a job at the brewer's. She went about it like it was a pull, even though it broke no laws. Something about wanting it that badly felt like crime.

Steady indoor work with enough coin in a week to afford a few rooms where she could eat bread that wasn't two days stale and cheese that wasn't half rind. Sometimes, on the edge of sleep, she would imagine her way into that future with the scent of lavender fresh cut from the herb gardens outside the hospital south of the city and a mattress of fresh straw sighing under their bodies as they shifted in languorous sleep.

In her dream, it was always the both of them. Her and Alys.

The old butcher trundled back toward her, a long, curved blade in his fist. She smiled as he cracked open the door and handed it through. She didn't know why he bothered with the cloth. There were as many flies in the shop as out of it.

"Take good care of my boy there," the butcher said.

"Always," Sammish said as she folded the blade into a sheet of leather the way Arnal had taught her and put it in her satchel with the others. "I'll have him back to you by sundown."

"Bring it before the market closes, and there'll be something in it for you."

"I'll do my best," Sammish said with a little bow, then turned back down the alley and left the blood and rot and flies behind. Her shoes were dark and sticky, and for a moment a fly was trapped in her hair. She'd never seen war, but she imagined it was like the alley behind a butcher's shop, only better because she liked animals more than she liked people. On a battlefield, the flies all danced on bodies that had had the chance to fight back.

She made her way in a loop, moving through Newmarket and east to the outskirts around the Temple where the gods of the city were worshipped and the grain stored against emergency, moving fast, but also looking through every crowd at every corner on the off chance she'd see Alys in it.

She passed through streets and alleys, thin private yards and streets that had been closed off and forgotten, all to avoid the bluecloaks who might stop her and ask for proof she'd paid the city's tax on her work. She hadn't.

Riverport, Newmarket, the Temple, Seepwater: there was no place east of the Khahon that Sammish didn't know, but she didn't brag about it. Pride was the poison of Longhill. To want better than life and death in the narrow, winding alleys was disloyalty. To try for even so small an escape as work in Seepwater seemed complicit in the city's contempt for Longhill and the Inlisc who lived there. She knew to keep her ambitions to herself.

She came to the whetstone man's shed just before midday. The heat was climbing, and the air had a thick humidity that stuck her tunic against her back. The afternoon would be as hot as midsummer, even if the night came a little sooner. The shed had no windows, and the air inside it was sluggish.

"What do we have today?" Arnal asked. He was older with white hair in tight curls that stood away from his scalp like they were trying to get away from him. She liked his voice. He always seemed like he was on the edge of laughing at something that wasn't her.

Sammish sat on the floor at his feet and undid the satchel's ties. "Shears from the tailor's shop under the chandlers' guild hall. She said to tell you these were for wool, not cotton. This hooked one here is from the cobbler's by the temple gate."

"Hard leather or soft?"

"This one's for hard. I've got another one here for soft. Soft has the red handle. There's the usual from the Newmarket butcher."

Arnal nodded, then pointed to the last remaining blade. "That?"

Sammish held up the ritual dagger with its false runes and glass gemstones. "Fortune-teller."

"Why do they need an edge on it?"

"Sometimes they bleed a chicken."

Arnal opened the little water sluice that kept his stone wet. Sammish stood, brushing the dust off her legs, and turned toward the door.

"You're not staying to run them home?" Arnal asked.

"I'll be back. I have to check something first."

"Death is division," the priest said. "Not only for the dying who passes from this world to the coming cycle, but within each of us. We are trapped between the life we had when our friend, our lover, our parent, our child was with us, and this diminished world without them. We are split in two, and bringing ourselves back to wholeness is the spiritual work of mourning."

Darro's body was already gone. The priests had burned it to ashes over the course of three days, chanting and praying over the kiln as it worked. What had been a man now fit in a box of stained scrap oak no longer than her forearm.

The pews in the little common temple had half a dozen

people in them. Alys's mother was there. One of Darro's old lovers sat apart, her eyes shining and bloodshot. A few others from the quarter who had known the man and either liked him better than Sammish guessed or enjoyed the ritual for its own sake sat together gossiping quietly.

Alys wasn't there.

"In the name of all the gods of Kithamar," the priest intoned, "and in the name of the man we knew as Darro, and in the names of those who remain in this world to carry his memory on, we now sing his soul to safety."

The death song was a single melody; the priest's voice was hoarse and low. The words were old Inlisc. Sammish had heard them before, but she didn't know what they meant. She lowered her head and pretended to pray to gods she didn't believe in on behalf of a soul she didn't care about. All she really meant was *Please let Alys be all right.*

At the end, the priest took a blade and carved a mark in the box. As Darro had been the name of his life, his deathmark would be the name of his absence from the world. The priest rubbed bright yellow wax to fill the new-carved grooves, and the full rites were complete. Neither the water nor the sky nor any spirit had claim on Darro's soul now. To Sammish's mind, that put him ahead of everyone else in the room.

Alys's mother went up to claim her son's ashes, but the priest only took her hand, murmuring soft words in a kind voice. He didn't pass the box over. Sammish saw a flash of humiliation in the old woman's face and felt something like joy leap up in her chest. The only reason Sammish could think that he wouldn't give the box to Darro's mother was that the old woman hadn't paid for the rites. Which meant that even though Alys wasn't here now, she would be. Alys would come for Darro's ashes, and when she did, Sammish would be there.

The others left, and the priests cleared ceremonial tools away. Sammish stayed. She'd take the knives back to their right places in the morning if she had to. The priest looked at her, a question in his slow, heavy eyes. She said nothing and waited before the empty altar with a hundred different gods and no one.

It was dark before she came.

The public door scraped, and Alys came in like a thief. The cloak over her head might have hidden her from someone who didn't know her, hadn't watched her from the corners of their eyes, wasn't hoping to see her there, but Sammish's heart tightened and relaxed in the same moment before Alys had taken three steps toward the altar. The priest came forward to meet her, the box of Darro's ashes in his hand. Alys took it, spoke a few words too softly to be heard, and let the priest return to his duties. She traced the deathmark with her fingertips and let the hood fall back a few inches. In the warm light, the darkness under her eyes looked like bruises, but they were likely only sleeplessness.

Sammish stood, and Alys started, noticing her for the first time. The fear in her expression was like Sammish had snuck up on a cat without being heard and tugged its tail. For a moment, she was certain Alys would race for the street and be gone. Sammish stood very still, met her friend's gaze, and nodded slowly.

She could see Alys weighing something in her mind, but she had no idea what it was. Alys moved forward with twitch-fast, uncertain steps, crowding close to her. Her eyes looked wild in the soft light.

"What are you doing here?" Alys said, her voice brittle and sharp.

"Looking for you."

"Why? Who wants me found?"

"I'm not hired. I just... You were gone, and I didn't know where."

"You're not being paid to hunt me down?"

There were hundreds of things Sammish had half imagined Alys might say, but this was none of them. "I wouldn't take that job if someone offered. We're friends."

Alys seemed to turn in on herself, like she was listening to voices only she could hear. Sammish chanced a step toward her, and Alys didn't shy.

"You can help me," she said. "I'll go to . . . I'll go to the square where Nimal's crew spends their days?"

"The dry cistern," Sammish said with a nod.

"You follow behind and watch. See if anyone comes after me. If you see someone, shout to me, yeah?"

"Are you in trouble?"

Alys shook her head, but she didn't mean *No.* "Let's find out."

In the street, the moon was little more than a sliver of white, the stars a scattering of brightness between the close-set eaves. What light there was came from the candle glow of windows. Alys was a shadow among shadows, and Sammish followed her by the sound of footsteps as much as by the glimpses she wrung out of the darkness. As they walked, she listened for anything else. Longhill at night was more nearly silent than in the day, but still Sammish heard voices. Two men shouting over each other about something. Someone else crying. Unnervingly close by, a single deep laugh that wasn't repeated. Running footsteps from the east that ended with the clatter of a closing door. Sammish followed and watched, imagining what she would do if she did see someone falling in behind Alys. She wished that she had a knife. Before her, Alys slipped in and out of sight.

When they arrived at the square, it was empty. In daylight, it was hardly more than a wider space in the street with a cistern that had cracked four years earlier, spilling water into the street and through people's homes on its muddy way to the river, and still hadn't been repaired. Now the place felt like something from a song—a space between worlds where the familiar and the eerie mixed and became each other. Alys sat on the edge of the dry cistern, her hands at her sides. From the way she held herself, Sammish guessed they were in fists. Alys tensed as Sammish walked toward her, and then relaxed a little when she recognized that it was only the girl she'd expected. Sammish sat beside her on the crumbling stone. The grit muttered against her thigh.

Sammish's eyes had adapted to the night, and in the weak glimmer of moon and stars, she could make out some of Alys's features. The tightness of her mouth, the wildness of her eyes. She was so clearly in the grip of fear that Sammish half expected some overlooked threat to lurch out of the shadows at them. She felt her own throat tighten.

"Anyone?" Alys asked.

Sammish shook her head, then saw that Alys wasn't looking at her. "No. No one followed you. Just me."

"Good," Alys said sharply. And then, more softly, "That's very, very good."

"What is going on? Where have you been? Is this to do with Darro?"

Alys took a long, shuddering breath made louder by the dark. When she leaned forward, it was as sudden as if she'd been punched.

"I don't know what's going on, but Darro was in something. A pull of his own, maybe. It was big."

"Is it why he was killed?"

"I don't *know*," Alys said, her voice breaking on the final word. "I don't know why it happened or who did it. I found things after he was gone, and I know there was something big happening. It might have been them. Or it could have been the bluecloak. The one from our pull. The one at the coronation. You remember?"

"Of course I do."

"Or he was looking for Orrel and something happened. It might not have been his work at all. It might have been me. I can't tell. I don't know if I killed him. Maybe I killed him."

Alys's voice rose with each phrase like a plucked string being pulled tighter.

"I've been moving from place to place, watching to see if anyone followed. I thought of going back to Aunt Thorn, but what if she was part of his pull or whatever it was, because who else could it be with coin like that? I couldn't even be in Long-hill where everyone knows me and I know everyone, or it feels like that, and then I wasn't going to come tonight, but..." She lifted the ashes and began to cry in earnest.

Sammish, heart aching, went to put an arm around her shoulders, but Alys flinched. Sammish made do with an awkward pat on her shoulder blade.

She couldn't make much sense of the words spilling out in the darkness. The details, whatever they were, would have to wait. What she could take as certain was that Alys had been frightened and alone for long enough that she was drunk on it. She'd spent too long with only her fear and her grief, and it was throwing her mind off. Alys was the sure one, solid and comfortable with her own judgment. The bawling girl in the dark beside her was an aspect that Sammish had never seen before. The older girl's vulnerability pulled at Sammish like a sudden rush in the river. She found herself weeping a little too, not even knowing what they were upset about. Only that Alys was broken by it, and so she was too.

Alys's sobs slowed a little. The shadow of her bowed head went still. The soft, saltwater smell of tears came to Sammish like the subtlest perfume, and she sighed. The slap of boots against cobblestone came from off to their left, but Alys didn't stiffen, and the footsteps passed and faded away. Some other poor bastard making their way through the dark on an errand that didn't touch them. Sammish sighed deeply and gathered herself.

"All right," she said. "Do you need money?"

Alys's one bitter laugh could have meant she needed it badly or that she didn't need it at all. Sammish didn't press that issue. Not yet, anyway.

"Whatever it is you need, we'll find a way to get it," Sammish said, making her voice sound more certain than she was. She didn't know if she was being strong for Alys or as a way to convince herself that what she said made sense. "We're clever, and it won't be hard. Then once you're not spinning around like a feather in a windstorm, we'll take care of the rest."

Alys was silent for a moment. When she spoke, her voice was still thick and raw. "You don't have to do that."

"We'll take care of the rest," Sammish said again, neither more forcefully nor less. "But first, if you can, tell me what we're looking at. All of it. From go."

Andomaka Chaalat, whom Darro had known as the pale woman, slept, and in her sleep she dreamed. She was very well practiced at dreaming.

In her dream it was winter, the great river in the heart of the city a single sheet of grey ice stretching north into the wilds and south toward the distant sea. She knew it was bitingly cold though she didn't feel it. Just north of her, a hole in the ice wide enough to fall through framed black, fast-flowing water. She watched threads of water weaving over one another, the turbulence shifting like the river itself was alive and restless. Something struck the ice she stood on from below like it was aiming for her feet, and she understood that Prince Ausai was in the water. That he was trapped there, swimming against the stream but unable to reach back to the catastrophe where the ice had collapsed beneath him.

Panic lit her, and she turned south, looking for some other flaw in the ice. Or for some instrument to make one. Around her on both sides of the river, the stones and buildings of Kithamar shuddered and cracked, and she knew with the logic of dream that they were being replaced. New buildings that, while they looked just the same, were not. Impostors made from architecture. The city itself was being eaten from within, and something alien, new, and malefic was taking its place.

The thump of punches from under the ice grew louder, and she sprinted, trying to find exactly where they were loudest, where Ausai was summoning her. And then her perspective shifted, and she was the one underwater. The Khahon carried her along under the gently glowing ice, and she saw no escape. She would be carried down to the sea that was also death and be lost in it.

She woke herself trying to scream.

She was in her room. Thin, milky moonlight pressed through the window like the glow of the ice she had just left. She pulled herself up from her bed and walked across the rugs, wood creaking under her with every step. Her private rooms looked out toward the east, the still-coming dawn, and the palace where her cousin Byrn a Sal slept in the prince's chambers.

Her cousin who was not what he seemed.

She felt the urge to go down to the private temple, as if anything there would have changed. She resisted. The servant girl who slept in the pallet at the end of Andomaka's bed muttered, stirred, and sat up.

"Lady Chaalat? Are you all right?"

"I had a dream," she said.

"Should I get your books, lady? Or wake Master Tregarro?"

"I don't need them. I know what this dream meant," Andomaka said. "It wasn't subtle."

Each year, a day came that marked the end of summer.

The city rose as it had for months, but instead of thick, heavy, unforgiving heat, there was a crispness to the morning air. Before midday came, the city would be bathed in its own sweat again, the taxmen at the gates would be fanning themselves as they had before and would again, and the dogs would curl in the shadows and pant. Children would swim in the canals and be chased out by mothers afraid that their babies would drown. The following morning might have the same chill, or it might not. There would be more warm days to come, but they would be warm autumn days. Summer had surrendered its crown, and the slow, lush, sensual slide into harvest had begun.

This was the first one in Alys's life that Darro wouldn't share. And after it, the first Longest Night without him. The first thaw he wouldn't see.

Since the night she'd found the knife and the coins, Alys had kept moving, spending her nights streetbound near the Temple or buying a place on a barge tied up on the Riverport docks.

Most recently, she'd found a room set deep into the flesh of Palace Hill in the quarter they called Oldgate: a vast fortification that rose up the eastern cliff face from the river to the palace. She leaned against the retaining wall that held the switchback road from crumbling down to the water, and looked out to the east and the rising sun. She wasn't even a quarter of the way up the black stone face of the hillside, but she could see out over the streets of Newmarket and Seepwater to Longhill. In the morning light, the roofs looked like a city of gold. It was an illusion. It was all stone and wood, brick and tile. It was only distance that made it beautiful.

And below her, on the southernmost of the four bridges that touched Oldgate—the one that spanned the northernmost edge of the Silt and reached across to Seepwater—she saw Sammish making her way toward her. Alys watched the little figure, small as a doll with distance, and felt a complexity of anticipation and dread, gratitude and resentment and growing restlessness. It was good having the girl as her accomplice in finding out what had happened, her eyes and ears where Alys was too wary to go herself. It gave her a path forward that she hadn't had before. Already, they'd found that no one seemed to have a price on Alys. The taprooms of Longhill weren't asking what had become of her except in the most idle, perfunctory ways. Nor had anyone come to her mother to dig for information about what Darro had been about when he'd died. All of it important for her to know, all of it calming in its fashion.

She should have been pleased, and in part she was. But Sammish wasn't Darro, and some part of Alys's heart felt betrayed by everyone who wasn't. Everyone in the city. The world.

Sammish reached the near end of the bridge and began the long trudge up the face of Oldgate, coming in and out of sight as the switchback carried her, and growing taller and less doll-like every time. Alys felt a vague obligation to go down and meet her, and resented it until it was too late and Sammish reached her. Then she felt a pang of guilt and resented that instead.

Sammish squatted beside her. The sun was fully risen now, the roofs to the east had lost their gold, and the river hadn't yet caught the brightness that it later would. A cart passed behind them, with the mule tied at the back as a brake against gravity pulling it down. The other girl pulled a tart from her sleeve and held it out to Alys almost tentatively. The crust was gold, and the center black with berries. Alys took it with a nod of thanks and bit into the warm, crisp salt-and-sweet. She hadn't realized until just then that she was hungry.

Sammish had a tart of her own, and they ate in silence for a moment before Sammish spoke. "I found the bluecloak."

Alys shifted to look at her directly. Pleasure danced at the corners of Sammish's mud-brown eyes. "At least I think I did. You said he called himself Tannen something?"

"The one Orrel took the belt from?"

"I think so," Sammish said. "I'm not certain. You saw him better than I did, and the one I found isn't city guard. But his name's Tannen, and he's the right age and frame. I think it's him."

"Where?"

"Camnit warehouse," Sammish said, gesturing across the water. "Do you know the one with blue doors next to the ropemakers' guild hall? There. He's new to the work. If that's because he lost his place in the guard..."

Alys put the last of her pastry into her mouth, leaning forward as if by mere will she could see across the water and make out one door from another. The thing in her head was moving now. She couldn't put a name to what she was feeling, but it was warm and high in her chest. And it didn't hurt. It was strange to feel something that didn't hurt. It left her lightheaded.

"Let's go see," she said. She rose and started down the slope to the river and the bridges. Sammish trotted after her.

At the bridge, the city guard eyed them suspiciously—two Inlisc girls on the wrong side of the water—then waved them past and went on collecting bronze tolls from the carters and laborers carrying cloth and wood and sacks of wheat to the eastern bank. Near the halfway point in the span, a street cleaner's cart was parked. Four young men—prisoners of the city—stood in it shirtless, throwing shovelfuls of shit and dead animals into the water. They whistled at Alys and Sammish, and one dropped his trousers to wag an unimpressive penis at them both until the bluecloak shouted at him and flicked his bare ass with a mule goad. Alys noticed them the way she did the sun or the sound of the river.

Once they reached the docks at Riverport, the activity stopped seeming like an anthill and grew into something more like a storm. Harvest hadn't come, but the preparations for it were stirring the streets. Boats unloaded barrels of sugar from island cities like Imaja and Caram far to the south. As soon as the holds were emptied, sacks of wheat and rye took their place until the waterline rose back up their sides. Fortunes were being made and lost in the chaos. A broken crane that slowed one family's pier might mean their ruin. A wise purchase of vinegar could let another family keep pickled eggs and vegetables through a bad spring when a mouthful of food was worth more than its weight in silver or silk. Mules dropped their heads and pushed through the crowded streets. Carters whipped away dogs and beggars. The warehouses stood with their doors open, and enforcers with chains and lead-dipped ropes guarded the goods. The air was thick with the smells of sweat and spice and the river.

It would have been a fine place for a pull, except that no one here carried a fat wallet. The rich merchants and skilled artisans were all in their courtyards and houses, playing at contracts and law. The silver and bronze remnants of Alys's one broken gold coin were probably the most wealth in the street. At the end of the second dock from the bridge, Sammish touched her arm. Alys let herself be led away from the river and toward the warehouses.

The Camnit family was well enough known that Alys had heard of it. They were Hansch merchants with family ties outside of Kithamar, but roots in the city that went back generations. They weren't nobility. Noble blood didn't live east of the water. They were wealth, though, and had the power that came with gold. Their warehouse was large, well maintained, and close to the water. Sammish put her head down as they walked past tall, wide doors painted the blue of a midsummer sky. Alys felt the urge to stare into the warehouse, searching through the shadows for a familiar face. Darro's voice came back to her. *Fifty steps.* She put her eyes to the street and counted fifty like it was a kind of magic. When they reached an intersection with smaller, less dignified warehouses and guild halls, she looked back.

A cart was coming up from the river, moving toward the Camnit doors. Two thick-shouldered men drove a pair of mules. The cart was piled precariously high with barrels of salt.

"The one at the back," Sammish said.

Following the cart, a younger man walked, his shirt off. He looked fresh, pale, and doughy compared to the older carters, and he used a long pole to steady the load. Each of those barrels was worth more than his season's pay. If one fell and broke while he was on the stick, he'd be working for less than free.

All the way over, Alys had worried that she wouldn't be sure. She wasn't worried now.

She remembered his voice as he threatened to cut her throat, and also his embarrassment and outrage when the shit and piss started raining down on him. He'd been humiliated. He'd lost his position in the guard. Would that have been enough to make him kill Darro? She imagined those pale hands holding a knife and the chagrin in Darro's eyes as he bled out at those thick-ankled feet.

"Well?" Sammish said. "Was I right?"

"Yes," she said, her heart feeling something like life for the first time since Grey Linnet had told her the news. "That's him."

"We have a start, then. I'm not sure what we do with him next. We can't exactly go ask him whether he's the one that killed your brother."

The cart rolled into the shadow of the warehouse. The once-bluecloak stepped in after it, the steadying pole in his trembling hands.

"Oh, I think we can," Alys said.

Tannen Gehart, once a city guardsman and now a junior laborer, ached. Every part of him from the soles of his feet to the place where his spine met his skull found some way to complain. His eyes were sweat-stung, his arms fly-bitten, and every muscle had been worked to the edge of collapse. The sun was gone, and the warehouse lit by moth-swarmed lanterns. His day still wasn't done.

"Not bad for a tadpole," the overseer said. He was a fat man named Hawls whose jiggling belly hid a terrible strength and boundless endurance. Tannen was well on his way to hating him. "A few more seasons like this, and you'll be a real man, eh?"

"Just doing my bit," Tannen said. He heard the others in the street, laughing at something. They'd all been paid out for the day's work. Tannen was the last, and Hawls hadn't taken his coins out of the paybox yet. He kept stalling.

"Your bit," Hawls said, chuckling. "Yeah, that. Thing is, there's always the sweeping up after. Used to be that was Darrit's to do, but with you coming on the crew, well, you're the newest, and it's the new man's duty . . ."

Despair deepened Tannen's weariness. All he wanted was his day's pay, a bowl of something with meat in it, and his cot. He knew when he took the job that it would be like this, for a while at least. Any whining he did now, he'd carry for years.

"Right," he said. "Tell me what needs doing so I don't miss anything."

Hawls handed him a broom, gestured at the warehouse piled high with barrels of salt and stacks of cut lumber, and laughed. "We'll be down at the porters' hall long enough to drink a little. Find me there for your pay. If you take too long, there's always morning."

Tannen tried to think of something manly and smart to say, but he was too tired and a quick wit had never been his strength. He marched himself back into the shadows and started sweeping. Hawls shared a couple jokes with the night guards and walked off into the darkness, smoking a clay pipe and humming to himself.

The temptation was to go fast, do just enough, and be done. He made himself be slow and thorough. Every time he found his attention had wandered, he went back over the last stretch he'd done. More times than not, it wasn't clean. True, they'd just be tracking in new dirt come dawn, but before that, Hawls would see what kind of job he'd made of it. If it was clean, he'd know Tannen was there to work. Suffering a little now to suffer less later was the smart way to go.

The night guards kept their watch. The city bluecloaks passed by once; a team of four that had Kannish and Maur in it. Tannen worked with his back to the street while they passed to keep from being recognized, or at least not to know that he'd been seen. Insects beat their bodies against the clear glass lanterns or found paths inside them and burned. The warehouse stank of their bodies and the cheap oil. Time lost itself. When he brought the last pile of dirt out to the street, he didn't know if he'd gone quickly or slow. One of the night guards took the broom from him as he blew out the lanterns, and they closed and barred the doors behind him as he left.

He turned toward the night and the porters' hall. His feet seemed farther away from him than usual, and harder to move. If Hawls were there, he'd get his pay and eat. If not, he'd go back to the bunks and sleep. Either one sounded wonderful.

The night was dark. What there was of the moon ducked behind high clouds, the shadows passing over the streets. He tried taking a few steps with his eyes closed to see if it mattered, but it felt too comfortable. He forced himself to open them to keep from falling asleep on his feet and stumbling into the river.

Oldgate rose on the far side of the water, a few torches and lanterns glittering on the switchback that rose up its face. The palace glowered at its crown, looking like the ancient war keep that it had once been. They were probably sleeping fine up there, curled in soft sheets on mattresses of quilted silk or something. He'd be lucky if the rushes on the bunkroom floor were fresh.

He noticed the girl stepping out from the gap between two ivy-choked walls, but she didn't alarm him until she stood in his way, her hands clasped in front of her. His first thought was that she was an unclean spirit thrown up by the river. His second was that she was a whore looking for work he couldn't afford to give her. He paused. The moon shadow passed, giving a little pale light. He saw an unremarkable, round face, neither pretty nor ugly. Her expression was something like chagrin.

"For what it carries?" she said. "I am sorry."

Through his weariness, a little thread of alarm came too late. Something hit his back, and he stumbled forward, hands out to catch himself. He skinned his palms against the pavement. If he cried out, he didn't notice it. A hand knotted itself in his hair and hauled his head up. A blade pressed against his neck.

Oh, Tannen thought, *this is how I die.*

But the blade didn't tug to the side. His throat stayed unslit. Instead a voice hissed at his ear. A woman's voice, but not the apologetic girl. Someone else. "Did you kill my brother?"

"Who the fuck are you?" he squeaked. And then, "No, I didn't kill anyone. I've never killed anyone."

"You were a bluecloak." The knife pressed closer. If she drew her arm to the side, he wouldn't see morning.

"For half a year," he said. "I saw maybe four fights the whole time, and no one died in any of them. I swear it. I'll swear by anything!"

The darkness around them thickened. He wondered, if he called out, whether any of his old friends would hear him. If they'd be in time to watch him die in the street. The first girl spoke again, but not to him. "I believe him."

Two long, shuddering breaths passed before the knife girl replied. "I do too."

The blade vanished, and a boot came down hard in his ribs. He felt something crack. Then another kick came, this one a toe-point to his kidney. The pain was brighter than fire. Tannen curled into a ball and waited for another blow. It didn't come. Through the sound of his own breath, he heard two sets of soft footsteps moving away. He rested his head against the stone of the street. As hard as it was, it still felt like the most comfortable pillow in the world.

Alys felt like she was flying, like her heart had widened to the size of the city and become fire. She wore the cool Kithamar night like a wide black cape and walked like she was still and the world moved under her. The long, empty days in her cell felt like a dream she'd had. Or the threat of a nightmare she'd fall into if she closed her eyes again too soon.

Sammish walked at her side, grinning. Alys remembered the weight and solidity of the bluecloak's back as she hit him as if it were happening again. The thin whine of his voice. The first time she'd had enough wine hadn't felt this good. The warmth and the broadness of spirit were both there, but the drink had left her muzzy-headed and sleepy. Now she felt more awake than she'd ever been, and she loved it.

"You know, then," Sammish said as they reached the river and started across. "It wasn't him."

"It's a good start," Alys agreed. The river roared against the stone under their feet like a god talking softly. Alys had the urge to jump over the stone lip and dive into the water as if she could command it. She knew better than to give the impulse life. She thought instead about digging the coin out of her safe cache and finding some taproom where she could sing and spend and be lifted up by what she'd done. That was a dream. The night was already full, and Kithamar in its beds. Any taproom she found now would be on its way to empty before she stepped in. Her own company would have to be enough.

She walked up the slope of Oldgate, her legs burning pleas-antly from the effort, and ducked into the thin inner streets within the hillside's flesh. It struck her that this was likely the longest she'd ever spent sleeping outside Longhill. When she was younger, she'd gone out to work harvest at an orchard east of the city that had taken her away for a time, but this harvest was longer, darker, and not yet at its end.

In her tiny cell, she lit a white candle—she'd need to buy more in the morning—and set it beside Darro's box. The yellow wax of his deathmark picked up the glow. Sammish sat on the cot, legs folded up under her. Her mud-brown eyes were brighter than usual, her smile an echo of Alys's own intoxication.

"You did good work," Alys said. "Finding him wasn't the answer, but you did good work. You shouldn't feel bad that he wasn't the one."

If Sammish's smile seemed to dim for a moment, it was likely just her mind turning to the path ahead. Alys leaned her back against the wall. The cell wasn't brick this deep in, but the native stone of the hill. She'd heard that in winter, the depths of Oldgate kept the cold at bay, but for now the wall felt cool against her shoulders. The elation was starting to fade, and she tried to hold it, willing it bright again like blowing on embers. She was suddenly tired.

"Orrel next," Alys said. "You said he was looking for Darro. If he found him—"

"Or the knife," Sammish said. "Orrel, we might put hand to, we might not, but the knife is here for certain. I could take it to the whetstone man I know. Maybe his clients. They might recognize it."

No jumped to Alys's throat, but she stopped it there. The thought of letting the weird blade out of her cell felt like a threat. What if it didn't come back? What if she lost that bit of Darro too? It was a mad thought. Her brother wasn't the blade. It couldn't call him back from his ashes.

"I don't know," she said.

"I'll be careful with it," Sammish said, and then, almost shyly, "And I know how to stay clear of a cutter's pull."

Alys chuckled, and Sammish smiled. It was the smile that did it. Alys took the blade and its sheath and handed them over.

"Do what you can," she said.

Sammish stood in the fortune-teller's back room shifting her weight from leg to leg while the old man who actually ran the place pulled the knife from its sheath and held it up to the light.

"Looked similar to yours," Sammish said. "I thought you might know it."

The actual fortune-teller was a Hansch girl with one blue eye and one brown. It made her look exotic and mysterious. She sat in a red leather chair, watching the old man with a look of amusement that Sammish liked even less than the old man's scowl. Sammish couldn't tell if the girl had had too much wine or if she was drunk on something stranger. Either way, she wasn't right. The room itself was dim, except for the one open-shuttered window. Tin mirrors lined two walls, throwing back twisted images of the three of them. A low black table had a wide silver bowl filled halfway with vinegar water that the fortune-teller would heat and pour egg whites into. The ghostly whorls were supposed to show the future. It stank of spices and incense.

The old man made a sour noise at the back of his throat. "These markings?" he said. "They're supposed to look like old gregate runes. Life and death, love and sex. Truth and cutting through the space between spaces. All the usual. The calligraphy's not bad."

"It's silver too," Sammish said. "You can see where it's tarnished up at the hilt."

"Plated, yeah. Not kept very well, is it?" the old man said. It wasn't plated.

He'd been running the fortune-teller's place for as long as Sammish could remember. The girl might have been his daughter or his lover or something odder. Sammish fought the urge to take the blade back. She didn't like the way he held it.

"Has to do with a murder, you said?" the old man asked.

"Didn't say. Might, might not," Sammish said, not looking him full in the eyes. "Someone had it."

"And now they don't." The old man chuckled. "All right, fine. The workmanship's not good. It's not likely to keep an edge, but as props go, it has some charm to it. I can give you eight bronze. Not more."

Sammish shook her head, confused. The old man didn't take it that way.

"Don't be like that," he said. "I'll go to ten because I like you, and Arnal's been sharpening my knives on the cheap for years. It's a favor, though. You'll owe me one back."

"I'm not looking to sell," Sammish said, and she snatched the sheath back. "That's mine. I only want to know what you thought about it."

"I think ten bronze of it," the old man said. "What's a girl like you going to do with something like this? You're not looking to come into my trade, are you? Because I won't have that. People like us might not have a guild, but that doesn't mean you can step into our business without consequences."

He was holding the knife by the handle now. He wasn't quite threatening her with it. Sammish felt her throat go tight. She couldn't win a scrap if the old man wanted one. She didn't want him to talk down to Arnal about her either. She wanted nothing more than to take his offer, however bad it was, and leave. If it hadn't been Alys's blade they were talking about, she might have.

"Not mine to sell," she said around the knot in her throat. "You can give it back now."

He hesitated. "A silver."

"I'd like to have it back now," she said, and the fortune-telling girl laughed. The sound was so unexpected, Sammish jumped. The old man snarled but at the other girl, not at her. He tossed the blade on the black table.

"Suit yourself," he said. "It's a shit blade with some nice drawings on it. Hope it keeps you warm in your old age. I've got work."

He stalked out. His footsteps tramped back through the hall and up the back stairs as Sammish scooped up her knife and put it back in its sheath. Even with him gone, she felt the threatening weight of his presence. She was about to leave when the fortune-teller spoke.

"Don't mind him. He's only angry because he thought he could turn a quick profit. He has a buyer for it."

"A buyer?"

The fortune-teller sat forward, languid as a cat. "Foreign woman came in a while back asking after a blade like that. Down to the markings."

"Foreign?"

"Not from Kithamar. Her accent sounded like something from the south. All clicks around the edges. She came asking after a silver knife marked with the same words as that."

"You can read them?"

"They say *Death of Death.* More or less. Translation isn't my work. She offered good money, too. Gold."

Sammish felt her gut tighten, thinking of Darro's secret coins. "How much gold?"

"Enough to be remembered. If you'd let that thing go for a silver, you'd have been getting the worst deal in Kithamar, and we're a city of cheats." The fortune-teller's smile was hazy. The old man's footsteps passed over them as he paced the floor above. Sammish had the image of him, weapon in hand, working himself up to violence. The smart thing was to leave and leave now.

"When did this southerner come?" she asked.

The fortune-teller shrugged.

"Please," Sammish said.

"After the word came about Prince Ausai being ill. Before he died. In there someplace. I don't remember."

That meant the woman, whoever she was, had been seeking the blade before Darro was killed. Sammish felt her blood moving faster in her veins, but couldn't tell if it was excitement or fear or both. "Did she have a name?"

"Saffa, I think. Or Sabba. She was an intense little thing. I liked her. I would have read her fortune for free, just to try working on a southerner. I like you too. Do you want to know your future?"

A louder thump came from above them, startling Sammish. "I should leave."

"I see death before you," the fortune-teller said, her voice suddenly deeper. "Death for you and everyone you love."

Sammish's breath went thin. Something must have shown in her expression, because the fortune-teller laughed and leaned back in her chair. She looked younger when she did it.

"Why is that *funny*?" Sammish said, surprised at her own anger.

"Because, green pea, it's true for everyone."

According to the vivisectionists at the university, the hearts of all animals were a kind of fist, relaxing to fill with blood and squeezing to push it out through the rest of the body. Alys imagined it working like a man flexing his hands before a fight he knew he'd eventually lose. The city had a pulse like that too, and harvest was the time when Kithamar filled.

The weeks before harvest saw the streets of Longhill and Newmarket and Riverport emptier than usual as everyone in need of extra coin signed up for short work on the farms. Carts from all the trading houses lumbered out, filled with men and women. The carts would come back filled with the produce of the year's growth, the men and women trudging exhausted behind them as spent as an army back from campaign. Then the race began: on one hand, the sugar and salt, pickling broth, and wax-sealed long pots, and on the other, the inevitability of rot.

Alys remembered being almost too young to walk, sitting in the great stone kitchen of some house in Stonemarket where her mother had gotten work stirring a vast pot of berries as they cooked down for the jars. The memory had the smell of the woodsmoke and the brightness of the berries. There had been a foam of pink on top of the boiling darkness, and the head cook had let Alys help skim it off. She could still taste the sharpness and sweetness from when she licked her fingers after.

Harvest was full of memories like that: the way the leaves in the Silt lost their green and fell; the Khahon flowing dark as tea; the slowly growing night and the fading day. The long weeks until the first freeze were a constant flow of wheat and barley, apples and squash, lentils and broad beans. Cows and lambs and pigs came to Kithamar on carts or tied by ropes, their eyes tired and incurious. The slaughterhouses in Seepwater and the Smoke poured blood into the river by the barrelful, and children helped pack the fresh meat into curing salts for a bronze a day. The pantries and larders and storerooms of Kithamar filled, and every shelf was the promise that hunger wouldn't come.

The rush would end near the first frost with a great celebration led by the prince, and since it would be Byrn a Sal's first, everyone was vastly curious how it would go. Would there be dancers and fire-eaters the way his uncle had done? Or would the new prince find some way to make the celebration his own? Longhill buzzed with rumors of the forgiveness for crimes, which there sometimes was, or the forgiveness of taxes, which never happened however much people dreamed. The first harvest festival without Darro.

Alys was in a Longhill taproom that everyone called the Pit, a beer in her hand. Ever since the bluecloak, she'd found her fear starting to ebb. She didn't start at shadows the way she had, and while she hadn't come back to a room in Longhill, she hadn't jumped from her cell in Oldgate either. It wasn't courage, so much as the growing sense that whatever dangers there were, they hadn't caught her scent. And also the growing, half-felt sense that Darro wouldn't have run, so maybe she shouldn't either. She'd had one victory, small as it was. She couldn't win others by running.

Around her, the younger men and women of Longhill were spending their coin and relaxing. She was at work. Sometimes she could forget what she was working at, as if digging into Darro's death could make it not have happened. Sometimes it just poured ashes on the cut.

"Did you hear about the sugar barge that sank?" Korrim Stara asked.

"I didn't," another man answered. "What sank it?"

"Some asshole in Riverport got happy, ran a flatboat into the barge. Didn't notice it was taking on water. Whole damned thing went down, is what I heard."

"Well, there's someone's fortune lost," the barman said philosophically. "Pity for them."

The trick to finding Orrel was that he clearly didn't want to be found. Asking after him was like touching a snail's horn; it would only make him pull away. The best she could do was be in the places that he usually was, and then listen and watch. They were the same taprooms and street corners where she had been, where her friends and petty rivals were. She entered into her life as it had been before Darro died, like she was impersonating the girl she used to be.

The Pit had half as many people as usual, which wasn't surprising for harvest time. Given the choice between begging in the richer quarters, scraping for work in the city, stealing, or going to the fields for the season's reaping, about half chose the hard and honest labor, and about half didn't. Nimal and Cane at the little table in the back weren't the honest type. Korrim had a bad knee that wouldn't let him do fieldwork. Calm Biran was there too, his hair pulled back from his face to let the early grey at his temples show. Everyone in Longhill knew everyone else, if not directly then at no more than a single remove. Korrim had lived in the building beside Alys's mother for three years when she was younger. Nimal and Cane had used Alys as a lookout when they were breaking into Riverport houses sometimes. Calm Biran had an older sister who had bedded down with Darro for a time before she took up with a student at the university. All of them knew who she was, and how Darro had died.

"Anything more for you, Alys?"

She shook her head, but the mention of her name shifted the room's attention toward her. Nimal stood, stretched, and slouched over to her. "Where've you been keeping yourself?" His tone and the narrowness of his eyes meant he was asking whether she was open to crewing up on a pull. Any other time, it would have been interesting.

She shook her head, answering the question he hadn't asked. "I've been here. Just have my hands full for the time."

"Heard about your brother," he said. "Me and Darro, we didn't always get along, but he was a good man."

"Thank you," she said, because it was expected of her, and because any more genuine answer would have invited him to keep speaking. He put a hand on her shoulder in a way that wasn't an invitation to a more immediate and physical kind of comfort unless she was open to the idea, in which case it was. When she didn't respond, he took his hand away and went to the barman for a beer.

Darro's name in someone else's mouth left her uncomfortable, itchy, and restless. She drained the last of her drink, straining it through her teeth and spitting the dregs on the floor, and walked out. It was still daylight, even if the sun was low and red. She could have spent some time down near the university where the girls Orrel had favored plied their trade, but it wasn't in her. Not tonight. She could have found Sammish, but even her company felt like a burden. She needed sleep and food and time for something like hope to find its way back to her.

She walked back toward Oldgate with her hands pulled into her sleeves. The evenings were getting cooler, especially near the water. A singer had put a little wooden dais near the bridge, and she paused to listen to him warble his way through an old Inlisc ballad that ended with two lovers stabbed and dead. A closed carriage with no crest on its side barreled past like it was fleeing from something, but no one followed on behind it. A group of older men in the good clothes and colorful cloaks of Riverport merchants strolled past, muttering among themselves with the gossip of trade and politics. Reluctantly, Alys went back to the bridge and her cell in Oldgate. The effort of finding food was too much for her now, even though she knew she'd regret later that she'd let her belly go empty.

Her small darkness waited, as it always did: cot, candle, and ashes. The time was coming soon she'd have to either pay to keep it or find another place to sleep. She lay down in the dim light and turned to Darro's box. It was such a small thing to hold a whole body. Fire left so little behind. She didn't weep. Her heart had many masks these days. Rage and sadness were the most common, though she'd also found herself giddy and restless or weirdly calm, like someone already dead herself and only watching her life from a distance. Her heart was as uncertain as weather, and tonight it had chosen the old numbness and despair.

She would have thought grief was just sorrow. She knew better now.

"Well," she said to the box. "This could be going better. At least Sammish found something. I don't suppose you'd care to tell me who this southern knife hunter is? What she was to you? Or where Orrel is? Anything that would help?"

Darro's box flickered as the candle spat and the flame wavered.

"Didn't think so," Alys said. "If you want justice, you could start by being more useful. You should have seen that bluecloak. He was so sure of himself when he came after me that day, but I left him crying in the streets. You should have seen it. You should have—"

Without warning, her calm gave way, and she wept. Even as the sobs racked her, she felt a deeper darkness growing beneath the sorrow. Grief was supposed to fade. Wounds—even wounds to the soul—were supposed to heal. She felt hers getting worse.

The candle spat again, the wick almost spent. She rose unsteadily to her feet and dug in her sack for another, but there were none. She'd neglected light as much as she had food. A hazy half-memory came to her, and she went to her hiding place. The knife was gone. Sammish still had it. The gold was there and the little stub of black candle. She took it and went back to the holder. She stood tracing Darro's deathmark with her fingertip until her old candle seemed to be in its last, fading blue, then lit the little black candle from the dying light. The dark wick sparked as the new flame took. She dug the old wax from the holder with a fingertip, ignoring the heat, and leveled the dark stub in its place. It was burning fast. It wouldn't give her more than a few minutes, but some light was better than none.

She didn't notice at first that the smoke was doing anything odd. The wisps and trails of it didn't dissipate, but narrowed, thickened, and wove together. Her attention was on Darro and her own self-pity. The woman's voice, gentle as it was, startled her as if it had been a shriek.

"Well now. Who exactly are you, little wolf girl?"

Alys spun. There in the gloom of her cell, a pale woman stood, her body made of smoke but solid as the stone walls. She was Hansch, with high, sculpted eyebrows and well-painted lips. Straw-pale hair cascaded down her shoulders, and even her gently smiling lips seemed bloodless. Her robe was silk the color of moss, bound at the waist with a beautiful belt of braided leather with a dove worked in bronze as the clasp.

There was a soft, throaty clicking sound, and Alys realized it came from her. That she was trying to speak, but the fear choked her.

"It's all right," the pale woman said, stepping toward her. "I won't hurt you, little wolf girl. Only tell me how you—"

The dark wick spat and reached its end. The pale woman blinked out with the light.

"We're in over our heads. This is too much," Sammish said. And then, "What did her voice sound like? Did she have an accent?"

Alys frowned, trying to recall exactly how the pale woman's words had sounded. It seemed impossible that something so astonishing could fade from her memory so quickly, but with each question that Sammish asked, Alys felt less certain of the answer. "She did and she didn't? Not like she was from Hyian or Bronze Coast, but not like she was from Longhill, either."

"But Hansch? You're *sure* she was Hansch?"

"I was until you pushed me on it," Alys said, more sharply than she'd meant to, and Sammish pulled back like she'd come too close to a fire. Alys tried to cover over her snapping by going on in a gentler voice. "She seemed almost...kind, really. Like she'd just found a puppy someplace she hadn't expected to and was trying not to scare it off."

It was midmorning, and they were sitting in the street outside the baker's house where Sammish slept. Alys had spent the night walking, and exhaustion was deep in her bones. Staying in her little room after the apparition or visitation or whatever it was hadn't been possible. She'd scooped up her things in the darkness and left, trotting down the wide path toward the bridges almost before she'd thought about where she could go or who she could stay with.

The night had been cold, but not bitter. She'd thought of going to her mother's thin, loveless squat, or Sammish's, or Aunt

Thorn. Every impulse that came to her had the same problem: they were places that she would go. In the darkness, being where she was known felt dangerous. The sense that someone or something out there had seen her, that it would be looking for her, made her want to keep far away from the places where anyone could expect her to be. Instead, she had made her way across the river, and through the streets of Riverport and Newmarket. She'd even gone to the Temple grounds. The only rest she'd taken was sitting in an alley between two ill-dignified minor churches there.

The morning light had taken away enough of her fear that finding Sammish felt like a risk worth taking. She'd found the baker's house when the scent of woodsmoke and yeast were thick in the air. The oven—a clay kiln set apart from the buildings around it to keep down the risk of fire—was only a few feet behind them now. Alys felt the gentle warmth of it against the back of her neck. The ground was pale with the residue of years of flour dust and rain.

"It might have been a Green Hill kind of voice," Alys said. "Like the magistrates when they're passing judgment or when the prince gives a speech. And she was pretty like they are."

Sammish scratched her chin like she was stroking a beard. "This is bad. I mean, it wasn't good before. Orrel gone. Your brother killed. But now foreigners looking for enchanted daggers and wizard women weaving themselves from smoke? Whatever this is . . . There might be some sense in letting it be?"

Alys felt anger in her breast, twice as vicious because she'd had the same thought. "Darro wasn't your blood. I don't expect you to do the same things I do."

Sammish looked down, scowling hard. "Are you certain Darro would even want you to do this? He cared about you. He *loved* you. No one wants the people they love to be hurt. Maybe he'd tell us to stop? You paid his rites. You took care of him. What if that's enough?"

On the street, the cleaner's cart ambled around the corner. The prisoners with their flat wooden spades scraped the horse manure and other shit from the paving bricks and hefted it into the dark-streaked, stinking cart while four bluecloaks walked far enough behind to avoid the worst of the stink.

"It's not enough," Alys said.

"All right."

"If you don't want to be part of this—"

"No. It isn't that. I just... I'm scared."

Sammish's gaze was fixed on the ground between her feet. Her hair was loose and falling forward like she was trying to hide behind it. Alys dug a finger in her belt, opening the hidden seam and popping a silver coin free from its hiding place. She held it out. "You've earned it."

Sammish took the coin like she was stealing from a temple box, never meeting Alys's eyes.

"Give me back my knife," Alys said. Sammish brought it out from under her tunic. It was warm from her body, and the leather sheath was dark on one side from her sweat. Alys stuffed it in her boot the way Darro had taught her, the hilt tight against her ankle and ready to be drawn if the need came. She was surprised to see the tears on Sammish's cheek and the shame in her expression.

Alys felt a rush of annoyance and then guilt at being annoyed. "It's all right. It would probably be too much for me as well, if I could get away from it. But I can't. Whatever this is, it's mine. Until I find the one who killed Darro, I have to follow this. You don't."

"But then you'll be going alone. I don't want you to be alone," she said, or close to it. She'd coughed a little on the *you*.

"How long have we known each other?" Alys asked.

"Since we were scrapping in the Silt with Grey Linnet," Sammish said.

"And how long have we been crewing up?"

Sammish laughed through her tears. "Since you stole that sack of onions from the stand at Newmarket and I pretended to be hurt when the seller knocked into me. You had that green cloak and red boots. You were amazing." She was still and silent for a moment, then reached out, the silver coin pinched in her fingertips. Offering it back.

Alys shook her head. "You've earned it."

When she didn't take it, Sammish balanced the coin on Alys's knee.

"Pay me my cut when the job's done," she said.

Green Hill spread to the north and west of the palace where Hansch villagers and farmers had once huddled close to the ancient keep, ready to run for its protection when the Inlisc raiders came. Centuries ago, they had dug the canal, a diversion from the northern reaches of the Khahon, built to protect the village's western edge and give clean water to irrigate fields and orchards that had long since become flower gardens and private groves.

Great houses stood on the bones of those almost-forgotten farms, and the trees and gardens that gave the quarter its name boasted of the wealth and power of its residents. To have open, living green space inside city walls verged on bragging, so while the stone towers and mansions with their vaulted ceilings and statues of fauns and spirits and serpents were designed to awe those who saw them, so were the oaks and alders that shaded them.

To the southwest, down the slope of the hill, Stonemarket spread out like a map of itself, streets and plazas arrayed like a field under a watchful farmer's eye. The Smoke, to the south, was hidden by the palace, a servant kept out of sight until something needed cleaning or mending. The eastern half of the city from Oldgate to the Temple could have been a rumor except for the accents of the tradesmen and round-faced cleaning girls and kitchen help.

Green Hill might bow to prince and palace, but nothing less.

The great families had their compounds—Reyos, Chaalat, a Sal, a Jimental, Abbasann—but old Hansch brotherhoods also kept their houses there: Clovas and Daris and Climianth-Sul. The brotherhoods were not families of blood descent, but of oath and custom. If asked, all would swear their loyalty to the gods of the city, but in private, each also kept their own mysteries and secret rituals. Tradition ran deeper than wells in Green Hill.

Tregarro had known that before he came to Kithamar, but some days it still astounded him.

He had joined the brotherhood twelve years before, still healing from the fire that had marked him. He'd answered the call to Kithamar seven years ago, and acted as Andomaka Chaalat's left hand for three of them. He had been inducted into the brotherhood's mysteries. He had drunk Kithamar's water and breathed Kithamar's air. He had celebrated the most holy rites in the private temple in the brotherhood's house here. He was as near to a native of the city as he would ever be.

He never would be.

He sat now in a drawing room at the back of the brotherhood's compound, in the building the servants and staff called the second guest house when the formal members of the brotherhood were present and the shed when they weren't. The joke was funny because in any other context the shed would have been a magnificent building: carved stone and polished wood.

It only seemed humble because it sat beside the formal gardens and the brotherhood's great hall.

Every now and then, he would amble to the window and look down into the courtyard. Andomaka was sitting in the shadow of a wide cloth banner placed there to shield her pale skin from the sun. Her cousin sat across from her. Elaine a Sal was daughter of the new prince, the next in traditional succession followed by Andomaka herself, and presently weeping quietly about something. They'd been talking down there for the better part of the morning.

But perhaps it was coming to an end. Andomaka stood and took the girl in her arms. They embraced for a moment, Andomaka whispering something in Elaine's ears before the girl stepped back. Tregarro retreated from the window. Being where the princess might notice him was bad tactics. It risked spoiling whatever moment Andomaka had been building between them, and he gained nothing by doing it. Despite that, he had to fight the impulse to drift back and watch. He wasn't a man who had gotten where he was by respecting the privacy of others.

Still, the sun had moved another hand's span in the sky before Andomaka came to him. Her lips were quirked in a little smile.

"That was unexpected," she said as she took a seat on a silk divan.

Tregarro poured out a glass of fresh water for her from the pitcher in the servants' closet. She took it from him without acknowledgment or thanks. "She seemed upset."

"My loving cousin isn't finding all aspects of palace life suit her, and I am fortunate that she feels at ease turning to me for counsel."

"I can't tell if you're joking or not," he said, and sat across from her.

"I am and I'm not," she said, and drank. He tried not to watch the subtle working of her throat as she swallowed. He was a trusted servant to the high priestess, not her lover. There were ways to look at things that exposed the observer more than the observed, and it was better that he avoid them. She put down the glass and settled herself.

"Your cousin coming here," he said. "Is it to do with the... the rite?"

The crisis that was upon them after Ausai's death and the failure of the brotherhood's mysteries wasn't something they spoke of openly even here. He expected Andomaka to disapprove, but she only seemed thoughtful. When she spoke, her tone was bitter.

"No, I think our failure was so complete it went unnoticed." She frowned, and her attention shifted. For a moment, he thought she was back in the Temple in the terrible hours after Prince Ausai had died, reliving the catastrophe again the way he did. When she spoke, he knew he'd been wrong. "I had a dream. The old god Shau had come to the city, and he'd taken on the form of two girls. They were both in grief, and that was the joke. And the beauty. One of them was the wolf girl."

"The one that used the candle," Tregarro said.

"I couldn't see the other one." Andomaka waved a dismissive hand. Tregarro didn't know if she meant the dream was empty of prophecy or just that she'd lost interest in it.

"Do we think the boy survived?"

"My wolf boy? I don't know," she said. "If he did, he wasn't there. The girl was younger than him, but of the same stock, I'd guess."

"A daughter? A sister?"

"Too old for a daughter."

"They start young down there," Tregarro said.

"She was surprised by me," Andomaka said, ignoring his words. "Frightened, even. I tried to gentle her, but there was very little time."

"She snuffed out the light?"

"I don't think she did, actually. I was looking at her when it died. I think it might only have reached its end. I think she wanted to talk with me."

"Well, if the candle's gone, she won't be reaching back that way. Did she have the blade?"

"I didn't see it. She might, she might not. She had an interesting face. I liked her."

Tregarro pushed away the little twitch of impatience. Andomaka often got lost in how things related to her experience of them. It came, he assumed, from looking at all the world as though it were a dream she was having.

"Was she in the boy's house?"

Andomaka narrowed her eyes as if she were trying to see again what she'd already seen. She shook her head. "She was someplace else. It was much quieter. And there was no wind. Little wolf always had the wind with him. And everything around her was stone."

"The west side of the river, then. Unless she was at the Temple. Was there anything else?"

"A cot. It was a narrow room. And a . . . box? It had a symbol traced on it. A deathmark, I think. Do you think that could have been little wolf?"

"Too early to say anything. That makes it sound like it might be the Temple. I'll go and look. Did she have anything remarkable about her?"

Andomaka reached out and touched the scars on his cheek and neck. He tried to be patient with her. "No," she said at last. "Her hair was at her shoulders. And it curled. Her face was round."

"That's half the Inlisc girls in Longhill."

"I'd know her if I saw her again."

"Well, that's something."

"You're angry," she said. "With me?" She didn't make it an accusation, complaint, or apology. She never did. If he had been angry with her, it wouldn't have bothered her. It would only have been another curiosity in a lifetime filled with them.

"I'm not," he said. "I'm frustrated. And I'm anxious."

"Hope," she said, nodding as if he'd confirmed something. "It was almost easier when everything was lost. The wolf boy and the blade with him. And Ausai. And the other boy, that one. Everything scattered and failed. Then we could mourn and build a new plan. If there's still hope, there's still something to be lost."

Tregarro felt an eeriness in her voice that was like an echo only of meaning, not sound. She found ways to say things that made them deeper than the words themselves. It was part of what fascinated him about her and a part of what he feared. He took her hand and gently folded her fingers away from the scars on his cheek. She didn't resist. She never did.

"I have my people," he said. "We will look for her as best we can."

"They may know the city. But they don't know her."

"They know she exists, and that's better than we had yesterday. The Bronze Coast boy's still in play. He's still kept safe, so if we can get the knife, we haven't lost anything we can't win back."

"Only if it's the right Bronze Coast boy," Andomaka said.

"If this girl had the candle, she may know where your Inlisc friend kept his other secrets. If he had the blade the way he said and it didn't get stolen when he got himself killed, maybe she can lead us to it."

"If and if and if," Andomaka said, and the dreamy quality had left her voice. She seemed only like what she was: a noble-woman of Kithamar whose will had been thwarted by circumstance. "They'll poison us if we let them, these ifs."

"Let me give you a few more, all the same," he said. "If this new girl is like your wolf boy, she may be greedy. If she is greedy, she may be looking for us as well. And if that's the case, you and I and the *city* have just gotten very, very lucky."

The foreign woman with the fascination for blades had passed through Kithamar, but she'd been careful about it. Every person the woman spoke to had suffered hundreds of fresher dramas and curiosities in the days since. A calligrapher near the Temple might have met with her if he wasn't mixing the question up with one that his wife's father had asked. A brewer in Seepwater had let a woman who had been asking after knives sleep in his back room for a night, but he didn't think she had been foreign. The street magician who sold amulets of glass and tin had seen a Bronze Coast woman, but she'd been looking for her son, not a blade. The petty blessing men and fortune-tellers who plied their trade in the markets—more of them frauds than real—had seen her, or pretended to have done until they could decide whether Sammish had money to trade for their story. Sammish knew better than to pay good coin for someone to echo back what she wanted to hear.

She didn't ask about the woman made from smoke. She told herself it was because Alys was following that thread, but that was more than half a lie. The truth was, Sammish didn't want to find that one. It wasn't only the high magic that disturbed her, though she didn't like it. It was the idea that the woman of smoke sounded like Green Hill. In the games of the noble and the wealthy, girls like her and Alys spent like small coin. What had happened to Darro could happen to them, and Kithamar wouldn't miss a meal. Putting herself into this would have a cost.

It already did.

"Nothing for you today," the butcher said.

Sammish laughed, then saw that he wasn't joking. She gestured at the flesh around them—sheep and pork and lamb unmade and ready for the pot. "All of this, and your knives are still sharp?"

He didn't meet her eye. "I have a Newmarket boy taking care of it for me. All my blades are fresh yesterday." Then, when she didn't speak, "You missed your day twice. Two times, I lost a morning's work because I didn't have my tools."

"I said I was sorry for those," Sammish said.

"You did, and you were, and I am too," he said. "But the Newmarket boy gets them back to me when I need them, and neither of us is trying to make chops with apologies."

"What about the skins?" Sammish said. "They go to the tanners, don't they? I could carry them there?"

"The tanner's boy does that. I don't have anything for you. Not today. Maybe...Maybe next week. I don't know. Don't count on it."

She stood there, trying not to show her humiliation and guilt. The truth was that she would probably have done the same in his place. A helper who doesn't help is less than worthless. She was less than worthless.

"I'll come back," she said, and left. She wouldn't come back.

She ran to the next house, feet slapping hard against the stone so that it hurt a little. She told herself she'd never miss her work again. She'd just push herself harder. If she only bore down more, she'd find a way to do all the things she'd promised...

It was the week of the harvest festival, and the streets were crowded. The men and women who'd gone off to the farms for the gathering in were returning, and the fat of the land came with them. A mule-drawn cart rumbled along before her as she walked, piled with rough burlap sacks and smelling of apples. The stalls of Newmarket were so filled with gourds and sacks of beans that the walkways were hard to pass through. Children sat on the corners with wicker baskets piled with honeyed walnuts and late summer berries that stained their fingertips. All the food was cheap, and everyone had coin. Now and for a few weeks more, all of Kithamar could pretend it was wealthy, or at least everyone who had spent the time to earn the extra silver and bronze.

It was wrong that seeing people she knew happy and thick with coin left Sammish feeling diminished, but it did. Even Alys had her secret cache of gold, though she was sworn not to spend more of it. Everyone had something extra except Sammish. She remembered something her father had said when she was very young and he was alive. *Plant daydreams, eat dreams.* He had meant *Don't be lazy*, but Sammish wasn't lazy. She'd been working as hard this last season as she ever did, only the payment she wanted wasn't coin. Not even the silver that Alys had offered her. She wanted to matter to Alys. Now, with all the wealth and plenty around her, part of her began to wonder whether she'd been foolish.

The festival itself began at sundown and lasted for three long, drunken days. Servants in the colors of the great families and laborers for the guild halls rolled tuns of beer along the street. Bright cloth banners were being hung from the windows. As long as it didn't rain, there would be music and dancing in the streets, lanterns hung at the prince's expense to push back the night, costumes and masks and open doors at every house with food and wine to offer to passersby. In a better world, Sammish and Orrel and Alys would have been out among them making their own harvest. Only they wouldn't, because Darro was dead, and Alys was drowning in it, and Sammish was a lovesick idiot busy trying to forge loyalty out of lust. She tried not to see all of them with contempt, and she succeeded a little where it came to Alys and Darro.

When she took the knives she had to the whetstone man, he was in a cloak of orange and blue. His hair was tied back by a woven leather thong, and he looked almost handsome. He was working, though, pedaling the little pump that passed the water over the pale flesh of the stone, holding the blades at just the proper angle, listening to the music as they hissed softly and took their edge. She imagined herself in his place, and the simple, pure sensuality of the movements. It wouldn't be so terrible to live her life alone, maybe, if she had some simple, well-practiced beauty like that to fill her days.

"You're taking these back tonight?" he asked as she unfolded the leather and removed the knives.

"I am," she said.

"Not going to be taken up by the festival? Put off delivery to after?"

"Fuck no," she said.

"Good," he said mildly.

"I'll be back before sundown."

"They'll be ready," he said.

And when she came back late that afternoon, they were.

The harvest festival's sun went down, and Kithamar changed its nature again, if only for a little while. Alys made her way through the streets of Longhill. She had rented costumes from a stitcher at the edge of the quarter. The seams weren't even and the thread was weak, but for the moment she was swathed in ribbons of green and blue and black that swirled about her like river weeds. Her false fingertips clicked like rain against stone. Her mask was sewn with grey thread that was supposed to look like silver and had polished stones in it that could pass as valuable in bad light. The other costume was pale as bone, and she carried it under her arm.

The baker's house was closed. He and his family were out in the streets and canals, and she rapped at the door to Sammish's little room until she was certain that she wasn't there either. The stars were out, filling the sky, and a wide, white moon was with them. The festival, like the wind, didn't reach into the depths of Longhill, but Alys could still hear it. The subtle sounds of merriment, far away. The city was enjoying itself, and the combined voices and violins, drums and pounding dancers were like listening to someone talking in the next room. She considered putting the pale costume at Sammish's doorway and going on her own, and wrestled with the reasons to leave and the reasons to be patient until Sammish arrived and the debate lost its importance.

Sammish had the leather satchel she used when she was carrying knives, and a sour expression. Alys could tell that she was trying not to snap when she spoke.

"You look ready for a night," Sammish said. "What're you meant to be?"

"Water nymph," Alys said. "You're a snow fairy."

"I'm a what?"

Alys held out the pale cloth. "Snow fairy. Now strip off your day clothes and put these on. We're going to Green Hill."

Sammish took the costume like she'd been handed a dead animal. "Why?"

"When else are we going to be able to pass up there?"

"Why would we want to?"

"To look for the smoke woman. What else?" Alys said, surprised that Sammish hadn't followed her thought. "Come on. You'll be cunning in this. And it's already paid for."

For a moment, Sammish looked so lost and despairing that Alys thought she would refuse. But she took the cloth and motioned Alys to wait as she undid the lock on her room and vanished into the darkness. A few minutes later, she emerged. The costume was fine—white cloth that caught the moonlight and yellow dye in patterns like light under water, a leather mask that made her eyes look wide and exotic—but she wore it like it was a sack.

"How bad?" Sammish asked.

"They'll bow down before you and ask for wishes," Alys said. It was a lie, but it was the right lie, and Sammish managed a smile. They walked together through the narrow and twisting streets until one opened onto a square, and they were in Newmarket. The harvest festival was in its full fever. They wove their way through the crowds and music until they came to the streets where open carts were letting anyone ride without charge. Alys found one heading toward the northernmost bridge over the Khahon, the one that linked Riverport to Green Hill, and clambered aboard, careful of her false fingers. Her heart beat a little faster with every street they passed, and she imagined what a hunter in the forest must feel.

Riverport was alive with torches and lanterns and firepits. The rich smell of roasting pork and the sweetness of sugar beet mash mixed with the smoke. The peculiar combination brought back memories of other harvest festivals through her girlhood, of running after her mother through a crowd, of dancing on a rooftop she'd climbed to while the owner of the building

shouted at her to come down, and of being carried on someone's shoulders through a dance while sparks and embers flowed
through the air around her. The flickering of the light made the
buildings themselves seem to sway, and bluecloaks marched in
force with a sand cart trailing behind them, watchful for any
untamed fires.

At every house, servants or younger children handed out bits
of sausage and ham, fresh-cooked game and bits of pumpkin-
and-butter still warm from the oven. Many of the revelers on
the street brought cups to dip into the bowls of hot juice and
spiced wine. Alys thought she caught sight of Nimal dressed as
an ancient Inlisc warrior, but it might have only been someone
who looked like him. It was early yet to be running a pull. The
city would be drunker the farther it fell into night.

Alys had lived in Kithamar from her first breath without
ever crossing its northernmost bridge. Going to Green Hill
was like walking to another world. Black water surged under
them, churning white where the old stone broke it, the river
cold and angry and filled with voices that had never known a
human tongue. The air was more than chill; it was cold. Alys
paused in the center of the span, looking west into the flow. For
a moment, she felt very small, like she was a rabbit and the river
a great dark owl that might kill her or might not, as its whim
took it. Sammish took her hand, their fingers briefly weaving
together. The uncertainty in Sammish's masked eyes made her
think she felt the same unease, and they walked the rest of the
bridge hand in hand.

It took no time at all for Alys to realize how badly she had
underestimated Green Hill.

If the life and light of Riverport had outshone the darkness
and emptiness of Longhill, Green Hill transcended the world
that Alys knew. The streets were lined with strands of tiny

lanterns, each of them glowing like a firefly. Acrobats tumbled and jumped in the darkness, and jugglers made bright-colored balls flicker through the air and tossed up knives that they caught in their teeth. Between two great houses, an archway had been constructed, its stucco painted to look like stone, and a man and woman either spectacularly nude or costumed to seem so stood on its apex, singing with voices like gods. There were no blue-cloaks; all the guards wore the red of the palace. The crowd that swirled around them wore costumes and masks unlike anything Alys had ever seen. If nymphs and fairies really existed, they would have passed here unremarked.

A man came by balanced on stilts and swooped improbably long arms down to offer bits of clove sugar to the crowd. A woman with long spirals of colored glass woven into her hair danced by, strewing flower petals. Palanquins shouldered by bare-chested men carried the highest families of Kithamar from house to house, weaving gracefully through the crowd. Everywhere she looked, she found people looking back. Some had disapproval in their eyes, some amusement. Alys glanced at Sammish and saw her own thoughts echoed there. In their rented costumes, they stood out like blood on a wedding dress.

"We could leave," Sammish said.

Alys squeezed her friend's hand and let it go. "Follow me."

With her head high and her jaw jutting out like she was ready to fight, Alys bulled forward through the crowd. She would make them cut her down in the street before she let a bad costume and the contempt of the rich stop her. Sammish trailed in her wake, a flutter of yellow and white in Alys's peripheral vision.

The palace itself rose up, high dark walls that blotted out the sky, and huge red lanterns that dripped from it like berries from a twig. As they came to its corner, the crowd grew thicker. Even the nobles were jostling for a better view. In Longhill, it would have meant there was a street fight. Alys didn't know what it meant here.

A huge shape loomed up, vast as a sailing ship and draped with bright cloth and pale banners. At its prow, a man stood. Prince Byrn a Sal, the light and lord of Kithamar, raised his hands, and the crowd cheered. Alys saw now that it was a massive cart, pulled along by a team of thick-bodied horses with silver woven in their manes. The wheels were as tall as she was, and the sound of its weight grinding against the street promised broken stones. Behind the prince, others stood, looking out over the city and waving. The crowd shouted its delight. A man behind her started chanting *It's our year. It's our year.* She couldn't guess what he or the ritual before her meant. It was like being in a dream.

She felt the panic almost before she knew why. She grabbed Sammish's arm hard enough that the other girl yelped. Alys pointed up to the top of the great cart. There, five back from the prince himself, a woman stood in a dress of green feathers and gold chains. She had pale skin and hair. Her arms were out, palms to the crowd, as if she were warming herself at a fire.

"Her!" Alys shouted over the clamor. "That's the woman from the smoke!"

Sammish looked up, then leaned close, her lips brushing Alys's ear so that she could be heard without anyone else being part of their conversation. "I'll look for servants. Find out who she is."

The woman in green smiled beatifically over them all. She was so *close*...Alys reached up and pulled off her mask.

"You!" she shouted, pointing up at the woman. "You! I saw you!"

"What are you doing?" Sammish hissed, but Alys ignored

her. Instead, she waved her arms and shrieked. The man next to her shied away, and Alys screamed again. She ran along beside the vast cart as it moved down the street, pushing aside anyone who got in her way. She lost track of Sammish, of the guards who watched the street, of everything except the pale-skinned woman floating along above her. Her throat ached with her shouting. With a sense of rising despair, she grew more and more certain that the voice of the crowd would always drown her out. The great barge of a cart came to a corner and paused as the horses were repositioned to make the turn. A huge stone statue of a Hansch goddess stood on a granite plinth, and Alys saw her chance.

She hauled herself up the stone, climbing it. She heard voices shouting at her, calling her to come down, threatening her. She reached the goddess's shoulders and rode them like a child being carried by her mother.

She still wasn't halfway to the height of the cart, but she thought the woman was looking at her now, amused and attracted by the commotion. Alys reached down and plucked the blade from her boot. When she lifted it up, the silver caught the light. Above her, the woman froze.

And then, like a flower bud blossoming in sunlight, the pale woman smiled.

The man who came for her had thick, ropey scars across his cheek and neck. At first Alys thought they were false, put on for the festival like a morbid kind of mask. He wore a sword at his side that wasn't a costume either. He found her in the crowd and walked her into the darkness with a grim focus that frightened her, though she knew better than to show it. Now he unlocked a gate between two great, thick hedges that stood taller than walls and nodded her forward. Everything she knew told her to turn and run. She clenched her jaw and walked forward into the darkness.

The roar of the celebration crested and turned to cheers behind them as some other astounding thing happened: an acrobat making some particularly terrible jump or a fire-eater blowing flame into the sky. Nothing of that mattered to Alys now, nor did it seem to matter to the man walking with her.

"What happened to—"

"Not here," the scarred man said. "Don't talk."

He led her down a narrow passage between thorny hedges and a rough stone wall. The green leaves were thick and leathery, and the twigs had cruel spikes. The pavement was wet and pebbled, and it glittered in the moonlight. If they meant to spirit her someplace quiet and kill her, she imagined it would look very much like this. She still had the knife in her boot. If he turned on her, she'd have the half-second while he drew his blade. She could try to cut his leg and run.

If he noticed her preparing for violence, he didn't show it. They came to a thin, dark wood doorway in a wall of carved granite. A metal bar held it closed, and the steel brackets had wept rust down the stone. He opened it and stepped through, clearly expecting her to follow. Alys stood for a moment at the mouth of the darkness before a brightness flared inside: the scarred man lighting a candle.

The room was small, windowless, and cold with a dark stain along one wall where something had spilled or seeped through. It smelled of mildew, and apart from a single rough wood table with a pair of benches at its side, it was empty. She guessed it might be an unused storehouse, unless the high families of Green Hill kept their own private jails. The scarred man sat at the table.

"You have it?"

"Have what?"

"Don't play with me. You have it."

Alys stood on the other side of the table from him. He looked at the low bench, but she didn't sit. She nodded.

"Let's see it, then."

She drew the blade, careful not to get close enough that he could try to grab it from her. She didn't know how quick he was. He didn't try for it, but leaned forward, resting on his elbows and squinting at the marks along the flat. Between the dimness of the light and the webwork of scars, she couldn't be certain, but he seemed to sharpen.

"What are you asking for it?"

"Who killed my brother?"

His eyes flicked to hers, evaluating and cool. "I see."

"Was he killed because of this?" she asked, gesturing with the knife. "Because of you?"

The scarred man stood, and she stepped back, not fleeing but wary. His scowl was contempt and pity.

"You'll wait here," he said.

"And if I don't want to?"

"We're past that," he said, and walked out, closing the door behind him. A moment later, there was a deep scraping sound, and when she tried to open it, the door was barred. She sat on the bench and scowled at it as if it might care. Slowly, her courage began to fade and a deeper fear welled up in her chest. She'd been impatient. She'd been carried away by the moment. She'd needed to see what happened more than she'd wanted to stay safe.

Keep your eyes down and forward for fifty steps, she thought, and sighed. Next time, maybe. If there was a next time.

The minutes stretched in silence. Her only company was the

single, slow candle and its buttery light. She strained to hear the celebration or voices. Even the scuttling of mice would have been better than the uncanny silence. It was like her cell in Oldgate, except that had been of her own choosing. It had been under her control. She wondered if she screamed whether anyone would notice, and if they came to her calls, what they would do.

The certainty settled into her bones that she had been impulsive and very, very stupid. Her only hope was that Sammish had watched everything that had happened. She might be making her way to the door to free her. She tried calling Sammish's name a few times, but the walls ate the sound. She was as good as buried.

Alys was more than halfway to deciding her best chance was to cut whoever opened the door and try to run for the shadows when the deep growl of the bar being lifted interrupted her. She stood, knife in hand, her heart fluttering against her ribs. The door was motionless for so long that she almost wondered whether the sound had been real. When it opened, it was startling. The scarred man entered first, took in the blade and her stance, and shook his head once. *No.* Behind him, the woman stepped in.

In person, she seemed less frightening. Her flesh was solid, and though she was older, she was a bit shorter than Alys. Her skin and hair were weirdly pale, her shaped eyebrows almost invisible until Alys looked for them. Her costume was gone, and in its place, a robe of fine wool bound by the same braided belt. The woman's smile wouldn't have been warmer if they had been sisters.

"Little wolf girl, you found me," she said, and it was the same voice Alys had heard in Oldgate. "It is so good that you found me."

"I'm not a wolf. I don't know who you are," Alys said.

"I'm called Andomaka, among other things," the woman said. She stepped forward and put her hand on Alys's shoulder, looking deep into her eyes as she did. Had Alys wanted to kill this woman, it would have been simple. The knife was in her hand, the woman's unprotected side exposed to her. The scarred man restrained himself, but his discomfort was in the angle of his shoulders and the deepness of his scowl.

"I'm Alys. Darro was my brother."

"Come, Alys," Andomaka said. "Let's sit together."

Alys settled on the bench. The light of the one candle glimmered in the other woman's eyes.

"How much did your brother tell you about our work?" Andomaka asked.

"Nothing," Alys said, and the word came out plaintive. "He didn't tell me anything."

"That's because of me. I asked him to hold what we did in silence. That he did so only means he treated me with honor. Don't think less of him because he was loyal to me."

Alys felt something shift. She tried to see the pale woman as if she were Darro. Could he have been in love with her? How deep had his loyalty to her run? Had she given him the gold coins?

"Why did he die?"

For the first time, something like distress entered the woman's expression. She folded her hands together on the table, leaning forward like she and Alys were at a taproom together and she wanted their conversation to be only between the two of them.

"There is a lie at the heart of Kithamar," Andomaka said. "There was a great injustice, and those who were meant to protect the order of the city have abandoned it. There are silent wars on these streets that the small and safe know nothing of."

"Don't know who the safe are. And there are some scraps in

Longhill you haven't heard of either," Alys said. It was an idiotic remark, born of fear and powerlessness. The smoke woman—Andomaka—was kind enough to ignore it.

"I am niece to the prince that died and cousin, we say, to Byrn a Sal, who has taken his place. There was more to that than it seemed, and there are prices to be paid for what happened. My friends and I have bent ourselves to serving the true powers of the city. In this, your brother was my eyes and ears. And, when the need came, my hands. When a thing needed doing, I could go to him, and it would be done."

"Darro was . . . fighting for Kithamar?"

The scarred man's voice was like a thing from another world. It startled Alys to remember that he was in the room at all. "We paid him. Let's not make this something it wasn't."

"He helped me," Andomaka said. "And I helped him in return. He fell when he was working in my name. To bring me the blade that was stolen, that you've brought. Since he fell, I have had to rely on others who I trust less, and whose hearts I do not know. But you've come, and I wonder if that was not fated."

"I don't know what you mean."

Andomaka took her hand. The pale eyes looked deep into hers. In the candlelight, they seemed almost colorless. "I think he sent you to me. I think you have come to take up his work. And to finish it. I do not know who killed him, only that it was an enemy of mine and of his. Come to me. Take his place at my side. We will find justice together."

"You . . . You want me to . . ."

The scarred man answered. "When we need work done, you do it as he did. We pay you as we paid him. And yes, it will take you and us against the same people that he went against. You have your chance to finish the ones that finished him."

"I didn't get him killed, then," Alys said. "It wasn't my fault?"

"It wasn't your fault that he died," Andomaka said. "Is it your work to avenge him?"

Alys couldn't put any name to the storm in her chest and her throat. All she knew was that it shook her. She nodded.

"One of his last tasks," the scarred man said, "was to bring us that blade. He didn't manage it."

"He did," Alys said, sliding the silver knife across the table and letting it go.

Andomaka put her hand on the hilt. "Thank you," she said.

"Of *course* she's going to say she's on the side of light and rightness," Sammish said. "No one comes in saying that they're a scheming bitch with plans to set the city on fire and charge for the sand to put it out. I can't believe you *gave* it to her."

The harvest festival was still going on around them, but the rush of energy from earlier in the night was gone. The lights still glowed in their lanterns, and music still played on the streets. The homes and guild houses stood open, but there were fewer people coming to take hospitality from them. The riverside was too crowded. The streets stank of half-eaten food and spilled wine. A pack of dogs feasting on the scraps eyed them warily as they passed. The moon had set, and the night air had taken on a deeper chill that spoke of the winter to come.

"I don't know why you're upset," Alys said. "This is a good thing. This is going to help us."

"Help us with what? Is there still something to help with?"

"Of course there is," Alys said, turning south. "We still don't know who killed Darro. That's what this was all about."

"We know it wasn't anything to do with you or me or Orrel. He was on a pull of his own, and it went bad somehow. That doesn't mean there's anything to pick up."

They walked in silence for a few long blocks. Sammish made small sounds like she was still chiding Alys, but under her breath. She was tempted to stop and demand that Sammish say whatever it was aloud, but she also didn't want to hear it. Instead, she walked, and she nursed her anger. Alys felt like something was gnawing at her breastbone from the inside. The pressure and the pain were better than whatever was underneath them. She tried not to think about that.

Andomaka and the scarred man—his name was Tregarro, it turned out—had thanked her for the blade, given her a few silver coins to mark the beginning of their new arrangement, and a black candle with a dark wick that she could use to speak to them as Darro had. Then Tregarro had taken her back to the celebrations in Green Hill where a group of young men, nude apart from masks that obscured their faces, were running a drunken race down one of the larger streets. Revelers in costume stood at the sidelines, shouting and cheering as they passed.

She hadn't seen Sammish. She hadn't even thought to look for her. When her friend appeared at her side as if she had never left, the relief in her eyes left Alys guilty, and when Sammish took her arm and said *Are you all right?* Alys hadn't known how to answer.

She'd told Sammish everything that had happened as they made their way back across the river. By the time she was done, her next steps had already become clear to her. She led them back the long dark way across the city to Longhill with a plan in mind.

The houseman who ran the building where Darro had kept his little room was known to Alys as he was to anyone. The land the building stood on was claimed by a merchant family in Riverport, but the buildings on it were run by Kennat Water.

He was a thick-bodied man, quick to anger, and he knew that Longhill viewed him as halfway between traitor and petty noble, taking their money to the wealthy quarters from which it would not return and with the power to choose who slept in shelter and who took their chances in the street. At least as far as the buildings he controlled.

Alys found him where she expected him to be: sitting on the steps outside his own house, half out of a costume that looked like it had been a warrior-priest and drunk on someone else's wine. He watched them as they approached with a vast incuriousness and cocked his head at Alys when she stopped before him. Sammish stood to the side, arms crossed and looking away.

"I know you," he said.

"Alys. My brother was Darro. He kept a room from you."

"Maybe he did, maybe he didn't."

"I want it."

"Good to know what you want. Already gave it to some of the roof girls. It's getting on toward winter."

"Move them someplace else. I want Darro's room."

Sammish hissed her name, but Alys ignored her. Instead she took one of her gold coins and placed it carefully in the center of the man's broad palm. Kennat looked at it for a long time, then up at her. His expression was more sober than his voice. "I'll have them out in the morning."

She considered demanding that he evict the other tenants now. With the money she was paying, he'd have done it. The hunger to have strangers out of her brother's room plucked at her, but something about having Sammish there made her feel odd about it.

"Good enough," Alys said, then turned and walked away. It was an odd thing to feel like victory, but it did. She had Darro's room. She had Darro's work, whatever it had been. Sammish's footsteps slapping along behind as she tried to catch up were the only flaws in the night.

"You're spending the gold now? I thought you were saving that."

"Andomaka didn't ask for it back," Alys said.

"Maybe it isn't hers. Maybe he was working for someone else as well. It doesn't make sense. He was supposed to give them the knife, but he had it and he hadn't passed it over. Why not? Who's the woman that was looking for it? Your brother had all this gold, but the people he worked for don't seem to know about it. None of it fits together. You see that none of it fits together?"

"Weren't you just telling me that I'd found out enough and there was nothing left to look for?"

"I was," Sammish said, and her voice was despairing. "I don't know what I'm saying."

"You don't like them."

"I'm not jealous."

"I didn't say you were. I said you don't like them."

They walked on for another half block. The buildings around them were largely dark, largely quiet. Here and there a window glowed, candlelight showing from the faults in the shutters. The stars swam behind clouds and peeked back out again. The only sounds were their footsteps and a man's voice somewhere, laughing at a joke they hadn't heard.

Farther south, there would be Seepwater and beer and fires in the streets to keep their hands warm by. There would be roasted sugar beets and honeyed walnuts, and enough beer to keep them both tipsy until dawn if they wanted. After all, it was harvest. Kithamar was as fat as it would be anytime in the whole year. It could afford to be generous.

"I don't like them," Sammish said.

PART TWO

WINTER

To know a thing—a house, a city, a street, a lover—
one must be with it for a full year. A street locked in
winter's ice is a different street than the same stones
under spring storms. A lover in the first flame of
passion is a different person when those fires have
cooled.

And even then, a year is only a year, and a lifetime
is only a life. With time enough, even gods may be
startled by the newfound sweetness of a well-bruised
heart.

—From the pillow book of Anayi a Jimental,
poet to the court of Daos a Sal

The first snow came early that year, falling from a low grey sky. The sunlight felt weak, strained through the clouds like milk through cheesecloth. Alys sat at her window—her window now, and her blackwood table, and her room looking out toward the distant river—with the shutters open and watched as the flakes passed from dark spots against the paleness above to white with the buildings across the street behind them. It seemed like a trick a street magician would do, transforming a thing to its opposite before her eyes and yet also invisibly. Her breath plumed, but only slightly. The cold made her cheeks feel like a mask.

She wore a dark wool cloak, not black but a deep grey, and fingerless gloves to match. Her boots were well made, with leather that was both supple and thick and a buckle on the side. Her shirts were three layers of cotton, and she had a dagger at her belt. It wasn't silver but steel, and it cost more than anything she'd ever owned before. All of it was newly bought. Given how unlike it was from her customary dress, it should have felt like a costume. Maybe it did, but it was comforting too. It was what she wanted.

The room was dark and close, and the walk up from the street was long enough that she didn't leave it without reason. There was a boy, thin-faced with pocked scars on his arms and neck, who brought around bread and cheese and water once a day if she paid him. The two girls from the roof had taken the room that shared her north wall, and they were willing to share their monthly cotton when Alys needed it. The night pot, she could empty out the window. The mattress on her pallet was thin, but it didn't stink and the bugs hadn't found it yet. Her blanket was soft and warm enough to keep away the bite before dawn.

It was the first room that she'd truly felt was her own, and she felt that because it was Darro's. She could have stayed the whole winter there and never left, except when Andomaka or Tregarro had need of her. She imagined her brother sitting where she sat, feeling the same combination of solitude and isolation that she did, or the same sense of his own adulthood. She imagined him watching the snow, and she felt herself changing.

Throughout Longhill, people wore heavier jackets or shawls against the chill. Shops and taprooms closed a bit earlier as the darkness pushed people to early beds. Frost began to whiten the morning cobblestones, but the first snow was the sign that said the inevitable had arrived, and all the comforts of autumn were gone. The best parts of the year had already passed. The river would run cold as death until the killing frosts came and sealed the city under ice.

On the streets below her, old Ubram Foyle rode his cart, whipping the same grey nag he'd had for years and calling out for bones and iron. Children ran out to him as he passed with handfuls of chicken and pigeon bones left over from their family meals or the longer, pinker ones from dogs that had died or been killed. The old man traded bits of honey rock for the bones. Iron scrap and chain, he weighed in his hand and paid for in coin. When the cart grew full, he would haul it to the Smoke and sell the metal to the smiths and the bones to the gluemen. Alys could remember being one of those children bolting for the street when his smoke-and-gravel voice called out, the anticipation of honey already making her young mouth water.

She wasn't that child now. Sweetness had less appeal.

Alys's mother had been born into Longhill, one of a half dozen children in a house large enough for three. She'd been called Nandy when she was a young child and Linly when she'd grown to be a girl as old as Alys was now. From all the stories, she'd been something of a beauty, dark haired and sharp-eyed, with a laugh that taught birds how to sing. Alys couldn't see even the traces of it in the soft jowls and greying hair that made up the woman she knew. Still, there had apparently been a time when a girl named Linly had skipped through the same streets that Alys travelled now, had drunk beer with her friends at the same bridges Alys crossed, and met and teased and loved young men who found her beautiful.

Linly had been born into Longhill; Alys's father might have been born anywhere. She'd neither known him nor known of him. When she'd been young and asked her mother—seeking the story of him if not the man—all her mother would say was that he'd loved her when he was here, and forgotten her when he was gone. He'd stayed long enough to make three babies, though: Darro, their sister Caria, who'd died of a fever before Alys was born, and Alys herself. The only memory Alys had of her father was as a wide back sleeping beside her and the smell of tobacco, and even that might have been from a dream. She didn't know why he had left, and if her mother did, she didn't say. She'd heard Grey Linnet say that there was a disgrace, and her mother had told her father to leave and not come back. That might have been true. Even if it was, it didn't affect Alys. All that was over before she could walk.

Longhill had a thousand ways for a girl like Linly to shape her life, and all of them were hard. It was the pride of the quarter that Inlisc cunning and ingenuity floated in the air and ran with the water there. Between the prince's taxes and the landlords in Riverport and Newmarket, coin flowed out of Longhill. It had to be coaxed back in. Or tricked. Working pulls was one way. Finding contracts on the barges or in the temples was another. Some people begged at the port or outside the walls. Others took work with the teams of oxen that towed boats against the river's flow south of the city. A few traded sex for coin. No one did only one thing, because no one thing could bring in enough to live off.

Most people slept in rooms they paid for, bringing as many others in as space allowed. Four people in a bed meant a fourth of the price for the house, unless you were someone with a child to care for. Or else two children. Unless you were Linly. In that case, a fourth body in the bed only cut the cost in half. The other one had to be someone willing to pay half the cost for a quarter of the space.

For all her mother's faults, Alys gave her credit for keeping her children safe from her lovers. Being turned out of the house for a night or two now and again, having to find someplace in the street to huddle while the darkness passed, wasn't the worst thing. Harder things happened, and more often than people liked to admit.

She was fairly sure the man had been named Otgar, but it might have been Uthar or Ausgar or something like. He'd been a trader from the east, carrying cargo to Aunt Thorn that didn't bear talking of. The gods knew what he'd found attractive about Alys's mother, and they weren't telling. Her mother had made it very clear that Alys wasn't to come home until morning. It was the end of her ninth year in the world, and Darro had already been away from them for years, living with a pack of boys who kept to the southernmost edge of the quarter.

Alys remembered her mother telling her to stay safe. She had been young enough that she thought if her mother told her to do something, it meant that it was possible. That safety could be had, and that it was within her control. That had been the night of the first snow too.

The flakes had been larger then; wide and thick as feathers. She didn't remember what she'd worn, only that she'd seemed almost warm at first, and then slowly grown colder until the cold seemed like everything. It had pushed down into her bones so deep that she'd wondered whether she would ever be warm again. Later that night, Darro would tell her that it had been a good sign, that if she'd started feeling warm again it would have meant she was dying.

She'd walked north, toward the Temple, not because she'd expected any gods to help her, or any priests for that matter. But the great stone building had fascinated her with the gentle glow of its windows and the solidity of its walls. Stone was how the Hansch built. Stone was meant to last forever. The idea of standing solid against the flow of time, unmoving as a bridge in the river, had appealed to her then. Her places were all wood. Wood floated on water and spun and washed away.

There was an empty place in her memory of that night. She remembered looking up at the Temple, and she remembered being by the north gate with its tall bronze doors streaked with verdigris and closed for the night. It was possible she hadn't been there. Darro might have found her by the Temple gate instead, and she was confusing it now. Before, when she could have asked him, it hadn't been important to her. Now that she couldn't, the question carried more weight.

Wherever she had been, there had been a niche between the buildings, and she'd backed into it, trying to stay out of the snowfall. She'd thought that the building would warm her, but it had made her colder instead, pulling the heat from her body more quickly than the air. She'd wept. She'd wondered whether to go to the bluecloaks and ask to be put in lockup for the night. If they didn't, she could kick them or threaten to start a fire. They might beat her, but they wouldn't leave her to die in the street afterward. They probably wouldn't.

She didn't know how Darro had found her. She'd been there in the grey darkness of the night watching the snowflakes fall on the black, shining cobblestones and melt. And then not melt. Darro had appeared out of the gloom. She hadn't seen his face, not at first, but she'd known him by the sound of his footsteps and the shape of his boots. They'd been dark leather with a buckle on the side. She remembered what he'd said, though. She'd carry it with her forever. *Tell me you can walk. I don't want to fucking carry you.*

If he'd said the secret name of God, she wouldn't have been more awed or grateful.

He hadn't embraced her or warmed her hands, but he'd put a thick leather wrap over her as they walked south for what felt like hours. They hadn't talked. She stayed silent because the cold and exhaustion and fear and relief had left her with barely enough of herself to put one foot in front of the other. He did because he was distracted or impatient or in a quiet rage at their mother for putting Alys out in the street to freeze and die.

Darro had been spending his days with a stable crew back then. Terryn Obst, before he got sick. Nimal, before he and Darro fell out. Black Nel and Sarae Stone. They'd all been more or less the same age. The children of Longhill grew up that way, making cohorts and crews and connections that complicated with the years. It wasn't strange for two old men to come to blows over an insult from decades before that had festered over time. Or to find two childhood enemies weeping in each other's arms at the end of a long night's drink. Everything connected in Longhill, and all the connections mattered. Darro had led her south that night in the silence and the snow to the alley behind the woodcutters' guild house. There had been a ladder against the wall, and she'd gone first with Darro behind to steady her if she slipped. She hadn't known where they were going besides up as the snow came down.

The topmost reach of the hall, four stories up, was all storage rooms and servants' quarters. Either they'd bribed someone for the use of the half-empty storage room or found it unguarded. Black Nel and Terryn Obst and two or three others were there around a little brazier in a stone firepit. They were all lounging on cushions and blankets they had stolen from someplace and laid over the rough wood. Terryn Obst cooked bits of chicken meat on skewers, dipping the pale pink flesh in powdered salt and fine-chopped rosemary. Black Nel had a bottle of wine that she passed around. Alys drank from it, the alcohol spreading warmth through her throat and chest.

For the most part, Darro and his friends ignored her as she snuggled into the pillows and blankets. They had talked and laughed and sung together, and she had been there with them. It had been enough and more than enough. It was the first time she'd understood why Darro spent his time away from her and their mother. He'd found something better, and as soon as she'd seen it, she wanted it for herself. She wanted to be the girl sitting at the fireside, trading bawdy stories with her friends and eating real meat and drinking until she was sated.

At some point, she'd fallen asleep there, and the others had too. She woke sometime near dawn with Darro's familiar body at her side keeping her warm. The snow outside the window had thickened, and the world seemed unnaturally quiet. There had only been the sound of his breath and hers. Alys had lain in the comfortable darkness, knowing that she might have spent her night in the niche by the gate and died in the snow, except that her brother had come for her.

Her brother, who had always come to help her when she found herself swimming in treacherous water. Her brother, who had a deathmark now, and who wouldn't see the thin snowflakes falling outside his window ever again.

In the street below her, Ubram Foyle turned the corner. His calls for bones and iron faded a bit, but not so much she couldn't make out the words. A pigeon flew past her window, a flutter of blue-grey wings. She tried to remember what kind of wine Black Nel had been drinking that night and whether the skewers Terryn cooked the pale meat on were wooden or iron. She tried to remember whether the smoke from the brazier had given her a headache or not. There had to have been a time when she'd known those things, even if it had only been in the moment. The details had faded or been replaced with false versions by an imagination hungry for more than was there. The thought tightened her throat and took the pleasure from the memory.

She stepped back from the window and the first first snow that Darro wouldn't see, and closed the shutters. The darkness wasn't total, but it took a few long breaths together for her eyes to adjust. She went to her safe cache, undid the hidden latch, and opened it. The remaining coins caught the faint light that pressed in at the shutters' edge. She took up the black candle and carried it back to the rough wood table. It was easy to light. The wick spat, the flame stretched up, blue then white then ruddy orange as it cooled into smoke. She waited, and it pulled back into a perfect sphere, just as it had before. She hoped Andomaka would come this time, or if not her, then no one.

The smoke shifted, narrowed, and darkened. It thickened. Alys found herself holding her breath as the smoke wove itself together, and Tregarro sat across the table from her. In the weirdly steady light of the candle, his scars looked deeper than they had before. When he smiled, the ropey flesh pulled down his eyelid. He seemed to notice her discomfort, and he smiled more deeply.

"Well," he said. "I see you're still open to work. She'll be pleased."

Alys didn't ask after Andomaka. Something about the man kept her wary of any sign that she cared about something or someone. Any connection would be a weakness, and any weakness would be exploited. She didn't know if that was true, or if it was only the man's uncanny appearance that made her think it. It didn't matter.

"I see you still have work that needs doing," she said, lifting her chin the way she imagined Darro would have.

"As it happens, I do," Tregarro said. "You don't object to working with other people, do you?"

"I don't."

His nod left her wondering whether that had been the right answer, or if she had just failed some subtle test. He took something from a pocket in his sleeve and slid it across the table to her. It grated as it moved across the wood. It was a black iron key as thick as her thumb with an animal of some kind worked into the top. It might have been a wolf or a lion; the metal was too worn to know. She'd seen keys like it used on warehouse locks. When she picked it up, it was lighter than she'd expected.

"Newmarket, two streets south of the main square, there's a soapmaker's shop. You know it?"

"No," she said.

"Well, find it. That key opens the door to the storage shed at the back. The others will meet you there tomorrow at sunset."

Alys put the key in the wallet hanging from her belt. "What are we doing?"

"There's someone we need. We've heard from the people who have him. You'll get the details then."

"Will it be dangerous?" she asked, and immediately regretted asking. She expected Tregarro to sneer at her and snap. Instead an expression passed over his face that might almost have been sorrow. When he spoke, his voice was gentler than she'd ever heard it.

"Everything we do is dangerous," he said.

The world didn't pause for Sammish. No matter what happened with Alys and her new people in Green Hill, Sammish needed money for food and to pay the baker for her room. Work only gave so much, and running a pull was always a balance between risk and reward. Festival days were an easy call; people were drunk and wearing their gaudiest jewelry. The bluecloaks knew to be on close watch, but they were also watching the empty warehouses and halls for burglars and pulling the intoxicated and aggressive out of their small celebratory riots. The usual squares—Newmarket or Riverport—were a more difficult decision. By their nature, they called people with coin in their wallets, sometimes there was beer and cider, but there was nothing like the abandon that a celebration brought.

Riverport in particular had its advantages and its dangers. Northernmost of the districts of Kithamar, there was more coin to be harvested there, but most of the people were Hansch, narrow-faced and straight-haired. The Inlisc who bought bread and fruit and meat, beans and herbs and knives from the stone stalls and tables there were usually servants of the great houses in Green Hill come across the river for the freshest goods instead of taking the scrapings of Stonemarket. A little fountain in the plaza gave frigid water to anyone with a bucket to carry it away and a place to sit and gossip, but few of the voices that rose above the splash and patter there had the accents of Longhill. The cloaks and embroidered hats and loomed scarves in River-port were a bit finer than the clothes people wore in New-market. And Newmarket was better than Longhill. For Nimal and Little Coop and Cane, Riverport was a more dangerous hunt-ing ground because they stood out there more.

Sammish didn't mind, though. She didn't stand out any-where. Even if she had, she needed the money.

Little Coop was the cutter, and Nimal was the flea. Sammish was the walk-away because she always was. They had Cane as the fish, which made it a little safer, but also meant they were sharing the take four ways instead of three. Sammish tried not to be resentful of that. Nimal had put the crew together, but Little Coop was the cutter, and the cutter called the go.

Sammish sat on the edge of the fountain, her hands in her lap, and watched whoever was close to Nimal, but never the man himself. There was a change in how he walked when he was moving in, and that was her signal. It hadn't come in half an hour. She'd been sitting there eavesdropping on the two old men next to her as they gossiped for so long that she was starting to form opinions about whether the thicker one's daughter really was treating her father poorly, or whether he carried some of the blame. Usually, in those kinds of family issues, she sided with the woman, but he was making a good case for himself. She was starting to waver when Nimal's back straightened and he turned sharply to his right. Sammish stood up smoothly, her shoulders a little hunched, her eyes a little down, and moved after him.

The safe cache was a cotton sack she wore inside her tunic, low enough that her breasts hid the lump. It already had two wallets and a silver necklace in it. She kept her eyes on the pavement near Nimal's boots. She never looked at the mark. To her, they were only ever blurs at the edge of her vision. Little Coop's feet appeared close to Nimal's, and she shifted toward them. The critical moment came. Nimal grunted and a woman's voice made a wordless sound of affront at the same moment Little Coop brushed by Sammish, passing something into her hand which she slipped into the little sack under her tunic through a slit at the seam. Three steps on, her hands were free and empty, the victim and her crew behind her. Cane's yelp was just part of the show, an extra distraction that added to the confusion. Even if the bluecloaks asked the victim what had happened, it would all be so addled and unsure that the story they heard would be more invention than truth.

This one was smart, though. Sammish wasn't more than a dozen steps away before the woman shouted for the guard. Of all the crew, she was the most at risk because she was the one carrying all that they'd stolen. Despite that, her heart didn't race. She looked over her shoulder with mild interest. The woman was Hansch, but broad across the shoulders. Her face was dark and her hands were in fists at her side, the very image of outrage. Nimal caught Sammish's eye and gestured that the pull was done, and to leave. Sammish made herself feel a mild curiosity—*I wonder what all that's about*—and then lose interest and turn away.

It was her secret. She had learned young how to trick herself. For the moment, and for several minutes more as she walked toward the low wall that kept city and river apart, she could genuinely believe that she was innocent, and that the commotion, whatever it was, had nothing to do with her. She could perform belief so deeply that she could even fool herself. There were only a few places in her life where her little talent failed her. She couldn't convince herself not to be afraid of the water snakes that lived in the canals or to stop craving the wheat beer they sold outside the university.

And Alys.

Alys was back in Longhill now, not across the river in her self-imposed exile in the cell of Oldgate. She always made a show of being pleased to see Sammish when they met. If she counted the minutes and hours they spent together, it likely wouldn't have been all that different from what they'd done before Darro died. It was only that Sammish felt herself being left behind, and it ached.

She had imagined that the search for Darro's killers would bring Alys closer to her. She'd imagined other things after that, and all of them seemed equally absurd and pathetic in cold daylight. As she walked along the street near the southern wall of the city, she let herself go over her fantasies again, but with a distance: examining them rather than surrendering to them, probing them like she was picking at a scab. She passed along the waterfront, looking out over the boats being made ready for the winter freeze. She paused, feeling the cold against her face and watching the men hauling at the dark, wet ropes, prying the wood and pitch that was their livelihood up out of the Khahon before the river squeezed them to splinters and ate them. Everyone knew water was hungry.

The sun was behind Palace Hill by the time she got back to Longhill and the Pit. The long walk had given her enough time to go from feeling sorry for herself to being angry to a kind of exhausted peace. The heat of the tavern's air was almost a shock as she stepped into it. It wasn't the fire, though a small one was muttering to itself in the grate. The Pit was thick with bodies, and the barn heat was enough to make the place almost uncomfortable. She slipped her hand through the slit in her tunic and kept it on her safe cache. More than once, someone had thought it was a clever idea to wait here and steal someone else's day's work. She wove her way back to the little table where Nimal and Cane were already waiting.

"Where's Coop?" she asked as she sat on the little stool that waited for her. It was too short, and the legs weren't even.

"He'll be here by the time we've counted out," Nimal said, and while it was likely true, Sammish bristled a little at his overbearing manner. Rules were you waited until everyone was there to make the split, but it wasn't her job to watch Little Coop's back. If he objected, he could talk to Nimal directly. She pulled three wallets, the silver necklace, and the leather pouch that the last, outraged woman had lost out on the table, and opened them one at a time while Nimal and Cane watched her hands. Palming a coin or two during the split was another pull, and while Sammish didn't do it, she didn't resent anyone being on the alert for it.

It was a decent haul. Bronze and silver coins for the most part, but also the necklace. One of the wallets had a little carved blackwood horse that probably wasn't worth anything, but it was nicely made. Sammish leaned back, and Cane made the division. Four piles that were as close as he could judge worth the same. Little Coop arrived while he was doing it. If he was upset that they'd started without him, he didn't show it.

With the four piles made, she and Little Coop and Nimal would each choose theirs, and Cane would get the fourth. Or that was how it was meant to go. After Little Coop took his, though, Nimal pushed one of the three remaining to Cane.

"Take it, and give us the table, yeah?"

They all hesitated, but then Cane shrugged, scooped up the pile he'd been given, and took Little Coop with him as he left. They vanished into the press of bodies like stones dropped in water. The sound of the crowd, conversations rising over each other to be heard, made a roar that would keep anything the two of them said from being overheard. Nimal leaned forward, careful not to put his hands near the coins.

"Had a proposition for you," he said. "May have something you want."

"You do," Sammish said, and nodded to the two piles still between them. "It's right there."

"Weeks back, you were asking about Orrel. Would it be worth your cut to find him?"

Sammish felt herself go quiet. This was why he'd told the others to leave. If she'd given up her part before, they might have wanted a three-way split. The question was, what did she want? Any money Orrel had from the pull on coronation day was more than likely already spent.

The only other thing he had was information about Darro. Whether Alys's brother had found him. And if he had, what had happened.

Sammish looked down at the coins. It was her room and her food. A fresh pair of boots. She wanted a beer and a roasted chicken and a warmer blanket. And a job at the brewer's taking wagers behind the iron grate. Alys wouldn't know if Sammish chose herself for once. She'd worked for it.

She put out her hand to grab up her share of the take, but what she did instead was pluck out a silver and two bronze. Something like shame or exhaustion sat on her chest, heavy as a cat, as she tucked the coins in her belt and left the rest for him.

Nimal smiled at her. One of his teeth was blue-dark and rotting. "Fair enough," he said.

Alys held the iron key with her fingertips, rolling it to feel the roughness of the metal. Her boots were soundless against the stones, and a cold wind from the east smelled like coming snow.

Newmarket was closing around her as she walked. The stalls and tables that lined the streets were empty now, the food and cloth and leather hauled back behind locked doors for the night. The canopies that weren't yet furled were being taken in. It made the street feel wider than it was, like she was a great lady with her way cleared before her.

She imagined Darro walking with her. She imagined that she *was* Darro. It brought her head higher and it straightened her back. It hid, she hoped, that she was so anxious that she hadn't been able to eat.

She was walking into a situation she didn't understand with people she didn't know, and whatever had led her brother to his death was waiting somewhere ahead of her. She felt like she was standing at the edge of a bridge, looking down into the dark, swirling water, knowing that she was about to jump.

The soapmaker's shop was dark and its shutters closed. Behind the windows on the second story, shadows moved. A family sitting down to their meal after a long day or else bowmen standing guard against an enemy. She had no way to know, and anything seemed possible. At the north side of the building, a narrow alleyway no wider than her shoulders opened like a crack in the wall. She stood before it, the key in her hand. How would Darro have held himself? Would he have smiled or lowered his head? Kept a hand on the hilt of his blade?

She stepped into the gloom, her senses straining. After a half dozen steps, the alley widened just enough that someone had built a wooden shed against the wall. Even though the sky was only a dark ribbon above her, the wood was grey with age and weather. She found the keyhole with her finger and fit the key to it. The soft sound of a voice came from the other side of the door, masculine and vaguely threatening. She felt the bolt sliding back as a vibration in her hand, and the door swung in.

Two men stood in the light of a single candle. They were older, and she didn't know them. One wore a cloak of worn leather like a coachman and a knit cap with a lock of grey hair at the temple. The other, shorter and broader in the face, was dressed like a laborer in a pale tunic and trousers of undyed canvas. The coachman held the familiar silver blade in his hand as if he'd been showing it to the laborer. It was the first time Alys had seen it since she'd given it over at the harvest festival. For a moment, all three were silent. Alys swallowed to loosen her throat.

"Andomaka sent me," she said.

"Don't say her name again," the coachman said, but not as a threat. "And don't ask mine. Or his."

"I won't," Alys said. "I'm sorry."

The coachman nodded to the door, and Alys closed it. The inner face of the lock had a wide iron lever. She pulled it down, and the latch slid closed. The shed itself wasn't as close as her cell in Oldgate had been, but it was nearly so. Thin shelves lined the wall, and the air stank of rosemary and lye. She was alone with two men in a place where, if they turned on her, help would not find her. She put her back to the door and a hand on the hilt of her blade as if she were only resting it there. The coachman's smile said he saw through the casual motion to the fear behind it. He tucked the blade into a fold of his cloak where it seemed to vanish. If there had been some conversation between the two men, her presence had ended it. She waited, and they waited, but the two stillnesses were different. She could feel their enjoyment of her discomfort. She might have left, if it hadn't meant turning her back to them.

The lock shifted and hissed as the latch opened. She stepped forward to let the door swing in, and a third man came in behind her. He was more nearly Darro's age, with close-cut dark hair and a smirk. She could have imagined him around the brazier with Black Nel and Terryn Obst. He lifted his chin at the coachman in greeting.

"I'm late," the new man said. He had an accent almost like Andomaka's, but lighter. As small as the shed was, Alys couldn't help brushing against him, though he didn't seem to notice.

"I knew that," the coachman answered.

"What's the work, then?"

"You come with me and keep your eyes open. If there's not a problem, there's not one. If there is, see to it that the silver blade gets out and back where it should be."

"And the money?"

"After. And we'd better be going," the coachman said, biting the words as he spoke them. "We should have been there by now."

The late one shrugged and backed out of the shed. Alys followed him, and the others came after. The coachman headed west with long strides, the laborer close behind him. Alys and the late one brought up the back. The sunset lit the western sky red as blood. Palace Hill and Oldgate stood silhouetted against the fading brightness like a god with his back turned. Alys walked fast, watching for movement in the windows and alley mouths without knowing what exactly she was looking for and too uncertain to ask.

The late one glanced at her, his eyes flickering to her boots and then back up her body the way men often would. On him, it didn't seem to mean what it usually did.

"You look like him," he said.

"Like who?" Alys asked.

"Darro."

They didn't speak, though the late man sometimes whistled a low, breathy melody. The night grew cold quickly. Though darkness came early this time of year, Alys felt as if they were travelling deep into night. They passed a patrol of city guard heading the other way, and though the bluecloaks watched them pass, they didn't call them aside. Slowly, street by street, she was able to put her unease inside herself and lock it away.

The Temple rose to their right, a darkness against the night sky except for a single glowing window, yellow as the sun and steadier than a star. Alys fought the sense that the gods were watching her.

The coachman stopped at a wide, dark building just off the Temple gate. It wasn't a part of Newmarket Alys knew. The cracked stucco walls and orange-stained lintels had little in common with the raw wood of Longhill or the unforgiving stone of the Hansch quarters. The roof was steep. No one would be sleeping on top of it. It was a merchant's house, but there was no trade sigil or sign to say what they traded in.

The laborer stopped walking first, looking back down the way they'd come. In the starlight, he looked grim.

"Would have preferred to do this in day," he said to no one in particular. Then, a moment later, "Watch yourselves."

A wide door at the corner of the house creaked and opened. Thin, buttery light spilled from it, and a woman stepped out with a lantern behind her. Alys couldn't make out her features, except that she was thick-bodied, looked more Inlisc than Hansch, and had her hair pulled back under a cloth. The coachman nodded to the new woman, then plucked the familiar silver knife from its hidden sheath. Alys felt a little bloom of pride that it was here. The woman, seeing it, stepped aside. The coachman went in, and the rest of the crew followed.

After the cold of the street, the interior felt hot and close. The air was wet and warm as a bathhouse, and dark mold dotted the walls at the ceiling. The woman let them through a hall past half a dozen doors with thick bars across them but no locks. They weren't made to be opened from within. Whatever lived behind those doors lived in a cage.

The center of the house was like a roofed courtyard: an open space lit by half a dozen lanterns and paved with baked tile. A stairway led to balconies on three sides, looking down over the lit space where the woman motioned them to wait. Dark wooden beams high above them took the place of the clouds. The late one squinted up into the gloom, and Alys understood. They were in the light. Anyone in the shadows above them would see them like they were actors on a stage but stay invisible themselves.

"This seems a promising place to die," the late one said.

"Dying's not the worst thing happens here," the laborer said.

The coachman scowled back at them and spoke in a calm, conversational voice. "Both of you shut the fuck up."

The footsteps came first, hard and sharp with nails in the soles. Then the sound of a door opening, and a short, harsh laugh. A tall man stepped into the courtyard, grinning, his arms wide as if he might embrace them all. Two men came after him. They wore straight, short, brutal swords at their hips and steel mesh gauntlets like animal handlers used to keep bites from cutting.

"This," the tall man said, "has been a long time coming." He had a mark inked into the skin of his cheek: two long lines crossed by a shorter third one. Alys had never seen anyone with the mark before, but she knew what it meant all the same. It was a Bronze Coast judgment mark. It was the kind they used when they caught a slaver. The tall man traded in the freedom of others. Alys remembered the barred doors and understood better what might be behind them.

"Sorry for that," the coachman said, and then waited.

The tall man tilted his head. "That's all? No explanation? No excuses?"

"None," the coachman said. "We meant to come before, but then there was a complication. Now we're here. You have the boy?"

The boy? Alys thought. She glanced at the late one and the laborer, but neither of them was looking at her. She couldn't say if they knew better than she did what was happening here or if they were only better at keeping their confusion hidden.

"I do," the tall man said. "You have the price?"

"There's a formality."

"All this time and worry because you wouldn't take my word?"

"Not my call," the coachman said. "You know that."

The tall man raised a hand, and a soft shuffling sound came from the darkness behind him. It wasn't only bowmen above them that the dark concealed. She had no way of knowing how many people were there, or how badly she and the others were outnumbered. The late one licked his lips, and she suspected he'd had the same thought.

A woman stepped out of the gloom with a boy at her side. He was younger than Alys by two or three years. His head was shaved, with only a rough stubble to cover his shining scalp. Long-faced and dark-eyed, he stared at the tiles. *Dumb as a sheep*, Alys thought, and then remembered the long rows of animals led on ropes to the harvest slaughterhouses. They had the same calm, incurious gaze. Exhaustion and fear that has lived past ripeness. The tall man stepped over to the boy and put a wide hand on the back of his neck, laying claim to him.

"This is the one."

"And still," the coachman said.

"Fine. Check for yourself."

The tall man shoved the boy forward, out into the space between the two groups. He stumbled on thin legs, almost falling. He didn't have ropes or chains, but red marks at his wrists and ankles showed where they'd rubbed wounds into him. He was too young to have a beard, but soft fuzz darkened his upper lip. If he'd been on a Longhill corner, no one would have looked at him twice.

The coachman stepped forward, and the silver knife—Darro's knife—was in his hand. For a moment, Alys thought he was going to kill the boy, but the coachman only steadied him with his left and gestured with the blade in his right. The boy didn't respond.

"Hold your hand out, son," the coachman said. The boy looked at him blankly. The laborer barked a half dozen syllables in a language Alys didn't know, and the boy shook his head. The coachman slapped him smartly across the cheek, and the boy lifted his hand.

The coachman steadied the boy's open palm with his hand and cut across it. The boy moaned and twitched, but he didn't try to pull away. Alys wasn't looking at him any longer. She was looking at the blade.

She'd spent hours in her cell in Oldgate considering it, tracing the arcane letters on its flat. She could have drawn them again from memory, she was sure of it. But the dark markings on the bloody silver now weren't those. The air around the knife shifted like the heat off a forge, and there was something like light but without the brightness that made it hurt to look at. She caught her breath.

Across the tiles, the tall man stepped back, his expression grave. Only the coachman wasn't unnerved. He knelt and sketched a symbol on the floor. It looked like a deathmark, but not for anyone she knew. The air thickened, and a sense of presence filled the room as if something vast was considering them all. The boy moaned and the mark began to blacken and smoke until the coachman rubbed it to nothing with his foot.

"Fair enough," he said. "He has the blood we're looking for. I accept him. Give him a cloak so he doesn't die in the cold, and I'll take him now."

"And I'll take the rest of my payment."

The coachman went still, and the late one at Alys's right made a small sound like he'd been stung by something small.

"That's not how it is."

"It's how it's become, though. I held this one for *weeks* more than we agreed."

"We didn't have the knife," the coachman said. "If we couldn't be sure he was the right one, you'd have thrown us one of your castoffs. We both know that's true."

"Might or might not. That's a world that didn't happen. The one that did had the boy with us longer than we agreed. Had to move and move and move to keep his people from putting hands on him. Now you want to take him and dance away, and I ask myself why I should think the payment will come on time when the collection was so, so late. I'm not asking for more than we agreed. But I'm asking for it now. And you, old friend, changed our arrangement before I did."

Alys saw something shift in the shadows. She kept her focus there, not glancing at the lantern flames and willing her eyes to adapt to the darkness.

"I don't have that option," the coachman said. He put the silver blade back in its sheath, but as he did, he looked back. The laborer nodded almost imperceptibly, as if to say he'd seen where the blade was, if he should need to grab it up and run. The tall man crossed his arms and scowled. Alys felt her breath coming faster.

She tried to imagine Darro, the way he'd been outside Ibdish's iron grate. The smile in his voice as he taunted the guardsman. His fearlessness. The late one at Alys's side made a small, almost contented-sounding noise and murmured to her, "Get ready. This may go poorly."

"I'll hold the boy a little longer," the tall man said.

"I don't have that option either," the coachman said, and Alys stepped forward, drawing her blade as she did. She took two long strides, casual and loose, as if she were confident. She took the thin boy by the shoulder, lifted her sword, and put its tip against the notch of his collarbone. Everyone in the room went still and silent.

"What...are you doing?" the coachman said in a voice that was calm and gentle, given the situation. Alys made her answer to the tall man.

"Here's a counter-offer," she said, picking her inflection to match someone she'd heard before. She couldn't recall quite who. "I kill this one. Everyone starts killing everyone else, and nobody gets paid for any of it."

"The fuck is this?" the tall man said, and the coachman shook his head.

"This is what my mother does when the children are squabbling," Alys said. "We came here in good faith, and now the both of you are barking at each other like two pit bitches with one bone. So here's your option. I kill him now and we all have a bad night, or else we leave with the boy. We do it now. And you get paid the usual way."

Whatever the usual way might be, Alys thought. The gods knew what those details were.

The tall man didn't speak, but his toughs didn't rush her either. Alys turned the boy to face the slaver, her sword never leaving his neck. His body pressed against her own felt weirdly intimate. His skin was warm. She put her blade across his throat and took a step backward, drawing him along.

The late one and the laborer shifted, falling in behind her as if this had always been the plan. A breath later, the coachman started back as well, his eyes on the tall man. The coachman was whispering a sewer's worth of obscenities, his gaze darting around the room. He didn't tell her to stop, though.

"You'll be paid," he said as he moved back. "We will keep our word to you."

"Fucking better had," the tall man said. His face was dark with rage. It made the ink on his cheek look angrier somehow. The laborer and the late one went slowly and carefully, clearing the way. The coachman walked backward, his face toward the enemy, and slowly pulled out a thick iron club as long as his forearm with a spiked hammer at the end from his cloak.

"It's going to be all right," Alys said in the boy's ear. So close to him, she could smell the muskiness of his skin and the oil of his body. The stubble on his scalp tickled her neck where it touched her. What he made of all this, she couldn't imagine.

"Door," the late one said.

"Head east," the coachman said.

The laborer's voice was a wheeze. "They'll come after us."

"They won't," Alys said because it fit the role she'd given herself. She didn't know if it was the truth.

The open air hit like a slap after the heat of the slave house. The wind was ice and malice. She felt the boy start to shiver against her almost as soon as they reached the street. Alys turned east, walking fast to leave the slavemaster and his blades behind, but also to get the boy wherever they were going. The night was fully dark. The stars spilled across the sky, brighter than the windows of Kithamar. Voices came behind them, but not, as far as she could make out, into the streets. With every step she took, the enemy receded.

"Put your sword away," the coachman said. "Unless you actually mean to kill the poor fuck."

Alys took her blade from the boy's neck and sheathed it as they walked. She felt the boy look back at her, but he was only a shadow among shadows. If he was smiling or afraid or still blank as a stone wall, she had no way to know. She didn't even see the carriage until she'd almost walked into it. It was under the eaves of a weaver's workshop, and if it had colors to it, she couldn't make them out. She was almost surprised when the one she thought of as the coachman actually hauled himself up to take the reins. She'd guessed him right.

The thick-faced laborer opened the carriage door, took the boy by the elbow, and lifted him up into the deeper darkness within it. He turned back, peering down the way they had come.

"No one and nothing," he said. "I think we got away with that."

"I'm not staying to find out," the coachman said, lighting his lantern. There were two horses in the team. They were huge black animals with blinders on. The coachman leaned over and pointed a long finger at Alys. "And if I see you again, I will gut you like a fucking trout. Do you understand me?"

"Then you should pay me before you leave," Alys said. "That was the deal, wasn't it?"

The late one laughed. "She might threaten to kill someone if you don't. She's wild that way."

"Fuck you too," the coachman said, but he took a pouch from his pocket and threw it on the ground beside them. Alys had to jump out of the way as the horses stepped out to the road and moved off into the night. Their hooves clattered against the stone, growing slowly quieter. It took her a moment to find the pouch. When she did, it jingled.

"Come on," the late man said, taking her by the hand.

"I don't think so," she said, pulling back, but the late man held his grip.

"My share's in there with yours, but we should get away from here before we start counting anything out. Don't worry. I wouldn't cross you. I've seen what that looks like." As much as anything, the merriment in his voice convinced her to follow him. The merriment and the fact that he'd known her brother's name.

The Temple was to her left now, and whatever glimmer of light had been in it was gone. To the east, the moon, almost at its half, began to rise. Kithamar at night was a different city, and in the cold of winter doubly so. The bustle and traffic of the day was gone, and the small sounds seemed louder. Rats scurried. Houses ticked as they cooled. The wind hissed across stones and over rooftops, a susurration that despite its randomness verged on music. Even when the moonlight was enough to cast little shadows and they didn't need touch to keep track of each other, the late one didn't let go of her hand. She didn't fight him. He seemed to have some destination in mind, and Alys felt warm and soft inside. It was like she'd finished a bottle of wine all by herself but without the muzziness. She was drunk on something better.

"I'm Alys," she said as they turned right toward the distant river.

"We're not supposed to share names," the late man said. "Mine's Ullin."

"Ullin. Good to know you."

"I'm best on first acquaintance. I don't age well. That, by the way, was the most awe-inspiring piece of not caring whether anyone around you lived or died that I have ever seen."

"It worked."

"Only makes it more astounding. They will tell stories of it forever, or they would anyway if we talked about any of this. Which we don't."

They walked in silence for another street. He let her hand go, and she found she was a bit sorry for the loss. He'd been warm.

"Who was the boy?" she asked. "Why is he important?"

"I don't know. We needed the knife to know we had the right boy, and we didn't have the knife. Then we got the knife, and so they sent for the boy, wherever he was being kept, and we came to see that he was the right one and gather him up. I don't ask where he came from or where he's going next."

"Just someone Andomaka wanted, then," Alys said.

"Is that her name?" Ullin said. "She must like you. She's never told it to me."

Y̲ou seem all right," Sammish said, but her gaze was fixed somewhere off to his left when she said it.

"No," Orrel said. "I don't."

He'd never been a large man. His body ran toward lean. People said his father had been the same before age caught up with him and thickened his gut. Orrel had never seen himself in the man who he'd called Papi. He looked even less like him now. Where he had been lean before, he was skeletal now, and his skin had taken on a greyish undertone except where the sores made an obscene pinkness. His hair hadn't fallen out, though the leech men said it might. The room had a small mirror made of beaten tin by the washstand, but he didn't look at himself in it.

The plague house stood in the forest south of Kithamar. In summer, the view from his little window would have been filled by a vast greenness of leaves. Now it was all black trunks and bare branches that rose toward the sky like a shriek. The only sounds were the soft settling of ashes in the brazier and the coughing of the woman at the end of the little hall. The pale stucco walls had glyphs and sigils that promised health and balance painted on them in bright blues and yellows. He couldn't tell if they worked. Maybe without them, he would have died by now.

Maybe that would have been better.

Sammish sat on the three-legged stool that the benefact used when she washed him. It was stained by the splashes of vinegar and lime that had dripped from her washcloth. If the room smelled of anything, his nose had grown accustomed to it long before. To judge from Sammish's expression, it stank of something.

"I looked for you and Alys both," Orrel said to fill the quiet with something. "After coronation day, I tried to find you. I wanted to give you your cut, yeah?"

"I know," Sammish said. She glanced at him, and then away. "I trust you."

It was a lie, and they both knew it. Just as they knew that anything he owed her had been spent weeks before. She didn't even ask for it. If she had, he'd have been angry. *Don't you see how ill I am? And you come here to squeeze my last coins out of me?* Since she didn't, he had nothing to push back against. That made it worse.

"I looked for you," he said again, gamely.

"What happened to you?" Sammish asked. And then, "Was it Darro?"

Orrel managed to get up some energy now, if only for the moment. "Fucking Darro."

"You heard what happened?"

Orrel didn't answer. His gut hurt, and his heart was racing. He couldn't tell if it was the anger and fear or the first sign of the fever coming back. The world narrowed until his skin was the horizon. It startled him when Sammish put her hand on his knee and pulled his attention back to her and the room.

"Do you know what happened?" she asked.

"It wasn't my fault," Orrel said.

It was the third day of Prince Bryn a Sal's reign, and pretty much everyone Orrel knew was waiting to see whether he made it to the fourth.

The story about Alys getting chased down by the guardsman was the first thing anyone who saw him talked about. The story ended with the guardsman running away from a rain of shit, or Alys getting a night pot dropped on her and the guard leaving in disgust. Or her brother Darro being caught in it. Or all three. What had actually happened, Orrel didn't know except that Alys was underground with Aunt Thorn, her brother had paid for it, and Orrel was very interested in not getting found by anyone involved.

But that hadn't worked out.

"I don't care," Darro said, putting down his leather bag. "That's not what I'm here for."

"Please. I'd never put my own crew in threat. It wouldn't be good for me, for one thing. Even if you think I'm the worst shit in the world, there's no call for me to—"

Darro looked around the little room. It was in the heart of Longhill, and less a house than a shack cobbled together where two other buildings hadn't quite met. When winter came, it would be too cold to live in, but until then, it was cheap and easy to overlook. Darro found a block of wood that Orrel had used for a table, turned it on its side, and sat on it like a stool. Orrel tried to crawl back farther into his sleeping shelf, but Darro reached out a hand and hauled him by the ankle.

When Darro spoke, he spoke carefully. "That's not why I'm here."

Orrel slowed, then stopped. Darro's expression edged on contempt, but he sat on the block and spoke in calm, friendly tones, like a man trying to gentle a spooked dog. "There's something I need to do. And you are in a position to help me."

"A pull?"

Darro's expression clouded, and his eyes seemed to take in something more than the room contained. "A killing."

Orrel swore under his breath, and it brought the older man back to himself. His smile was apologetic, though Orrel couldn't have said who he was apologizing to. "It's also a pull, but this is the dangerous part. I'm going to have to end someone, and I'm going to have to do it in the street where I can be seen. I'd rather not be stopped, and I think you can arrange that for me."

"The fuck am I? A wizard?" Orrel said. "What are you into, Darro?"

"I have an opportunity is all. Someone stole a thing, and I recovered it. Now I have two people who want it. I've pledged to give it to both of them. One of them's paid me. The other one is too dangerous to cross. So I'm keeping the coin and knife, and making very certain that no one is around to suggest I had any but the most loyal intentions."

"But *killing* someone?"

"No one will miss her. And people die for money every day. Just the coin usually goes up to the palace instead of rolling down to Longhill. If anything, this is more justice than the city usually sees."

Orrel's panic had thinned and burned away. He sat with his back to the wall, his legs crossed under him. He didn't even think about fleeing. Not now. "Is it a lot of money?"

"It could keep me for years," Darro said, and there was no

boast in his voice. There might even have been dread. "She knows the risk of it. It's why she won't meet me in private. Which means I have to end this in public. And I have to do it so that no one whistles up the bluecloaks."

"How—" Orrel began, and in answer Darro leaned down and pulled a length of blue cloth from the bag at his feet.

"I understand you have a badge of office. No one calls the guard when the guard's doing the killing."

Orrel felt his eyes go wide. "That's brilliant."

Darro pushed the cloth back into his sack. "Let's not get too happy yet. I haven't managed it. Now. The badge."

Orrel scrambled to his feet, and Darro let him. A part of him wanted to take the chance and run. It was a reflex. His safe cache was under a board in the corner of the sleeping shelf, and the bluecloak's belt was in it. He held it out to Darro like a man putting offering bread on an altar.

"Do you..." Orrel began, and faltered.

Darro took the badge and fitted it to his own belt. It looked wrong there, but to other eyes, it might pass. With the cloth around it, Darro might look less like a Longhill knife in a costume and more like an actual guard. Orrel swallowed to loosen his throat and tried again to speak.

"Do you think you'd want a fish? Someone to watch the crowd and raise an alarm if you needed one?"

"Are you offering?"

"Are you paying?"

"I am," Darro said. "Spin this wrong for me, and I'll kill you before the guards do."

Orrel grinned. He remembered clearly that in that cursed moment when he should by right have run, he'd grinned.

o   o   o

The next day had been hot, but the river had the deep smell of rotting leaves that it got when the turn of seasons was close. The meeting was in a square by the northern wall, beside the bridge that crossed to Green Hill. Orrel didn't wear the blue, because he had no badge to justify it. Instead he wore his good shirt in hopes of passing for the son of a merchant house or a worker at the store yards. The sky had been white with summer haze. Darro had stationed himself at a corner, sweating himself thin under the guardsman's blues and a darker cloak to hide them until the moment. Orrel had gone ahead.

The corner of Riverside nearest the docks meant good money, but low blood. The people there were healthy and washed, but their clothes had a tradesman's cut, and there were no silks or fine linens. Orrel's attention skipped to the best marks—a boy with a basket of food he kept putting down, a girl with a belt that hung slack enough that a deft hand could lift out her wallet, an old man sleeping in the shade with his mouth open. But they weren't the job. First, he saw that there weren't any bluecloaks nearer than the bridge, and those just a pair of men collecting tolls for the prince. Once that was clear, there was only finding the woman.

It wasn't hard, since he knew to look. She had a hard face with crow's-feet at the eyes and a mole as black as tar on her cheek. Her braid was as thick as his arm, wiry hair that was black where the first frost of age hadn't touched it. Her clothes were well made, but subtly wrong. She held her body for a different outfit, even if Orrel couldn't guess what it was. She was in costume as much as he was. As much as Darro. They were players in a little drama put on for an unsuspecting crowd. Orrel made his way back through the streets quickly, trying to reach Darro before any patrol bumbled into the square and took the whole thing down.

When Darro met his eyes, Orrel nodded. Darro didn't smile, just shrugged off the brown cloak from above the blue, put his hand on the grip of his club, and strode into the square like a man who owned the place, the way the guardsmen did. The costume wasn't bad. The only thing that spoiled it was the dark stripe of sweat down the back. The badge of office glittering at his hip more than made up for that. Orrel followed a few paces behind, his heart tapping at his chest. The promise of violence was sharper than wine. More intoxicating.

The woman didn't recognize Darro as he walked across the square. Her gaze didn't shift to him until he was almost on her. He spoke then in a loud, booming voice, "You there! Put your knife down! I said *down*."

She didn't have a weapon drawn, but Orrel knew the pull. If Darro said it for enough people to hear, they would remember a blade into her hand. Darro raised his club and brought it down hard. The sound was like a butcher's meat hammer. The woman spilled out across the filthy stones of the street.

Orrel thought she would cry out, or scream and try to run. Darro shifted his club in his hand and struck her twice more in the ribs and once, aiming for the killing blow to her head, on the shoulder. The girl with the loose belt squeaked and danced away. The boy with the basket turned, confused by the shouting.

Orrel saw something in Darro's eyes. A horror, perhaps, at what he was doing. A fear that it was taking too long to finish his prey. Maybe sorrow that he had come to this as his best choice. Darro swung his club up with both hands, aiming at the back of the woman's head, and the dark woman lifted herself toward him. She had the grace of a dancer, an economy of movement that made everything she did seem like she was only being carried along by a soft breeze.

She ducked inside Darro's swing and punched him once in the chest as she did it. Only afterward, Orrel saw that she did have a knife in her hand after all. And it hadn't been a punch. She walked briskly away, the speed of running without the effort of it.

"You! Stop!" Darro shouted, and went after her. She didn't look back, but made her way along the riverbank, swimming between the men and women and children at their business like a fish through river weeds. Darro ran after her, and Orrel followed. Because he was behind, he didn't see the blood on Darro's chest until the older boy stopped and sat on a low stone wall that overlooked the water. The woman was almost lost in the crowd.

"She pinked me," Darro said, but his cloak was soaking red. He lost his grip on the wooden club, and it fell into the water. He didn't try to catch it back. "I just...I have to catch my breath."

When he slumped to the side, Orrel tried to catch him, but Darro was already dead weight.

Was already dead.

Someone shouted, and Orrel stood. His hands were covered in Darro's blood. The two bluecloaks from the bridge, too far off to know what had happened, were looking toward the river wall. With a clarity that mimicked calm, Orrel realized how much trouble he was about to be in.

"Get a healer!" he shouted. "This poor man's been hurt!"

A crowd was starting to form, and getting out under its cover before the guard found him was his best chance. He grabbed a girl who came near, pressing her toward the corpse with a terse *Do what you can for him*, and then began weaving his way south, touching as many sleeves and backs as he could. A single bloody man stood out, so better that there be twenty people with stains on their clothes.

As he slipped from the edge of the crowd, a man shouted and a woman shrieked. A splash came as Darro's body fell into the Khahon. Orrel paused for a moment to look: dead skin pale against the tea-dark water, blue cloak billowing as the ripples from the bridge folded Darro into themselves and pulled him down. A sorrow found its way through the fear: maybe for Darro, maybe for the gold he'd promised that would never come.

When he looked back up, the woman was watching him.

She was at the corner of a stall where a boy was selling wheat-cakes and honey, her braid pulled over her shoulder like a huge snake. She gasped for air like a fish hauled up from the water, and her face was striped with blood. Darro's or her own, he couldn't say. It might have been only the distance and his fear, but the whites of her eyes seemed black.

Her lips moved, and he swore he could hear her whispered words cutting through the roar of the crowd and the rush of the river as if her lips were against his ear. Weird, oily syllables that made his head spin. She turned and walked away, vanishing like a flame when the candle's snuffed.

Orrel took another half dozen steps, his legs unsteady, and vomited on the street.

"That's why you came here?" Sammish asked. "Because you got sick?"

"I came because I have a cousin who tends their medicine garden," Orrel said with a thin laugh. "I thought it was just...I thought it would pass. And no one's looking for you in a plague house. It wasn't you and Alys I was dodging. It was *her*. Darro's fucking witch. Only I kept puking. It didn't stop."

He lapsed into silence. Sammish moved her stool a few inches closer and took his hand. Her fingers felt cool in his, which probably meant the fever was coming back.

"When they found him," Orrel said, "did he have the badge still?"

"No," Sammish said. "The river took it or the guards did."

"Good. That thing was bad luck from the start. If I could live it over, I'd have stayed in bed that whole day, and never mind Byrn a Sal and his coronation parties."

"Yeah," Sammish said. And then she laughed. "It was a good pull, though. I mean, a guardsman's badge right off of him? Who'd even try that? We did it, though. The three of us. Not even a fish to help."

Orrel let himself smile and remember being that boy in the sunlight, more drunk on his own daring than on wine. It seemed like a memory from someone else's life. He sobbed, and Sammish squeezed his hand. She was crying with him.

"She cursed me," Orrel said. "We tried to kill her and she cursed me."

"You're living in a sick house," Sammish said. "Someone passed their illness to you. It happens all the time. You'll get better."

"It started when she spoke. You don't know what it was like. I haven't been right since then."

"You will be," Sammish said, but she said it with pity. She saw him as clearly as he saw himself.

He could dream of taking a boat south when the spring came or riding with a team of towing oxen, but it wouldn't happen. Before thaw came, he'd be in the ground or in the river. Whatever else he'd imagined or expected for his life—half-noticed ambitions for love or sex or comfortable old age—this was what he'd have instead: a few more days or weeks in a cold stucco room with floors that stank of lye and vinegar and the herbs the benefacts burned to cover the stink of corruption. Soon, he wouldn't even have the will left to be horrified at the thought. He let Sammish's fingers go. He felt too weak to hold them.

"Did..." Sammish began, then let it trail away. She squared her shoulders and tried again. "Did he say why she wanted the knife so badly? Or what it was that made it special?"

"I don't remember."

"It's important," she said. Then, "You didn't pay me for that pull. You owe me. Just try to remember."

Orrel opened his eyes. He didn't remember closing them. "Something about a rite? It was supposed to be some sort of religious thing like they do in Bronze Coast. Ancestor worship."

"Are you sure about that?"

"No," he said, and let his eyes close. They felt very comfortable closed. He heard Sammish's stool clatter against the stone floor. Her footsteps hushed toward the door of his cell.

"I tried to find you," he said, or else dreamed that he was saying. "You and Alys both."

In her rooms at the Daris Brotherhood, Andomaka neither woke nor slept. Her mind did something else entirely, feeling the world as if it were a part of her body. The same act of will that lifted her finger and arched her foot might squeeze snow from the clouds or shift deep-buried stone. It was a beautiful way of being, and she had practiced it since she was a girl. Her uncle the prince had taught her. Prince Ausai a Sal, who had dreamed once as she did now. He had shown her that Andomaka was an illusion. What they called her self was a series of impulses as wild as a rainstorm, and as transitory. She had practiced letting go, just as all those of royal blood did when they were inducted into the Daris Brotherhood.

Her cousin Byrn a Sal had not, because his father, Tallis—brother to both Prince Ausai and her own long-dead mother—had turned away from the rites. Ausai had told her that it would make no difference. The unprepared vessel of Byrn a Sal would carry what it had to carry just as well. The only price was that the invocation would be more uncomfortable for Byrn, more frightening, less beautiful. The thread of Kithamar, Ausai had promised her, would be unbroken. But that was before Prince Ausai's final illness, before the discovery of the blade's disappearance, before the rite had failed and Byrn a Sal ascended to the prince's house unhallowed. Unsanctified. Wrong.

The thread of Kithamar was broken. It was hers to repair it.

She felt him there, in the room with her. Ausai, and more than Ausai. The spirit that had dwelled within him and within his city. She felt its fear and its rage. She felt its distance. It was like hearing the desperate pounding from the wrong side of the ice. She reached out her focus, pulling her will past her skin and into the dry water in which the whole world swam. *I am here* she thought to the spirit of Kithamar. *I am faithful. I will find you.* And perhaps the rage lessened.

She opened her eyes, and Tregarro was there. For a moment, she was too broad and diffuse for her own body, and she couldn't keep from drifting into his. His banked lust and the complex knot of self-hatred and pride at his core were unpleasant, and she pulled back quickly.

He held out a goblet of hot mulled wine, and she accepted it.

"Well?" he asked.

"No. Not yet."

His impatience was palpable even when she was wholly back within her own flesh. "We have the boy and the blade. We could perform the ceremony tonight. It doesn't need to be perfect. It's not like we're keeping the bastard once it's over."

"Not now. There's a reason we do this after the funeral and before the coronation when everything is thinnest," she said, and didn't add *And what if we do it all correctly and it still fails?* The memory of Ausai's last days—his desperate struggle to recover or remake the lost blade, his death, and the failure of the rite—haunted her to the degree that she could be haunted. Her dread was another illusion, and she was aware of its impotence. "Longest Night, maybe. Or first thaw. Thaw might be better."

"The first thaw is too far," Tregarro said. "Longest Night. It has to be."

She rose from her couch. The candles around her, thick and dark and smoking with perfumes, were low and guttering. Her room went darker as the small fires failed.

"Are you advising me of that?" she asked. "Or was it an order?"

"I don't order you."

She tightened the sash at her waist. The wine was thick and rich, and her belly warmed with it. A shudder passed through her, as it sometimes did in these moments.

"Longest Night, then," she said.

Ullin slept in Stonemarket, west of the river. He shared a common barracks with twelve other men his age. They paid a bronze a day to keep claim to a sleeping shelf, a box the size of two balled fists for their things, and the protection of the landlord. Alys didn't want to take him back to the room that had been Darro's before it became hers, and there was more than one reason for that. First was that it was Darro's and it was hers and she didn't want too many other people in that communion. Also, it felt like bragging to have a place all to herself when Ullin was breathing in the dreams of a dozen strangers.

And though it never quite rose to the surface of her mind, there was a flavor to Ullin's friendship that could have turned to sex if the opportunity had presented itself. While she found herself hungry for his company, what she needed from him wasn't that. Rubbing up against him would have ruined it. So instead, the Longhill knife made her long way through Seepwater and the Smoke to Stonemarket.

It was the farthest quarter of Kithamar from the ones she knew. Even if she paid to ride in the back of someone's cart, it could take more than half of the winter's short day to pass through the canals of Seepwater, over the river's southernmost bridge, through the filthy soot-blackened canals and streets of the Smoke, and into its squares and lanes. Travelling back at night would have been walking in the dark through the bitter cold. Instead, she rented a bed from a merchant family that would eat through half of another of Darro's gold coins before springtime came. When Ullin or one of his friends asked, she pretended to be staying with a cousin who apprenticed with a coppersmith. No one questioned her story. The only qualm she felt came from leaving the box of Darro's ashes by itself. She hated imagining Darro lonesome.

The cold and dark of winter slowed Kithamar's blood, but Stonemarket was a revelation for her. She had passed through it before, run pulls by its grand fountain and sold stolen cloth at its marketplace, but she had not lived there. A thousand small things made it different from Longhill and the city she knew. She felt like she'd been transported to some foreign country. The buildings here sounded different. The bread they baked here rose from soda, not yeast. Even the landmarks she knew meant something else here. She'd gotten badly lost twice before she realized that Palace Hill was to the east here, and her whole life it had been a synonym for sunset. She caught glimpses of round Inlisc faces like her own, but they were few. All humanity seemed Hansch in Stonemarket.

She was a stranger here, and so she could be anyone.

"So there I was," she said, gesturing toward the fire as if it were the summer streets of Longhill, "running like hell, and this baby guardsman screaming behind me with his cloak billowing out like a sail because we'd cut his belt off him."

Ullin was laughing so hard, tears were running down his cheeks. Two of the others from his barracks were with them: one tall and thin as a sapling tree, the other with a scar that pulled down his right eyelid when he smiled. She didn't remember either of their names, though they'd said them earlier. They all sat together at the mouth of an alleyway, bundled in wool and leather. Their breath was white and thick as clouds, but she didn't feel the cold. Ullin had brought a rough iron pan to hold a fire, and they had cooked strips of meat over the dull red coals before moving on to burn bundles of herbs whose fragrant, soft smoke left her feeling warm and expansive and pleasantly outside of herself.

"He must have shit himself!" the one with the scar said.

"Funny you should say that," Alys said, "because let me tell you what happened next."

Ullin leaned back against the frost-crazed stone of a building, his head in his hands, and only the edge of his grin showing past his wrists. She couldn't tell if the hiccups of laughter were telling her to stop or go on. She went on.

It was what Ullin and his crew seemed to do in the long darkness: tell stories and drink. She liked it that the stories were almost evenly weighted between tales of victory and comic stories of their own humiliations. When Ullin laughed at her, it didn't sting, because he laughed at himself too. As she reached the part of her story with the night pots of Longhill opening up like a yellow-brown raincloud over the guardsman, an old man hurried past on the street. He wore a foxfur overcoat and an embroidered hat that covered his ears. He scowled at the winter cold or at the four of them, or at both. When the tall one made a little bow, the man only hurried his steps. Alys saw Ullin weighing whether to go after him and relieve him of his wallet and furs, and then deciding it wasn't worth the bother.

"Ah, Darro was a one, wasn't he?" Ullin said instead. "I didn't know him except through..." He gestured vaguely with one hand. When he'd said they didn't talk about Andomaka and the work for her, he'd been very serious. More serious than Alys had seen him be about anything else. He also knew or guessed that what Alys wanted from him was her brother. He was right about that. Any story, any scrap of the life he'd lived and kept from her was worth more than the gold he'd left.

The one with the scar took a small brown bottle from his pocket and drank from it. He didn't offer it around. Ullin took a deep breath, then blew it out. It looked as solid as a feather in the cold.

"I remember one time I was out with him," Ullin said. "Would have been about a year ago. I'd just met him."

That was interesting. Had Darro only been taking work from Andomaka for a year, then? She realized Ullin was waiting for her, that the pause had gone on a heartbeat too long. "Yeah?"

"We had done a thing, and after, we stopped at a taproom in Seepwater by the canals."

"Won't see me going to the fucking river," the tall one said. "Water's hungry. Stay in my place, me."

"Well, my place is where I'm called," Ullin said. "Anyway, there was this girl there, hair dark as pitch and straight as spooled thread. Don't recall her name."

"Nel?" Alys said.

Down the street, a small woman turned the corner, wrapped in grey rags and a hood, head lowered against the cold. Alys noticed her and ignored her in the same moment.

"Could have been. Don't recall. But she was looking for a fight with whoever came in range of her. Now this place, the keep had a rule: You left your blades at the door. So we were there, Darro and me, not a knife between us, and this girl with her teeth out and her fists cocked. Darro said something about it too, and she came at him like he was her best enemy with his belly showing. Only he picked up his club. You know the one?"

"Hard oak," Alys said. "One end dipped in lead."

"Thought you said you left your arms at the door," the one with the scar said.

Ullin lifted a finger like a university tutor making a fine point of public rhetoric. "*Blades.* I said we left our *blades* at the door. Weighted stick's not a blade, which was Darro's point. So this fine young woman sees how she's just started something that won't finish well for her, and her eyes—"

"*Alys?*"

The woman in her grey bundle of rags had stopped near them and, improbably, Sammish's face appeared from under the hood. Her cheeks were dark with the cold, her upper lip shining with snot. Snowflakes clung to her eyelashes. Alys noticed that it was snowing. She tried to stand, but it was more difficult than she'd expected. She wondered how many bundles of herbs they'd burned and whether she'd been sitting downwind without noticing.

"You know this one?" Ullin asked at the same time that Sammish said, "Are you all right?" Alys took a moment to untangle the two questions in her mind, then turned to Ullin.

"I'll be right back." She stepped forward and took Sammish's arm. She'd meant to pull the girl away, but found herself leaning against her instead. "What are you doing here?"

"Looking for you," Sammish said. "What are *you* doing here? No one's seen you in days."

"I'm...working," Alys said, but it wasn't quite the right word.

Sammish glanced around, alarmed. "You're doing something for *them* now?"

"Not that kind of working," she said.

"I was worried. I thought something bad happened to you."

Behind them, Ullin said something. The tall one laughed his long, braying laugh. Alys had missed the joke, and she saw Sammish seeing her impatience. Alys smoothed her expression like she was playing at tiles. "Nothing bad. Just learning more. About Darro. What he was working." Her heel landed on a slick bit of ice, and she stumbled. The road seemed to shift and roll like the river after a storm. She shook her head to clear it. Sammish started to say something, but Alys, annoyed, cut her off. "How did you find me?"

"Tamnis has a cousin working in Green Hill. He said he'd seen someone that might have been you by the fountain a few days ago. And I didn't have any place else to try."

"How long have you been looking for me?" Alys asked.

Sammish shrugged and repeated herself. "I didn't have any place else to try."

A rough clanging made Alys turn. Ullin was upending his iron pan, scattering the coals in the gathering midnight slush. Embers rose in the air like bright insects and then went dark. It wasn't something that would ever have happened among the wooden structures of Longhill, and it made the stone walls around them seem magical. Things that were impossible in the world she knew became possible here. The tall one fumbled with his belt, hauled out his cock, and started pissing out the few coals that still glowed. Ullin met Alys's gaze, raised a hand in farewell, and turned away. The night, it seemed, was over. She considered the two who were still there. They didn't take jobs from Andomaka and they hadn't known Darro. They didn't mean anything to her. A breath of wind set the falling snow swirling.

"Well, you found me," she said. "I'm here, and I'm healthy and whole. So . . ."

"I can't believe you were sitting out in this weather. People die like that."

"They don't."

"They do. Especially when they're too drunk to feel the cold. Yarro Connish did two years ago. They found him curled up outside Ibdish's house with half a skin of wine in his hand."

"I'm not him," Alys said, and started walking southeast, toward the Smoke. She was steadier on her feet now, and Sammish had to trot to catch up. Her heart was a complex of resentment, amusement, and regret. Part of her wanted to be back with Ullin and the necessary evil of his friends, trading stories and laughing and getting drunk on smoke. But part of her, she now realized, wanted badly to sleep. She didn't know how long she'd been out in the alleyway, or how far into the night they'd come. With the clouds low overhead, there was no moon or star to tell her. Ullin had the trick of making the night seem brief.

"Long walk home," Sammish said.

"I'm not going home," Alys said.

"Oh. All right," Sammish said, her voice pulling back like Alys had touched a cut. "Then I should..."

"Fuck's sake, you're not either. Stop whining and come with me."

The streets of Stonemarket were calm and quiet in the darkness. A few people made their way on foot, and Alys led Sammish past one slow-moving cart drawn by an ancient, tired-looking mule, but the doors of the markets, workshops, guild halls, and warehouses were all closed. There were glimmers of light in the higher windows where families and servants hadn't yet gone to bed, but only a few. For the greatest part, the city was saving its candles and oil. Alys stopped at a private alley with a high iron gate and took the key from her sleeve. When she closed and locked the gate behind them, Sammish looked as lost as a rabbit, and Alys took her hand to lead her into the darkness.

The merchant family she'd taken her room from traded in salt and private loans, and they'd bargained hard for her little shelter. It was close as a grave, but it backed against the kitchen. The stone radiated a little of the cookfire's heat even long after the cooks had gone to bed. Alys wondered whether Darro hadn't also had arrangements like this. Little places to go to ground scattered all through the city. She imagined that he might have. She hoped that he had.

There was no candle or lantern, so she led Sammish to the straw mattress in darkness, and in darkness, she brushed the melting snow off her own cloak sleeves and shoulders. The mouser that lived in the alley scratched at the door, and Alys let it in too. A few fleas weren't much to risk if it meant a little more warmth.

"There's a night pot in the corner if you need it, and some water on a stand beside," Alys said, lowering herself into the bed.

"Are we supposed..." Sammish said, as if the words were too big for her throat. "Should we undress?"

"If you want to freeze to death, go ahead," Alys said. "There's only one blanket, and it's thin."

"All right. I didn't know." And then, "I'm sorry."

Alys found the blanket and hauled it up over the both of them. "For what?"

"I'm in the way. I shouldn't have come looking."

"You could trust me better to watch out for myself, that's true," she said. Then, because it had come out harsher than she'd meant it, "These are good people."

"Are they?"

"They aren't like us. They're rich and they're smart, and they didn't spend their lives grubbing for their next meals the way we did. They're bigger than we are is all. They're better. It's why Darro was with them. They care about the whole city, not just their corner of it."

"Those boys?"

"Not them. Andomaka. The people who matter."

Sammish didn't speak, but Alys felt her shift and thought it was a nod. Alys closed her eyes, and the world didn't get any darker. The mouser crawled between them, turned around twice, and settled down, purring. Alys's body felt heavy and slow. Sleep tugged at her, but having Sammish there, another flesh next to her own, felt odd. She'd grown used to being alone.

"How much do they know about us?" Sammish whispered. "About why you're really here?"

"As much as they need. I don't go around launching into it every time, but there's no call to hide it."

"They know about the gold?"

"I don't know. Maybe, if it came up. I wouldn't keep any-thing from Andomaka. There's no reason to. We want the same things."

"So you wouldn't keep secrets from her?"

"Of course not. Why would I?" Alys said, and shifted. "Did you find something?"

Sammish was quiet for so long that Alys thought she'd fallen asleep, and when she did speak, her voice was small and oddly sorrowful. "No. I didn't find anything."

Back in Longhill, Alys drew the club through the air as hard as she could and enjoyed the feeling of its mass. It made a soft noise like the flutter of wings.

"You like it?"

It wasn't quite like Darro's, but then it couldn't be. Darro had carried his for years, and use had changed it. The wood had been darker, and shaped to his hand. Even if she'd had it, it wouldn't have been quite like it had been for him. Her arm was a different length, her hand had its own grip. The most she could hope for was a translation: a tool that was to her as his had been to him. As far as she could recall, Darro had bought his from Merrian Haldin, whose son Jiam stood before her now, Merrian having died last season from a cut on his leg that wouldn't stop bleeding. It was the same little shop, though. Darro's club had been oak, as was hers. His had an end dipped in lead to give weight to its swing, just as this one did. And it was a good piece of work. It was as near to her brother's as it could possibly be. And still, the gap between what she could have and what she wanted chafed.

"It's good," she said, and wished she could have been more enthusiastic.

"It will do everything you need, that," Jiam said, almost defensively.

It wouldn't, but Alys would take it anyway. She smiled because smiling was polite, and gave the boy his money. Trees that had been lush and green when Darro died were black sticks now, and she still had enough money that she didn't have to save for the club or trade for it. She walked back out into the streets of Longhill with the weapon across her shoulders and her arms resting on it like a yoke.

She had come back to Longhill for the club and to be in her own room again. Ullin had teased her for leaving, pretending an affront he didn't feel. She took it as a sign of friendship—or at least companionship—but it sat poorly with her. And now, walking through the familiar winter streets and alleys of home, her irritation grew.

Ice had settled into Kithamar with the deepness that meant it was there to stay. Snow haunted the shadows, and the shit that people threw from their windows froze in the street, waiting for the prisoners' cart to come by and clean it away. It didn't even stink.

The preparations for Longest Night were apparent in the windows and doorways. Bits of ribbon hung from the mantels, and candleholders sat outside the shutters, waiting to be filled. There was a comfort in knowing that the days would be stretching out again, even if the coldest weeks were still between them and the thaw. But Alys found herself feeling tight around the throat and strangely ill at ease as she looked at the little signs of celebration. She didn't put her thumb on why until she saw Grey Linnet walking ahead of her. The old woman wore a shawl of woven, bright yarn across her shoulders as if she were going to a celebration, but her face was sorrowful. She carried a bouquet of thistle.

Alys remembered what she had been trying to forget. She knew—of course she knew—that Longest Night was five days on from where she stood. And that five days before Longest Night was also Darro's naming day. It would have been his twenty-second, and instead it was the first of his absence. Another moment of traditional mourning that Alys had tried to erase from her mind through a clench-jawed act of will.

And she had failed. Looking back at all she'd done in the past days, she thought the impulse to buy the club in her hands today of all days hadn't been as random as she'd pretended.

She felt as if she were two people at once: one who had forgotten the course that mourning her dead brother would take, and another who had followed the pattern of ritual, seeking out a token of the dead man and walking now toward the place where her quarter would end their debts and their mourning.

Alys resolved not to make the turn that Linnet had. She was her own woman now. The customs of Longhill didn't command her. She could walk back to her room—Darro's room—if she saw fit. Or buy a place on the back of a cart and make her way back to Stonemarket and Ullin. Or Green Hill and Ando-maka. Or even walk to the cheap little room by the baker's that Sammish still used. Kithamar had ten thousand different things happening that day, and her brother's nameday was only one. She didn't have to choose it. At the intersection, she hesitated like her feet had stuttered.

She turned toward her mother's house, her teeth clenched.

The first nameday celebration she'd been to after someone had died, she had been too young to understand. It had been for Coward Holt, the long-faced man who had lived across the street from them back then. A fever had taken him in the height of summer, filling his lungs with water, like the river stealing in and drowning him from afar. Alys hadn't liked or disliked the man, but her mother had forced her and Darro both to go to the funeral. It had confused her then when, just after harvest, her mother had told her to plait her hair and put on her good skirt, that they were going to Coward Holt's nameday. She'd done as she was told, thinking that maybe there had been some mistake and the old man hadn't really been dead. Or that he had, and death wasn't as irrevocable as she'd thought.

In the event, it had been the dead man's son and widow welcoming people who'd known Coward Holt, giving them cheap beer and stale cake. Instead of nameday gifts, the guests brought what the dead man was owed: the leather punch that Coward Holt had loaned to Fat Stanni, a few bronze coins with Prince Ausai's likeness going a little green for want of polishing in payment for the door Coward Holt had fixed for Ibdish, a wool coat to replace the blanket that Tamnis Couard had taken from him and lost. Alys's mother had owed the old man nothing, but she took a handful of thistle bound in ribbon as a token and a jar of salted fish. *Whatever you think you owe, give a little bit more,* her mother had said. *We're Longhill and we're Inlisc, and it's how we take care of each other.*

In her memory, Alys had been surprised to hear that they took care of each other at all, but that might not have happened. It had been years ago, and she had been a child.

Alys hadn't seen her mother since the day she'd seen Darro dead and learned that the woman hadn't been willing to pay the full rites. Her mother had moved since then, but only a few doors down, where she seemed to be sharing a thin-windowed, one-storied converted storeroom with two other women her age. Alys might have walked past it without knowing what it was, except for the symbol drawn in black over the doorway.

She'd spent hours looking at that same symbol herself, where it was carved into the box of ashes and filled with wax. She was almost surprised that her mother had bothered to learn Darro's deathmark.

She went in with a sense of resignation, like a prisoner who had failed to win the mercy of the judge. The group within was smaller than the one that had gathered at the news of Darro's death, but the faces were all familiar. Damnis Oltson. Nimal. Sarae Stone, with a baby on her hip that must have belonged to her. Ibdish and his wife. Alys looked for Sammish and was surprised by her absence. Her mother's reed-thin lover was also gone. He'd left her, or her mother had told him to go; it made no difference. Her mother was sitting on a high stool, her hands folded on her lap, leaning close to Aunt Daidan the better to hear her old friend's thin, watery voice saying, *It's so hard losing them young, isn't it, Linly? So very hard.*

Her mother caught sight of her, and for a moment fear bloomed in the old woman's eyes. Then maybe relief, and at the end a shyness like a girl at a taproom finding the courage to talk with a beautiful man. Her mother had lost weight in the last months, even with the fullness of the harvest. Her cheeks looked deflated and papery. She motioned Aunt Daidan aside and stood. Alys took two short steps and was at her side.

"Mother."

"Alys. I wasn't sure if you'd..." She trailed off, then tried a smile. "You're looking well. You look..."

Like him, Ullin finished in Alys's memory, and she stood a little straighter. "I've been busy."

"Yes, of course. Of course you have. It's so good to see you."

Alys nodded, acknowledging the words more than responding to them. Her mother's gaze cut away. They stood neither together nor apart for a moment. Alys felt a sudden overwhelming sorrow, as crushing as it had been in the first days after Darro's death, and then a rage she could barely restrain. She kissed her mother's cool cheek and walked to the wall, leaning against it with her arms crossed. Sarae broke the silence, turning to an older woman and praising the wooden rooms. Ibdish moved across to Alys's mother and murmured something as he pressed a cloth wallet into her hands. The rituals and ceremonies of Longhill found their feet again after Alys had tripped them, and she watched with a storm in her chest that she could not name.

Damnis left. Pocked Chelle and Bastard Leah arrived. Linnet took Aunt Daidan's place at her mother's side, and started telling a long story about when Darro had been a boy out on the Silt with her, and the day he'd caught a fish with his bare hands and tried to use a stick to gut it. The story should have been funny, and Linnet told it with a warmth and affection that had the others laughing and weeping, but not Alys. More people came, and the heat of their bodies began to warm the room, but Alys still felt the cold against her back. Ibdish's wife went to Alys's mother, took her by the hand, and talked quietly about how hard it had been when her own son had died. He hadn't gone to the river as Darro had, but slipped off the top of a building where he and his friends had been daring each other into more and more dangerous tricks. His neck snapped against the cobblestones, and he'd died before anyone could bring her word. The two mothers shared their grief, and Alys watched them like they were beetles with particularly eerie shells.

Alys was born to Longhill. She'd lived in its streets her whole life, almost, only leaving for beer or to work pulls. It was only since Darro's death that she'd slept her nights in Oldgate and Stonemarket, visited Green Hill. Not half a year had passed, and yet it was enough that she looked at this last celebration of

Darro's life and felt herself out of place. She'd always known that the other quarters of Kithamar looked at Longhill with contempt, but she never had until now. Nor could she put a name to what had changed, except that every time Grey Linnet laughed or said some empty platitude about the brightness and dark of life, Alys felt embarrassed for her.

She stayed there as long as she could stand it, then, between one heartbeat and the next, the warmth of the bodies and the air just spat out from other people's lungs made the room feel like she was buried alive. She lurched for the door, and then out, stopping on the street and turning her face to the white winter sky. The cold bit her, and she welcomed it. She gripped her new club in her hand like she was drowning and it was the last rope. An emptiness she had let herself forget opened in her.

Once, when she was very young, she'd known a girl who had been cut by a fish knife. She had seemed on her way to heal-ing, but then the scab split open, and the pus and blood were worse than the fresh wound had been. She felt like that now. She'd thought she was happy. She'd thought she was doing bet-ter. Now, every bright feeling she'd had—every triumph, every laugh, every good night—seemed like a cheap song bellowed out to cover the weeping. A small voice in her mind calmly said *This is only a hard moment. Ever since it happened, there have been hard moments. This one will pass too.* But she didn't believe it.

She didn't notice that her mother had followed her until the old woman put a hand on her elbow. Alys wiped away the tears freezing on her cheeks like they'd betrayed her. She expected to see pity in her mother's eyes, or need, or something. The uncer-tainty and fear that had marked her inside were gone now. Alys could almost imagine this was a wholly different woman.

"What?" Alys asked.

She thought her mother wouldn't answer, that the two of

them might stand in the cold Longhill street until night fell. When she did speak, she sounded the way exhaustion itself might have, if it had its own voice. "I've lost two of my children. I can't stand it again."

"I'm fine."

"So was he, until he wasn't. If you're walking in his footsteps, you'll end where he ended. Be careful with yourself."

Alys scowled and stepped back. Her mother didn't try to hold her. Instead, she seemed to grow smaller and greyer, her face losing what little expression it had, before she turned to her rooms and trundled back under Darro's deathmark, closing the door behind her. Alys closed a fist around her club, squeezing until her knuckles ached. She didn't know what she wanted to hit. She turned out into the bright, ice-bound streets, and as she walked, she raged.

The focus of her anger shifted. Between one intersection and the next, she imagined herself shouting down her mother for treating Darro's death as another way to get a few cheap coins to spend on drink, never mind whether it was tradition or no. Then for half a block, it was Sammish, who could have been there, could have warned her, could have stood by her instead of being off wherever she was doing whatever she did. Then Grey Linnet for acting like she had a right to grief. Ullin for living on the ass end of the city where Alys had to walk half a day to see him, like all the gods kept him west of the Smoke unless Andomaka was paying him to go. And all of them at once, down to the last breathing soul, for treating Darro like he was dead. She muttered to herself and swung her club. Dammis Ragman passed her going the other direction, and gave her a wide berth.

Nothing she felt was justified, all of it skirted the edge of madness, and she knew it. But knowing didn't dam the flood.

She reached the corner where her room waited and hauled herself up the thin, dark stairwell, taking the steps three at a time. When she undid her lock and pushed her door open, she was almost warm.

The shutters were closed, but a ray of milky light came through the crack where the hinges were. Dust motes floated in it like snow that wouldn't fall. She sat at the table, shaking. In the niche across the room, Darro's ashes stood. There was dust on the box, and the deathmark was little more than a few lighter bands of shadow. A vast guilt washed over her for leaving him alone so often and so long. She embraced the pain. That Darro was past caring whether she was there or not was sharper than her self-reproach.

"I'm sorry," she said. Nothing replied.

The winter hours were short. The sun would drop behind Palace Hill soon, and the long, frigid night would come. There was no trekking back to Stonemarket, and the prospect of an evening shoulder to shoulder in some Seepwater taproom made her flesh crawl. Staying here in the dark with Darro conjured back those first days after he went: her cell in Oldgate, and the numbness she longed to have back again and also feared.

She didn't open the shutters, finding the safe cache by touch alone. The coins were still there, though there were fewer. She had to be more careful how she spent them. They had to last. She lit the candle, and the little room filled with a warmer light that turned her breath the color of honey. The flame shifted as it always did, and the smoke from it gathered. Alys felt herself reaching for it, willing it to take a solid form. Even the scarred, caustic Tregarro would be better than sitting alone.

But the smoke thickened and wove, and Andomaka was sitting across from her. The woman's pale hair was tied back and wet, as if she'd just risen from a bath. Alys wondered whether the noble houses of Green Hill had their own private bath-houses. She had to think they did. Andomaka's robe was formal, though, and her expression vague. Maybe drunk.

"Did I call for you?" the pale woman asked, and didn't seem to know the answer.

"No. I've been away. I thought there might . . . I thought you might have wanted to talk with me and I wasn't here. So . . ."

"Oh," Andomaka said. "No."

"If there were something. Is there anything?"

"Are you out of coin, little wolf? Because—"

"I'm not. I have money. I need something to do. I need work."

"Work?"

"I need anything," she said.

The city changed for Sammish when her questions did.

When she had haunted the ports and gates, the market-places and taprooms to ask about the mysterious foreign woman who'd pay gold for a silver knife, the question that drove her had been *Where am I most likely to find someone who knows something?* and she'd been asking it with Alys in her mind like wine fumes. Now, she asked *Where would you go if the man who tried to kill you had been wearing a blue cloak and a guardsman's badge?* and she asked it for herself.

It led her to very different places.

Dawn came late and bitterly cold. The crook-tailed cat that haunted the end of the street had decided that Sammish was sleeping in his bed, and she didn't mind the company. She rose carefully, so as not to disturb him too much, dressed herself against the winter's chill, and went out into Kithamar. The long, frigid hours of the winter night held sway over the streets even after the light came. Frost glazed the cobblestones, and icicles as thick as Sammish's wrist hung from the eaves where no one had knocked them down yet. The baker's oven was warm, though, and the smell of raisin tarts still hung in the air.

The baker had left her a cloth sack of stale rolls, and she set aside an extra coin to pay him. In other times, she might have carried them to taprooms and houses, tried to sell them on the cheap to people who didn't want to brave the cold: the sick and the elderly and the sadly hungover. It was a small profit, but it was reliable. It wasn't the work of that particular day.

Instead, she put the sun at her back and headed west as the winter city hauled itself to wakefulness around her. She had heard stories of the towns out in the countryside where nothing might happen at all in the long, dark snowbound months. Maybe the dark and cold meant a kind of weeks-long sleep elsewhere, but Kithamar was a city, and cities were restless.

By the time she reached the edge of Longhill, carts lumbered, and the horses that drew them sighed out great white plumes beside her. Children ran in packs, screaming and jumping and keeping the cold at bay through boundless energy and will. She passed a Hansch lightman pulling a handbarrow stacked with finger-thin wax candles wrapped in grey paper and a huge tin jug that stank of lantern oil. He didn't notice her, because she didn't want him to.

It was Longest Night, and so it was also the shortest day. There were families all through the city that would be celebrating their rites, depending on which gods and icons they worshipped. She passed doors with the evergreen pine sprig of Lord Kauth and the yellow smear of the Pajanic Rite. Some corners had old men, shirtless and blue with cold, declaiming the chant against the darkness that was supposed to turn the year back on its path toward summer. Sammish gave one of them a stale roll for free. She wondered whether, if the men of faith ever chose not to stand on their corners, the world would really slide into permanent night. She didn't think it would.

It was midmorning already when she reached the river. The river was ice stretching south of her and forward into the northwest, flatter than a road. Far ahead by the piers, she saw the bright figures of Riverport skaters gliding over it. Sunlight glittered from the blades on their boots, and their embroidered jackets reminded her of the spring flowers that wouldn't bloom for months. She walked carefully down the quayside to the ice, the cloth sack over her shoulder, even though there were no guardsmen on the bridges. There was no point collecting tolls, after all, when anyone could walk across the Khahon. Sammish kept on, placing each foot down squarely so she wouldn't slip and trying not to think too much about the vast dark water that flowed invisibly beneath her. Across the ice, the thin, bare trees of the Silt reached up toward Oldgate or Palace Hill or the sky.

It was days since Sammish had even seen Alys. At a guess, she was gone off to Stonemarket again, to smoke and laugh with the other hired knives. Or maybe the pale woman had set Alys some other violent, risk-drunk errand. Either way, Sammish was almost pleased. Not because she wasn't aching with jealousy for whatever had captured Alys's attention, but because what she needed to do now, she needed to do alone.

And worse—or stranger, anyway—she felt herself changing. At night, she still dreamed of Alys. Alone in the darkness, she studied the marks for the brewer's board, as she always did, and imagined that she would wake in a house of her own, and in the circle of Alys's arms. But something about her dreams had shifted. It felt like the subtle greening of early spring bark, or the first yellow leaf on a summer tree. She saw that it meant something, but she couldn't yet say what. There was joy in it, though.

And fear. Whatever the change in her was, she walked with it to the Silt again, as she had every day for almost two weeks now.

Every quarter of Kithamar had its streetbound. Sammish had spent more than a few nights in niches or under the bridges herself, when she was younger. The few who made their camps on the Silt had chosen to live with danger. A river flood could wash away a sleeper before the warning came. A fire among the trees—which happened sometimes—would bring the bluecoats to the walls with pails of sand ready to tamp out embers that came down on the better quarters, but no one would bother trying to save the Silt. It was the wilderness within the city walls. The only ones who lived there were the wild, the desperate, and the mad.

And, perhaps, those who had reason to fear being elsewhere.

Sammish reached the shore where the shallow ice creaked under her, and when it broke, there was sand beneath it, not water. At the edge of the trees, she paused and looked back. The sun hung in the sky not far from the Temple. Plumes of smoke rose from a thousand hearths. If she closed her eyes and turned her face to it, the sun gave her some warmth, but not as much as winter air took away. She walked into the trees, and the city disappeared around her.

Another few steps, and the wild man was there.

It was, she told herself, like trying to make peace with a dog. Be friendly, be patient, be kind, and be ready to kick it in the jaw if it decided to try being her enemy. She'd made a habit of coming with her gifts. Sometimes no one met her and she left the bread for the first person to come or else the birds. Sometimes there were a few. The wild man was the one she saw most. He had hooded eyelids and dirty grey hair. His robe was filthy, but it was wool. He wore sandals as if the cold couldn't touch him.

"Hello," Sammish said.

"Yes, yes, yes. You're looking for a woman," the wild man said. "I know. You keep saying it."

Sammish opened the sack and started laying the stale rolls out on the snow and dirt. "She isn't from Kithamar. She might have been hurt."

"Mm-hm." The wild man's eyes didn't leave the rolls, and his tongue flickered on his lips.

"She's been in the city since summer. Maybe longer." She stepped back the way she would have from a dog, and the wild man moved toward the bread. His gaze flicked between her and her offering—hunger at war with distrust.

He grabbed up the first of the rolls and tilted his head. "What would she be here for?"

This was new. It was progress. Sammish pushed down the leap of hope before she started to trust in it. "She's desperate for something, I think. She was looking for a knife. And maybe a boy. And she doesn't want to be found."

"You're her enemy?"

"No," Sammish said, and then, because she saw the glimmer of distrust in his eyes, "I don't know. Maybe."

The wild man squatted beside her offering, picked up a thick, gold-brown roll, and tapped the dirt from it. His look was challenging. "Why look, if she doesn't want to be found?"

"Because I'm a little desperate too," Sammish said. She was a little surprised at her own honesty. It was as if the wild man could see her in a way that most people she met couldn't. As if he could command a deeper part of her than her own will allowed.

"For what?"

"A friend of mine is in trouble, and I don't know what the trouble is, except that it involves this woman."

"And the trouble your friend is in. What's that?"

"I don't know," Sammish said, hearing how thin she sounded. How lost.

"Maybe you should stay out of things that could eat you," he said, and bit the roll. Something red ran down his cheek. Sammish started. He turned the bitten bread toward her, and it was the raw red of living meat.

Sammish cried out, but wordlessly. The voice that spoke wasn't hers.

"Stop."

The wild man scowled. The bread was only bread. The blood, if it had been blood, was gone, and perhaps it had never been. "We talked about this. If she can be scared away, she should be."

"It's cruel," the woman said from behind Sammish. "We can kill her if we must, but I've had too much of cruelty. What do you want from me, child?"

Sammish turned. The woman stood beside a thin, black-barked tree, and her robes were the color of bone and snow. Her hair was dark, and her skin was brown and dry, and she had a single dark mole. She held a blade in her right hand casually, like a butcher who'd paused in her unmakings to talk for a moment, and her eyes were dark and weary. Sammish thought of pale Andomaka. This woman could have been her shadow. Sammish tried to speak, but nothing came out. After all her searching, she'd given up hope of ever really winning through. Now that she had, the woman seemed too solid and real to hold all the dreams and fears about her.

"You have a friend?" the dark woman said, prompting her. Her accent was thick, but it didn't hide the words. "I'm supposed to do something for her?"

"No," Sammish said, and it was hardly a whisper. She coughed, cleared her throat, and tried to stand taller than her fear wanted her to. "But I want to know what she's folded herself into. And you know."

"I do?"

"The woman she's taken work for says that they're protecting Kithamar, but I don't believe her. Andomaka, that's the woman. Not my friend."

"And what's your friend's name?"

"I'm not going to tell you that," Sammish said.

The dark woman tilted her head a degree, like she was solving a puzzle in her head. "Come with me," she said.

"No no no," the wild man said. "This isn't happening."

"Goro," the dark woman said. The wild man sighed and gathered up the rest of the rolls.

"This is a mistake," he said, and led the way deeper into the trees.

The Silt was smaller than any other quarter. Oldgate towered above it to the north. It was impossible to truly lose her way here, but there was a sense of displacement as they walked, as if the wilderness went on longer than the thin land it grew upon. It seemed however long they walked, the bridges glimpsed between trees didn't change their angles, that Oldgate showed the same stony profile. It was an illusion of her anxiety and the unfamiliar path they walked. Not more than that. Probably.

The shed they reached was white wood, dry and a little rotten. It was only barely larger than Sammish's room in the baker's house. Letters and glyphs were carved into the old wood and colored with wax rubbed into the grooves—red and yellow and a weird, vibrant blue. When they stepped into it, the interior was warm and comfortable. A little table, two beds with fresh straw, an iron stove no larger than a dog's chest with a fire already burning in it. Sammish remembered the fortune-teller's rooms. This place felt like what the old man and his mix-eyed accomplice were only playing at. The door closed behind her, and she felt a deep certainty that she would only leave this place if the dark woman and the wild man permitted it. It wasn't a stone room with an iron door like the one Alys had been taken to at harvest, but it might as well have been. A wave of vertigo rolled through her, or else the earth below them spun.

The dark woman sat by the little stove and fed a bit of wood into it. The flames leapt. "Now, child. Tell me what you know. All of it, except, I suppose, the name of your friend. I'll know if you leave something out."

Sammish sat, her hands between her knees. She felt a deep unease, but it was too late to pull back now.

"It began in summer," she said. "There was a guardsman the day that the new prince took his place."

She told everything—Alys and her brother's death, the gold coins and the silver knife, Alys's cell in Oldgate and the candle that summoned the pale woman, the night they found Ando-maka and the way Alys had taken up her brother's work. She had expected it to all come out disjointed, but it didn't. She told the tale like she was a storyteller who'd said it all a thousand times over, and the dark woman sat, listening. After a while, the wild man took a paring knife from under his bed and a dry apple from a box and started cutting bits of the fruit into a bowl. The smell was sweet and rich, and it reassured Sammish in a way she couldn't put words to.

She told of Alys's errand for Andomaka, the slave house and the boy.

The dark woman sighed then, and it was more profound than tears. Sorrow and despair radiated from her like heat came from the fire. Sammish stuttered to a halt. The man offered up a bite of apple, and the woman wordlessly pushed it away.

"Is that..." Sammish began, and then found she didn't know what question she was trying to ask.

"I wanted it to be otherwise," the woman said. "I knew my hopes were thin. Go on."

Sammish told of finding Orrel, candle-skinned and weak, in the hospital and his story of Darro's attack and death. It was a surprise that the woman from that tale was sitting before her, but it was a satisfying one, like the last word of a good joke that pulled the whole thing into a new perspective. It brought the whole tale together, as if it had been meant to be this way. As if the gods had planned it. And still, the dark woman didn't interrupt or speak until Sammish reached the point in her story where she'd gone to Stonemarket and found Alys among Andomaka's knifemen. When Sammish had lied about finding Orrel.

"Why?" the dark woman asked, and her voice was soft and weary.

"Why what?"

"Why didn't you tell her about what her brother did to me?"

Sammish shook her head. "I didn't know what Darro did, not really. I still don't. I mean, was it your knife? Was Orrel telling the truth about you making him ill? Maybe it wasn't even true."

"No."

Sammish shook her head, not certain what the woman meant. The dark woman lifted her eyebrows. "I told you that I would know. That isn't why," she said. "Try again."

Sammish looked away. The wild man, cross-legged on his bed, scratched his bushy beard. Sammish felt a blush rising in her throat and cheeks. "I didn't want Andomaka to know. Alys told me that she'd pass it along, and I didn't want that."

She realized a moment too late that she'd called Alys by name, but neither the man nor the woman commented on it.

"Closer," the dark woman said instead. "But try again."

In the stove, the wood popped and crackled. A breath of wind shook the door. It was already dark outside. Sammish didn't know how long she'd been talking.

"I want to help her the way I know her," she said. "I don't want to help who she's become."

"Yes," the dark woman said. "I understand."

"It may not be as bad as it sounds," the wild man said, and Sammish knew he didn't mean Alys.

"They have the knife," the dark woman said. "They have Timu. I have nothing."

The wild man hung his head and sighed, but he didn't disagree. She opened the iron stove and fed in another stick. By the light of the fire, Sammish saw that there were tear tracks streaking her cheeks. She didn't know how long the woman had been weeping. She hadn't given any other sign.

"The moment I kissed that man," the dark woman said, "this was inevitable. I was young and foolish and caught up in things I didn't understand. The world is rarely kind to people like that."

Sammish tapped her fingers together to draw their attention. The dream of her story was gone now, and she was very aware of the naked sword that still rested at the woman's side and the short knife in the wild man's hand. She should have felt fear, but she didn't. "Are you going to kill me?"

"I wouldn't ask," the wild man said. "You're into this deeper than you can swim already."

"I know," Sammish said. "But I still don't know what it is."

"What more can we lose by telling her?" the dark woman said.

"You? Nothing. I still have things worth living for," the wild man said, and the regret showed as soon as the words were past his lips. He ran a liver-spotted hand through his hair.

The dark woman gathered herself. "The thread of Kithamar your friend spoke of is real," she said. "But it is not a thread."

"This city," the wild man said, "is a shell around a partic-ularly nasty crab. Only someone's played a trick, and it's not all safe in its armor anymore. That blade is what keeps it safe. All those people out there drinking their usual wine and eating their day's bread don't know it, but this city is on a knife edge."

"Thank you," Sammish said crossly. "That makes everything clear."

The wild man laughed and tossed her his bowl. There were still strips of dry apple in it. She ate one.

"Ask what you want," the dark woman said. "I will answer what I can."

Sammish thought of the thousand questions that had haunted her. "What's your name?"

"I am Saffa Rej of the Bronze Coast, priest of the six, and sworn of the spirit house."

"Who is that boy?"

"He is my son," she said, "and the son of Prince Ausai. By blood, he is the heir of Kithamar."

The Khahon ran south from the city, flowing wide and slow as it moved toward the sea. Other, lesser rivers lost themselves in it, eaten by the broad water. It passed through Mastil and bent in a lazy S around Haunamar. Dozens of villages clung to its side, using its water to drink and irrigate and run little mills. And when that didn't sustain them, they took coin from the boats that tied up for the night at their little piers and the oxcarts that worked the towpaths. Far in the south, it broadened into a rich delta, its water lost in the vastly greater expanse of the sea.

To the west of the delta were the black-soiled islands of the Iustikar—Caram and Imaja and the plague-struck ruins of Lithou. To the east, the land curved gently, cupped by high, cloud-forested mountains. The great cities of Dulai and Ghan marked the beginning of the Bronze Coast. Kithamar the cold, city of wood and stone, sheep fat and forge smoke, was as exotic in the courts of the Coast as the beetle hunters and night markets of Dulai were to the citizens of Longhill. The stories of the northern city's wealth and

power, its bloody past and the beauty of its men, were half entice-
ment and half threat. Kithamar, seen from so far away, seemed to
have only one face, and it was as sinister as it was enchanting. To a
girl born to the warm waves of Ghan, it was only slightly more
real than the drowned jade-and-gold cities that were supposed to
house the spirits of the first people and the king with eight bodies
from before the sky was broken.

The sky was broken? How was the sky broken? asked Sammish,
and the wild man put a finger to his lips. She went quiet.

It was of no particular importance to be a priest of the six.
Nearly every household had someone who had attended the
rites, drunk from the cup, and spoken the oath in the grand
circle. It had a cost, but not one so high that any but the poor-
est couldn't find a way to save the temple's fee. Only priests of
the six could sit on juries, speak before the council of elders, or
contribute to the fires that marked the end of the season of rain.
Since many people wanted the things that came with the priesthood, many accepted it and then went on to ignore it for the
rest of their lives.

To be sworn of the spirit house was another thing altogether.

Unlike the brotherhoods and petty temples that had their
houses in every city, the spirit house belonged to the Bronze
Coast and nowhere else. Every initiate was a priest of the six, but
more than that. They had to have been in the world. The keepers of the spirit house had all known lovers. Many had borne
children and had families. Some had cared for their parents
as they died. The spirit house was a place people came to find
peace from the world. Saffa had watched her young husband die
of a bloody flux. She had carried his body to the fire without
even a sister or brother to help her with her burden. The peace
that the spirit house offered and its teachings of loving the world
but not engaging with it called to her as if by name.

Even so, the keepers had not been convinced that she belonged. She was young, for one thing. And her grief had been fresh. It is easier to renounce those things with which you are already weary, and they had feared that as her hurts healed, she would find herself restless in the house. In the end, she had convinced them.

Young, hurt, and turning her back to the world. Looking back, it was clear what Ausai a Sal, prince of Kithamar, had seen in her. What he had thought she was, and why he had chosen her.

The news that the prince of Kithamar was coming to the Bronze Coast had been a curiosity and a wonder: the ice and dark of the northern waters walking the roads and sitting in the sun of the coast. The council of elders remained placid and calm, but that was their job. Everyone else quivered and fidgeted like children waiting for permission to eat their honey sticks. Or that's how her memory had it. Knowing truth from the story she made after seeing the ending was difficult, if not impossible.

It was the middle of the dry season, which meant it only rained once or twice in a week. The ship that came in from the delta was tall, and its wood was dark and intricately carved. It cast anchor in the bay of Dulai. The council of elders had arranged for representatives of all the factions to gather on the wide, white sand as skiffs carried in the honored guests. Prince Ausai himself stood in the first skiff to shore. He wore a shirt of black and indigo. His head was shaved to the skin. Saffa had expected him to wear jewels and gold, but he walked to shore unadorned and accepted the welcome of the Bronze Coast as casually as a fisherman cleaning his catch. The white-haired, ice-eyed man who followed him was larger, stronger, and still seemed like a child beside the prince. That had been the prince's

brother-by-law, Drau Chaalat, and as much Saffa's downfall as
Ausai himself.

Who? Sammish asked.

Drau Chaalat, the wild man said. *Husband to Ausai's sister, Hanan,
and father of your pale woman, Andomaka. How do you not know these
things? These people have the power of life and death over you.*

*Does knowing which of them married who make my bridge tolls
cheaper?* Sammish snapped.

Seen in retrospect, the seduction was expert. Prince Ausai's
attention to her had been casual and polite at first, and then
more aware. Nothing more than that at first. If he had expressed
his desire for her as a demand or a point of diplomacy—these
things happened—she would have refused him, but he didn't.
He invited her to his dinners and laughed when she made her
little sallies into the conversation. He appreciated her as a man
appreciating a woman. He was beautiful in his way. He was
older than she was, but not an elder. He moved with the careful grace of a strong man who knew how to use his strength.
He was a man of overwhelming importance and some mystery
who had noticed her. If she didn't believe all his little admira-
tions, she did believe that he thought her worth flattering.

Above all else, he was brief. In only a few weeks, he would
return to Kithamar and be gone from her life. Nothing permanent was possible with him. Any dalliance between them would
turn with the season and be gone. The stakes had seemed low.

His brother-by-law, Drau Chaalat, joined them some nights.
He was, Saffa learned, the priest of the Daris Brotherhood. She
recognized that it was a position of status. She didn't know its
mysteries, and he didn't offer to tell her. He performed a few
little cantrips after their dinner, no more than a fortune-teller
on the street might offer, and she'd pretended to be impressed.
And then he would leave them alone together.

Those nights had been sweet and left her with a sense of the expansiveness of life and of her own body. It made all that came after a deeper betrayal.

Ausai left, as she'd known he would, with fondness and respect and no empty promises. Drau Chaalat, on the other hand, had stayed on some unspecified work of the brotherhood. She hadn't suspected that his errand was her.

He arrived at her home unexpected, but not unannounced. He had his servants with him. His white hair and beard weren't the signs of age. He was simply pale as bones. She poured him wine and water and he made a gift of meat tarts bought that morning in the day market. They'd talked about...something. She didn't remember what. And then, calmly, he'd explained that so long as the brotherhood had no need of it, the child was hers to love and raise as she wished. But that if the time came when Ausai had need, it was her duty to surrender it. The sacrifice might not be required. Probably wouldn't. But if, then without fail.

She hadn't understood at first, and then when she did, she still didn't believe. It was another month before she was certain that she was pregnant. Chaalat gave her gold and silver, treated her with the respect due to a prince's chosen lover, and then climbed on a ship headed for the delta. She had told herself that it was only the politics of succession and bloodlines that woke her in the dark hours before dawn. She felt Timu kick for the first time when she was lying in her bed listening to the thunder of a distant storm, and it felt like an omen. She couldn't say later what made her decide to study the Daris Brotherhood except that it was Ausai's chosen mystery and her memories of Drau Chaalat disturbed her.

Timu was born healthy. Everyone knew who his father was, and no one cast blame on Saffa for bearing a child to a foreign prince. The world was woven of such things. This was only one curiosity among many. Her work continued at the spirit house, though she found it was harder now to release the world. Her son was in it. She might meditate for hours on her own eventual dissolution and death and even find some peace in the idea. Picture the same thing for her boy, and she was made from animal panic, and the best she could do was observe that terror and try to accept the fact that she was a woman who feared for her son.

As Timu grew, Saffa learned of the Daris Brotherhood and of Kithamar. The deep mysteries of the house were kept close, but there were those who whispered of a darkness there. Ancestor worship was a common enough thing. The Richian mysteries, the creed of Amnen Toh, even the respect afforded to the council of elders had an aspect of owing homage to those who came before.

The Daris Brotherhood was something else.

She found old tales with uncertain sources, some little more than ancient gossip. They told of child sacrifices and lineages of more than blood. Tales of a knife that was also a needle, capable of stitching an unclean spirit to a child's flesh. The eerie promise of the death of Death. She came to believe that the diplomatic mission Ausai had led to the Bronze Coast had been an excuse. That what he'd been seeking was a secret place for his blood to live away from the intrigues of his cold, dark home. If the brotherhood needed Timu, who played in the surf with the other children of Dulai, it would be for a rite. And not one from which he would return.

Saffa, who had dedicated herself to a philosophy of release, found herself unwilling to consider letting her son go. Instead, she hoped that the issue would never arise. The source of her comfort was Drau Chaalat saying *Probably wouldn't*. And so she comforted herself until the day that *probably wouldn't* became *would*.

The message had come from Ausai himself, not long after the word of his illness had reached them. All it had said was *I have need of our child. Send him.* She put the paper into her fire. She'd told herself that the Bronze Coast was her home and her place of power. The cold fingers of Kithamar wouldn't reach here, and if they did, they wouldn't be strong enough to pull Timu back.

In her heart, she knew she was trying to shout down a storm.

Timu vanished without another letter coming or any further warning. One day, he was present with his friends, running down the paths between the trees, and then no one knew where he was. Everyone thought he'd gone the other way. Tragedy struck many people, and by many means. He might have swum into the sea and been caught by a riptide, or gone walking and fallen into some secret and terrible cave, or eaten some spoiled fruit that drove him mad. There were a thousand ways to lose a son. Saffa didn't doubt for a heartbeat what had happened to hers.

She went to her family and to her friends. She begged the high priest at the spirit house and the general priest of the six. She sold everything she had and borrowed against what she might gain later. Divesting herself of everything was easy. She'd trained for it her whole life. She bought a traveller's cloak, a knife that she carried in her sleeve, a leather hat that she'd lost the same day she got it, passage on a trading ship, and all the coins of Kithamar she could find. It was a fortune, if a small one. It was her life, translated into a handful of gold. It was her hope of seeing her son's living face again.

Fuck, Sammish said. *That's where Darro's coins came from. That's what he stole.*

Thieves steal, the wild man said. *Start being angry at that, you'll end up angry at the wind for blowing.*

She went to the delta and took working passage with a flat-boat, taking a turn with the team of oxen that hauled them against the current. She talked to anyone who would talk, and she listened to the rest. She learned that Drau Chaalat was years dead, and his daughter presiding over the brotherhood's house in Kithamar. She learned that Ausai was dying, and heard rumors that the prince had been searching for a missing knife. She also heard that Bronze Coast slavers had been seen on the river, heading north.

She used the petty magics she'd learned in the spirit house to hurry her travel, to find signs of where her son was or had been, to ask the powers behind the world for guidance and hope. Or if not hope, then freedom from it. She slept little.

Kithamar had been everything she'd been told, and less. Cold and close. Beautiful in its way, and forbidding. As a foreigner, she'd met distrust and avarice. For weeks, she'd hunted the chill streets, buying information about the knife or her boy or the fate of her once-lover Prince Ausai, dying in his palace that overlooked the city. She'd found the too-clever young man, and told herself that because he was Inlisc and hated by the powers of the city, he might be a true ally to her.

And then Prince Ausai died, and the night between princes came, and she'd suffered a terrible dream. Black wings and the scent of fire. It had been a premonition of death, and indeed, days later, the Inlisc man had come in the costume of the guard and tried to kill her. Betrayed and injured, she'd gone to an herbalist in the Smoke. The woman had taken her pulse, touched a wand of woven sage to her brow, and told her to get the fuck out. That the help she needed was on the Silt or it was nowhere.

She'd found her way there, and Goro had taken her in.

What is Goro? Sammish said.

The wild man raised a finger like a student at the university declaring himself present at a lecture.

Death had been close enough to smell her. Even with Goro's kindness and protection, it took weeks before she found strength enough to walk on her own. Her injuries had brought on a fever that came back just when she'd thought herself well. And when she recovered, she reached out into the city again, but so much was in flux. The new prince, Byrn a Sal, was alarming the high court with his erratic behavior. The knife she'd sought had been seen and actually held by one of her sometime contacts. Her strength grew, and with it her despair.

Fear stalked her through the autumn streets. Its teeth were colder than winter, and she felt them in the night when she tried to sleep. The ache had been more than she could stand, and Goro had helped her, lending what power he had to help her pray for guidance.

And then, guidance had come in the form of a plain-faced girl with a sack of stale bread. And it had told her that her son was in the hands of the enemy. Her son had been given to her by the palace intrigues of Kithamar. She had broken her oath to separate herself from the world, and now she would be punished. Now her task was to find a way to live with the grief she had carried with her, unacknowledged, from the sea.

The woman went quiet. A tear fell down her cheek. There were already a dozen and more that had leaked from Sammish's eyes. Saffa's sigh was worse than sobbing.

"We have to make a decision," Goro said. He wasn't looking at Sammish.

"Do we?"

"You're still in danger. Maybe you will be for the rest of your life. Maybe you won't. But you are now, and this one is part of it. She knows where you are, and if we let her leave, other people will find out."

"They won't," Sammish said. "I wouldn't tell anyone."

Goro shrugged. "I can trust you, or I can trust myself. The first one's better for you. Second one's solid for me. And for her."

"You can't kill me," Sammish said.

"I really can."

"No," Saffa said. "We asked her here, even if we didn't know exactly what we were asking. She came to our summons."

"Or she showed up by coincidence. Not that it matters. The problem of your situation stays the same either way."

"Killing her might be wise, but it would also be ungrateful," Saffa said. She turned her dark, tired eyes to Sammish. "Go. Save your friend, if you can. Don't mention me, and don't come back."

The central temple of the Daris Brotherhood's house was open to the public. Its columns were carved marble the color of butter, its altar covered with fresh rosemary all year round, and the chimes rang at the sacred hours with a celestial harmony. It wasn't where Andomaka and her acolytes within the mysteries did their important work. That was for the private temple.

It rested deep within the compound, a round room without windows or doors, secured by a series of maze-like hallways. The rites performed there required that the room not be sealed from the city, but the path in could be made obscure. The air was fresh but motionless, as if under a thick forest canopy during a storm. Lanterns burned at points of focus, drawing the stars of the sky and the paths of the gods into the small circle of the temple. Birth and death, betrayal and loyalty, the pure and the complex, everything was represented in the subtle relations of the lights and the darkness, the altar stone and the tapestries and the high, arching ceiling. Andomaka had spent days in the private temple when she was young. She had been consecrated there, learning secrets that had formed her. It was more than a home. It was the heart of her city and her god. That it was also just wood and wax took none of the miracle away from it. It was a place meant to call forth the thinness of the world. The way moments of change—Longest Night and Shortest; the first freeze and the first thaw; the night between the funeral of a prince and the coronation of a successor; the moment between a birth and first breath—invited disruptions in the order of the world, the private temple made that potential welcome.

And now, in the darkness after the year's swiftest sunset, she was supposed to be there.

Instead, she was in a minor drawing room of the palace, drinking lemon tea and sharing the heat of the fire with her young cousin Elaine a Sal, daughter of the prince. The girl's eyes were red from weeping, and there were bruise-dark bags under her eyes. She had fallen in love with a man below her station, and her father had been acting strangely. She was afraid that, to protect her lover—whom she wouldn't name out of some misbegotten superstition or belated attack of discretion— she would have to abandon him. The pettiness of it verged on comedy. The fate of the city was in doubt. Titanic forces of history and magic were at play like an invisible storm, and the girl was oblivious. Andomaka's training let her see her own contempt as if it belonged to someone else, and then add it to her understanding of the city and of herself.

"He's asked me to come, and I went to him," Elaine said.

"To his barracks?" Andomaka said, feigning confusion.

"No. His family house in Riverside. I don't know what to do."

"Follow your heart," Andomaka said. "It's a better guide than I am."

Elaine nodded, as if the meaningless words were deep. Ando-maka squeezed the girl's hand and retreated, careful not to sigh until she was out of earshot. She walked quickly, aware that she had been expected in the brotherhood's house. It wasn't why she hurried. She hurried because she wanted to.

The palace was closer and darker than the compounds of Green Hill. Its past as a fortress showed in thick walls and narrow windows. The lamps swallowed the air. It felt more like a prison than a seat of power, and she was pleased to leave it for the open, frigid street. Her carriage was waiting, and Tregarro with it. The servants lifted her up, and almost before the thin door latched, Tregarro thumped the roof and the coachman called the horses to a fast trot. The darkness of the palace gave way to the darkness of Green Hill. Andomaka felt the subtle difference.

"I don't like this," Tregarro said. "They suspect."

"They don't."

"They know."

"They don't."

"The same night we choose to attempt the rite again, she decides to pull you in for a talk? Tell me that's not meant to rattle us."

"You were never young and in love, were you?" Andomaka said. It was a cruelty, but Tregarro pretended that she hadn't meant it to be.

"Never like that one."

"She's half in the nursery and half in the marriage bed. The world she knows stops at her skin. None of what we're doing exists to her. It was coincidence."

"Magic and coincidence. I don't like it."

The carriage hit a rough cobble, jouncing hard and then coming back to true. Outside her little window, she saw the house of the Daris Brotherhood with torches burning at the door. Andomaka felt a pinch of real anxiety. *What if the rite fails again?* She pushed it away.

"If a girl's lovesick gossip is enough to distract me, I deserve to fail," she said.

Andomaka had never worked the weaving of the thread before Prince Ausai's death. There had never been a reason to. She had studied the rite, as she had studied all the rites, certain that she would be ready when the time came. Neither she nor Prince Ausai had anticipated a hidden enemy within the palace. But as her uncle's health began to fail, the rot in the city began to show. The knife had gone missing. By its nature, it could not leave the city without raising an alarm, but sometime in the decades between Prince Ausai's ascension and his final sick bed, it had been taken from its sacred resting place. In his last weeks, Ausai had overseen the forging of a new blade. And, more urgently, the collection of a secret of his own: a child of his blood from Bronze Coast.

Before the old prince could put the rest of his wards and protections in place, death had come. The world had reached another of those moments of thinness, and Andomaka had taken the new blade, a vial of Byrn a Sal's blood, and the death-name of Prince Ausai.

The continuity of the city, its hidden heart, had rested in her hands. In her hands, it had broken. The new blade had shattered. The next morning, Byrn a Sal stood his coronation with his own spirit, the first to do so in centuries. The conspiracy against Kithamar had won, if only for a moment. Now, at the turning of the year, she could take the first real steps to understanding why. It began by giving Kithamar its voice, if not yet its throne.

The carriage pulled through the gates to the inner courtyard of the Daris Brotherhood, rose through the long pathway, and came to a stop by the temple's gate. Footmen were waiting for her in the colors of her house and the brotherhood's. Tregarro didn't wait for the steps to be placed, dropping from the carriage door to the gravel and striding forth to make certain everything was in place before she came to it. Andomaka let him go. It was his role to worry and fret, and hers to make reality bend to her will and the city's. It was as important that she let servants like Tregarro and the footmen serve as that they respect her power. Everyone in their place, everyone playing their role.

When she entered the private temple, the candles were lit. A minor priest sat on a stool by the altar, playing a bowed harp in a complex drone. She felt her body relaxing by long habit. She stretched out her hands, reaching her will past the tips of her fingers to caress the air, the world, the spaces between the spaces. Reality felt soft. Fragile. Easy to remake. Tregarro looked at her, his expression a question. She smiled her answer. *Yes.*

"Bring the boy," he said. "It's time."

Andomaka walked to the altar. The knife was already there, the way it should have been on the night of her uncle's burning. His deathmark was written on a small, yellowed scroll beside a black cup filled with water from the Khahon. She didn't need the scroll, but she was pleased that it was there. If all it did was give her a degree more confidence, that was enough.

The boy came in. He looked healthier than when he'd first come from the slavers' camp. There was more strength in his gaze. The shape of his face wasn't right, nor the cast of his skin, but she could see the echo of Prince Ausai in his lips and eyebrows.

"Be welcome," she said in his own tongue. Hope flared in his expression, and then, seeing her more closely, snuffed out.

"You're going to kill me now?" he asked, still in the words of

Bronze Coast. He had a good voice. Musical, and deeper than his frame suggested.

"What is death?" she asked. And when he didn't answer, "Give me your hand."

The boy stood unmoving. She hadn't expected more from him, though she had hoped. At her gesture, two temple guards stepped out of the shadows. The drone of the harp became richer, the overtones complicating in the fragrant air. A shiver of anticipation washed through her. Just anticipation, she told herself. Not fear. The guards forced the boy to his knees.

"You are my blood," the boy said. "You are my cousin."

"Yes," Andomaka said, taking up the blade.

"You don't have to do this. We could escape together. You could be free."

She drew the blade across his shoulder. He barely winced, but a thin line of blood welled up where she had touched him. The fabric of the world shifted around them, and Andomaka shuddered with something like pleasure. She turned back to the altar. Blood called blood. But the rite had failed before . . .

Gently as a calligrapher, she drew out Prince Ausai's death-mark on the stone. As soon as the last line was complete, the blood darkened and began to smoke. Relief poured through her body. The true blade had returned, the blood carried the thread, and the bridge between the living and the dead had been made. The air thickened with the attention of things without form. Old things. Ancient. The candles seemed to dim as something like cold smoke filled the space. She felt the energy and hunger as if they were her own. Her body felt loose and warm, like she'd drunk half a bottle of wine.

"You could get away," the boy said. "We could both get away. *Please.*"

She wiped the blood from the knife with a square of cloth that had never been touched by sunlight, then dipped the knifepoint in water. She knew the boy's name because Prince Ausai had taught it to her. She wrote it—Timu—across the deathmark, blackened blood and pale water flowing into each other. Like the wake of a huge fish disturbing the surface of a still pond, something moved the smoke. The boy's eyes widened in pain and alarm, but only because he had never been prepared. He cried out, and when he drew in his next breath, he wasn't the one breathing.

"Andomaka," Ausai, dead prince of Kithamar, said in the boy's lovely voice. "You've done well."

"Thank you, my prince," Andomaka said.

The guards released the thin frame, and Ausai walked through the temple slowly, becoming accustomed to his new skin. The harpist put away his bow, and Ausai's footsteps were the only sound. She would have known him by the way he moved, no matter what body he wore. The flood of love she felt for him had been something she'd trained herself to since she'd been a child. That it was constructed and practiced made it no less real.

"All of you, get out," Ausai said, and his gaze locked on her. "You stay."

Within a dozen heartbeats, the temple stood empty except for Andomaka, the spirit that had ruled Kithamar for centuries, and the candles still burning in their places.

"It took time finding the original knife," Andomaka said. "The new blade shattered. I don't know what we did wrong when we consecrated it, but—"

"It wasn't the blade."

Andomaka shifted. "Master?"

"The knife didn't fail, though I suspect we were intended to think it had. The theft of the sacred blade was theater. It gave us something to blame so that our enemy could hide the true cause of the catastrophe." He shook his head, a smile that was equal parts anger and disgust on his unfamiliar lips. "If I hadn't thought to put a secret line of my own into the world where we could use it, you'd have been left to blame the knife and spend your time and effort searching for it or trying to remake it, and failing again. Or the rite, looking for some error in the ceremony. Or yourself, your confidence shaken. Eventually, the ceremony would be abandoned."

"The brotherhood would never let that—"

"This is *my* city. I have sat that throne since the Temple was *built*."

"If it wasn't the blade or the rite..." Andomaka said.

"The blood," he said.

"The vial?"

"The man. We failed because I had no connection to the new prince. Byrn a Sal is not our line. At least my sister-by-law and quite possibly my mewling cunt of a brother have betrayed the city and put a bastard on the throne. If they weren't already dead, I'd haul them over a live fire to ask the details. But..." He gestured with one young hand. She had seen that movement so many times done by a different arm. For a moment, she felt a wave of vertigo. Ausai rubbed his palms over his eyes.

"He's been crowned," Andomaka said.

"Yes, and what proof do we have of his treachery that doesn't also reveal my secrets? Are we supposed to go decades back in time and set a watch on Irana to see who she fucked besides my brother?"

"There could be letters..." Andomaka said.

"Letters burn. Proofs can be altered. I didn't suspect anything for the decades I sat the throne. Who'd believe me now? Look at me. I'm a Bronze Coast whelp. I wouldn't believe me."

"I'll stand," Andomaka said.

Ausai lifted himself to sit on the altar. For anyone else, it would have been blasphemy. No rules that applied to other people constrained him. "You will, but not that way. This war began in the shadows, and it has to end there. A false prince sits the palace, and we will take him from it. Byrn a Sal may not even have known what he is, but it doesn't matter. He has to die."

She grasped at the thought. Byrn a Sal might not even know he was a bastard.

"He wasn't brought up in the brotherhood. It will be simpler if he isn't already on guard against us."

Prince Ausai scowled with the young boy's face. "If he didn't know then, he may by now. I wasn't expecting to have anyone else's eyes on my private things. If he's found them...yes, he'll know there's something. Not the details, but even those he may come to suspect, given time."

"He has an heir."

"His daughter dies too. The House a Sal will have to end. It's time for a new family to guide the city. Chaalat is honorable and old and carries my blood. It is time for the ages to turn in Kithamar, and you are the axis around which history will spin."

Silence reigned in the temple as Andomaka took the thought in, held it in her mind.

"It can be done, and better quickly," she said. "But it can't be discovered. The city wouldn't understand."

The boy nodded. Or Prince Ausai did. Or the thing that had worn Prince Ausai's skin—the thread and spirit of Kithamar itself. The god that she had been raised to worship.

"When they fall, you will be prince of the city, Andomaka," it said. "And I will be you. It's the only way this works."

Three days after Longest Night and a week still before Tenthday, Alys walked unsteadily back from her night's drinking.

She'd thought that being around people would be less awful than being alone, and she'd been partly right. The soup had been warm, and they'd had meat tarts with spiced pork that she could still feel burning pleasantly on the back of her tongue. There had been wine with only a little water in it. The wash of bodies and heat made a welcome change from Darro's hole, for a few hours at least. Korrim and Calm Biran had sung a drunken round, celebrating the coming of the light, and she'd felt the tension growing at the back of her neck.

As she walked, she realized that part of what drove her back into the dark and the cold of her room was guilt. It had come in mouse-quiet. She'd enjoyed herself for a little while, and she'd forgotten Darro. For the time it took to eat a bowl of soup and drink a cup of wine, she'd lived in a world where Darro was truly forgotten. It was a mistake she couldn't allow herself again.

As she took the dark stairs, she heard a man's deliberate cough. It came from behind her own door. Darro's door. She took her club in her fist, rage and fear flowing into her like she'd found a spider in her hair. She kicked the door open.

Tregarro sat at her table. His scarred face caught the light of a little oil lamp. He wasn't woven from smoke this time. He'd actually come in the flesh. Magic would have been less alarming.

"How did you find me?" Alys asked.

"Fuck you," he answered calmly. "And close the door."

She did, but she didn't sit. Her gaze shifted, checking to see that Darro's box was where she'd left it, closed and undisturbed. She relaxed when she saw it was safe.

"What do you want?" she asked.

Tregarro nodded. "She said you were hungry for work. Is that still true?"

"Yes," Alys said without pausing to think.

"There's work. In Riverside."

"All right," Alys said. "What is it?"

"Are you loyal to her?"

Alys frowned. "What do you mean?"

"I am. I'm loyal to her. If I think for a moment that you would put her or our work in danger, they would never find your body. You know that."

With a shock, she realized the scarred man was frightened. She didn't know what of. "I know," she said.

"There's a girl who's been trysting with a boy while his family's elsewhere. It's a merchant house. You're to find the house."

"What can you tell me of it?"

"Just that."

Alys scowled.

"If it was simple, I'd have done it already," the scarred man said. "Find the house. Watch over it, and when they make their little love meeting, you'll interrupt them and kill the girl."

Alys shifted her weight. Part of her was already refusing. Find a merchant house with young lovers freshening up the luck? That had to be half of them. And walking into danger was one thing, even anticipating a fight. But the prospect of murdering someone—of seeking them out in order to leave them dead—was like looking over the edge of a cliff. It left her head spinning and her heart beating fast. She told herself it was just excitement. "Kill her?"

"Yes."

"Is she one of the people who killed my brother?"

"She's one of the people who's against us. That's all you need to know."

"And her boy?"

"I don't give a shit about him. But the girl dies."

She tried to imagine what Darro would have done. What

he would have said, and how he would have said it. He would have been fearless. He would have been hard. She wasn't either of those things, but she could learn to be. She could pretend she was until it came true. She smiled his smile, leaned against the wall, her hand resting on the club. Her breath was short, and her heart tapped against her chest.

"A girl who's with a boy?" she said. "Next you'll be telling me to look for someone who's breathing."

"I know it isn't much to start from. But do what you can, and you'll be paid."

She shrugged the way she imagined Darro might have. "Then I'll do what I can."

There's plague in the Stonemarket," Black Nel said. "Palace guard shut down three streets for quarantine. Anyone that wants can go in, but try to come out and they fill you full of arrows and burn your corpse."

"Bad omen," Deva's Quinn said.

Seems like there's a lot of those these days, Sammish thought. She almost said it aloud, but she was afraid people would agree. It was six days now since she'd sat with Saffa and Goro, and she hadn't been able to get the woman's dry voice out of her ears.

We're in over our heads. That's what she'd said to Alys, it seemed like years before. She hadn't understood how deep they'd really been, or how dark the waters were.

The Pit seemed almost comforting. Longhill and Seepwater might be desperate in their poverty. People might risk freezing if the weather turned cruel or starving if their coin ran out. People caught knives in their guts over a wallet of bronze or a romantic betrayal or a mad, angry sense that this was all the life they would ever have coming out in impotent rage. What they didn't have was dark magic and the prince's throne.

Sammish sat in a corner, her eyes on her bowl of broth-and-onion. No one noticed her because she didn't want them to. She didn't want anyone to, ever again. Her mind kept circling back to Saffa, sitting in the strange little hut on the Silt. Her voice as she said *She came to our summons*. Had she? Sammish had lived her whole life around the petty magics of Kithamar: the fortune-tellers and the rat wards and the herb sellers whose tea promised health or love or the return of whatever else you'd lost. Most were pulls by a different name, but some were true. Had Saffa doomed Orrel to a slow, ugly death, or had he only been unlucky? He'd puked after watching someone he knew die. So what? He hadn't stopped, but he'd hid himself in a plague house. People got sick all the time. Had Sammish put together the better hunting grounds to find Saffa by herself, or had some spirit drawn her? She didn't like to think of herself as a small piece in a larger game, driven by forces she didn't control. And when she did, she'd rather the forces be gold and knives and politics. But hadn't Grey Linnet called the way she could choose not to be noticed a little magic? Could that be truth?

Sammish's mind skipped and jumped around her skull like a trapped sparrow looking for a window out. Her stillness was a mask for her storms.

"I heard there's rot in the granary," a thin Hansch man said. He was sitting by the fire. Sammish didn't know him, but some of the others seemed to. "Green rot. The kind that makes you sick up and go crazy."

"That's bad, if it's true," the barman said. "If the brewers can't get the temple priests to sneak them out cheap grain, I'll be charging all of you two fingers and a nose for a tun of beer come summer." His voice was jovial to pull the sting.

"It's shaping up to be a hard year," Black Nel said. "We'll all be thinner before harvest comes again, you can count on that." And then, "Plague better not fucking spread. A quarantine in Stonemarket's all to the good, but the palace starts thinking it's here, and they'll burn Longhill to the ground and us inside it."

"Hey," the barman said sharply. "No talk like that."

Sammish sipped her broth. It wasn't that odd for someone to be a little tipsy and start railing at the atrocities the nobles and merchants rained down on the Inlisc of Longhill. It meant more that the barman was worried about reprisals for it. Or maybe it was only that Sammish was frightened and uneasy, so that everything seemed soaked through with menace and portent.

The street door clattered open and closed, and then Alys herself pushed through the folds of cloth that kept the heat in.

If Sammish hadn't known her, she'd have guessed Alys was one of Aunt Thorn's crew. Leather and good wool, black boots and a thick belt. The only thing that made it seem like she might not be wealthy in her own right was that she carried a lead-dipped club instead of a blade. She looked around the taproom, her eyes fever-bright and a smile on her lips that left Sammish anxious. Alys didn't see her, and Sammish took the moment to stare.

Alys's hair was tucked under a woven cap except for a curling lock that had escaped at her ear. Her broad cheeks showed a little color where the cold had bitten them. Her body, hidden though it was, left Sammish aching in a way she didn't like to think about. All that was usual. Alys was beautiful, but she'd always been beautiful. Today, she was sharp; hard and brittle as cracking ice. And that was new.

We should have run, Sammish thought. *As soon as Orrel cut the bluecloak's belt, we should have run for the city gates and never stopped.* Sammish lifted her palm and let herself be seen. Alys's smile flickered into something more genuine. Relief, maybe. It was odd. Usually Sammish was the one who took comfort in it when they found each other.

"You've been thin on the ground," Alys said as she slipped onto the bench across from Sammish. She didn't quite make it an accusation, but she didn't keep it from being one either.

"I've had things," Sammish said. "Figured you did too."

Sitting close as they were, Sammish could see the seams on Alys's coat. Black, thick, and triple-stitched. It was good work. Expensive work. Sammish had known that before, but now when she saw it, she thought of Saffa begging her friends and family for the coins that had bought it, and it made the jacket less in her eyes.

"I'm making progress," Alys said. "Tregarro came to me. The scarred one."

"I know who he is."

"I think they're preparing for something big. The people that killed Darro are about to suffer a real loss. I don't know all the details, and what I know, I can't...I can't speak of. You understand."

Sammish didn't laugh, and if she had, it wouldn't have been mirth. "I do."

"They're going to suffer," Alys said, and to her it was a good thing. Sammish felt something shift in her gut. She must have made a sound, because Alys looked up at her, an apology in her eyes. "It's not that I don't want to tell you. I've promised not. Once it's done, I maybe can."

"It's all right," Sammish said.

Alys reached across the table and put her hand on Sammish's arm. Her eyes had taken on an expression that was almost a plea. "Don't be angry with me. I know you've been with me on this. Even when I had to do parts of it by myself, I know you've been there. I'm not looking to keep you out of it."

She's frightened of something, Sammish thought, and it brought a bitterness that surprised her. When Alys was strong or sad or angry, Sammish was tolerable: worthy of a warm bed in the Stonemarket cold or a beer if there was no one better about to drink with. When Alys was frightened, Sammish mattered. The kindest way to phrase it was that she was who Alys came to when, for whatever reason, the stakes were highest.

She could think of other less charitable ways to describe it.

If I told you everything I know, she thought, *you would run to the Silt to try your hand at killing Saffa. Or worse, to your pale woman to spill it on the floor for a pat on the head.*

"You don't have to tell me," Sammish said. "It's all right."

"You aren't angry?"

"I'm not," Sammish said, surprised to find it was true. Something was complicating her heart, but it wasn't anger.

The conversations in the Pit all found a pause in the same moment, and the barman's voice cut through like he was an actor on a stage. "There's gods on the streets these days. Be careful is all I'm saying." He looked up, embarrassed to have spoken so loud in the sudden quiet, and the mutter of voices rushed back. If Sammish had been in the mind to look for omens, it would have been one.

"We need something to drink," Alys said. "You want cider or wine?"

"I'm fine with the soup."

"You're sure? I'm paying."

The dark-eyed, brokenhearted woman hiding in the Silt was paying, she just didn't know it. Sammish remembered the day Alys had offered her a coin for helping. She was glad she'd given it back. "I'm certain," she said.

The yearly rituals that followed Longest Night took up the palace and most of Green Hill. The great families had their turns hosting the prince Byrn a Sal and his retinue, and in return the palace was opened for the private rites and observances of the brotherhoods. Crystal lanterns hung at the street corners, and music filled the galleries and temples. It was a seventh year by the reckoning of the Clovas brotherhood, so its members were out in masks and rags, giving out charms and bits of sage-scented candy. Tregarro had heard that the apparent charity led to a vast orgy on Tenthday, but he'd heard similar rumors about the Daris that he knew from experience to be false.

Andomaka was out among the celebrations somewhere, standing for the Daris Brotherhood and Chaalat. The double duty meant that the little time she could spend at the brother-hood's house was in its public halls and temple. On Sixthday, Byrn a Sal himself came to the house with Halev Karsen at his side, and Andomaka had welcomed them both as if there were no dark war between them. It made Tregarro's neck ache.

There were rumors of unrest. The quarantine in Stonemarket set a nervousness about the season, and Byrn a Sal did little to reassure people. There were stories of him drunk and shouting in the palace, as if his unclean conscience haunted him. Maybe it did. But the most dangerous animal was a cornered one, and if the prince lashed out, he would do it with the force of law behind him. Tregarro was pinned to the brotherhood's house, protecting not Andomaka but the boy who had been Ausai.

That one kept to the most private rooms of the brotherhood's house, sitting in the temple itself for hours playing a game with red and white glass beads on a complex board. It was one Tregarro knew, though he wasn't expert at its strategies. Some-times, Ausai would play against himself, shifting one red bead and then a white with equal concentration. Other times, he would invite Tregarro to take a color. They sat across from each other, passing the long, anxious hours, and vying for position on the board. Sometimes, they drank beer. Sometimes, they talked.

"I keep wanting to call the palace guard," Ausai said, taking one of his beads to a corner spot where it could shift to a different circle. "It's habit, you know? I haven't been cut off from my guard for... well, for a very long time. It chafes to think Byrn has their loyalty and I don't."

"You should have," Tregarro said. "You will again." He reached for a white bead, ready to block the corner transit, but stopped himself at the last moment, pulled his fingers back. The corner move was a trap. He chose a different bead on an inner circle.

Ausai smiled mirthlessly. "It's a dangerous moment. I hate relying on stealth. Give me a chance to open a few necks, and I'm fine. This... waiting? I feel the risk in every minute of it." He moved not the corner bead, but one beside it, then rocked back a degree and passed an open palm across his chin and cheek. Tregarro felt a moment's vertigo at the gesture. He had seen it many times when the prince had done it. Though he knew better, some part of his mind had rebelled at this deep magic. Without intending to, he had put the boy in the same class as street-corner actors and performers for the court, aping the expressions and cadences of their betters. Having that one unconsidered gesture come again in this unfamiliar body drove the strangeness of their situation home.

Ausai looked up at him with a question in his young brown eyes. Tregarro moved one of his beads. "We will not fail you again."

"You'd better not. The farther the blood connection gets, the harder the transit. Children and siblings are best. Nieces and nephews are good too. Cousins like this start to get tricky. Having a few disposable offspring is good as a storm port, and I have enemies. There are gods in the streets these days. And look at me." He lifted his thin, boyish arms. "If you think anyone's putting this lump of skin into the palace of Kithamar, you're drunk. Until I am in the palace again, I'm at risk, but being this child is worse. Put me in a noble skin, and I have some status at least. If Byrn a Sal threw some Bronze Coast boy in a dark room for a few decades, who'd object?"

Tregarro understood that Ausai didn't need an answer from him. The prince was using him as an excuse to talk to himself. Also, he was more than a little drunk. Ausai shook his head and shoved the corner bead in a level toward the center of the board.

"Irana has to have known that Byrn was a bastard," Ausai said. "She was there at the getting of him. But maybe Tallis knew it too. He was a strange one from the time he was born, and looking back, Byrn doesn't even look much like him. The mysteries unnerved him. But can you imagine letting your wife fuck another man and then raising the child as your own, knowing it all the time, and swallowing it all just to spite your brother?"

"The issue's never come up," Tregarro said.

"Or your father, maybe," Ausai said as if he hadn't spoken. "Maybe it was something I did when they were children, and he hated me as his father before he hated me as his brother." He sighed. "They were good children, those three. Two boys and a girl. Tallis and Ausai and Hanan. But maybe I did Ausai too many favors, and left Tallis jealous. He was a sensitive child. There was the hound of his that Ausai wanted, and I let him take it. Maybe that was the seed of all this shit. They say it of girls, but mark me, young boys are pettier. The gods all know I've raised enough to see it."

Tregarro felt another wave of strangeness as he realized the boy wasn't speaking as Ausai any longer, but as Ausai's father,

Prince Airis, dead almost a century ago. The wistfulness in the young boy's voice was born from memories of things his grand-father by blood had seen and said. Prince Ausai had once had his name written in water and welcomed this spirit into his flesh. The man he had been before that, Tregarro had never met. Ausai moved another bead, trapping one of Tregarro's white ones. He plucked it from the board like it was an insect and tossed it into the dead pile.

"You're losing focus," Ausai said.

"You'd beat me even if I didn't," Tregarro said.

"True, but it means more if you give it some effort."

"I will do my best to defeat you, my lord," Tregarro said with a smile. It took him some time to find a good counter-move, but he did. Ausai nodded in approval when he saw where the white bead landed, but did not otherwise respond to Tregarro's little joke. The scarred man grew concerned that he had given offense. "I don't mean to presume."

"You might as well. I'm not prince of anything right now."

"We both know that isn't true, but thank you for your permission."

Ausai waved him on with a thin Bronze Coast hand. Tregarro was already beginning to regret the curiosity that had brought him this far. But there wouldn't be another moment for it. "Andomaka has no children, my lord. When she becomes prince of the city…"

"Yes, I'll have to take care of that. It's been a long time since I was pregnant. It will actually be nice. There are some very pleasant aspects to it."

"You've been women before, then?"

"Men, women. Fathers, mothers, daughters, and sons. I've watched my children grow and become my siblings, and then my aunts and uncles. Great-aunts and great-uncles. I've held babies for their first breaths and held their weary, bony, liver-spotted hands at their last. Birth to death. I've seen its whole arc, again and again and again. I know what we are better than anyone."

"Who were you? First, I mean. Who were you born as?"

Ausai, or the boy, or Airis, chuckled. "I am Kithamar. I was born a city," he said, moving a red bead at the center of the board, and Tregarro saw how the game would be lost.

In the palace of Kithamar, the great hall was lit by a thousand tiny candles, each no larger than Andomaka's smallest finger, and half a tree burning in a long iron grate. The air was thick with the scent of burning sap and spiced wine and the low, earthy perfume that seemed to be the fashion this year. A singer moved through the crowd, crooning hymns to half a dozen gods in turn, with a drummer following along behind him as accompaniment.

In the side galleries, people clustered and spoke. An Inlisc woman in gaudy scarves cast little spells or else little sleights of hand while the nobles appreciated or ignored her. A juggler cracked jokes crafted to offend no one. A priest from the common temple passed the charity bag, taking coins of silver and bronze and giving a sense of absolution in return. Even those in the finest silks and furs, with jewels on their necks and wrists like flakes in a snowstorm, could feel generous.

Servants carried shallow plates of beef and boar to the noblest mouths in Kithamar, and then took the plates away to have the grease toweled off. Nothing used or soiled was allowed there for long. Even the little candles had a team of unobtrusive young women walking with eyes turned away from their betters and waiting for a flame to gutter and be replaced. The palace guard wore their red cloaks like costumes, with flares of embroidery at the collar and sleeve special to the occasion.

The walls, by contrast, were stone and old and dark. They remembered war and violence. Light, they seemed to say, passes quickly. Soot and scorch endure. At times like this, the palace reminded Andomaka of an old soldier forced to wear a frilly dress. The decorations were beautiful and bright. They promised lightness and gaiety. The frame beneath them suffered the illusion but didn't share in it. The palace was hope, as worn by history.

Ten days had passed since Longest Night. Most of the city had already fallen back into the rhythm of its usual life. The garlands were either down from the walls and windows, or still there but turning brown and losing their leaves and needles. The markets were open for those who had things to buy and sell in the cold. Only Green Hill and the palace held on to the festival air, celebrating a moment that had already passed because they could. It was, by common keeping, the first ten days of the new year, and the beginning of the long, slow cold that would lead eventually to spring. There were other ways to mark years, though.

The legal calendar began on the day Byrn a Sal had stolen his crown. Followers of Shau or Lannas or the Emurian mysteries counted theirs from the day the river froze. The Dajan, from the equinox. There were a thousand ways to describe the cycle of seasons and the motion of the sun along its arc, and someone, somewhere championed each of them. If it had been music, it would have been cacophony. But palace and temple kept the common calendar, and so they celebrated Tenthday, when the prince opened the city's private rooms, but not too wide. Enough to let the nobility in. Andomaka had heard that Riverport merchants had started a feast of their own, since none of them were welcome here, as an echo of the real thing. She wondered whether that were true, and whether Elaine a Sal's clandestine lover would attend it. It would be interesting to see, even if she had to go in disguise.

"You're looking lovely tonight, Andoma," a voice said, and she pulled her mind back from the imagined merchant feast to where she actually stood. Barasin a Jimental was at her side, his sharp cheeks a little softened since she'd seen him last. Marriage was thickening him.

"You're very kind," she said, bowing her head. They both understood that he'd just made her an offer, and that she had turned it aside. Anyone who understood the court would have seen it, but it had been done correctly. No offense could be taken by anyone except perhaps Barasin's new wife. He smiled, nodded, and returned to the crowd. She had kissed him once when they were both children, and he'd never quite let go of it. It was sweet, in its way.

All around her, the companions and families of Green Hill and the palace moved and spoke, touched and avoided touch. Micha Reyos, head of her family now that her husband was ill. Andomaka's own cousin, Ober Chaalat, his smile a little too wide and his face sheened with sweat, already drunk. Little Jabin Karsen with a ceremonial sword at his side that would probably bend if he tried to draw it. Every one of them had secrets and intrigues, loves and hatreds. The party was as many different parties as there were people attending it, and only a few had much in common. Andomaka found it all beautiful and comic and melancholy in more or less equal measures.

The one person she wanted to find, however, wasn't there.

She tried the lesser halls, with no better luck. The palace, for all its majesty, was denser and closer than the compounds of Green Hill. It had been made when Kithamar was a smaller, less forgiving, and less civilized place, and it wore its history in thick, cold stone walls and galleries and meeting halls that had been grand when they were built. There were few places among the music and entertainers, wine and beer and cider that a girl like Elaine could go, and fewer still where she could be alone. Andomaka knew many of them, but not all. Not yet.

She felt herself getting close when she went up the narrow stairway to the stone gardens that stood on the palace roof. A bonfire roared there, thickening the air with its smoke, and the heat of it radiated without warming. One cheek could feel almost burning, and the other bitten by the cold. The older cohorts of the noble families stayed below in relative comfort while their children danced in steady blue moonlight and red flicker of flame.

It hadn't been so many years since she had been among the new generation of noble blood. She clearly recalled breaking away from the dour, slow, dull conversations of her elders and finding where the others of her age were meeting. Of course the constant eyes of the palace guard and the house chaperones were on them. The freedom they had was a performance, but it was the closest they would have until they reached majority. She strolled in the play of light and darkness. The wind at the rooftop of Kithamar was cold, and there was nothing to break it.

Elaine was at the eastern edge, far from the bonfire, in a gown of yellow and blue. Her hair was plaited with silver threads, and she wore a scarf around her neck against the cold. She was speaking with one of the palace guard, a young man whom she dismissed when she saw Andomaka drawing near.

From the rooftop's edge, the western half of the city spilled out like a map of itself. At their feet, the long fall of Oldgate, its switchback avenue like a child's drawing of a snake, and just beyond it, the pale ice of the river. The farther quarters glittered past its banks, torches and lanterns and candlelight. From here, the divisions between Riverport and Newmarket, Longhill and Seepwater all faded away. Only the Temple stood as a landmark, rising in stone above the night-dyed wood of the Inlisc buildings. And then the city walls, and the long, rolling darkness of the land beyond them. Seen from here, Kithamar was a single, vast organism, and they stood at its head. Above them, the waning moon and the vast spread of stars. It was beautiful and it was eerie. Elaine broke the silence.

"Andomaka." Not *Greetings, Cousin* or *Blessings for the new year* or any of the more formal etiquette that could have passed between them. The girl was at ease with her, her guard down. It was like seeing a mouse trained to enjoy the company of cats.

"Elaine," Andomaka said, matching the girl's tone and cadence to keep her feeling at ease. "How is your heart?"

The girl's laugh was short and hard as a cough. "It's been better. I have..."

Andomaka waited, thinking that she was searching for words, then looked over to see that she was weeping. Andomaka made herself take the girl's hand. Elaine's fingers were strangely warm. Or maybe it was only that her youth kept the cold at bay.

"It's all right," Andomaka said. "Whatever it is, it will be all right."

"It's stupid. I shouldn't be...I should be happy."

"Why?"

"Because I'm free."

Annoyance pricked at Andomaka's breast as she began to guess the shape of the girl's distress. "You've ended things with..."

Elaine looked up at the sky, her lips a quivering smile. "I have. It's the only way to keep him safe."

Well, that was inconvenient in a morbidly amusing way. As long as the girl had been sneaking out to meet her clandestine lover, there had been a time of vulnerability when she wasn't under the eyes of the redcloaks. By protecting her lover from her father's wrath, she'd made herself safe. Or safer, anyway. Andomaka looked down over the edge of the palace, to the cliffs below, and then back toward the bonfire. It wouldn't be impossible to shove the girl over the edge and call it an accident. There were so many eyes on the rooftop, though, that it would be a gamble. Even an accusation that she'd killed the girl would come back to haunt her when she—or Ausai in her body—took back the city. She considered the girl's hand in hers. Pull the arm straight to lock her elbow, and then turn at the waist. Elaine would have no choice but to swing forward. Would she let go when she fell? Or would she pull Andomaka over with her?

No, she thought. There were too many risks. It was better to be careful. She didn't realize she'd sighed until the girl squeezed her hand.

"Thank you," Elaine said, and Andomaka understood she'd taken the sign as sympathy.

She leaned over and kissed the girl's brow. Perhaps there was another way. "Are you sure of this?"

"I'm daughter to the prince. What else can I do?"

You are not, Andomaka thought. Such drama and dudgeon to protect the honor of a bloodline that was already corrupt. She looked down toward the lights of Riverport. Right now, somewhere on those distant streets and low towers, a lovestruck boy was likely staring up at the palace, his heart twisted in the same petty grief as Elaine's. It would have been endearing if the future of the city didn't ride on it.

"You wouldn't be the first person to have a lover," Ando-maka said with a gentle laugh. "Ausai shared his bed with more women than his wife. Everyone knew."

"It's not the same."

"Because he's a man?"

She thought she saw a blush on the girl's cheek, but it was hard to be certain in the moonlight. "That makes it different."

"It does. But it doesn't make it impossible." She turned the girl to look at her. The whites of Elaine's eyes were shot with red, and her eyelids were so puffy it looked like she'd been struck. She was an ugly weeper. "We give our lives to the city, you and I. We marry for the city. We bear children for the city. And our family, and our blood. It's the sacrifice we're called to, and it's our duty. But it isn't everything we are. You have to take the pleasures you can in this life. They won't be given to you." Andomaka coughed, surprised by the passion in her own voice. She sounded almost angry. That was interesting. "What is his name?"

"I'm not...I don't..."

"Name him."

"Garreth."

"Go to your Garreth," Andomaka said. "Not as Elaine a Sal, daughter of the prince. Go as a woman to a man. Show him what there is in your life that he can claim, and what there isn't. And find what there is of him that will sustain you."

"You...do you...I mean, have you...?"

Andomaka understood the question and fought to keep the contempt from her voice. She would be who she needed to be for the moment. She could be someone else later. "I'm a woman too."

The girl's face seemed to blossom with surprise. No, not sur-prise. Hope. So that was something. A little permission to sin was all she'd needed. Just as effective in the long run as inviting her over the edge and into the air.

"Elaine!" They turned together to see a man silhouetted against the fire, striding toward them. Elaine pulled back her hand sharply, which was interesting in its own way. Andomaka looked from the dark man to the girl and back again, and the figure resolved into Halev Karsen.

She had known the man from the time they'd both been children, but always at a remove. He was known to be Byrn a Sal's best friend and closest advisor. At the moment, he looked as angry as she had ever seen him. Or perhaps worried. He started to speak, then seemed to think better of it. Andomaka would have bet gold that the words he finally gave weren't the ones in his mind. "Kint's been looking for you."

"I'm sorry," Elaine said.

"Please attend your father now."

Elaine nodded and walked away. Andomaka half expected her to look back, but she didn't. She more than half expected Karsen to go with her, but he stayed.

"You're looking well, Andomaka," he said, and from him it was not an invitation.

"As are you, Halev. Power suits you."

"I don't believe that's true." There was something here she was missing. A hardness in his tone, and a care in how he chose his words. She couldn't see what was behind it, but that he was on his guard was something. If Halev Karsen was concerned, then Byrn a Sal would be as well. And if they were concerned about her in particular, they were already a good way down a road she didn't want them to travel. She smiled and took his arm, walking back toward the celebration and the fire.

"They're beautiful, don't you think?"

"What?"

"The young ones. It's hard to believe we were that age once."

"We aren't old yet," Karsen said. And then, more softly, "No matter how it feels."

"You sound weary?"

"It's the time of year," Karsen lied. "I'll be glad when the darkness has passed. That's all. Do you remember when my sister decided she'd join with the chanters? Out there on the street corner with her shirt off, calling back the light."

Andomaka smiled and shook her head. "I do not. And I'd recall that, I think."

"I suppose our parents got it quieted down. It was all the talk in our house anyway. You're still with the Daris Brotherhood?"

"On and off," Andomaka lied.

"You should come to the palace more often. I know Byrn would appreciate your company."

Was that a threat? Was it a test? Andomaka smiled emptily. "Perhaps I will."

They reached the stairway back down into the warmth of the great hall. He took the opportunity to take his arm back from her, and she didn't cling. It was interesting watching him, like reading a poem in a language she only slightly knew. She wasn't sure if the unease she saw in him came from him or from her. But she saw his jaw go tight when the first shouts came from the great hall—laughter and a wild whooping. They walked a little faster with Karsen in the lead, and the scene they walked into was perhaps the least expected thing in the evening.

In the great hall, Byrn a Sal, prince of Kithamar, was galloping through the crowd like a child in a playroom. He had a broom between his legs that he whipped like a horse as he ran. The palace guard cleared the path for him as best they could, but he was erratic. His face was pale, but with patches of unhealthy redness as if he were wearing makeup that he was in the process of sweating off. His grin was wide and drunken, and all the people he passed laughed and clapped him on. They had to. He was the prince. He was the city.

"Excuse me," Karsen said, and made his way into the crowd. Andomaka watched him, and the prince, and the community of all the highest families in the city. The sense of wrongness had to be more than hers. The sense of anxiety and illness was as much in the air as the scent of wine and smoke and bodies. Only a few knew that a false prince sat the throne, and she couldn't be certain who they were besides herself. She clapped and laughed, and acted as though it was a lovely joke. In the privacy of her mind, she thought *You are a traitor by blood. I will kill you and yours and remove the stain of your rule from history. You will be forgotten.* And the thought made laughing easier.

The prince whooped again, turned, and started galloping in the other direction. The redcloaks scurried to get ahead of him, and in one of the near galleries, a drummer struck up a beat. Someone began to sing a traditional song so old that half the words were fallen Hansch. Slowly, the whole great hall joined in. They'd all heard it from their cradles so it had a sense of home and comfort, though the words, looked at carefully, were a call to war and slaughter. Andomaka joined in, closing her eyes and letting the music wash over her. There was nothing more she needed to do. She had headed off the unexpected threat by giving Elaine the permission she needed to continue her dalliance. And more than that, she'd found something of the lover's name. Garreth. A scent to put before the little wolf girl and all her other hunters.

It was such a small mistake on Elaine's part. Easy to overlook. The prince's daughter would never understand the role it had played in her death.

The new year ran cold. Sammish knew from trust that the days were growing longer, the hours unfurling more slowly. She didn't experience it that way. The bright, clear skies that came with Longest Night and the days that followed vanished. Clouds crowded down over the city, dark as stones. The snow that fell from them was small and dry, like numberless tiny teeth. The wind that carried it was sharp and merciless.

All through the city, the decorations were gone. There were no celebrations now, just the long durance of winter and distant promise of the thaw. The dogs that haunted the streets grew thinner, and the rats grew hungry and bold. The charity houses gave out thin soup to the streetbound who could find a bowl or cup to carry it away in. The shelves and cabinets that the bounty of harvest had filled continued their long annual exhalation. Each jar that came down, each crate of salt that gave up its bit of pork and beef to the stewpot, was one less to see the city through to summer. The quarantine in Stonemarket seemed to be holding in the illness; it hadn't spread to the rest of the city. But the men and women of the Smoke and Green Hill were forced to make their way across the river to buy food, and the extra custom drove the price of bread and cheese higher for the citizens of the east bank. Even if the warehouses were opened and Stonemarket declared clean and healthy, it might be a starving spring in Longhill. Food only went so far when the coin to buy it ran out.

The city was out of balance, and everyone seemed to sense it. No one seemed to know what to do, least of all Sammish. All she could think was keep her head down and do what she had always done: survive. In the mornings, she took the stale bread that was left for her, if there was any, and made her rounds of the poorer streets. If she saw any of Aunt Thorn's people or even just the normal denizens of Longhill who looked a bit more desperate than usual, she'd shift her route around them. The little profit she made wasn't worth dying for, but if she went without for too long, she wouldn't be able to pay the baker's rent. And without her rent, he wouldn't be able to buy his flour and honey.

Everything depended on everything else, and all of it was fragile.

In the afternoons, she studied the chalk marks from the brewer's window or cleaned ash from the boilers of a bathhouse near the Temple or ran her ice-bound track through the city gathering knives for the whetstone man. Tramping through ice-grey streets with aching hands pulled up into her sleeves, Sammish could almost forget Alys and Saffa, Andomaka of Green Hill, and the whole vast, dark mess that had spilled into her life after Darro's death. When she did think of it, she told herself it wasn't hers to carry anymore, and she was lucky to be done with it. Sometimes she was almost convinced.

She folded the blades into the leather satchel: a pair of straight blades from the cobbler's shop, a set of cloth shears from the tailor, and—to her advantage—a set of five blades from a tanner's house at the edge of the city. The stink of the place got into her clothes, but they paid well, and the extra work made up for the butcher's trade that she'd lost.

She stepped into the shed just as she had a hundred times before. The winter cold pushed in from the walls, radiating like heat from a fire. Arnal sat at his stone. The iron brazier at his side was enough to keep the water from freezing onto the stone, and its fire cast a little light. The old man was wrapped in wool blankets and a leather hat with patchy fur trim over the ears. His hair pushed out from under it like a vine growing between bricks. His eyes flickered when he looked at her. It wasn't even a real expression. Just a moment of pain or regret. He put down the knife he'd been working—a thumb-long, three-sided dagger that grooms used to trim their horses' hooves—and waved her forward toward him. Sammish felt a sudden rush of apprehension, but Arnal's face seemed kindly enough. She went to him, holding the leather satchel out before her.

"Good load today," she said. "The tanners must have had a heavy month."

"Or bad technique," Arnal said, taking the satchel from her hands. "Nothing dulls a blade faster than a bad hand. Sit down with me, eh? We should talk a little."

Sammish swallowed an apology. She didn't know what she'd done wrong. If she'd done something wrong. Arnal pulled a little wooden stool over next to the brazier and stopped working the little iron water pump. The flow over the stone died. Sammish watched the subtle tooth of the stone come clear as the last of the water sheeted off it. It felt like an omen.

"I've...ah...I've decided to make a change," Arnal said, not looking at her.

"I can get more knives," Sammish said. "I haven't been going to the kitchens in Riverport, but I can. Half of those people have their own kitchens. If I go out at daybreak, I could get you a dozen more every week."

Arnal raised his palm, silencing her. "It's not you. It's me. My hands are getting weak. They have been for a few months now. And I'm starting to get the shakes. See?"

Now that he said it, she did. She'd never looked at his fingers before. They were thick and callused all the way to where they met his hand. The nails were yellow, and the flesh where they met his skin was white and cracked as a dropped tile. The shiver in them made her think of leaves in a slight breeze, or a candle flame in a draught. He looked at her looking at them, and his smile was a kind of grief.

"Have you seen a healer?"

"I've been drinking a tea for it every night since first snow. It helped for a while. But it's getting worse now, and the tea tastes like mule piss. I can't do good work. Not like this. You didn't do anything wrong. I'm just old, and the time's come to step back."

"Oh," she said.

"I've got a son who works for a tinsmith in the Smoke. He's got room for a cot, and he said I could stay there. Might be able to do a little work around the smithy on the days I'm feeling right. But this"—he gestured at the little shed; the stone; the pump; the grey, sandy water—"this is over for me."

"All right," Sammish said. Her voice sounded calm, given how fast her mind was going. She wasn't ready. This wasn't supposed to happen this way.

"You've done fine work for me, these last couple years," he was saying. "You're smart, and mostly reliable. I'm sure you'll find a spot someplace to make up for the shit I paid you."

"Your brother."

Arnal tilted his head.

"Your brother runs a brewer's shop," Sammish said. "I've been practicing the marks for the bettor's window. Maybe he's looking for someone?"

Arnal put his trembling hand on his knee. There was sorrow in his eyes that might have been for her or for him or for the way the world ground people like them down. "I can ask him," he said, and the way he said it meant: *No.*

Arnal gathered up the satchel and unfolded it, considering the blades as he pulled them out one at a time. Now that she knew to look, she could see the light fluttering on the flats of the blades as he shook. When he was done, he counted out a half dozen bronze coins. Five were old, with the face of Prince Ausai. One was newly minted, bright, and carried Byrn a Sal's profile on it. Or she guessed that was what it was supposed to be. It didn't look much like him.

"I can be back for the blades tonight," she said.

"They can wait for tomorrow. If we run a little late, and they take their coin somewhere else..." He shrugged. *What does it matter?*

"Tomorrow, then," Sammish said. As she left, she heard the squeak of the pump and splash of the water. It would probably be the last time. She turned east, toward Longhill and home. As she walked, legs working a hard rhythm to keep her heat up, she thought that she'd have to find some other way to get money. She'd have to ask who had a place for her. What she could do. What she was good for. She didn't exactly feel the sadness or the humiliation or the loss. She only knew they were there, acknowledged them, and gave them a little space within her.

The rooms in Seepwater, the job at the brewer's, the bed where she'd imagined herself waking beside Alys's sleeping body. All of it swirled and scattered like the little angry snowflakes caught by the wind. It hurt, but not as much as she'd thought it would. It was as if she'd known all along that the dream was only a dream, and that someday she'd have to wake up. The only difference between then and now was that the day had come.

"That's harsh," Alys said, her breath steaming as they walked.

It was one of the nights she was back in Longhill instead of wherever else her work took her. She had a new red wool scarf at her throat, and a cloak of lined leather that was almost a request that someone knock her down and take it. She swung her lead-tipped club like a Green Hill dandy with a swagger stick.

Sammish shrugged. "It happens."

"Lots of things happen. Doesn't mean they're good."

Other people had noticed the time that Alys was spending outside the quarter and the money that flowed from her finger-tips. Sammish had heard the laughter and the whispers and the speculation. Aunt Thorn had hired Alys on as an assassin. Alys had met a girl in the palace who looked exactly like her, and they'd traded places. She'd started fucking a rich man in Stone-market who liked the idea of a girl from Longhill dancing on his leash. None of them were right, and all of them meant that something was happening with her. She didn't fit in Longhill the way she used to.

For Sammish, it was as if there were two Alyses now. There was the angry, hurt, beautiful, funny, soft creature she'd longed for in silence for so long, and then there was this girl—half thug and half fop—who actually sought her company now and then because Sammish knew the truth behind her transformation and apparently Alys didn't have many people to talk with.

Sammish knew it was an illusion, but she couldn't get rid of the sense that that first Alys was somewhere in the city, maybe even in Longhill. Walk into the right taproom or market, go to her room at the right moment, and she'd be there, the way she'd always been. They'd go drink hot wine down by the theater and cut some purses and laugh and fall into each other's arms.

"I mean," the real girl walking beside her said, "it's not worth pouting over. I was being sympathetic."

"Sorry. I must be in a mood."

"I might be able to help," Alys said, and her voice dropped to a murmur. "We're looking for someone in Riverport. I can't tell you why, but he's son of a merchant family. We know his name's Garreth, but that's all we're sure of."

The implications rolled out in front of Sammish like a rug. A mysterious young man who was the new focus of Andomaka and the scarred man, the next job that Darro would have been on if he hadn't died. The new pull. And if Sammish wanted to help, there might be some table scraps left for her. The way she bristled wasn't entirely fair. Alys had invited her into pulls before. This wasn't all that different. It only felt as if it were.

Sammish shook her head. "Doesn't mean anything to me. The closest I know is a tailor's boy down in Seepwater called Garret, but I'd bet my right foot that's nothing to do with yours. Sorry I couldn't help. Good luck hunting him, though."

Alys blinked, and Sammish willed her to let the subject drop. There was no path that led from here to Sammish working one of Andomaka's jobs, and the more Alys pushed her on why, the more Sammish would want to explain it, and anything she said would go straight back to Green Hill and the Daris Brotherhood. Better not to talk at all. Sammish hurried her steps a little, and Alys matched her pace.

The street bent to the left around a dry cistern, and then opened to a tight, uncomforting square. The dark lines showed where wagon wheels had crushed snow against stone. Crows huddled at the roofline, three stories above them, shifting their feet and muttering complaints at the low white sky.

Ullin was leaning against the wall, sending greyish smoke up from a bone-yellow pipe. When he saw Alys, he hitched up his chin in greeting. He didn't acknowledge Sammish, and she didn't want him to. At her side, Alys shifted her gait, sinking lower into her hips like she was another lank young man, easy in her joints and ready for violence. Everything she did was a performance. Ullin pushed off the wall, but didn't step forward.

"We have a thing we need to do," Alys said.

"Won't stop you," Sammish replied.

"Think about what I said, though, yeah? You're good at finding things out. We could use someone like that."

"Good luck," Sammish said, and didn't mean it. Or at least didn't mean it as *Find what you're looking for.* Alys slouched over to Ullin as Sammish angled her way back east toward home. Alys and Ullin traded words, but she couldn't hear them, only see their breath in the cold and the falling light. Ullin laughed and moved to put his arm around Alys's shoulder, but she shifted out of his reach. Sammish could still smile. She felt a pang of jealousy, but even that seemed like habit.

By the time she reached her room, the night was falling. There was no sunset, only a slow dimming of the world. The cat had found comfort elsewhere, or else had finally crossed a dog he couldn't outrun. Sammish lay in her bed though she wasn't tired and thought about what she would do now that the knife running had gone away. There were other sharpeners in the city. If she could find one that was looking for more work, she might be able to keep her regulars. Even if it wouldn't open a path to something better later on, it would bring in coin to keep her fed. Or she could go back to the hospital and see if they needed someone to clean up after the sick and the dying. She could see if, against all chance, Orrel was still alive. Or she could go begging for cleaning work at the merchant houses, though those jobs were jealously guarded by the people who had them, and she couldn't think of anyone who'd speak for her.

She closed her eyes and willed the sleep to come. It didn't. Thought after thought after thought rose and fell away, none of them connected. She didn't plan it when, still in the darkness, she rose and dressed. She only knew she had to get out of her little room. The night air was bitterly cold. Her nose and ears ached with it. By memory and the few lanterns that burned outside taprooms, she trudged west. By the time she reached the frozen canals of Seepwater, she was almost warm. When she lowered herself down to the Khahon, the sky was starting to lighten. She fell twice on the way across the snow-covered ice, but she didn't get hurt. She did imagine what would happen if some bizarre warm current from the north had weakened the ice enough that she fell through it and how the ice would look above her as she drowned, but that was only being morbid. Thaw hadn't come. Rotten ice was the least of her worries.

The bare, black trees of the Silt were stark against the pearl-grey sky. She used the looming darkness of Oldgate to put herself near where she'd been the time before, but the city seemed to shift around her. She was always too far north or too far south, too near the river or too far from it. She considered going back to her room. Not to rest, but to get the stale bread the way she had before, as an offering to the residents of the Silt. To Goro. But her feet ached and Longhill was far and, more than that, something in her gut rebelled at being a supplicant anymore. She'd drunk too much of that already.

With morning turning the still-falling snow ash-grey against the sky, she planted her feet at the treeline, cupped her hands to her mouth, and shouted his name. Nothing happened but a stirring of bird wings. She shouted again and again, repeating the syllables until they lost their meaning and she was only making noise at a world that wasn't listening. When the cold began to creep up her legs, she walked and shouted. When her voice grew hoarse, she shouted hoarsely. If the wild man didn't come, she didn't know what would make her give up. Exhaustion, maybe. Or some bluecloaks sent along to gather up the latest madwoman and put her in a cell until she calmed down.

But he came, trudging out from between two trees that she wasn't certain had been there before. He wore a stained wool cloak and walked with a staff of gnarled wood, and his frown could have lit fires.

"The fuck are you doing?" he spat when he came close enough to speak.

"Is she still here?"

His eyebrows rose. "Of course she's not. You found her here. If you did, someone else could. She's been gone from me since the night you came."

"Has she left the city?"

"I'll say this again," Goro said. "She left here. I don't know if she stopped inside the walls or kept going until she put her feet in the sea, because she didn't want to tell me and I didn't want to know."

"I think she stayed."

"What does it matter to you?"

"I'm going to help her," she said. "And you're going to help me find her."

The wild man's beetled eyebrows rose in astonishment. "Well. Look who lost her milk teeth," he said. And then a smile as if he'd seen something pleasing or had a long odds come good. "All right, then. Let's talk."

F inding a merchant house in Riverport was like finding a raindrop in a thunderstorm. If it didn't matter which one, it was easy. Finding one in particular was hard.

The first problem, and it wasn't a simple one, was to understand what *merchant house* meant. Riverport was thick with trade on every scale. There were only a dozen great compounds that aspired to echo the noble houses and brotherhoods of Green Hill, and if those were the only merchant houses, then the job wouldn't be that difficult. But for each of those, there were twenty family businesses focused on one or two goods with buildings that were both the center of commerce and the shared hearth. Add again the little shops for the tailors and cobblers, the leatherworkers who sold belts and caps from their own homes, the healers who passed tinctures and powders from their kitchens, the butchers and lamp oil carts and soap-and-candle men, and almost anything with a door and a window might be called a merchant house, excepting only the public temples where the residents of Riverport gathered to perform their piety at each other, and those weren't merchant houses only because it was rude to say what the priests were selling.

Of all the quarters of Kithamar, winter touched Riverport least. Snow and ice clung to the shadows and the edges of the streets, but wagon wheels, boots, shovels, and sand cleared the way. As long as there was daylight and the snow and wind weren't too vicious, the corners boasted musicians playing for spare coins and criers announcing the virtues of some particular taproom or private baths or tea house. Longhill might be poorer than dogs, Alys thought, but at least they wore their station with dignity. They were who they were. Riverport had money and a kind of power, but at the price of wearing a bright mask until the face behind it faded to nothing. Comfort, yes, but never ease.

"What about this one?" Ullin asked, pointing down the corner with his chin. Alys considered the mark. A yellow stuccoed warehouse with broad, red-painted doors presently closed to the street. The windows above it had shutters open despite the cold, and bright curtains with awnings that had likely once been the same shade of red but had faded to something nearer to dark pink. The rows of windows above that were for the family's sleeping rooms and the last, thinnest, and nearest the sky for servants and visitors of no particular dignity. A flight of worn stone stairs led up from the street to a double door on the family's floor with thin columns on either side of it like an echo of the compounds of Green Hill.

Alys looked up and down the street, not for any particular threat, but to recall as best she could what other houses they had tried nearby and how long ago. Down on the left, there was a larger compound they'd tried four days before, but nothing else nearby.

"Might as well," she said. "You or me?"

"I'll take this one," Ullin said. "You come with me and back me if I need it."

She nodded once and sharply, the way she imagined Darro would have. It felt natural to her now. She walked a bit down the street and leaned against a wall where she could see and hear all that happened without seeming to and nodded Ullin on.

Ullin stepped smartly to the warehouse doors and slapped them twice with an open palm. Alys waited. A wagon rolled by, a load of cloth bales covered with an oiled tarp against the wet. The carter didn't so much as glance at them. Ullin pounded again. They'd been running these pulls long enough that she could read the angle of his shoulders and the way he held his weight. He was about to turn away when the door scraped open and an older man's wide face looked out.

"Looking for Garreth," Ullin said.

"Fuck yourself," the wide man said, his tone conversational and without heat. He started to close the door.

Ullin blocked it with his boot. "No offense. I don't need to speak with the man. Just give him a message for me?"

"There coin in it?" the wide man asked. This was a trap. All they wanted was to know whether there was a Garreth in the house, and if there were, if he was the son of the family and not a groom or kitchen boy. If they offered money, the servants were just as likely to take it, promise to deliver a message or a package to someone who didn't exist, and call themselves clever for their own little pull. Alys couldn't blame them for the impulse, but she did have a little contempt for their amateur ambitions.

"There's thanks if I know he gets it," Ullin said, which wasn't a yes or a no. "Is he here?"

The wide man considered, and sloth won out over greed. "No one here called Garreth. You've the wrong house."

"You're certain? The son of the house, I heard it."

"Then clean your ears, and get your leg out of my door before I break your kneecap, you little Inlisc shit," he said amiably.

Ullin laughed, stepped back, and made a false and elaborate bow as the red door pulled to. Alys slapped his shoulder. "Don't show off," she said.

The hunt they were on had rules—don't use the same approach too often, let a street cool for a few days rather than hit every door at once, don't make trouble, don't say anything you can't take back, stay dull enough that no one starts telling stories about you—and they all cooked down to one central edict: Notice but don't get noticed. She wished Sammish were with them. For one thing, she was a genius for work like this, and Alys found herself weirdly missing the girl's company. It would have been good to run a pull with someone from Longhill.

"North?" Ullin asked. "Been a while since we saw the city wall."

"Fine with me."

They turned down the street and fell into step together, Alys stretching her legs to match Ullin's longer stride. She could tell the work was hard for the Stonemarket knife. For one, he stood out on this side of the river. There were plenty of Hansch here, but Ullin knew he was out of his circle, and it made him puff up. He acted out his ease and comfort so much he seemed uneasy and discomfited. It annoyed her, but she wanted his company more than she didn't. With the quarantine closing down half a dozen streets in Stonemarket, she knew she should have been grateful he was there at all. As they walked, they spoke. With Ullin, it was mostly steam and piffle, jokes at the expense of whoever was out of earshot and stories that didn't stand up to too much inquiry. But enough of them had Darro mentioned that Alys was happy to sift through the dross.

Ullin, according to his own account, had been born the third son of a coppersmith, and spent his early days splashing in the polluted canal that ran through the Smoke. His brothers had taken the family places in the guild, and left him to make his own fortune, which so far he'd done by running jobs for himself or for people willing to pay. Tregarro had found him four years before, when the old prince was still firmly in power and there weren't even rumors of illness. The pale woman hadn't come into his circle until after Darro had, which Alys tucked away. Andomaka hadn't taken any interest in Ullin, but in Darro she had, and it left Alys feeling quietly pleased. As if she'd won a point in a game she didn't fully understand.

To hear him tell it, Ullin had broken hearts and lifted wallets and windows all through the western half of the city, excepting the palace. Crossing the redcloaks was more than he was paid for, he said with a laugh.

At a thin house with only two stories just outside the northern gate, Alys pretended to an old woman that she was bringing a note from a physician to Garreth, son of the house, about a girl they both knew. The implication was that this fictional girl might have caught a whore's pox, and while the old woman was alight with curiosity, there was no Garreth there to give the message to, but maybe she meant Gaucin who worked at the grocer's at the corner? Along the long, curling street that bent back toward the river, Ullin was there to give a warning to young master Garreth about a rumor that he'd heard from a mutual friend who might not be the friend he seemed, but the only Garreth there was comfortably into his sixth decade and cared more about his own gout than what anyone was saying about him in the taprooms.

The winter sun went down more slowly than it had at Longest Night, but it was standing at the shoulder of Oldgate and a cold wind was picking up as they made their way back toward the river. Alys found herself thinking of the salt warehouse where she and Sammish had braced the disgraced bluecloak. It hadn't been half a year earlier. It seemed like something from a different life.

"One more, and then soup and beer," Ullin said.

"Works for me," Alys said as if he had made an offer and not an assertion. She pointed ahead at a four-story compound with pale blue shutters and white walls warmed by the colors of the coming sunset. "That one?"

"Your turn," Ullin said instead of *yes*. "Pretend you're carrying."

"No," Alys said.

"Oh come on," Ullin said. "You can't be embarrassed for bedding down with someone you've never actually met. It's a lie. You're pregnant. Garreth may be the father. Go."

He pushed her, and she stumbled forward. She hated the story, but it wasn't one they'd used before, and nothing better came to her as she walked the half block to the house. She reached the door. No stairs on this one, but a bracket where a lantern could be hung and a fresco of a wreath with red berries and pale green leaves over the doorway. When she glanced back, Ullin was watching her from across the street. His smile was halfway to a smirk, and she felt a little stab of anger toward him. But she put a hand to her belly, and with the other she slapped the door. A few breaths later, it opened.

The woman looking out at her wore a servant's clothes in the same pale blue as the shutters. Her hair was white, but had enough curl in it to speak of Inlisc blood. Her face was thin with age. She hoisted an eyebrow. Alys imagined herself being a brave idiot girl, there to demand that the man who'd planted his seed in her be there to help care for the child. She squared her shoulders the way that girl might, lifted her chin—but not too far.

"I need to speak with young master Garreth," she said with just a little tremble in her voice.

The old woman glanced at the hand that cupped Alys's belly and her lips thinned. Disgust, but not, Alys thought, for the troubled girl at her door. That was interesting.

"Try the barracks," the servant said. "He's had no place here for months."

"Wait," Alys said as the door began to close. "What do you mean?"

"I mean, Garreth made his decision when he entered the guard. If you have business with him, talk to his captain. He may be part of this family by blood, but his business belongs elsewhere."

And then the door closed. The rasp of a bar falling into place made the degree to which her presence was unwelcome clear. Alys turned back, forcing her shoulders forward in mimic of a sorrow she didn't feel. She walked away with bowed head in case anyone were watching. Ullin stepped toward her, but when she ignored him, fell back. Alys walked slowly and sorrowfully until the curve of the street took her out of sight. Then she straightened and grinned.

Tregarro, woven from smoke, sat across her table from Alys. As he listened, he rubbed the scars along his cheek and neck. When she was finished, he leaned forward onto his elbows, his gaze cutting from side to side as he thought. "What else do we know about the house?"

"Belongs to a family called Left. They trade in wool with a side in spices, mostly. They've just made an alliance with some northern village that's supposed to have good sheep."

"That's all?"

Alys didn't shrug. It felt too much like an apology. "We didn't want to be too obvious asking."

She wished it had been Andomaka who'd come for her report, but the pale woman hadn't seen her for weeks now. Alys tried not to feel disappointed by that, and mostly she succeeded.

"And he's the only one?"

"Someone named Garreth, son of a merchant house in River-port," Alys said. "He's all you asked, but there may be others we haven't found yet. It's not as if we've tried every door in the quarter."

"And he's a guardsman?"

"That's what I hear. I didn't want to get my fingers too close to that, though. Bluecloaks don't tend to love people like me." The room was cold enough that her breath plumed. Tregarro's didn't. She wasn't sure if that was because he was only there by candle or if he just got along with frost better than she did. When he didn't speak for a few long breaths together, she said, "We can keep looking if you want."

"No," Tregarro said. "Not yet. Take a few days. Learn what you can about the streets around the house. When the family is away. If our man Garreth is meeting his lover there, she'll have a way to sneak in and back out again. Find that."

"And if I see him with a girl?"

Tregarro weighed some thoughts he didn't speak. "Kill her if you have the chance. It will be worth the risk."

"Who is she?"

"She's the one you're supposed to kill."

"Best hope he's not stepping out with more girls than one, then," Alys said, trying to make it a joke.

"If he is, we kill all of them. As long as the one I want is among them, the others won't matter."

"Anything you can say so I know she's the right one?"

"She's Hansch," Tregarro said shortly, and pushed a wallet across the table. It was warm, and solid, and the coins in it clinked nicely. "You did well. Keep going."

"Am I paying Ullin out of this?"

"I don't care," Tregarro said. He stood and, walking away, unwove. The black candle spat, and she lit a normal wax one from the flame before she blew it out. In the less eerie light, she counted out her pay. Across the room, the box of Darro's ashes sat on its shelf. It had grown dusty over the weeks.

She wanted to feel the victory of the job. She'd won the pull, but something about it chafed. She kept imagining Darro going up to the house, asking after the missing son. She didn't know how he'd have done it, but it wouldn't have been by pretending he was pregnant. She was glad enough that she'd done the work Andomaka needed of her, but she hadn't done it the way her brother would have, and that tainted something.

She looked over at the box, and the deathmark stood out in the darkness. A few lines, straight and curved, that in the dark seemed like a strange and unblinking eye considering her. She went to it and rubbed the dust off with her sleeve until the wood was clean. She put Darro back in his place.

"Sorry," she said. "I won't do that again. It was...I don't know. Sorry."

Darro, of course, didn't answer. She made a little dinner of a bit of bread, cheese, and mustard, then wrapped herself in a blanket against the cold and blew her candle out. Through the wall, she heard a man and woman talking seriously to each other, but she couldn't make out the words. As she faded into sleep, the voices became her and Darro. Hovering between the world and dreams, she listened to herself and her brother, the conversation becoming more nearly comprehensible and less connected to the living voices in her ears.

In the dream, they were walking side by side down a hallway that was also a street. She was bragging to Darro, telling him how well it was all going, how she'd managed her pulls and taken up his work. She was desperate that he understand how it was all going to be well, and that he say it back to her so that she could know it too. Instead, the dream-brother answered her with indulgence and amusement, but never the approval she needed. Her frustration grew.

There were no actual words in the dream, but the sense of talking was immediate and powerful. She found herself having to shout, and realized that there was a roaring sound that came from above them, and that their pathway had led them underneath the river. The great, dark flow of the Khahon was above them, and she couldn't make herself heard. She had to convince Darro that things were going well, that it would all come out right because of her. The sense of being thwarted was deep, and she found herself growing angry with her brother and the way he treated everything she did so lightly.

When he spoke, his words were perfectly clear and crisp, as if his mouth were almost against her ear: *Why won't you look at my face?*

Alys's scream woke her. Her heart was beating hard and fast, and she was sweating though she felt terribly cold. She sat in the darkness, her blanket pulled tight around her, and waited for a terror that she didn't understand to pass.

The quarantined section of Stonemarket was a rough triangle not far from the western gate. At its most, it was three streets wide, almost twice that long, and narrowed to a stone-paved common that was hardly more than a wide place in the road. It was marked by thick rope with yellow rags tied to it every few feet. The guards who walked its perimeter had whistles and swords and the badges of office that hung from their belts. Their cloaks were not blue, but red. The prince of the city had closed these streets, and the palace guard enforced his ban. It was a measure of how dangerous the illness was, though Sammish hadn't yet been able to get a clear description of what had raised the alarm.

The most reliable story she'd heard—which only meant that more than one person had repeated it before her—was that it was a fever that turned into thickening, greying skin. She had also heard that it was a cough that rattled the ill so badly they couldn't sleep or a bleeding in the mouth and asshole that wouldn't heal. Whatever the details, it was the source of fear and dread, and the people of Stonemarket kept their distance from the plague quarter, even if they only lived across the street.

Sammish walked the whole rope, looking down the forbidden streets as she passed. In more than one, the bodies of dogs and cats lay lifeless on the stone paving where the palace guard had thrown them. In one, there was the corpse of an old man among them. Sammish couldn't say if illness or a redcloak had ended him, only that he was dead in the street, and no one had come to carry him away. The story was that water was hungry, and whoever died in the river could lose their soul to it. That might have been true, but Kithamar had more than one hunger in it, and the stones of Stonemarket carried a death of their own and would until the palace said otherwise. Now and then, she caught sight of someone farther down the street, inside the quarantine. Sammish didn't call to them, and they didn't come forward.

She carried her cloth sack over one shoulder, the weight of it bumping against her back as she walked. It had food in it, along with fresh water and incense she'd bought from the hospital. All she had to do was duck under the rope. It should have been easy.

"You," a man's voice said. "What are you doing?"

"Waiting for my grandmother," she said, the lie coming easily to her lips. She turned to see a group of three redcloaks on their patrol. They were large men, all three of them Hansch, and one carried his sword unsheathed. She tried not to look them straight in the eye.

"Your grandmother?" the bare-bladed man said. It was his voice that had spoken before. "If she's in there, she stays in there."

"I have things for her. To help. She knows to meet me here, but she hasn't come."

The redcloak stepped close to her. He had scars on his knuckles and an unnerving kindness in his voice. "She may not know anything anymore. So you listen here, yeah? Toss the bag over and go home. If you cross in looking for your old grandmother, we will let you, but you won't come back out. Not unless the order comes."

"She needs to eat, though," Sammish said.

"I hope she does. But she may not. Don't go in."

Sammish nodded, staring at the man's boots.

The redcloak sighed. "Or if you do, keep some of the medicine in a sleeve or in your shoe. They're desperate in there. They'd kill you and drink your blood if they thought it would help them."

"I know."

The redcloak sighed. "Be careful. And don't try to come back out. I don't want to be the one that kills you."

"Thank you," Sammish said, and ducked under the rope.

"Well. Look who lost her milk teeth," Goro had said. "All right, then. Let's talk."

Back in the Silt, Sammish had followed him with her heart in her throat. The cold had pressed itself so deeply into her feet that she couldn't feel the ground she walked over. The old man led her along pathways she didn't recognize. They passed a huge carved stone statue of a Hansch god that had cracked through at the chest and been abandoned. She was certain she'd have remembered it if she had seen it before, and yet only a few yards more and he was at the door to his little cabin, and waving her inside.

The little stove popped and snapped; the cheerful sounds of fire. Sammish sat beside it. Her cheeks hurt. Her ears hurt. She found herself weeping not from sorrow or distress, but the terrible awareness of how nearly frozen she had been now that the first bits of feeling were coming back. The old man closed the door.

"You can stay long enough to get warm," the wild man said. "Then you have to go. I have business today you've got no part in."

"Get a lot of custom here, do you?" Sammish joked, but Goro didn't laugh.

"People find me who need me. Sometimes I expect them. Sometimes I don't. You . . . you're a hard one to see. What does that come from?"

"I don't know what you mean."

The wild man sat on a little stool and hauled off his boots. His feet were pale as ice. "Never mind it, then," he said. "Let's try this instead. Why in the name of all gods together do you think I'm going to help you find Saffa now that she's gone?"

"I'm going to help her," Sammish said. And then, "If I can."

"You said that, but what's that to me?"

"She's your friend," Sammish said, but there was a sense of confusion growing in her. "You gave her shelter. You were trying to keep her safe."

Goro shrugged. "I did what I did. That doesn't say what I'm going to do. Saffa paid for everything she got here. Not in coin, maybe, but there was a price for it."

Sammish felt a sinking in her stomach. She was suddenly very aware of being a girl alone in a man's home. Goro must have seen the thought in her eyes. He barked out a laugh.

"No," he said. "I don't trade in that. But I do trade. You want my help, I'll want something back. A dream, maybe. Or a memory. Your best day, if you want. Or your worst."

"Are you serious?"

Goro shrugged. Sammish remembered the illusion of raw meat when he'd bitten into the stale bread the last time she'd been here. She liked magic better when it was fortune-tellers' pulls and the empty piety of priests.

"One memory's not too much," he said. "You forget things every day, and then forget that you forgot them. Everyone does. Feed me one, and you won't even notice it's gone."

Sammish leaned forward. Her feet ached now, which was better than feeling nothing. "I'll bring you bread for a week. It won't be fresh, but it'll keep you fed."

The wild man's smile seemed both feral and inexplicably affectionate. "You drive a hard bargain, but I'll take it if I can ask you a question. I won't eat it."

"You won't eat a question?"

"I promise. But, no offense, you're a Longhill street rat. I've known ones like you since I was young, and I'm older than you think. People like you live on the edge of not living at all. Three things go wrong, and the prison cart will be hauling your frozen corpse away with the horseshit. What are you doing this for?"

Sammish felt her jaw move, but she didn't know what she was going to say. If she was going to say anything. It seemed like something she should already know. She thought that she did, but now that someone—anyone—cared enough to ask, it was hard to find words for it. Only that it was bound up with Andomaka and Darro and Alys. And a little apartment that she'd imagined so many times that she could walk through it in her mind even though it didn't exist.

"I want to," she said. "I'm doing it because I want to."

"Best reason I've heard all day," Goro said. His feet were getting some color back in them, and he flexed and curled his toes half a dozen times before he hauled his boots back on. "All right. I'll help. But I'm not leaving the cabin, much less the Silt. It's my place here, and I like it. Also, I don't know where she is."

"So how are you going to help?"

"Why did Saffa come here?"

"To the city?"

"To the Silt."

It might only have been lack of sleep, but Sammish thought it was a stupid thing to ask. "Because Darro tried to kill her."

"That's what came before, true. But maybe there's a relationship, maybe there isn't. What makes you think that your boy Darro acting poorly would make her come *here*?"

"Someone's trying to kill you, you go where they can't."

"Seems wise, yeah? The way your friend holed up with Aunt Thorn when that bluecloak was looking to open her skull for her. Only Aunt Thorn has iron doors and guards. I don't. Did I lock you out?"

"She was just being hard to find," Sammish said. "The Silt's no place."

"Wasteland," Goro agreed. "Hard to find anyone out here, because there's no one here to find. No good way to get here. No reason to stay once you do. So there you are."

"Where I am?"

"Now you know how her mind works. Glad I could help. Now warm your hands up and get the fuck out of here. I told you, I have business. And don't think for a moment I'll let you off bringing me that bread. You agreed."

And in fact, Sammish had brought the bread. With all that and knowing what had happened to Orrel, it still took her days to understand where the Bronze Coast woman was hiding.

On the other side of the rope, the streets stank. No prison carts had made their way down these streets in weeks, and the shit and trash were piled on the paving stones. If it had been summer, the reek would have been terrible. With the winter still in its depths, the bodies of dogs and the turds and the sacks left on the ground after the food and water had been taken from them all had a white coating of frost. With no one leaving the quarantine, the people unlucky enough to live in these houses survived on a grain and water allotment from the Temple tossed in by the guards and whatever their friends and family could spare them. For someone whose neighbors disliked them, who had no one to help with their survival, plague was the second most likely thing to kill them.

Sammish turned a corner. The harsh, clean sunlight pushed through between the buildings on a little widening in the street where a dry cistern stood, its pipes capped by the city. The shutters around it were closed, but Sammish had the sense of people behind them. There were eyes on her, she was sure of it. If she'd been wrong in coming here, she'd been very, very wrong. She walked to the cistern, clambered onto its low stone wall, and tried for once to be seen.

"I've got medicine! Herbs from the hospital! And fresh water!" The white steam of her breath caught the sunlight, swirled, and vanished.

A set of brown, cracked shutters opened behind her. A girl no more than seven years old looked out. Sammish lifted a hand in welcome, but the girl didn't react. There was some movement at the doorway of a house, and then another a little farther down the street. Sammish dug through her bag and pulled out a little water jug. She held it up.

"I don't need money! I just want to talk!"

And find a foreign wizard woman who doesn't want me to find her. And get out of here without getting sick. And not have anyone put a knife in me so they can take all my things. Weirdly, the unspoken thoughts made her smile.

A thin man leaned out of a doorway. He might have been sick. He might only have been hungry. His hair was filthy, and he wore a tunic that might have been yellow or white or green once. Sammish smiled to him and held out the jug. He walked with a hitch in his step, like something had gone wrong with one leg. He made his way to the cistern and looked up at her. For a long moment, she wasn't sure he was going to speak.

"I'm Dannid."

"Sammish."

"I've lived here my whole life, and I've never seen you before. You don't have people here."

"I don't. And I'm looking for someone else who doesn't. She's older than me, and she'd have come just before the quarantine came up."

"Did she bring the plague?"

"I don't think so," Sammish lied. "She's older than me. Not from Kithamar. She has a mole on her face."

Dannid looked at the water jug, then back at Sammish's eyes. She saw the calculation going on in his mind. As tired and weak as he was, if it came to a fight, she thought she'd win. As long as no one came to join him. But there were more shutters opening now. Another door, farther down the street.

Sammish held out the water jug. "Ask your friends if they've seen her. I'll be here."

Dannid took it like he'd been given something precious, and not a double handful of baked mud around four swallows of water. "I'll ask," he said. It didn't matter much if he did. Another man came out into the street, and a thin woman behind him. Sammish wished she'd brought more to trade with, but she had what she could get. Wishing the world were different was a luxury.

The woman came forward next. She hadn't seen Saffa either,

but her child had the fever. Sammish gave her some of the herbs. And then a young boy came from another building. And then an older man. Sammish handed out something to each of them with a growing sense of fear. Every time her sack grew lighter, she was that much closer to failure.

She was giving a jar of nettle tea to a grey-haired man when she noticed another figure in the street. She hadn't seen what door the woman had come from or seen her step out around a corner. The woman no one had seen was simply there.

"Wait," Sammish said, grabbing the grey-haired man by the shoulder. When he turned back, she took a jar of water and some salt pork from the sack and handed him the rest. "You give it out, yeah? You know this place better than I do."

"Bless you," the old man said. "Thank you for this kindness."

Sammish hopped off the cistern wall and trotted toward Saffa. The attention of the street stayed with the sack and whatever might still be in it. Saffa turned her back and began to walk away, but not so quickly that Sammish couldn't catch up. She fell into step beside the Bronze Coast woman as she turned down a side street. The boundary rope cut across the next intersection like a line inked in the air.

She had thought so much about how to reach this moment, and now that it was here, she wasn't sure what to say. Saffa didn't seem inclined to help her either. At a narrow wooden doorway with a chain across it, she stopped, pulled at one of the boards, and the chain went slack enough to open. Saffa ducked inside, and Sammish followed before the door was closed against her.

Inside was a tiny room with a mattress of old straw, a night pot, and little else. Prisoners lived better than this. Saffa sat on the mattress with her legs crossed under her. Sammish stood. The silence between them was unbearable.

"Did you do this? The fever? I mean, did you make that happen?"

"I used what I found. Why are you following me?" Saffa said, and her voice was hard as stone.

"To help," Sammish said. "I have a plan. I mean, part of one. The shape of one." She paused, but the Bronze Coast woman didn't speak. Sammish balled her hands into fists and bulled ahead. "Andomaka took your boy. Probably he's at the brother-hood's house in Green Hill. I know where that is."

"As do I. How does that help me?"

"I can find their house, get in, draw you a map. If he's there, it'll help you get him out. If he's . . . if it's too late, it might be useful in other ways."

"You will be caught and killed."

"I won't. I'm good at not being noticed."

Saffa leaned forward, her elbows on her knees. It was a small shift, hardly more than a few inches, but it left the older woman looking exhausted instead of enraged. Sammish saw the softness of Saffa's cheek and the weight in her shoulders.

"He may be gone already. It is too late."

"Might be, might not. It doesn't matter," Sammish said. "You'll be trapped here until you know one way or the other. You'll live the rest of your life in ratholes like this. If all I can do is help you go free, then I can help you go free." Saffa shook her head, and Sammish felt an unexpected surge of frustration. "You thought the gods sent me last time. Maybe they sent me again. It's something to try."

"Why would you do this?"

"To get the plague out of my city, apparently. If I were smarter, I'd do it for money," Sammish said sharply.

"Why really?" Saffa asked, and there was a humor in her voice Sammish hadn't heard there before.

"You know, you and the old man seem awfully happy pushing after all my whys. Maybe let me worry about that," Sammish said.

The Bronze Coast woman bowed her head, but she was smiling.

Sammish found herself smiling back. "I assumed if you were here, you had a way to sneak back past the quarantine line. Hope I was right about that. Now, tell me what you know about what this blade is and how it works and what we're looking for."

Saffa did.

The first winter of Byrn a Sal's reign went on cold and harsh. Even as the days grew longer, the chill sank into the bones of the city. Old snow piled in niches and turned to grey and stinking ice. The air reeked of smoke from thousands of hearths. The brewers, whose trade never stopped, hired boys to chop through the ice on the canals and draw up the water from below that would be next month's beer. Andomaka stretched her awareness over it all like a skin over the mouth of a drum.

Now that she was to be prince of the city and carrier of the thread, what had been a lazy, soft spreading of her mind through the world had grown harsher. She drilled it like a guardsman or a soldier, but training for something stranger than war. With her eyes closed and her flesh relaxed, she pushed herself in ways she'd never done before. She felt the forges of the Smoke and tasted the brightness of the waste metal that poured into the river from them. The lectures at the university were like little headaches. The palace was a numbness. She tried to extend herself out past the city walls to the hospital and down the river to the south. Some days she could manage, but most she couldn't. On rare occasions, she knew something else, something from far away that wafted into her mind like a tendril of perfume from another room.

"Good," Ausai said with the young boy's throat. "You're doing very well. Slow your breath. Try to slow your heartbeat."

She tried, but it was difficult. Being aware of her body and the world at the same time was like breathing in and blowing out at once. She felt her concentration shift and slip. A grunt came from her throat, though she only heard it. It wasn't a thing she felt.

"It's all right if you can't," the boy who was the prince who was the city said. "Just try, and then be what you are. Know what you know."

She let her body go, and now her awareness was broader. She felt the world in ways she couldn't have without her mentor at her side. To the west of the city, a space of warmth and the smell of animals. She drifted to it, astounded to be so far from Kithamar.

"A caravan's coming," she said. "Three days?"

"A winter caravan?" Ausai said. "Someone took a risk."

"They have...peppercorns. And cloves."

She swirled back inside the city walls, carried like a dried leaf on the wind. She was dreadfully tired. She wanted to stop. But Ausai hadn't said she could. For a moment, she was in a dark place. Cold, and filled with rats. It was like using the candle to be in two places at once, but without the warmth and the light. There was a woman there, curled in the dark. The thought passed through her *Grey Linnet is dead* without knowing quite what it meant. If it meant anything. She felt a self-annihilating impulse like looking down from the top of a tower, and the terrible urge to step out into the void.

"I have to stop," she said. And then, "Please."

"Come back," Ausai said.

Andomaka opened her eyes. The feeling of nausea and being stretched too thin passed quickly. She rolled to her side. Her body felt heavy and slow. Waterlogged. But Ausai was sitting at her side, his boy's smile familiar. The eeriness of the prince's expression on this new face was fading, and she found herself thinking of Ausai as if he were the young man. As if he always had been.

He took her hand. "You've done very well. You have a talent I haven't seen in generations."

"Thank you," she said. She sat up.

The temple was cold despite the braziers and lanterns. Or perhaps that was only her. Tregarro stood against the wall, his arms crossed. When she nodded to him, he brought her a thick black mug of heated wine. The first sip of it felt like it might burn her, but then the warmth spread through her throat and chest.

"You are the most honored and powerful woman of your age," Ausai said, and his voice sounded like he was almost awed by her. She noticed her own pleasure at the compliment, felt the warmth of it like it was a different sort of wine. Ausai turned his attention to Tregarro. "Nothing more of my false grandniece?"

"Not yet, my prince," Tregarro said, and there was something odd about the color of his voice. First, that it had a color at all. Andomaka closed her eyes and let the oddness of that pass through her. Tregarro's words were the grained brown and beige of polished wood. Beautiful and hard. "The guardsman Garreth Left is Elaine's lover. We're certain of that. But they haven't met at his family's house since we found him. It's possible that there were more opportunities during harvest when the family house was empty. But our eyes are on it, and our knives are ready. When the moment comes, we will be there."

Something else tugged at Andomaka, but the dizziness was coming back. There was something about the winter caravan and why she'd been able to feel it when anything outside the city walls was so difficult for her. Tregarro took a step toward her, and she felt his concern as if it were her own.

The boy made a soft chucking sound deep in his throat. If he had been in the body Andomaka had known when she was younger, it would have been impatience. Perhaps it was still. He said, "We can afford to wait better than we can to hurry," but he said it with distaste. As if he were trying to talk himself into believing it.

Ausai's gaze softened, seeing something she couldn't imagine. Where the world and Tregarro and her own flesh were all weirdly present, Prince Ausai seemed to stop at his skin. What was within him was hidden from her like a face behind a carnival mask. As if he had heard her, his attention returned, and he put his thin young hand on her shoulder. "You are everything I had hoped for. You are going to save Kithamar."

The news swept through every quarter west of the river. Every taproom was alive with it. The guild halls were filled by meetings where merchants and artisans decried or defended it, and more than once the city guard were called to keep the arguments from spilling onto the frozen streets. The shutters in the magistrate's office and the tax post showed glimmers of lantern light well into the night as clerks and lawyers read through contracts, guild agreements, and city law.

A winter caravan had come.

Outside the temple gate, a rough corral had been built. A dozen small, shaggy Inlisc horses stood in it, snow caking their coats. Half as many wagons made a rough circle, their leather sides rimed with frost. The caravan master was a thick man with a beard as scraggly as his horses, and a calm that said he'd anticipated the scandal and thought it was funny.

Three merchant families had quietly commissioned it. The risk had been huge, and the gamble had paid out. Now, with the river still locked in ice and spring little more than the occasional less-biting afternoon breeze, the sponsors of the caravan had a jump on spice contracts. By the time the boats and wagons arrived, orders would be filled and markets glutted. Fortunes had just been gambled. The audacious had won, and the houses and families who stood to lose were all frantic as a kicked ant-hill as they looked for some way to unwind what had already happened. The brewers' windows had started taking bets on whether the issue would end in murder, and while the odds weren't good yet, there were plenty of people in Longhill and Seepwater willing to put a bronze or two on it as a kind of prayer. *Please let the wealthy and powerful suffer a little bit too.*

For the rest of Longhill, it meant groups of people meeting, which meant a chance to run a pull. It meant sneaking messages and money over the city wall to cut side deals with the caravan before the guilds approved or the taxes were levied. It meant the anger and fear of men and women with money to spend, and there were more ways to shave a bit of silver off that than there were stars in the sky. All it took was being clever enough to find them. For Alys, what mattered was that one of the families behind the caravan was called Left, and their disgraced son was a bluecloak who had been spilling salt with the girl she was meant to kill.

Andomaka hadn't been able to find them a time when the assignation would be most likely to happen, so Alys and Ullin had set up a rough watch of their own, trading day for day. She'd spent the morning before finding plausible reasons to pace through the streets of Riverport, circling back to the house with blue shutters. Everyone she saw, she cataloged. There was the old man, the pinched woman, the rooster—that was a small man with angry eyes and a chest that preceded him through the doorway. There was an Inlisc girl whom she'd seen more than once with porcelain-smooth skin and full brown lips who looked like she could be someone's lover, but Tregarro was adamant that the one they wanted was Hansch. And once, three streets over, she'd seen a group of three bluecloaks, the youngest of whom bore a resemblance to the old man. She'd even spent part of an hour following him, but the city guards had done nothing more than harass a vendor who was shy on his tax bill and break up a fight outside a taproom. She'd committed his face to memory, though. If she saw him again, she'd know him. If he was being discreet with a Hansch girl, she'd know that too.

That and feet so cold they'd gone numb and bloodless were all the day had brought her, and Ullin's turn was up now. The next day she'd be out again, and there was more than one problem with that.

"A few days in a row?" Alys said, keeping her voice low enough that it didn't carry even as far as the next table. "I can be overlooked. But every time I go is another chance that someone will take note. And then what happens?"

Sammish shrugged. Her gaze seemed to focus somewhere off Alys's left shoulder. Her friend had grown thinner since they'd seen each other last. It was a look Alys had seen before when someone's fortunes had started to slip. When the choice was between freezing in the street or not eating, starvation killed you slower. In the summer, it might have been different. Sammish might have taken the coin that paid for her bed and used it for a bowl of trout or a sack of walnuts. Warm nights in Kithamar had their dangers, but they were easier to live through than the cold. But here Alys was, with good work for solid money, and Sammish couldn't be bothered to pay her full attention.

"You're perfect for this," Alys said. "It's like being the walkaway, but there's not even that chance of getting caught. You didn't do anything. And when the time comes, you won't be the blade. You'll be here, or at some brewer's house, or sitting on a bench with half a dozen bluecloaks. It won't matter. You come be our eyes for a few days, and I'll see that Andomaka pays you."

Sammish shook her head, and Alys's impatience ratcheted up again.

"This will get you enough to last to thaw. It's not even a hard pull. I don't know why you're being stubborn about it."

"Stubborn," Sammish said. Alys was starting to wonder if maybe the girl was drunk on hunger. It happened. Someone hadn't eaten in a few days and their mind went soft sometimes. Maybe what she needed to do was get a bowl of broth and a crust of bread, then explain the offer again. But when Sammish spoke again, her words were clearer and sharp at the edges. "What are you doing?"

"I just told you," Alys said. "He brings the girl to his old house. We're learning the place. When we see the rhythm of it, we can—"

"You can *what*? Murder a girl because your Green Hill friends told you to?"

"Keep your voice down!"

Sammish did, leaning forward and speaking low, but her words had a serrated edge. "What do you tell yourself this is? You went into it because you wanted to know Darro didn't die because of you. You've known that for months. You think this girl you're stalking after killed him? She didn't, and what's more, you don't think she did. You don't *care* whether she did."

The same irrational fear she'd felt in her dreams poured into Alys's chest like ice water filling a cask. She leaned back on her bench and scowled at Sammish like she was scolding a dog that had nipped at her.

Sammish wouldn't be stopped. "You've never killed anything

more than a rat, and now you're some kind of assassin? A year ago, you'd have turned away from a pull like this in half a heartbeat. Now you don't ask anything about it, just put your head down and bull forward. And do you know why?"

"I don't know what's wrong with you. I'm done with this."

Sammish's hand was quick as a snake; her fingers wrapped around Alys's wrist like a guardsman's rope. "Because you're so afraid to stop and look. This whole plan to take on your brother's work isn't about getting justice. It's not even about getting revenge. It's about not having him be dead, but he is. He's *dead*. You're turning yourself into him so that he'll still be in the world, and who gives a shit if it eats you while it happens? And what's more, it's not even working. You're not him. You aren't, and you never will be."

Alys made her voice deep and hard. It barely shook at all. "You're hurting," she said. "Take your hands off me. Now."

For a moment, it seemed like Sammish wouldn't. Like she'd grind Alys's bones together in her grip out of spite. Her scowl looked like hatred. Worse, it looked like contempt. She let Alys go.

"He wasn't this, Alys. What you've become, with your swagger and your intrigues? He wasn't like that. You're being what you wish he'd been, but Darro was just another Longhill knife running the pulls he could find, same as the rest of us. He wasn't loyal. He wasn't powerful. He wasn't your pale bitch's lap dog. This that you're doing? It doesn't even rhyme with him."

Alys stood up too fast. The bench scraped against the brisk floor. From the next table, Nimal and Cane looked over, curiosity and amusement in their eyes. Alys leaned in, towering over Sammish as best she could and pointing a hard finger at her with each word. "I tried to help you. *I* helped *you*."

She turned to the door, wide steps and head high to convince herself that she didn't feel the sting of tears in her eyes. She more than half expected Sammish to call her name or rush over to take her elbow and pull her back to the table. If she had, Alys would have gone, but the taproom door opened on the frost-bound street and nothing came. When she glanced back, Sammish was sitting where she had been, her face in her hands. It wasn't grief or regret. Maybe exhaustion. Alys let the door close behind her.

For the first few streets, her heart felt like the raw spot where a scab had been ripped off too soon. But each corner she passed, each wagon and wheelbarrow that creaked in her way, each voice raised in the cold, the pain turned warmer. By the time she passed into Newmarket, her mind was red with rage. Sammish was jealous. Of course she was. She'd been half a step from streetbound while Alys was paid from the coffers of Green Hill. But that wasn't Alys's fault. She'd offered to share. She'd tried to. When Sammish had wandered over to Stonemarket in the killing chill, Alys had taken her in.

Besides that, Alys hadn't needed the girl's help in any of this. Everything important that she'd done, she'd done on her own. If Sammish hadn't wanted to be part of it, she could have kept her narrow ass in Longhill where it belonged. Alys would still have found that first black candle. She would still have taken the knife to Green Hill. Sammish hadn't been the one to catch Andomaka's eye. Sammish hadn't taken Tregarro's contract or faced down slavemasters for the Bronze Coast boy. And every-thing that Sammish had said about Darro...Alys didn't want to think about what Sammish had said about Darro.

Why won't you look at my face?

A dog darted out ahead of her too close, and she swung her club, catching its side. The dog yipped and ran away. If Alys felt a flicker of regret, it didn't last. "Next time stay out of my way," she called after it. But she kept watching long enough to reassure herself it wasn't limping.

The houses that lined the streets grew a little taller. The streets grew wide enough for two carts to pass each other and room between them. To the west, she heard the high whistle of the bluecloaks summoning help to a fight, and she tacked east away from it. At some point, she must have been weeping, because her cheeks ached now where salt and cold conspired against them. She rubbed her face with her palms until the pain went away. And before Ullin saw her.

He was lounging in a doorway, smoking a clay pipe with the half-impatient air of someone waiting for a late friend. When he saw her, his eyebrows lifted a degree. Alys found a bit of wall beside him and put her back against it.

"Didn't think you'd be here today," he said.

"Life's full of these little shocks," she said acidly, and he laughed.

"Well, then I don't have to wait to share the good news. I saw them."

Sammish and the humiliation of the taproom vanished like a candle flame being snuffed. Ullin smiled and spat smoke.

"The old man and the young one—the pretty boy—took the Inlisc girl off in a carriage. I think to a guild meeting or the magistrate. Sun hadn't moved two fingers in the sky before our boy Garreth was at the door. And a woman travelling alone not long after that."

Alys felt her breath grow shallow, but Ullin shook his head. "They're not there now. The carriage came back before I could manage anything, and I don't like going into this sort of job by myself. But if our love dogs come here when those three are gone, we have a way to predict the meetings. And I saw how the happy couple snuck out. Which means I know how we can sneak in too."

The day had been hard, that was all. The sick feeling in Alys's gut was only the whiplash of Sammish's unexpected cruelty and this happy surprise. *You've never killed anything more than a rat* rose in her mind. For a moment, she felt younger than she was, and alone in a way she didn't want to understand. She realized Ullin was waiting for her to say something, so she answered him.

"Good."

S ad Linly walked—trudged, rather—through the frost-bound streets, her knees aching to announce a change in the weather. The cold bit, but not as sharply as it had even last week. Any breeze more powerful than a breath had the killing threat of winter, but find a patch of sunlight and still air, and it was almost warm. If she had gone outside the city walls, she would have seen no leaves on the trees, and underbrush like twigs with only the crisp brown remnants of the last year clinging to it. But the bark might have had a touch of green on it. The withered limbs might have been just a bit less withered. It wasn't springtime, but it was the promise that springtime would appear. And her knees ached. Change was coming.

Every doorway she passed, she knew. She'd lived her whole life in Longhill, and rarely gone even as far as the eastern side of the river. Some deep, atavistic part of her still thought of it as the Hansch city rather than another part of Kithamar. She liked being where the people all looked like her, slept like her, ate the foods she ate even if they were the cheapest parts the butcher had on offer. Growing up, she'd felt safe in Longhill. Now she'd lost two of her three children and was on her way to losing the third. And still, she was out of her little room, away from her housemates, and looking for her friend.

Grey Linnet hadn't always been Grey Linnet any more than she herself had been born Sad Linly. She'd known the woman since they were both girls. Linly and Linnet, drinking to match the boys in the taproom and breaking hearts and cocks. The memories were bawdy and distant and more than a little shameful. They kept her warm.

These days, Grey Linnet kept a little room not too far from Seepwater. Big Salla had come to Linly yesterday asking if she knew where Grey Linnet was. No one had seen her, and the children wanted to go to the Silt and look for treasures. She'd told the children that the river was solid. It wouldn't be washing up anything new until after thaw, but Big Salla wouldn't be moved. And it was best to check on Linnet. She might be sick or hurt, and Longhill looked after its own.

Linly reached the alley and turned down it. Linnet's door was old wood with a leather hinge, and she slapped it with the palm of her hand. "Linnet? Are you in there, you old bag? Are you all right?"

No one answered. The door was latched, but the hinge was weak. It wasn't hard to make enough of a crack to slide in her boot knife and lift the catch. It had been a long time since she'd forced a door, but it was a skill that faded slowly.

She knew before she saw the body. It wasn't rot; the world was too cold for that. But death had a smell all its own. The only light was from the door, and it was enough to see Linnet there on her cot, curled up. The brazier beside her was scorched where the wood had been, and ashes lay in the bowl. The rats hadn't taken to her, which was a kindness. In death, she looked younger. Or if not younger, at peace. Spring was coming, that was true. But not for Linnet.

Linly sat on the end of the cot and patted the dead woman's thigh as if she could still be comforted.

"Good work, you," she said. "No more Linly and Linnet, I guess, but that's mine to carry. You did good work. You should rest proud."

There was no answer, nor had she expected one. Everything that rose, fell. Everything born, died. The only questions ever were when and who was left behind.

She sat there, communing with the dead woman for a time, then went to find a bluecloak who could call for the body men.

The weather was foul and threatening storm the second time Sammish went to Green Hill—low, angry clouds and a wind damp enough to leave the cobbles slick.

She'd thought that taking away the banners and decorations of the harvest festival would leave the quarter looking less than it had, but the truth was the absence only changed it. It was like seeing someone in a gilt mask shaped like a wolf, and then removing it to discover they'd been a panther all along. Green Hill in the midst of harvest had been a cacophony of magic and illusion. Green Hill at the trailing edge of winter, standing as it was under a low and ominous sky, was wide and austere. Its houses were clad in stone, its streets so clean it was hard to believe they'd been used, and the servants and low courtiers who walked under its bare arbors and leafless trees would all have been beautiful in Seepwater or Longhill.

Sammish felt like an impostor just breathing the same air that they did. Which, fair enough, she was.

She and Saffa stayed off the larger avenues where the carriages and litters travelled, keeping to the narrower alleys and back ways meant for servants and mules. The brotherhood's house had been designed to be seen from the front, but even this oblique view of it impressed Sammish. It was less a building and more a small quarter to the city in itself. Ivy rose along its walls, and a patio in carved marble led to its public temple. Its private rites and mysteries were available only to those invited in, but Kithamar had more gods than sparrows, and most of them gave out a free taste to whoever wanted it. The fountain at the patio's side was empty, the pipes dry against the winter cold. In summer, it would have been astounding.

The nearest thing to the Daris Brotherhood in her experience was Aunt Thorn's little fortress beneath Longhill, but even that would have needed ten of its own kind stacked one atop the other to match the brotherhood's compound. It would have been the central fact of any other district of Kithamar. In Green Hill, it was one ostentation among many.

Sammish wore a servant's dress she'd borrowed from Averith, who'd kept it from when her sister had taken a place at a Riverport merchant's house. The sister was dead now from a bad childbirth, but the dress was decent, and it almost fit her. Saffa walked at her side, a brown cloak pulled tight around her, a hood concealing her hair and her features. Sammish could feel the anxiety in the older woman's walk and see it in the way she held her shoulders. She tried to imagine what it would be like, coming so close to the home of your enemy. Whether the urge to run back from the danger or forward into the fray would be stronger. She didn't know, and it didn't matter.

"I should wait for you," Saffa said.

"You shouldn't," Sammish said. "You should walk around the outside of the compound with me once the way we planned. You should look for any signs your son might have left to guide a rescue. And then you should go back to your hole in Stone-market and wait for me."

Saffa didn't answer. She didn't need to.

"We'll be fine," Sammish said. "This will work."

"You don't know that."

Sammish shrugged. Of course she didn't.

Riverport wasn't quite in riot, but the energy in every passing stranger spoke of its anxiety and unease. The magistrates were taking up the complaint against the winter caravan, just the way everyone had known they would. The guilds and merchant houses were in array against each other. Fortunes were going to be made and lost before the sun set. Even if Garreth Left's family hadn't been at the center of the controversy, they'd likely have gone to watch. Everyone else would be there. As it was, the house was as good as promised to be empty for the lovers to use. The sky was dark with low, blue-grey clouds that blotted out the sun, and the breeze had a thick, eerie texture that told Alys worse was coming. More snow, maybe. Or something worse.

"You're upset," Ullin said.

"I'm paying attention. You should be paying attention too."

They were walking around the household of the family Left the way they would have if they'd meant to rob it: changing their appearance a little each time they passed, coming together one time and apart the next, never looking quite the same way twice. If she was still angry—not that she was, but if—it was only that Sammish should have been with them on the pull. But Sammish was too busy being a little shit, so never mind her.

What Alys hated was the way her once-friend had corrupted her own tools. She'd spent months now growing into Darro's shoes. She walked the way he'd walked, swung her club the way he'd swung his, held herself the way she remembered his body. But now when she did, Sammish's voice threaded its way into her mind like a thistle in a wool cloak. *This that you're doing? It doesn't even rhyme with him.* How would she know? Darro wasn't her brother. Sammish hadn't grown up around Darro and his friends. No one liked Sammish. Not even Alys, now.

But it irritated her that Sammish had been able to put that grit into her wheels. Trying to make her doubt her connection with her brother was unforgivable, and that Sammish had almost, sort of, halfway managed it was worse.

"To the right," Ullin said. His voice was light and casual, but the words hit her all the same. And yes, there ahead of them was the bluecloak, only he wasn't wearing his blue cloak or his badge of office. He was just a young man with a sword at his hip and an anxious look in his eyes. Alys looked down and started counting her steps to fifty the way Darro had told her. The way Darro would have done himself.

"Girl?" she said quietly.

"Not that I've seen yet," Ullin said. She could hear his smile. "We will, though. Today is our day."

She imagined telling Andomaka it was done and saw the pleasure in the pale woman's face. The gratitude. She knew she had to hold that image if she was going to get through to night-fall. *You've never killed anything more than a rat.*

"We're strong. We can do this," she said, and took a firmer grip on her club.

Sammish felt bored and a little bit put upon. Normally it was easy. She would just be the girl who was like that, and it happened, simple as putting on a jacket. Today it was hard. Her body was vibrating with fear and hope and an anger that she'd been carrying so consistently that she was starting to wonder if it would ever pass. Taking all of that and fitting it into a version of her that was just moving through another dull day in order to reach an uninteresting night was like pulling a sock over a street cat. Might be possible, but it also might not.

It didn't help that she'd had two stale rolls and a finger's length of dried fish for food in the last two days.

She trudged down the pathway to a servants' entrance where a man and woman were talking. She didn't look at either of them, just moved forward like she'd rather be doing something else, shifted by the man and in through the doorway.

"Hey!" the man said, which was a bad sign. He shouldn't have noticed her at all. "Where do you think you're going?"

"Need my pan," she said, and shrugged. She trundled into the shadows of the house and the man went back to his conversation. The hardest part was done. Once she'd passed into the space that the brotherhood commanded, the assumption would be that she belonged there. She made her steps slow and not particularly stealthy. Thieves were quick and quiet. She wasn't a thief. She was just trying to get back her pan from the girl who'd borrowed it. It was only because she was low and small and unimportant that she walked quietly but with purpose, as though she knew where she was going and required neither help nor permission. She wasn't trying to hide, just not to give offense. Inoffensive was, as far as Sammish saw it, another word for invisible.

She knew in general terms what she was looking for. The pale woman, her scarred chief servant, the temple they served, and the secure rooms—a pit, a jail, a barred room—where the boy prisoner might be held. But she wasn't searching. She was just going to get her pan back, and it was always just a bit ahead and down another turn or two. She knew the way, even if the understanding changed with each corner and hallway. Sammish, bored and a little put upon over her panic, made her way through the brotherhood, committing every bit of it to memory and waiting for something interesting to catch her sharp and secret attention.

The Hansch girl came soon after, as if blown by the first gusts of storm. Ullin pointed her out as soon as she came around the corner, but he didn't need to. Her cloak had its hood up to hide her face, and she walked with a bad actor's version of casual ease. If she'd been on a pull, she'd have been caught by the guard before she'd had a chance to do anything. Alys imagined herself walking down the street toward her, killing her there before anyone could stop her. In her imagination, she felt the club come down on the girl's skull, hard and soft at once. Instead, she bent down and pretended to be working something free of her boots as the girl went to the same low point in the wall that her lover had crossed. She actually stopped there, glancing up and down the street before she hoisted herself over.

"Not the smartest thing, is she?" Ullin said. "Taking her out before she can breed will be doing the world a favor."

"How long do we wait?" Alys said, and then felt stupid for asking. It was something she should have known already. Darro would have.

Ullin shrugged. "The magistrates are going to take all day. They've got the place to themselves, more or less. But true love gets its skirts up quick, and I'd rather catch them distracted."

"So, now?" Alys said. She didn't feel right. Usually she could imagine Darro and then mimic him, but she felt bright and tense and nauseated. She couldn't imagine her brother ever skating the edge of fear like this. Ullin rested his hand on the pommel of his blade. His eyes were as bright as a drunkard's.

"Now," he said.

Alys watched the street one direction, Ullin the other. When both looked clear, they stepped out of their niche, made their way across the street, and swung over the wall. Not running, but moving quick and smooth. Purpose didn't draw eyes the way thrashing did.

The far side of the wall was a kitchen garden. Herb beds stood bare and empty, ready for planting. A black iron stove and a clay oven stood at the wall. Alys could hardly imagine the luxury of cooking in your own courtyard. Longhill's relationship with fire would never have allowed it.

Ullin passed over to a red lacquered door that opened under his hand. He drew his sword. It was a little shorter than his forearm, and had no adornments. It looked brutal. She hefted her club. Ullin passed inside, and she followed.

The hallway within was stuccoed the warm yellow of summer sunlight made sullen by the low, angry sky. They moved down it quietly. The floor was smooth stone, and Alys rolled her feet heel to toe to keep her steps from tapping. She was sick with the fear of a servant opening a door or coming out in front of them, but the house was silent. It made sense. The disgraced son of the family had chosen this moment for his tryst because the place would be empty. The same things that covered his transgression would cover theirs.

The hall reached two sets of blue doors and a thin stairway leading up to what Alys assumed were the household's family rooms. As Ullin put his hand to the nearer of the doors, gently lifting its latch, Alys saw something on the stairs. A smudge of dirt hardly longer than her thumb, but fresh and the same rich soil as the garden. For a moment, she hesitated. If Ullin led them the wrong way, they might run out of time. They'd have to try again another day. It wouldn't even be her fault. The idea of leaving with the deed undone was almost worth having to do it all again. But only almost.

She put a hand on Ullin's shoulder, and when he glanced back, she pointed up. He nodded, and carefully, they ascended.

She really did want her pan. That it didn't exist, had never existed, didn't matter. It was hers, and she had need of it, and she wanted it back. If anyone stopped her now, she wouldn't even be lying. Magic knives and foreign wizards and stolen boys weren't any business of hers. Just her pan.

Behind that, Sammish's fear was starting to fade. She was in her element now, dull as dust and twice as common. In her mind, the brotherhood was coming together corridor by corridor, room by room, window by courtyard by stair. Here was a sculpture in marble of a chained god whose name she didn't know. Here was a shuttered window that looked down over the street, its glass fogged by time and wear. Here was a door with a complex brass lock and a stool built into the wall at its side. Landmarks. She held the map in her mind, and drew it there.

And it was in that map that she began noticing something odd. Curved halls and straight but without doorways between them. They almost reminded her of the way the streets of Longhill had been built to tame the wind. She imagined it all had some religious significance. The part of her that wanted her pan back didn't particularly care, but her secret self pricked up its ears and led her deeper in. She'd heard of temples built this way—open to the air, but also not.

The walls there were rosewood with lanterns that looked like tin and glass but were probably silver and crystal. Voices carried from behind her, but only in talk. Not alarm.

She made another turn and came into a wide, round room.

Even if the altar stone hadn't been there, she would have known it for a temple. Tapestries hung along the wall with images worked into them. Some seemed to be weird, near-human forms. Others were more like the drawings the university lecturers drew when they were talking about the relationships between numbers and shapes and music and stars. The floor was wood inlaid with curves of white stone that made interlocking circles and ellipses, and where the lines met, lanterns burned. She half expected to find a god sitting in the shadows and playing dice.

Instead, she found the boy.

He was sitting on the altar like it was a table, and he was playing some little game, but it wasn't dice. He wore a simple robe, warm against the chill air. A brazier on high iron legs was beside him, and the smoke from it was fragrant. She turned to leave, and he looked up. His expression was mildly curious. *Sorry. Need my pan* was on her lips, but she saw his eyes and the shape of his face. The color of his hair. He was older than she'd imagined him from Saffa's stories.

Her heart beat like bird wings and any thought of her false story blew away like ashes in a high wind. The boy's eyebrows rose as he saw her better.

"Timu?" she said.

"Who are you?" His voice sounded a bit like Saffa's too. The same reed-like music in it, but without her accent.

"Your mother sent me," she said. "I've come to get you home."

There were voices. Alys heard them as they reached the landing. A man and a woman, too indistinct to make out words, but the tone wasn't of love. If the hope had been to catch them together in the throes of passion, it didn't seem likely.

The floors at this higher level were of dark wood sealed with oil and hard wax, and they shone like stones in the river. Windows with a dozen palm-sized panes set in lead filled the hall with soft light and looked out over the herb garden below. Window boxes with living green plants stood in the light and brought a sense of the garden into the space, protected from the hissing winds outside. It was beautiful.

It occurred to Alys that this was a home. People lived here, with these solid walls and bright windows. The grand halls of Green Hill never struck her as human. They were too grand, too strange. But this was like Longhill could have been if it had been richer, surer, less desperate. It made the house feel obscene.

Ullin shot an angry look at her, and she realized she'd made a little sound—grunt or laugh or growl—deep in her throat. She nodded, half apology, half merely acknowledging that she'd made a mistake. But the voices hadn't changed. She and Ullin had gone unnoticed so far. They crept forward, trying to keep the floor from creaking. Her hands ached.

The closer they came, the clearer the voices grew. Both were distressed, but in different ways. The guardsman spoke in a low, controlled voice, less anger than tight frustration. Or fear. The girl's voice was higher. Not shrill, not chiding, but rich with pain that bordered on despair. Whatever they were to each other, it didn't sound as if it was going well.

"It's the same for me," the boy said.

"Nothing is the same for us," the dead girl said. "It can't be. We aren't the same."

"That isn't what I meant."

"I know." And then a long breath later, and more softly, "I know."

Ullin reached the door that the voices had come from, even as they stopped. There was some softer sound. A rustling of cloth.

Maybe the two were finally done talking and getting around to the business of sex. Alys felt almost dizzy, with a growing sense of not being the one inside her body. Her mouth was dry.

"Do we go in?" she whispered, and from the other side of the door, the boy said *What's that?*

Ullin pressed his lips thin—annoyance and disappointment. She'd gotten it wrong again. She didn't have time to say she was sorry for it. Ullin took a step back, kicked the door open, and they charged inside. Alys—shamed, frightened, divorced from herself, and ready for murder—followed after.

Timu blinked, shook his head, and laughed once as if at a joke only he understood. For a tense moment, she thought he was going to refuse her. Then he took her hand, and she smiled, trying to be reassuring. This wasn't her plan, and never had been. Sneak in, map the place, sneak out, and then make a plan was very different from sneak in, grab the boy, and run like hell.

"If we find anybody, let me talk," she said.

"What will you tell them?"

"That..." Her mind danced. "That they saw lice in your hair, and Andomaka's having me bathe you and shave your head."

"That's good," Timu said. "You know Andomaka's name."

"We have friends in common," Sammish said, and led him back along the way she'd come. "I mean, not always friends we like much, but there you have it."

"Not that way," Timu said. "Follow me."

He tugged her toward the back of the temple. She didn't like it. Retreat was never the time to go exploring, but he'd been in the house longer than she had, and apparently with enough freedom that they left him unguarded. Which was odd.

"Hurry," he said, pulling at her, and Sammish let herself be led deeper into the brotherhood's house. He ducked behind one of the tapestries, and back to a curving hall that it concealed. She went ahead of him. For the story to make sense, she had to be the one taking him. He had lice. She was fixing that. She tried to believe it, but something was wrong. The back of her mind wouldn't let the new story fit.

"Where is she?" Timu asked quietly.

"What?"

"My mother. Where is she? She's in the city?"

"Yes," Sammish said. Once they got out of the brotherhood's house, they'd either have to head south through Green Hill toward Stonemarket or north to the bridge to Riverport. The first got them to Saffa faster, but it meant going through more of Green Hill. Leaving the quarter fast might be better, even if it meant half a day's walk through the eastern half of the city. But she shouldn't be thinking about that. The pan or the lice or something else. She was thinking like someone trying to escape, and so if anyone saw her, that's what they would see.

"Where?" the boy asked.

"She's safe. I'll get you to her."

"But where is she?"

They turned another corner and what had been a hall opened into a narrow courtyard with winter-killed ivy climbing up the face of the walls. There was no one there. Their luck couldn't hold much longer. The sky was the grey-blue of slate, dark as twilight though the sun wouldn't fall for hours. Distant thunder rumbled. The first real storm of springtime. It would help if it kept people in the homes and taprooms. Assuming they got that far.

"How do we get to the street?"

"It isn't far this way. But where is she?"

She was reluctant to answer, and she didn't know why. Maybe

only because she was in the heart of the enemy's place, and it seemed like bad luck. That, and it kept her from thinking about the lice. Fortunately, the boy was at ease. Bad enough that she couldn't focus, but if he was acting like a prisoner slipping his chains, they'd be caught for certain.

And he wasn't. He wasn't acting that way at all.

Sammish's skin crawled as she understood what the back of her mind had been screaming since she stepped into the temple. The thing looked back at her with the boy's too-innocent eyes.

Alys saw it all in an instant. The bedroom larger than any she had ever seen; the rooms she'd taken from Darro could have fit inside it. The bed with four posts holding up thin, gauzy fly netting. A scholar's desk under a window with paper shutters that let in soft light while hiding the room from prying eyes. The walls painted with flowers.

The girl, on the end of the bed, had taken off her cloak. Her gown was pale. The city guardsman, her lover, had rough canvas trousers and was naked from the waist up, and held a sword in his hand.

All this between one sprinting footstep and the next.

And then, chaos.

Ullin went for the boy, swinging hard for his ribs. The boy parried with the speed of instinct, pushing in toward the attack to get inside Ullin's guard. The girl—the target, the reason they were all here—stood as if she were about to command them all to stop.

Alys swung her club, cracking the girl on the shoulder and spilling her to the floor. She was aware of Ullin and the guard to her right, and one of them shouting. Her hands ached from the blow she'd delivered. The girl looked up at her from the floor with fear and surprise and something else. Rage, maybe. Alys lifted her club, ready to bring it down on the girl's skull, but when she swung, her victim was bolting for the door. Alys shifted, but only caught the girl a glancing blow across the neck, and that with the haft of the club. If it had been a blade, it would have opened her throat.

Ullin shouted something, but Alys was grabbing at the girl's collar, trying to haul her back. If she could just knock her down again, she could finish it. They pulled at each other like children wrestling in the street, but without the play. The girl slipped loose, slammed out the door, and Alys, shrieking, followed. The girl was down the hall, head lowered and sprinting. Alys loped behind her. They went down the wooden stairs in a tumble, and out into the herb garden. The girl went for the low point in the wall, but Alys knew she would. She swung her club in a fast, vicious arc just ahead of her fleeing victim. The stone at the top of the wall split under the blow. The girl pulled back, and Alys put the wall behind her, cutting off the girl's escape.

They faced each other, feinting to one side and then the other. Alys really saw her for the first time. Thin Hansch face. Light hair. She looked vaguely familiar, but not so much that Alys recognized her. From the house, someone screamed, but whether it was Ullin or the guardsman, she couldn't tell.

If the girl turned to the house, Alys could cock back her club, swing, and take her in the back of the head. If she pushed through to climb the wall, Alys could bring her down there. She was sure of it. She only needed for the girl to choose which way she was moving when she died.

Only she didn't. Her arm hung wrong from the shoulder. Broken, likely, from the hit Alys had landed. Mud streaked the girl's face. Alys didn't know where that had come from. The girl stood there, looking Alys in the eyes. Somewhere far away, thunder rumbled.

You have to kill her, Alys thought in Tregarro's voice. *You don't have a choice.*

And then Darro. *Why won't you look at my face?* Despair radiated from the girl's expression.

Alys stepped to the side, clearing the way to the wall and the city beyond it. The girl didn't take the bait, and Alys was shocked to realize it wasn't bait. It didn't matter what Tregarro or Andomaka wanted. It didn't matter what Darro would have done. They weren't in the garden and Alys was.

"Why are you waiting?" Alys snapped. "Run!"

"This isn't the right way," she said, trying to keep her voice from shaking. "We have to go the other way."

"No," the thing in the boy's skin said, using the boy's voice. "Keep coming. This is right."

"You can go on your own, then. You don't need me. I'm going back."

Sammish tried to pull her hand free, but the boy's grip tightened, and his eyes went hard. The pretend game was over. When he spoke again, his voice was lower. "You are going to tell me where she is."

"Fine, then," Sammish said, stepping toward him, then dropped her full weight against his hand, pushing where his thumb and fingers met, just the way she would have against a bluecloak's restraining grip. Whatever the thing was, it hadn't practiced holding a Longhill street rat in check. Her arm free, she turned and bolted. Its voice rose behind her, screaming for the house guards. Good. Better that it call for help than that it follow on her heels. By the time they knew what they were looking for, she had to be someplace else or she'd die. She was certain of that.

She made it to the temple, hopped over the altar stone, scattering the beads of the game and knocking over a lantern as she passed. If she was lucky, they'd stop to keep it from putting the house to fire. The map she'd built in her mind was of a place she'd only seen once now, and that from the other direction. Fear muddied it. A wrong turn could put her at a dead end or in a guard tower. She didn't think. She only ran.

She'd passed a window coming into the temple maze. The one with the foggy glass and the shutters. It was where she headed now. Behind her, more voices were rising loud. A horn blatted the alarm. She couldn't outrun sound. The window came before her. It wasn't as wide as she'd remembered, but the glass was old and the wooden shutters thick. She yanked the wood down, putting all her weight on the hinges until they bent and gave way. A plank of wood half the size of her body with splinters at the edge. She braced herself against it and ran, putting her shoulder behind it, shouting as if her voice alone could shatter the glass.

The window broke, and she scrambled up through the hole where it had been. It was a longer drop to the ground than she'd expected. This part of the brotherhood's house was built on a hill, and the alley below her was lower than it should have been. She didn't hesitate. For a long, terrible second, she fell. There was time enough to wonder if it had been the best idea.

The alleyway hit the bottom of her feet. Her knees snapped up into her chest, knocking her breath out. She had to run, but she couldn't even stand up. The horn sounded behind her again, and a roll of thunder.

She pulled herself up to standing, swung one foot forward, put her weight on it. She could walk. As she did, she pulled her cloak off, pulling the sleeves through so that the paler fabric on the inside faced out. By the time she reached a corner where the alley joined a larger way, she was wearing what looked like a different cloak. She took a length of string from her pocket and tied back her hair. She was limping, but that was fine. It didn't seem like the glass had cut her, or if it had, she wasn't bleeding badly enough that it showed.

The house of the Daris Brotherhood boiled with guards and servants like a kicked hornet's nest. She glanced back at it with mild curiosity, wondering what all that was about. Whatever it was, it was nothing to do with her. She turned south, trundling down the street. Her feet ached. Her knee hurt. There was a storm coming.

All that, and she still had to get her pan.

The bluecloaks came even before the family returned, their whistles calling guardsmen and curious citizens alike. Even when the first fat raindrops fell, the citizens of Riverport huddled under awnings and lifted their hoods rather than look away. The trading house at the center of the winter caravan appeared to have some new scandal. Freezing rain wouldn't keep curiosity from having its day.

When the family did return, they weren't allowed into their own house. Not at first. Ropes had been put up, and bluecloaks stood at the iron stanchions to keep them in place. The older man—the head of the family, Alys guessed—refused all shelter even as the younger one tried ineffectually to hold a blanket over his head. The water plastered his white hair to the old man's scalp. The pretty Inlisc girl was weeping, and the old, pinch-faced woman looked ready to take a knife to someone. Alys watched them from the middle of the crowd of onlookers, leaning on her club like it was a cane.

The wise thing would have been to do as Darro told her: put her eyes down and walk away. Ullin would know to look for her, if he could. There was nothing to gain by being here, and on the off chance that Garreth Left had survived, he might be able to point her out as one of the assassins. But with so many people to stand behind, he probably wouldn't.

She got ahead of me at the stairs, Alys rehearsed, planning the inflections she'd use and the gestures with them. *By the time I got close, she was already in the street. We'll find her next time. Next time, she won't get away.*

Now that the moment had passed, she regretted letting the girl live. It wasn't that she had suddenly become bloodthirsty, but if she'd beaten the girl's head in, all this would be over. She wouldn't still be dreading it. Or feeling the shame over letting the pretty Hansch girl slip away. If she'd have been feeling the shame of something else, that was for a different time. Today's failure was today's ache.

A murmur passed through the crowd and brought her back to herself. Garreth Left was stepping out into the street. A wide-set bluecloak with an oversized silver badge of office at his belt and a scowl the shape of murder had him by the elbow. The young man's face was pale. He walked carefully, like movement hurt him, and there was blood in the brown hair over his left ear.

The old man of the house said something, but between bodies and raindrops, she couldn't make it out. The boy straightened and replied. Two more bluecloaks emerged from the doorway, hauling a cart behind them. The crowd pulled her forward like a swimmer in a current as they tried for a better look.

Ullin was on the cart, covered in blood. He wasn't moving, but she told herself he might only be hurt or unconscious. They stopped him before the old man and sluiced Ullin's head clean with a bucket of steaming water. The old man took a moment, then shook his head. Ullin didn't move. Would never move again.

The horror and sorrow were overwhelming, but at their heart a tiny relief glimmered. She wouldn't have to lie to him, anyway. She turned her back to the merchant house, pushing through to where the crowd thinned, and then south and east toward her room and Darro's ashes, and a storm in the back of her head to match the thunder outside.

The night was long, cold, and terrible. Sammish had wanted nothing more than to turn south toward Stonemarket and Saffa, but the danger of being followed or tracked sent her north and across the river. By the time she reached Riverport, the storm had joined her—thick, slushy drops that froze as soon as they touched the paving stones. Her cloak was sodden, and she was shivering. Snow would have been warmer. Snow would have been kinder. There would be people dead on the streets by morning simply for not having the coin to buy shelter or the friendships to borrow on. It would be a sad joke if she was one of them.

Her fears kept her walking. First, her fear that the guards of the Daris Brotherhood had found a way to track her through the city streets. Then that the cold and her hunger would overwhelm her. And then, as her pace warmed her and the narrow streets of Longhill grew near, the fear of the thing in Timu's skin.

It was always like this, even if it wasn't always this bad. While she worked a pull, her mind was calm and detached, lost in the role she imagined herself into. And then after, her two selves had to come back together, and all the fear and danger shook her. If it had been a close thing, it might have made her feel sick. Sometimes she woke in the night with the memory of some particularly near miss with the bluecloaks or an angry touch, and she sat up, shuddering against what might have happened, until sleep came again. Tonight was no different, except that there was a growing dread of the future as well. Saffa was in Stonemarket, waiting for her to come back with a report of the brotherhood and its layout. Sammish had something terrible ahead of her to add to the ones behind.

She made it back to her room by the baker, stripped her soaked clothes off, and crawled under the blanket. Her body felt thick and heavy as a woman drowned. Sleep came on with a pull so sudden and profound, she wondered if it might be death. Only she woke afterward, so it wasn't.

She put on her other set of clothes and hung the still-wet ones to dry. Her body ached. The rain was still falling in a thin, frigid drizzle. Not sleet any longer, but not much better. It was a long walk to Stonemarket and the quarantine. It would have been easier not to go. The angry clouds and filthy weather were an excuse. But then she imagined Saffa waiting, wondering if she had been caught. With her luck, the older woman would vanish again out of an overgrown sense of caution, and Sammish would have to track her down just to give her bad news. Better that she do it now.

She had a strip of dried pork that she'd been saving, and she chewed it as she walked, working it like a dog gnawing wood and then sucking the salt and old fat out of the gristle. Living like this was dangerous. She'd be streetbound before summer if she didn't find a way to get coin, and whatever she was doing with Saffa and Alys, the dead prince and the live one, it wasn't going to buy her food. She'd die, and the city would close around her like she'd taken her finger out of water. She wouldn't leave a hole.

As she walked, memories of Alys floated through her exhausted, cold, hunger-drunk mind. They left her sad. A carter let her ride from the Seepwater bridge halfway through the Smoke and waved to her when she hopped off. It was easy to forget the little acts of kindness in the city, but they were as real as the river, even if they weren't enough to make up for the darkness and the rot. Sammish made her way west and then north as the clouds broke and an improbably warm sun shone down on a Palace Hill washed clean by the rain. Or as clean as it could ever be, anyway.

A day almost to the hour after she had left Saffa's plague-guarded retreat, she returned to it. The full circle of Kithamar left her feet hurting, her legs tremblingly tired, and her mind eerily clear. Now that she knew where to find her, slipping unseen past the ropes wasn't hard. The quarantined streets were quiet and empty. A few new sacks lay on the ground where the priests had brought grain and water from the Temple and thrown it in for the locals to part out by whatever method they could. She thought of Orrel sweating himself to death in his little room to the south of the city and wondered whether she shouldn't be more worried about the sickness that Saffa carried with her like a sword.

The Bronze Coast woman sat in a doorway, waiting. Her dark eyes brightened with relief and hope when she caught sight of Sammish. Then, reading her face, they dimmed. Sammish lowered herself to the street, sitting with her back to the wall. For a time, the only sound was the trickle of meltwater as ice gave way to sunlight. Sammish kept reaching for a way to begin—*We're too late* or *I made it in, but the news is bad* or *I'm so sorry*—and kept failing to find the right one. Eventually, Saffa broke their silence.

"He was a kind child. He would have been a good man."

"I'm sorry," Sammish said, and the way the woman sank at the words said she'd been hoping for different ones, despite the acceptance in what she'd said.

"Tell me," Saffa said, and Sammish did.

When she reached the moment where the not-boy had asked too much how to find her and it became clear that Timu's body wasn't his own any longer, Saffa hung her head low over her knees. She took deep, gulping breaths. Sammish found herself weeping in sympathy as she went on. When she was done, she took the older woman's hand, and Saffa didn't pull back. The grief was overwhelming for a time. It had been more than a year that this thin, strong mother had sought her son. Sammish tried to imagine how unforgiving hope would be to drive someone forward like that, alone in a foreign land. Sammish made herself a witness as that hope died.

"I'm sorry," Sammish said for what felt like the hundredth time. Only this time, Saffa was nearly enough herself again to answer.

"Thank you. At least I know. At least I can stop now. It isn't the kindness I wanted, but it's the one I have."

"Couldn't we . . . I don't know. Put him back?"

"My son is not what his father was. And even if he were, Ausai's hiding place has been found. He won't stay there. Timu is gone."

"It's over, then? You're stopping?"

"I have nothing to do here. Everything I loved is gone. This city is death for me now. I'll go home. I'll . . . I don't know what I'll do."

"Or," Sammish said.

Saffa's eyes, watery and bloodshot, found hers. The woman pulled back her hand, and Sammish let her. The thoughts that had been turning themselves over through the long, cold walk found words. Sammish thought each sentence before she spoke them, leaning forward with her fingers woven together.

"Hear me out. You aren't the first to fight this thing. That one you were talking about, Andomaka's father. He said they *probably* wouldn't need the boy, but then they did. Something went wrong for them. You didn't steal the knife. Someone else did that. I don't know who they were or what made them take the chance, but they took it. You're not alone in hating this thing." Then, a moment later, "We're not alone."

"This isn't your fight."

"You don't know what my fight is," Sammish said, and the words were sharper than she meant them to be. She started for an apology and stopped. "All I'm saying is that other people have stood against this."

"Who are they, though? Are they alive? Do they still fight?"

"I don't know, but...I mean, we're here."

Saffa looked at her hands, rubbing her palms together slowly with a sound like the hiss of wind in a loose shutter. She shook her head. "You are kind to offer, but no."

"I'm not offering you anything," Sammish said. "I'm telling you something. There was a plan to break them. All right, it didn't work. That doesn't mean it can't ever work. And if it can, I'm going to do it. You can stay and help me, or you can go home. I'm not your jailer. But I'm going to fix this."

It was astonishing to hear herself say it and feel her own sincerity. She couldn't remember the last time she'd spoken something aloud that mattered to her. She always kept it so quiet. It felt like breathing in after swimming too long underwater. She saw the question forming in Saffa's expression, and she thought it would once again be *Why?* She was wrong.

"How?"

"Not sure," Sammish said. "But I'm going to start by taking that fucking knife back."

Tregarro stood on the stone stairway, his lieutenant quietly behind him. Sleet had come in through the shattered window and darkened the stone. Two girls in servants' robes were mopping it up with rags, wringing the freezing water into an old tin bucket. Their hands were raw from the cold. The window itself was a ruin. Time and weather had weakened the lead. When the spy or assassin or whatever she'd been had thrown the shutter through it, it had shattered like a pitfighter who'd taken coin to fall at the first punch.

It had been a bad day. Something had happened with Elaine a Sal. No one had announced anything, but servants' gossip became masters' gossip faster than a stone dropped, and Green Hill was alive with speculation.

Andomaka, in her role as cousin to the prince and high blood of the city, was at the palace, finding out what she could about her false cousin. If they were lucky, the little bitch was dead, but he hadn't heard from his hired knives, and every hour they didn't come for the rest of their coin made it seem less likely. The better guess was that her assignation had been discovered, and the so-called prince was having her punished or spirited out of the city until the problem could be addressed. She might even be pregnant, which would mean killing her while she carried or else having a baby to slaughter before Andomaka could take the throne.

And also this.

"How many men did we have on duty?" Tregarro asked.

"Eighteen, sir. We have fifty on the force. Fifty-three. Three watches, but at night most doors are locked, so there's a few less on patrol. And they all take days off to rest. It's tradition."

He was a younger man, and a dedicant to the mysteries of the brotherhood without yet being advanced enough to know the deepest of them. And he talked too much when he was anxious.

"And yet," Tregarro said, and gestured to the window.

"They say she was dressed like a servant," his lieutenant said.

"I know she was. I'm the one who told you that. What I'm asking is how eighteen of our guard let some girl slip into the private temple just because she was wearing a cheap cloak."

"I . . . they didn't see her."

"She's a witch now too? Made herself invisible? Turned herself into a mouse?"

"They just didn't notice her."

"Well, maybe if we whip a few of them, it will sharpen their eyesight."

The hesitation before he replied was enough to say he expected to be first man tied to the post. Which, if it came to that, he would be. "If you say, sir."

"Double shifts. No days off for anyone until I say so. And nobody goes into or out of the private temple without being known. Anyone that tries to sneak by either way, open their throat and we'll question the corpse."

His lieutenant nodded sharply, turned, and walked stiffly away. Likely he was still more than half ready for the whip. Fair. Tregarro was more than half ready to wield it. But after a failure as utter as this, it was better to consult with his master than run ahead and risk doing something Ausai—*Kithamar*—didn't desire.

The scars on his cheek itched the way they did when he was

getting sick, but this wasn't an illness. His body was only telling him that he was frightened, and he was doing all he could to ignore the message. He walked back slowly, following the path the spy had run, looking for anything that seemed odd or out of place. Any sign she might have left that would lead back to who she was and where he could find her. It was only hallways. The girl had been a shadow.

In the temple, Ausai sat cross-legged on the altar. His young body seemed at ease, and his expression was almost mischievous. The glass beads of their game were in a complex position, caught at midgame as if the two players had only stepped away from the board. Tregarro looked at the board, trying to guess which color would make the next move.

"Red," the boy said, as if hearing the thought. "What do you think he should do? Attack or entrench?"

"The attack is almost always more dangerous," Tregarro said.

"I agree," Ausai said. "What did you find?"

"Nothing you don't already know, my lord." He felt the urge to report that he'd doubled the guard, that he'd punish the men who'd failed them, that he apologized for the failure. He didn't let his chagrin loosen his tongue, though. He only waited.

"Still, that isn't nothing. She said we had friends in common, if not friends we liked. She talked of Saffa and she knew Andomaka's name. That's two places we touch. And she knew to look here. Three. That's actually quite a bit. And she didn't trust me." The spirit wearing the boy's skin cracked his knuckles like a workman about to turn to a hard job. "It's fascinating that she didn't trust me. There are gods on the streets these days, Tregarro. They sense the thinness like fish sense the worm. I can feel them bumping against me sometimes. They think they can take this place back, but they're wrong."

"Gods, my lord?"

"Gods. Philosophies. Stories of the world that shape it. Ghosts that wear kingdoms instead of flesh. Whatever you want to call them. It doesn't matter to me."

"Whatever they are, they won't get in here twice. Not while I'm breathing."

"Careful," Ausai said with a grin. "They'll hear you. What is it? You're so glum."

"I failed you, my lord. I thought you would be displeased."

The thin, boyish shoulders shifted in a gesture that meant yes-and-no. "I should be. But it was interesting. And I'm young. It's been so long since I was this young, I almost forgot what it felt like. And a boy. Boys have a thirst for danger, so for now anyway it's easy to let go of the mistake. Nothing bad happened, after all. We got away with it. I was so old when I was Ausai. I would have been angry if I were still him. I could smell death with his nose, especially at the end. Youth can't feel what age does. So you're lucky I'm still what I am, I guess."

"If you say so, my lord."

"And *Saffa*. Saffa's come all the way here. She was a beautiful woman. Bronze Coast priestess. Smart. Deep. Beautiful with her robes off. I never thought she'd come after the boy. She was so much of the place she lived, you know? I couldn't imagine her stepping out of it."

"You sound as if you loved her?"

"I liked her, anyway. We'll have to kill her, but I enjoyed her company. I'd almost want to see her again. Seeing your lover through her own child's eyes. You discover so much more when you can have different perspectives that way. Who she was when she was letting herself be seduced. Who she is trying to save her son. A lover and a mother are very different people, even when they're the exact same woman. And the eyes. Ausai's eyes were hungry for her. These eyes won't take her in the same way at all. That's why this is all worth doing. It's like eating a good meal. The world is so much rounder when you have more than just the one life in it."

"It sounds . . . it sounds astonishing, my lord."

"Yes. But it won't happen. There's no time. Not with this weather."

Tregarro felt his gut tighten and didn't know why. Not at first. "It's pissing down sleet," he said, lulled by Ausai's manner into forgetting both his formality and his chagrin.

"It is. It's warm enough to. I can feel the change. The air smells different. If I listen deeply enough, I can hear the river *creaking.*" The joy and anticipation and longing in his voice sang like a viol.

Thaw, Tregarro thought. *He's talking about the thaw.* The moment of transformation when the passage between what has been and what will be is thinner, and easier to breach. For a moment, he thought of Andomaka, and the knot in his stomach grew worse. He pushed the image of the pale woman away. This was a *good* thing. It was what they had been waiting for. They would be one step nearer to taking the false bloodline off the throne, and putting the true spirit of the city in its right place. They were saving the city. That was all he had to remind himself of. Andomaka would be prince, and he would guard her then as he did now.

These were the mysteries, and he was dedicated to them.

Like a fox fleeing a farmer's stone, Elaine a Sal had vanished. The whispers of it rippled through the court, but what it meant, no one knew. The plague had spread to the palace, and she was the first to grow ill. Or she had gotten pregnant by one of the redcloaks or an Inlisc servant or one of her half dozen suitors from the court. Or she was dead.

Andomaka's little wolves might have taken the fox. Or something else might have happened. She didn't know, and the people who did weren't telling.

"You are many things, Halev," Andomaka said. "You aren't my cousin."

Despite the goldwork on the wall and the oil lanterns, the palace meeting room was small and dark. The thick walls held the cold of winter so that she hadn't taken off her cloak, nor had Halev Karsen removed his jacket.

"The prince is very busy," Halev said.

"I don't remember Ausai being so constrained by his duties," she said. It was a barb that might pass for innocent, and if Halev felt it, he hid the sting with a shrug.

"It's Byrn's first year. Once he's been through the cycle a few times, he'll get the knack for it. It's always like this when something's genuinely new."

Genuinely new. Was that a barb in return? Was Karsen saying that the bastard who wore the name a Sal like a mask was the new order of Kithamar? That she couldn't tell made it seem more likely that he was.

"Well, then perhaps I'll ask after him again next year."

"If there's something I can help you with, I'm pleased to do it," Halev said. And then, a moment later, "What does bring you, Andomaka?"

The question seemed to resonate, like the room had suddenly grown larger. She'd meant to answer with a triviality, but that false echo gave her pause. What would it mean if she'd dreamed that someone like this—an acquaintance since their mutual childhood and now perhaps-enemy—had asked her why she was coming to the palace? If her sleeping mind had conjured Halev and his question, what would it have been trying to tell her?

It was the kind of question she'd been trained to ask, but since Ausai's return, her training had become harsher and more rigorous. There were whole days now when she felt like she was barely tethered to her body at all. She saw things, heard things, found meaning in things that she never had before. It felt like growing suddenly wise, except she sometimes had trouble remembering the lessons she was learning. They all seemed to run a little, like fresh paint in a sudden rain.

"Andoma?" Halev said, and for the first time, he seemed almost unguarded. "Are you all right?"

"What brings me to the palace is...Elaine, I suppose." And

that was true. Elaine would bring her there, if only by her death. So that made sense. "We have been talking, she and I."

"Have you now?"

"You knew that."

"I did. What do you two talk about?"

"Byrn never followed the brotherhood," Andomaka said. Which was true. All their conversations with their threads of love and sex and death, politics and magic, were about her father and his false blood. They had been talking about the betrayal of the city and her family's role in it, even if Elaine didn't know that. "It would be better for the city if she followed custom."

"I hear what you're saying," Halev replied. She didn't think that was true. He didn't trust her, she could feel that, but he was also distracted. She couldn't see the things in his mind that were drawing him away, not quite. There were glimpses of them. Something about wax and pig's blood. Knowing it left her feeling lightheaded. "I'm afraid Elaine isn't available either. Not right now."

"Is she well?"

"She's young," Halev said. "Being young is always hard. Every generation fights to survive it." Another odd answer. Evasive. Something had happened, there was no doubt, but it didn't sound as if the girl was dead. Not yet.

"Another time, then," Andomaka said, both to Halev and to herself in their different conversations. She would come back another time. The girl would die another time. There was a little thrill as her mind that drifted and her mind that lived in the world came together for a moment.

Halev made his bow and left. When he was gone, a redcloak came in to escort her out. They both pretended it was a sign of honor, but the sword at his belt wasn't ornamental. The palace was on alert, and she had the sense—much as she'd sensed the winter caravan's coming—that they didn't know what they were guarding against. Like a sword fighter trying to parry with his eyes bound.

"What's your name?" she asked the man as they reached the black, squat gates that led north from the palace and into Green Hill.

"Marback, lady."

You will answer to my voice, Marback, she thought. *This mouth will command you, and you will do what these lips say.* She didn't speak it aloud. He would only have misunderstood.

As she stepped out of the palace and into the openness of her quarter, most of the compounds stood elegantly to her left, bright stone and bare trees pregnant with leaf. She turned to the right. To the north and below her, the white ice of the river was darker. Bluer. A sound reached her, faint but vast. A giant the size of the world, whispering. The ice groaning. The living water restless in its sleep and ready to see the sky again.

If she had dreamed that her enemy had asked what brought her to the palace, and that the river had answered, it would have been prophecy. The thread of Kithamar had brought her here, at the moment of the thaw, when the world could shift again to keep her here but as prince.

All the way back to the compound, water ran. It was everywhere. Dripping from gutters, sliding down the streets. Filthy snow that the months had crushed into ice was transforming. The air itself felt lush with promise, and the world was changing. The implacable hold of winter had slipped. Thaw had come. A moment of change, and moments of change were dangerous and full of wonder. When she arrived, Tregarro was waiting. And Ausai was too.

She bathed before the ceremony, not because it was needed, but because it was beautiful that way. Warm water in a copper tub. The heat sinking into her flesh. She remembered her first initiations into the mysteries of the Daris Brotherhood. She'd been a child then. Her father, Drau Chaalat, had told her to put on her best clothes and come with him. That it was time. He had been the head of the brotherhood then, as she was now. He'd taken her through the doorless path to the private temple for the first time, and she had been astounded to find Prince Ausai waiting for her there. His hair had been thinning even then, but it had still been dark. The illness that had turned his skin dry as paper hadn't declared itself. He'd been a man, strong and hale and vibrant with power. He had been the city.

That first ceremony had been little enough. He'd given her the words, and she'd mouthed them without understanding their significance. What she remembered best was the sense of him. His masculinity and grace, and the shivering sense of a great puzzle just beginning to solve itself before her.

That day had been the first step on the path that led to the last stone of today.

She rose from the water, dressed herself in ceremonial gowns and a jacket of red tapestry embroidered with gold. She brushed her pale hair for the last time, and a sense of peace descended on her like the first spreading warmth after a drink of wine. Life was made bearable through meaning, and the meaning of her whole life was this. There was no fear in her. Only the certainty that everything was as it should be. Everything was well.

She walked the doorless path alone this time. Her father was long since dead, his deathmark worked in stone. Still, she imagined him at her side. His calm approval. His certainty which was, after all, an echo of her own. Candlelight filled the temple, and a stray breeze that had somehow followed her in made the little flames shiver and dance like they were laughing. Tregarro stood at one side of the altar. Ausai, in the body of the Bronze

Coast boy, at the other. Knife and scroll and cloth were all laid out. Her uncle nodded to her with the boy's neck, and she bowed before him.

"This is the most important thing you have ever done or will ever do," Ausai and Airis and every prince of the city back through the centuries said. She more than half expected the words to echo as Halev's had, but they were only words. "We are proud of you."

"Thank you, my lord," she said, and began weeping from gratitude and joy.

"Be strong," the boy said. The same tongue had once said, *You don't have to do this. We could escape together. You could be free.* It had never been true.

The boy stepped to the front of the altar and knelt. Tregarro stepped behind him and put the cord across the thin, youth-smooth neck and tightened it. The boy's face grew dark as he was strangled. She had wondered if there would be a struggle at the end, but apart from a moment's reflexive and impotent gasping, the thread of Kithamar met this new death with calm. The stink when the body's bowel loosened should have been disgusting, but it wasn't. It was only an indignity of flesh, and almost endearing. Tregarro gently drew the corpse down to the floor at the altar's foot and placed a dark cloth over the dark face and protruding tongue. They were alone in the temple, the two of them. She found herself weeping, but neither frightened nor sad.

When Ausai had died before, he had been older, ill, and sur-rounded by the members of the court. He had suffered then, fighting to remain on this side of death's dark waters until the missing blade could be found, until the boy who was his secret refuge could be brought, until the conspiracy against him could be understood and defeated. His other caretakers and physicians hadn't been initiates of the brotherhood, and he'd been too weak to visit the brotherhood's house. There had been so few moments when she could sit with him and whisper their progress into his failing ears. She wondered now whether Byrn a Sal had called for a close watch on their uncle in order to keep his false claim to the throne secret, or if it had only been the care and attention it had seemed.

In the end, the old man's flesh had failed him. He had drowned far from water, refusing anything that might ease his passage in a bid for just a bit more life. He had died with his hands in claw-like fists, not knowing whether she would find the way to bring him back, or if the thread of Kithamar was cut forever.

Byrn a Sal hadn't suffered so much as a strange dream when the rite failed. And the boy—Ausai's son and not Byrn's cousin—had been left with the slavers hired to bring him. Everything she'd trained for, everything her father had raised her to do, had become meaningless.

And now, this new death of Ausai's, quicker and without fear or illness. It was a death without struggle and with faith in resurrection. Andomaka was, before all other things, a priest. Her life was in the service of her god and her city. She sat beside the dead boy now, her hands wide above his empty body, and began his funeral. His soul was made safe, as it had to be. She sang the hymns and cleaned the body, Tregarro at her side with scented oil and fresh cloth. The dead boy-child who had been her uncle, she treated with reverence and respect. And when rite found its end, she drew his deathmark.

As she did, she felt something deep within the temple shift. Ausai was at peace again, and would be until she drew him forth. The thaw was in the air as well, a moment of change. Of thinness and possibility. Of renewal for the city, and of culmination for her. She let her eyes close and felt her own body, her awareness moving through each limb and joint like a hostess preparing a room for an honored guest.

"Are you well?" Tregarro said.

"I am perfect," she said, and it was true apart from the one unsettled echo. *What does bring you?* She had answered that, hadn't she? She'd understood the prophecy. But the echo of the question remained. That was strange. Why did it remain?

"We can wait if you like," Tregarro said.

"There's nothing to wait for," she said as she opened her eyes. He gave her his hand. She rose to her feet. There was a scar on his thumb too, wide and pale and ropey as the ones on his face. He was a beautiful man, in his way. She was grateful that he had been here to stand by her and the brotherhood.

The rite itself felt like images of itself drawn on onionskin and laid one atop another. In all the history of the brotherhood, there had never been anyone who performed the ritual three times. Her first, failed attempt the night that Byrn a Sal had taken his crown, then the actual redemption of Kithamar, after they'd recovered the blade and the boy, and now this third and final time.

Souls faded. Even now, with the child's body still warm, the thread would be falling from the world. She had saved it before. She would save it again now. She took the blade and drew in her own blood the deathmark she'd only just bestowed. It darkened. It burned. The cold smoke that came with the attention of the dead complicated the air. She shivered and told herself it was only the chill of the passing winter. Or joy at the approaching transformation. She cleaned the blade with a cloth that had never been touched by sunlight. She dipped the silver into a basin of river water. Anticipation lifted the hair on her arms and neck.

She crossed the deathmark with the letters of her own name. Herself, her life, all that she was or had been, written in water. After the last line, she put down the blade and placed her palms flat on the altar. The stone bit her skin like ice.

For a fraction of a breath, she was afraid it had failed. She almost called out to Tregarro. But only almost. The cold smoke that wasn't smoke thickened, billowing into the air from no place. Or from a place that no living eyes had seen. She'd never been aware of this before. She felt as though she were falling from a great height, and the smoke was a vast and turbulent sea waiting to receive her.

Something moved in that sea. At first, she couldn't make out its form. And then she could.

The question was answered. She understood what was bringing her to the palace. She saw what she had spent a lifetime serving, and the sense of betrayal was deeper than seas or skies. Her regret was instantaneous, complete, horrified. She tried to turn back, willing herself into the flesh she'd already half abandoned. She tried to scream.

The thing that called itself Kithamar, the thing that had eaten its rotting way through generations of her ancestors, caught her in grey-white teeth. It shook its vast head like a terrier killing a rat, and the thin, bright connection of herself to herself, already made tenuous by years of grooming and effort, snapped.

Andomaka Chaalat, great lady of the city and high priest of the Daris Brotherhood, didn't die. It wasn't so gentle as that.

Tregarro watched as she made the deathmark, drawing it in her own blood, and at once, it darkened and smoked. If anything, the effect was faster and more violent than before, as if the blood might catch fire. A sign, he guessed, that Ausai's spirit was close. She cleaned the blade, and perversely, he felt the urge to tip over the little basin of water. Ruin the rite. But it was only a moment's perversity, and it passed. She drew her name in water. The deathmark spat. She put down the blade, leaning forward with both palms flat against the altar. Something shook, but the candle flames didn't waver.

Andomaka shifted forward with a little cough like a gasp. She straightened, and she stood. The laugh that came from her throat was as familiar as his own voice. But it wasn't her.

"Oh, it is good to have that done with," she said, then stretched. On the floor, the dark cloth had slipped off the dead boy's face. Andomaka stepped over, looking down at the corpse with something like compassion in her eyes. "I would have been beautiful in that one, given a few more years. Such a waste. We'll want that burned and the bones ground down."

"Yes, my lord."

"Lady," Andomaka said. "Your lord is now your lady, after all. Kithamar has become a woman again."

"Yes," Tregarro said. "Of course. My apologies."

"It's always an odd transition. It's been a long time since I've been in a body like this. It will be a pleasant change," she said, and sat on the altar as the boy had so often done. "We'll want to put the blade someplace much safer than last time. With any luck, we won't need it again for a very long while, but I'm not too proud to learn from my mistakes. I don't want to do this all again a few decades from now."

"Of course."

Andomaka rubbed her arm idly, as if she were feeling the cloth sleeve of a new jacket. "And with this behind us, I think we can turn to the other work at hand. My nephew and his daughter..." Andomaka stopped, shook her head, and laughed again. "My cousins. Byrn a Sal and Elaine. And also Saffa and our unwelcome visitor."

Tregarro took up the knife, wiping away the last clinging drops of water with the ritual cloth. His throat felt thick, and he wasn't sure why. He hoped he wasn't getting ill. If Andomaka noticed, she didn't say anything.

"Saffa's girl," she said. "She was Inlisc with a Longhill slant to her vowels. We have some of those in our coin box, don't we?"

"A few, yes," Tregarro said.

"Well, gather up our hired knives, Tregarro, my friend. It's time we sliced off some loose threads."

PART THREE

SPRING STORMS

Violence is the nature of the world. Peace is the pause between blows.

—From "Aunt Thorn and the King of Crows," a traditional Inlisc folktale

I don't know," Alys said to no one for what had to have been the thousandth time at least. "He didn't tell me that he was doing it. We found the place together. The plan was to go in, the both of us. But Ullin's Ullin. Sometimes he changes the plan. I guess he went in without me."

Her room was silent apart from the distant rumble of carts in the street and a man's muffled laughter that came through the wall. Alys shifted on her mattress, trying to find a position of comfort. She couldn't.

"The girl that was with him?" she said, answering the question no one there had asked. "I wasn't sure there was one. Anything could have happened to her. You'll have to ask him."

And could they? If anyone could haul the dead up out of their graves, it was Andomaka. If Ullin rose from his own ashes, she didn't think he'd likely cover for her.

It would have been so much better just to have done it. A few swings of her club, and the girl's brains would have been ready for a sausage casing. Alys would be dreaming at ease instead of worrying at a story that she wouldn't have believed if she'd heard it. Only she wouldn't have been. That was the hell of it. She'd have been losing the same sleep for different reasons.

"I don't know," she said again. "I don't know what happened." And then, to Andomaka or Ullin or Darro, "I'm sorry. I'm so sorry."

She didn't weep. She was done with that. The shock and sorrow had been hard as a fever at first, but they were gone. All that was left were the bone-deep dread and the shame of her own cowardice. Darro would have followed through. Darro would have killed the girl. The box of ashes was on the table. From where she lay, she could just catch sight of it. One of her shutters was open, and the sunlight fell on Darro's deathmark like the gods were pointing a finger at it.

"You would have, wouldn't you?" But even in her imagination, her brother was silent.

The ache and emptiness she'd felt that terrible day at the temple when she'd seen Darro's corpse had been pure and overwhelming. Something had screamed in her then, and gone on screaming for weeks. She still felt it sometimes, but she had to work for it now. She had to will the pain back to its fresh, transcendent rawness. The ache was duller now. Grey as ashes.

She was losing him. Darro's face, his voice, the way he held his weight over his feet like he was always on the verge of running. She could remember them, but they didn't intrude on her the way they had. The grief was in her, but it was weary, and she was weary along with it. And Darro wasn't there to help her remember. She wanted the pain back. She wanted it to whip her on, because if it didn't she might decide to stay in her little bed in the shadows and let herself starve or else eat her own shame until it poisoned her.

"I don't know what Ullin did. You'll have to ask him," she said.

She wanted to feel bad for Ullin, and she did, a little. She'd liked him well enough, and seeing him dead was a blow. But she'd felt pure grief before this. She was a proud citizen of grief, and flew its flag in her heart. With Ullin, it was nearer to embarrassment that she'd let him down.

"I don't know what happened," she said. And then, "Fuck."

With a grunt, she hauled herself to sitting and pressed the heels of her palms against her eyes. The candle was in her safe cache. All she had to do was light it, tell Andomaka what had happened and what hadn't. Or tell her lies about it and brazen her way through. Anything would be better than waiting and worrying and chewing her own tongue with all the ways it had gone sour for her. Maybe she'd do it. She just needed a drink first. Beer or strong cider. A bowl of something warm in her gut. Then she'd do it. Get it over with. Be done.

Or maybe she'd light the candle, and the scar-cheeked Tregarro would appear instead. Or maybe he'd knock on her door.

"I have to get out of here. Get some food," she said, opening her cache and grabbing up a few bronze coins. Darro didn't answer. When she went, she left the shutter open as if he might enjoy the cool breeze and the light. If she felt a twist of disgust at herself for that, it was only one among hundreds, its significance overlooked.

The wooden walls and roofs of Longhill were dark with the runoff as old ice became fresh sludge. Rivulets of dark water ran down the streets, carrying away the dirt, shit, and food scraps of the long winter months. Rats gamboled in the shadows and in the sunlight, then scattered as dogs rushed in, barking in something part play and part hunt. The city was still cold, but the promise of spring made people want to believe it was warm. Men walked without jackets, their breath only smoking a little bit. Here and there, a girl had taken a summer skirt out, mended the winter's damage of moth and mouse, and suffered goose-flesh for her optimism. The chill hadn't gone, but the city was bent on pretending it had. If they did it long enough, it would become true.

Alys bought a cup of thick soup from a cart by the east wall and ate it while she walked. To the north, the Temple glittered in the sunlight, and the looming presence of Oldgate and Palace Hill was hidden by the wooden buildings on her left. She could almost imagine that everything west of the river had been washed away, and Kithamar become an Inlisc city the way it would have been had the Hansch never come.

She saw the funeral before she knew what it was. She crossed an intersection of two curved, shifting roads, and there almost at the bend a few people stood together. It could have been anything—a conversation about the weather or how to remake a wall thin with dry rot, a pull being organized or paying out, even just a collaboration of chance. But there was something in the way the people—adults and children both—stood and bowed their heads toward each other that spoke of sorrow. Alys slowed, turned, and walked toward them.

As she drew near, she knew some of the faces. Danna. Cane. Nimal. They stood outside an open door that someone had draped with a red cloth, talking in low tones. Nimal had tears on his cheeks, which was unnerving. Nimal was too worried about seeming strong and manly to weep easily. There were children with them—two girls young enough that they would have been genderless in different clothes—holding each other by the hand, a thin boy with bright white hair, an older girl with thick braids framing a broad and angry face. Alys knew them, even if she didn't recall their names at first. The girl with braids was Danna's daughter. The two holding hands had the same name, but she didn't remember what it was. It would likely come back later, when she'd forgotten to think about it. She sucked down the last of her soup and shoved the empty cup in her sleeve. Cane saw her and nodded. Nimal saw her and looked away.

"Who passed?" she asked the thin, pale-haired boy. Elbrith. That was his name.

"Grey Linnet," the boy said.

The name hit Alys like a stone thrown at her breastbone. "What happened?"

"She went to sleep, and she didn't wake up," Elbrith said. And then, with a solemn, knowing nod, "She woke down."

Alys had known Linnet since she was younger than this boy. She'd gone to sweep the shores of the Silt with her and the other children. Nimal and Black Nel and Darro had too, before her. And this child, standing in front of her. How many generations of children had gone looking for mundane treasures at the side of the water with Linnet? There would have been a time not long ago that the idea Linnet could die would have been as ridiculous as the river dying. Linnet was a part of the city. Only she wasn't. Hadn't been. She'd been a woman, same as anyone, and just as mortal.

"I'm sorry," Alys said, and the pale boy nodded as if she'd spoken a password or a reply in a religious rite. She'd said what she was supposed to say, and he approved. Odd child.

Alys went to the open door and stepped past the red cloth into the room beyond. It was a small space, narrower than her own room, with a cot and a thin mat of rushes on the ground, but it was filled with people. The air was hot, and it tasted like someone else had just breathed it out. There was little enough room to move through, but no one would run a pull here. Grey Linnet had lived alone, fighting for her food and a place out of the weather, but she had been known, and to judge by the press of bodies in the space now that she'd left it, she would be missed.

Alys would miss her.

She almost didn't recognize her mother at first. The winter hadn't been kind to her. She had looked wan on Darro's nameday and lost more of the flesh from her cheeks since then. Her hair had been grey, but now it was thinning. Alys could see the shining, oily scalp back past her mother's hairline. The whites of her eyes had taken on the yellow of old ivory, but her hands were steady and her eyes were dry. Caught up in conversation with an old, thick-bellied man, she didn't see Alys.

She's also dying, Alys thought. *Even if not from anything in particular just yet, she's still dying.* It was so clearly true that it should have been trivial, but it stopped her like a slap. Her mother laughed at something the man said. There was a dark gap where her left eyetooth had been. She looked older than the image that Alys had in her mind when she thought *Mother*.

Alys turned back, edging her way out to the cold street. Her mouth was set in a scowl so profound it ached a little, but she wasn't angry. Not quite. She lowered her head and started walking, counting the steps in her head until she reached fifty, then looking back. The group outside Grey Linnet's room ignored her. Black Nel had Nimal's arm, and they were leaning on each other. A new child that Alys didn't recognize was sitting on the paving stones, weeping with her head forward. No one looked her way, much less called her back. Alys wondered whether Sammish had gone to pay respects, and if she hadn't, if she would. She wondered who would pay for Grey Linnet's rites, and if they'd opt for full or stay with partial since the old woman hadn't died in the river. She thought maybe she ought to, but the coin she had from Darro would only last so long. She had herself to think of.

She walked back south, the Temple behind her now. Her shoulders ached. She had been born in Longhill. She'd lived her whole life there. But Darro was gone, and she didn't want to speak to her mother or Sammish. Ullin was dead. Somehow, Alys had built a life that didn't have anyone in it for her to sit with except a box of ashes. It felt unfair, but she didn't know who she could blame for it. It hadn't been her plan. It just happened that way.

She reached her corner more quickly than she'd expected, lost as she'd been in thought. From the street, she looked up at her own window. The shutter stood open, as she'd left it. It was one of hundreds she'd walked past, and nothing to lend it meaning or significance apart from that it had been Darro's and was now hers. Every other one she could see had another room behind it, with someone else living out a life that meant as little to her as hers meant to them. She felt small.

As she made her way up the steep, lightless stair, she thought about where she would go when Darro's gold ran out. A little rat-haunted cot like Grey Linnet's, maybe. Or someplace like Sammish's little closet by the baker's kiln. Or a place in a barracks like Ullin had kept in Stonemarket. Or the deep holes and tunnels of Aunt Thorn, if she found it in herself to be the killer she pretended. Or the street. Or her mother's floor until her mother *woke down* herself someday.

It was strange to have spent seasons with her focus always on Darro's ashes, and only now to feel the sense of her own life's boundaries, still distant but coming closer breath by breath. *Why won't you look at my face?* She shuddered and opened her door.

The air in the room was cold as the street, but dark. Smoke filled the space, but there was no fire for it to come from. Her throat went tight, and her less immediate fears flew away like sparrows.

"I didn't know what happened," she said under her breath,

willing the words to come naturally. "Ullin didn't tell me he was doing it."

She closed the shutter enough that only a thin slice of light came in, then went to her safe cache. The black candle was there. When she picked it up, it was cold to the touch. She had an impulse to put it back, leave it in its drawer, and pretend she'd been out in the city someplace and hadn't seen the summoning gloom. It would be easy enough. She could even make her way down to the taprooms in Seepwater or to the river where the old men and women played at stones and watched the river flow again now that the ice had broken.

But that would only invite Tregarro to find her again in person, and that would be worse. She put the candle in its place on the table, lit it, and waited. The smoke shuddered and shifted, thickening and weaving itself into a human shape. Alys relaxed a degree when she saw the pale hair and eyes.

Andomaka's eyes clicked over Alys's face and body like she was reading words written on her skin. Her smile was tight and thin.

"You haven't made a report recently," the pale woman said. Her usual dreamy quality was gone, and a harshness had taken its place. "Where do things stand?"

Ullin did something stupid. I don't know what it was. I wasn't there. All the lies she'd practiced crowded at the back of her tongue, bumping against each other so that none of them could get through. Andomaka tilted her head, a little frown tugging down the corners of her mouth.

"We tried," Alys said, and wished the words back as soon as she'd spoken them. It was too late. "We watched the house when we knew the family would be away. The bluecloak came, and his girl did too. We went in for them, but...they fought. Ullin was killed and the girl got away."

Andomaka was still as stone, pale eyes locked on Alys with a focus that itched, and she rested one thumb in her braided belt like a swordsman putting hand to pommel. Her pale tongue darted out, wetting her lips in a brief, lizard-like swipe, and she shrugged. "Well, that explains some things. Did the girl see you?"

"She did," Alys said.

"Did you see her?"

"Yes."

"And?" Andomaka said. Alys shook her head. Andomaka sighed. "Did she look familiar?"

Alys reached for something to say. It wasn't a question she'd expected. "She looked... rich? She was Hansch."

Andomaka was still again, and then smiled. When she spoke, it seemed more than half to herself. "I love this city. Well, we'll have another chance later. She can't stay hidden forever."

"If you say so."

"I have another job for you. You can make up for your failure with the girl who looked rich by tracking down an Inlisc girl who looks poor." There was a laughter in the words that uneased Alys. It might have covered anger or disappointment or something else, but it was sharp-hearted, and it made Andomaka seem different. As if Alys were seeing a side of her that had been hidden until this moment.

"Any particular one?" she said, trying to match the tone.

"We had a little mouse come visit my temple. Brown hair, brown eyes, so absolutely unremarkable that the guards hardly took note of her while she walked in past them. But she knew me, and my enemies. She knew my business. And she knew my name. My understanding is that not many people know my name. But you do, don't you?"

"Only because you told it to me."

Across the table and across the city, Andomaka lifted a reassuring hand. "I'm not accusing you of anything. But I am asking if you might have mentioned it to anyone."

"Ullin, once," Alys said. But her thought was *Sammish, by all the gods, what did you do?*

"Anyone like our unwelcome visitor?"

"May have," she said out loud. "I don't know. I know a lot of poor Inlisc girls."

"With whom you discuss me and my work?" The edge on the words could have cut cloth.

"No," Alys said. "Just one, maybe. She wouldn't do anything against you, though." Except that she might. *He wasn't your pale bitch's lap dog* floated up in her memory. Her breath was coming fast and shallow now. Her head felt light.

"What's her name?"

"She goes by several," Alys lied. It was a reflex. If she'd been able to think, she wouldn't have, but her body knew the smell of a predator. Instinct led her to the strategies of the Longhill street rat that she was. "But I know where she sleeps. I can find her."

Andomaka leaned back on the bench, stroking her chin as if she were a man touching a beard. For a moment, the silence between them was brittle. The pale woman came to her decision.

"Hunt her down," Andomaka said. "Bring her here."

T hat's all you can tell me?" the coachman said. He had a way of scowling that Tregarro found annoying. It was as if the man was making a mask of his own face. They stood in the yard nearest the stables, the late morning sun pressing down from a blue-white sky. If there had been even a breath of wind, it would have been frigid. With only sunlight and still air, the day could have been mistaken for warm.

"It's what you can start with."

The coachman scowled again and shook his head. "There's a lot of Inlisc girls who don't look like much of anything, boss. Wasn't there anything about her that stood out?"

"She was in the private temple without anyone stopping her. That was exceptional."

"How am I supposed to look for where someone was before they got where they are now? It's not like there's a mark on her from it."

Tregarro scratched his cheek with a casualness he didn't feel. The coachman had been one of his most trusted knives for half a decade. The impatience he felt now was likely more about himself than his hired man's impertinence. "Try going to taprooms near Longhill and listening. If someone's drunk and bragging, maybe you hear it. If someone stops talking when you mention the Daris Brotherhood, maybe you notice it. I'm giving you the place to start from. If I knew the whole path to the finish, I wouldn't need people like you."

If he put a little roughness into the words *people like you*, the coachman didn't notice. He only shook his wide head in a performance of despair. "That's going to be a hard fish to hook."

"You aren't doing it alone. Everyone is on this. If you're the one to haul her in, it's well worth the time."

"I'll do what I can," the coachman said, as if there had been an option.

Tregarro wasn't offering work that his people could pick up or turn down at will. He was instructing them. But he was also aware that he was raw and itching. When he felt like this, it was too easy to start fights he regretted later. "I trust you to."

Mollified, the coachman nodded, turned, and trundled back across the courtyard to the stables. Tregarro stretched his shoulders, trying to get the tightness out of his joints. It had been there for days.

Thaw was past, and the vines that climbed the courtyard wall were already wrapping themselves in fresh green so bright they looked false as a child's memory of leaves. The early flowers were already blooming, and the air smelled like the promise of summer that hadn't come. He had the sudden and visceral memory of walking through this same space only a year before and finding Andomaka here. She had been sitting with the corpse of a bird, looking at it as if it were singing to her.

The true thread of Kithamar—the founding spirit that had held the city safely in the world from its first days—had

returned, what had been broken was mended, and the idea
that anything could turn the avenging blade of the Daris aside
seemed impossible. If the price of that was that he wouldn't find
Andomaka kneeling over dead feathers in a springtime courtyard, it was what he'd sworn to suffer. He would be fine with it.

He made his solitary way around the perimeter of the house
compound. Half a dozen buildings from the great central house
to the carved granite toolsheds. Some were connected by covered walkways, some by buried passages, some not at all. They
made up his little nation. Kithamar was bounded by its walls,
by custom and status and its boughs and branches. The Daris
Brotherhood was bounded by Tregarro's will, and it had been
breached once already. It wouldn't happen again.

Turning the corner at the eastern edge, he found two of his
guard leaning against the wall, scowling at the traffic on the
street. Their narrowed eyes and casual posture, the hands they
rested on the pommels of their blades, made them look like a
weak man's idea of strength. Tregarro's half-formed sorrows
shifted easily toward them, and he strode along the edge of the
street. His guards' eyes were dazzled with servants in the colors
of half a dozen houses, carts piled high with flowers and vines
with black soil clinging to pale roots ready to be planted in the
kitchen gardens of the powerful, and a small company of redcloaks marching in north from the palace. Tregarro was fewer
than a dozen steps from them when his slouching guard caught
sight of him and straightened.

He stopped before them, waiting with the same calm, silent
attention a houndsman might use to scold a pup. The two men
tried nodding their salute, then a more formal raising of their
hands. Their eyes were bright and anxious, and their relief was
unmistakable when he returned the gesture.

"Anything?" he asked.

"No sir," the senior of the pair said. "Nothing of note."

Tregarro let his gaze move along the roadside. His gaze lingered for a breath or two on the retreating forms of the palace guard. If Byrn a Sal knew for certain the secrets and intentions of the brotherhood, he wouldn't be seeing the redcloaks from the back. They'd either be facing him or they'd be as invisible as wind. He allowed himself a thin smile. Other than that, a servant girl who stumbled and was steadied by her mother. A merchant's cart pulled by a beautiful grey mare worth more than everything she hauled. A flight of geese, high above the city, honking and calling in their ragged line. One of his guards swallowed uncomfortably.

"Well enough, then," Tregarro said. "But stay sharp. You're not a pair of taproom knives. You're the face of the Daris Brotherhood."

A flicker of shock passed through the young one's eyes, as if Tregarro's scars made even the mention of the word *face* a dangerous choice. He was sorry he hadn't been harsher with them, but changing his course now would seem petty. Would be petty. Would seem petty because it was.

"Report in at the end of your guard," he said. "I'll want a full account."

"Yes sir. Of what, sir?"

"Make it as full as you can," he said. "I'll tell you whether it was enough."

He turned on his heel and walked back the way he'd come. Well, fine. Just a bit petty after all.

Sammish didn't change her stride when the scarred man came around the corner, but her heart sped up. It was their third time around the brotherhood's house, this time with Sammish dressed as a servant girl and Saffa as her mother. Before, Sammish had been blind and Saffa led her. Before that, they'd been hauling sacks of laundry. No one had taken notice of them as Sammish had made her study.

The change in the brotherhood's compound was the difference between sleeping and wakefulness. Where she had walked into the Daris Brotherhood before, there were double sets of guards now. And worse, the guard had the too-sharp manner of men in the shadow of the whip. Any cutter worth salt would call off a pull when they saw the intended victim come alert. It was madness not to. And if the compound had been complacent before, it was sharp as a needle now. The side door that had stood open with servants gossiping through it was closed. The watch stations where men had played dice and traded jokes had no games in them. The brotherhood had even put mercenaries on the public street. If a house in Longhill had changed its demeanor so much, everyone from the southern gate to the Temple would have known there was trouble brewing, but Green Hill seemed to think that noticing such things was beneath its dignity. Or maybe they smelled trouble differently than Sammish did.

The scarred man—the one Alys had called Tregarro—made his soft way to the guards, and the swordsmen went stiff with fear. Sammish became very aware of how easy it would be for the captain of the enemy guard to glance over at them. She wondered if he'd ever seen Saffa before, or drawings of her.

A merchant's cart clattered down the street, heading toward her, a great grey mare stepping proudly before it. The scarred man turned his gaze to the street just as Sammish's foot caught a loose stone, her ankle rolling. She stumbled just when he was looking toward her, and for a few knife-bright heartbeats, she was sure he'd seen her for what she was. Saffa took her arm.

"What's wrong?" the woman muttered, but as she did, the guard captain looked away. Sammish felt the fear in her throat like she was going to be ill. She shook her head, not trusting herself to speak in case she did something else stupid that drew attention to them. Sammish tried to keep her body from trembling, but the shock added to her own hunger made her weakness hard to conceal. Saffa said nothing, but her face hardened.

"We should go around once more," Sammish said.

"We should get food and a place to rest," Saffa said, and this time Sammish didn't fight. She only wanted to walk the compound's perimeter again because she hadn't seen the flaw in it that she needed. She'd had the chance to slip into the enemy's rooms once, and she had wasted it. No matter how dearly she hoped to find a chance to do it again, it wasn't there. She let Saffa turn her away from Green Hill and the palace and trudge south toward Stonemarket, where they would attract even less attention.

"Maybe you're right," she said as they turned into a slowly curving street that led toward the cistern. "I should eat. I'm not thinking straight."

They stopped on a bench near the market square, but not in it. Saffa left her for a time and came back with little bowls of oats and egg. They weren't seasoned, but Sammish ate it all down to the shine all the same. A girl with a handcart sold them fresh water with crushed mint to wash it down. Saffa paid with a bronze coin going green at the edge.

"I'm sorry," Sammish said. "You shouldn't have to do that. It's my city. I can feed myself."

The Bronze Coast woman didn't answer. In the afternoon light, she looked old. The creases by her mouth were like bloodless cuts in her flesh, and her eyes were thick with fatigue. Sammish guessed that her own were too. It had been a hard year.

Around them, the traffic of Stonemarket flowed—carts and sacks and wagons. A yellow cat dashed by with something in its mouth, and Sammish noticed how much her city had grown in the months since Byrn a Sal had taken the throne. Her life had been Seepwater and Longhill and Riverport. The Temple had been outside of her private Kithamar, and Oldgate practically a foreign land. Now she was planning a pull in Green Hill and sitting on a Stonemarket bench among the Hansch without so much as feeling odd about it. Strange how things turned.

She thought of Alys, and sighed. Strange how things turned.

Without preamble, she said, "That was disappointing."

"Yes," Saffa agreed. And then, "What are your eyes seeing?"

Sammish leaned back and the springtime sunlight pressed itself against her eyelids as she spoke. "They're watching. It makes things hard."

"Possible, though," Saffa said. "It has been done before."

"That's not what makes it possible. Someone put hands on the blade before, yes. But they're like me."

"How?"

"They did it and they got caught. Have you ever seen a street player doing false magic? Hiding a stone in his fingers or making birds come out of a girl's skirts? Once you find the trick of it, that's all you see. So it has to be something new every time. What the other ones did before, even if we knew it, it wouldn't help because those fuckers know it too. If I'd slipped in and out before without them catching wise, I could get in that way again. But since they know, I have to find something else. If it were a normal pull, we could switch target. But these are the only bastards who have what I want."

Saffa let the silence between them stretch, and Sammish felt her mind starting to come together. Whether it was the food or the rest, she couldn't say, but she felt clear and solid.

"What we have against us is that they know to watch for us. More guards, more discipline. And they have power. Coin alone would be bad enough, but they're like you. They know mysteries we likely don't, and if there's something sacred in that space, it's sacred to them, not me." She opened her eyes and turned to Saffa. "You don't have anything you can do? Like with Orrel, or the plague street?"

"Ausai and Drau Chaalat knew me. This is the heart of their power, not mine."

"Figured as much," Sammish said. "That's all right."

"Is it?" Saffa said. "It sounds like doom."

"That's just what's against us," Sammish said. "There's for us as well. There are house mice in Longhill we can go to if we need to. Calm Biran and Adric Stone. The compound's large. Something that big is hard to watch. That means there's more people."

"That's bad."

"It's good. We only need one hole to flow through. Each of those guards is a chance for the enemy to slip. And . . ." Sammish rubbed her fingertips together, feeling the grips of her fingers catch against each other. There was something else. Something at the edge of her mind that she hadn't put words to before. Now the words came. "And they're scared. Frightened. It puts them on guard, but it tempts them to make mistakes."

"What mistakes?" Saffa asked, but Sammish didn't hear her. Not really. Her mind was running ahead. If they couldn't pull away, push in. They were on alert. How could she control that? They were afraid. How could she frighten them?

"The captain. Tregarro," she said. "Do his scars look to you like they came from fire?"

W here is she?" Alys asked.

"Sammish?" Little Coop said. "Should I know? Sammish is more your friend than mine."

It was still too cold for the shutters of the Pit's common room to be open, but open they were. The keep's hunger for the coming season drove him to pretend the warmth that had come was enough, and the drinkers and thugs and street rats of Longhill played along, throwing a little more wood into the grate and keeping their jackets around them. Some took their cider and beer out to the street to stand in the sunlight, where the spring had more nearly come. Finches no bigger than Alys's thumb buzzed through the open windows and out again, chirping to one another. Lanna's Hoel had returned from a winter's contract clearing ditches for a farmstead east of the city, and was spending his bronze like he'd never run out.

Alys leaned forward, elbows on the scarred wood of the table. She scowled the way she would have around Ullin's friends in Stonemarket to show that she was a woman to be feared, but

Little Coop had known her on and off since they'd both been digging the edge of the Silt with Grey Linnet, and he only shrugged.

"Last I heard she was talking about some kind of pull with Adric Stone," he said.

"She's captaining her own pulls now?"

"Maybe. It's just something I heard. Might be a lie."

"What kind of pull?"

"Am I Adric? How would I know? She didn't talk with me about it," Little Coop said. "She's no blood to me, any more than you are. She's a good walk-away when you need one, and otherwise, she's just another turd on the float, same as any of us. If I needed to find her in a hurry, I'd be asking you."

Alys shifted on the bench. The keep made his ponderous way over to the fire and threw on another log. A little cloud of embers flared and went grey. Just past the shutters, a pack of street dogs was barking at a prison cart. The wind shifted, carrying the smell from the cart through the Pit, but only for a moment.

"There's money in it if I can find her quickly," Alys said.

"Well, aren't you the prince of all things," Little Coop said, but he said it with a smile. "Look, I don't have anything worth paying for, but the last time I worked with her, it was a crew Nimal put together. Just a day of cut-and-run. Was months ago, but he could find her then. Maybe he'll know how to find her now."

Alys took a bronze from her belt and put it on the table with a click. "You run into her, you let me know, yeah? There'll be more once I find her if you're the finger that points the way."

Little Coop looked at the coin, then up at her. When he picked up the coin, it was with a shrug that meant *Who am I to turn down free coin?* and it didn't give her much hope he'd reach out to her if Sammish lifted her head above water.

"What about Nimal?" she said. She should have asked before she gave him the coin. But Little Coop didn't seem to expect payment for every word he said.

"Last I saw, he was in Seepwater. Down by the stage. They're putting up a show, and he's good at building crews for show times. For all I know, Sammish is with him."

Alys nodded, rose, and walked away, swinging her stick a little too wide, even if she didn't hit anything with it. She felt the eyes of the others on her as she headed out for the street, but when she looked back, she caught no one's gaze. She turned south and west, walking the thin, curving streets with her chin high and her chest out, making a show of filling the road from side to side in part because she didn't actually feel right.

There was an uncomfortable buzzing feeling in her mind—distress without any clear idea what she was distressed about—like a beehive sounding its alarm. She did her best to ignore it, but it wouldn't fade, and whatever it meant was wrapped up with Ullin's bloody face being sluiced clean on the street and the girl she didn't kill and Andomaka saying *Hunt her down and bring her here.* And with Darro whispering *Why won't you look at my face?* in her dreams. She didn't like the confusion, and she didn't know how to clear it away.

A street-corner magician produced a pigeon from a burst of green flame, holding it out to the people and horses as if he'd done something special. Alys kept walking without tossing a coin in the old man's box, and then felt an unexpected stab of guilt. As full as her wallet was, maybe she should have.

The stage stood in the middle of a wide square near the university, its boards ribs-high from the ground so that no one had their view blocked by the head of someone standing before them. And, Alys guessed, because it gave the impression that the women among the players might risk someone peeking up their skirts. The performance at the moment was a tumbling act: large men tossing small girls high enough that they were in more danger of crashing into the roof above them than falling to the ground. She didn't pay them attention. Her eyes were on the crowd. If Nimal was working a pull, they'd likely be near the back, and dipping into the little pond of audience like birds diving for fish.

She saw Dammen first. Last spring he'd been too young and small to work pulls, but now he was old enough. A mop of dark, curly hair over a round face. She thought at first that he'd seen her and was coming to talk, but a movement to her left caught her. He wasn't the only one walking her direction. Disbelief, outrage, and amusement leapt through her like the tumblers on the stage. When Dammen was three steps away, she turned, meeting Nimal with her full attention.

"Is this a joke?" she spat.

Nimal's eyes went wide, and then he laughed. One of his teeth was missing.

"Alys! I didn't recognize you. By all the gods, I mean it. From the back you looked like a Riverport girl come down for the show."

"Did I?"

Dammen looked from one to the other, panic in his eyes. Nimal waved him off, then put his hand in his sleeve. The cutter's blade flashed as it disappeared. "No harm, no harm. Honest error. And you can't tell me this is how you wore your cloaks before. You stand out in this bunch like you owned the place; yeah? Moved up in the world."

His smile seemed genuine, but it still felt like a dig. Alys crossed her arms. "Need a word with you. Not here."

Nimal scratched his arm, and there were words in it meant for the others in his crew. His pull would wait. She nodded him toward one of the stands at the edge of the square where a brewer had set up for the day. Alys bought, and Nimal drank.

"I'm looking for Sammish. Have you seen her? You know where I can find her?"

"She still has the room by the baker's, but I know she's been straying outside Longhill. I thought she was following after you." His voice was friendly enough it almost hid the edge. The buzzing in Alys's mind seemed to grow louder. She was supposed to press on Sammish, but what came out of her mouth was different.

"I go where the work is, that's all. You aren't running your crew in the quarter either. You're coming here."

"No insult," Nimal said, lifting a palm like he was ready to deflect a blow. "Didn't know the plan was yours. Looked from outside like maybe you were hiring on with someone else."

"What's the difference? The coin spends the same."

"One of them's a Longhill pull, and one's not. But you do what you do. It looks to be working out, and I don't judge."

Alys scowled hard enough that her cheeks ached. "Sammish, though. When was the last time you saw her? Little Coop said you'd had her on a crew."

Nimal shook his head. "That was forever ago. Between harvest and Longest Night. I brought her on as a walk-away, paid her with how to find Orrel, and haven't seen her since. She might have taken some offense that I didn't give her the full cut."

"Orrel?"

"Yeah, there was a time she was sniffing around about a fortune-teller's prop knife, and asking where Orrel had got to. I didn't know anything about the one, but I did the other. Offered it to her instead of her coin. We haggled, but you know how it is. Sometimes you regret the things you agree to." He shrugged elaborately.

"Where is Orrel?"

"The earth and the air, now. They burned his corpse just after Longest Night. Sammish saw him before that. I don't think she got what he owed her, though."

"When did she know?" Alys said, and the man behind Nimal turned to look at her. "When did you tell her?"

"Like I said. After harvest. Just before your brother's nameday."

If he'd slapped her, it would have stung less. She and Sammish had hunted for Orrel together, but Sammish had found him and kept it secret. She found herself touching her wallet like she was making sure it was still there. Like she was seeing whether she'd lost something.

Nimal drank the last of his beer, handed the cup back to the boy at the brewer's stand, and looked at her, tilting his head. "Are you all right?"

"I'm fine."

"Look, it's none of mine. Your work's yours. But is this about what happened to Darro?"

It was. It had been. It had all been about Darro, about losing him and the pain of his being gone. About making it right. *Why won't you look at my face?* The buzzing was louder than the crowd that cheered the tumblers. The spring sun was too bright and too hot. She turned her back and stalked away, not caring what Nimal thought. Not caring about anything but the tightness in her chest and the trembling in the world. She bumped into someone as she passed through the crowd, and didn't look back to see who it was.

She walked toward Longhill. The afternoon sun shifted toward the palace. The streets reeked. Her hands ached, and she forced herself to unball her fists. She had been angry for weeks, it felt like. She couldn't remember not being angry; even if there had been stretches when she'd forgotten it, the rage had always been there at the back, hadn't it? It didn't seem possible that she could be so consumed by it now if it hadn't always been there, waiting in the dark of her soul and growing.

Sammish had betrayed her. Sammish had known where Orrel was, had gone to speak with him, and kept whatever he'd said from her. Well, she'd find Sammish and whatever plot Sammish was working, and she'd turn it over to Andomaka like a shovel turning up grubs. She marched to her room, climbing in the darkness, unlocking her door. She would grab the candle, reach back to Tregarro and Andomaka, and tell them all she knew and hadn't said about who and what Sammish was. They would set the dogs on her.

Darro's ashes stood where she'd left them. The yellow wax of the deathmark caught the sun that pressed in through the cracks in the shutters. She went toward her safe cache, but the storm in her head and the presence of her brother's small, dark box distracted her. She sat on the bench by the little table. Her breath was ragged, and she didn't know why.

But Andomaka had set the dogs on Sammish already, hadn't she? That was Alys. Green Hill might call her little wolf girl, but what they meant was dog.

"I'm angry," she said to the darkness, to the ashes, to Longhill all around her. "I'm so *angry*."

But she meant a hundred things more than that. She was angry and confused. Angry and embarrassed. Angry and, though she couldn't think why, ashamed. The urge came upon her to lash out at Darro's box, shatter the wood under her club and spill the ashes onto the floor. She'd cocked her arm back before she reined the impulse in. She bared her teeth at the deathmark instead.

"Fuck you," she growled at her dead brother. "*Fuck you*."

She went to the safe cache, but not for the candle. She took the coins instead. All that was left of them. She would spend them all if that's what it took to find Sammish. If that was what it took to throw a wet cloth over the fires burning in her head. She'd find another way to pay for the room, or if she didn't she'd leave them. Nothing mattered now but making this right. Making it stop.

She went back down the chimney-dark stairs, swinging her club against the walls as she went, taking pleasure in the violence of the sound and the jolt in her hand. There was a way. There was a path through the city that began with her and led to Sammish, and all she had to do was find it.

The spring streets were fuller than the cold of winter or the steam and sweat of summer would allow. A few mule-drawn carts, but mostly the men and women and children and dogs of the quarter filling the narrow, curving streets. The voices and wheels made a murmuring like the river's. She passed the turn that led to Ibdish's, and for a moment she was the girl who'd fled there on coronation day, a city guardsman with bare blade and violence in his eyes at her heels. It seemed like something from a dream.

A wide-faced, thick-shouldered girl not more than ten years old squatted against a wall. A thin, white-haired boy sat at her side. Big Salla and Elbrith, trading something back and forth between them with the seriousness of gamblers at the brewer's window. Big Salla looked up at Alys as she passed, the young girl's eyes narrowed in suspicion. Alys ignored her and kept walking.

But she was aware in a way she hadn't been before of the richness of her cloak, the worked leather of her belt. Even the stitching on her boots spoke of money spent, of status, of power. She'd known that when she bought them. It was what she'd wanted. What she'd paid for. It felt like a costume now, and she became aware of how much gold was in the little wallet folded at her hip. If someone had been foolish enough to walk past her with that much coin when she'd been Big Salla's age, she would have made a try for it, crew at her back or no. If the little girl came for it, Alys would crack her skull and be grateful for the chance to. She didn't know what that said about her, only that it was truth.

She imagined Sammish appearing in the street before her. Why not? Longhill was her home too, and there weren't so many streets and alleys that finding each other by chance would have been odd. The baker's house where Sammish kept her room was only a few corners from where Alys was now. If she didn't want to talk to anyone, to ask anything, she could just pace these streets until the inevitable happened...and then...

And then she wasn't sure. Grab the girl and march her to Green Hill? It was a long way. Beat her until she broke, and haul her back to Darro's ashes where she could use the candle to summon Tregarro and his swords? Maybe that. The details hardly mattered. She'd find Sammish.

And do what Darro would have done?

The thought came through the blare and haze like someone had whispered it in her ear. In truth, Alys didn't know what Darro would have done in her place. She couldn't picture him in it, and that as much as anything frightened her.

She turned down the street she'd been going toward, only realizing as she did that she'd had a destination in mind. She walked down the street she hadn't passed since five days before Longest Night. The ice and snow that had been there then was melted and gone and forgotten.

The door was narrow, and it hadn't been oiled in years. The pegs had been bored out and replaced, and the latch was old iron that streaked its rust down the wood. Alys hefted her club, feeling its weight in her hand as she readied it to knock. She hesitated, put it back down, and used the back of her knuckles.

A voice came from within, but there were no words in it. A grunt, maybe, or a muttered curse, then footsteps. Her mother opened the door and met Alys without expression. There were red marks on her cheek where she'd slept too long without moving. The room behind her was dark, and the air that came from the house smelled of old, stale wine.

"I'm looking for Sammish. I thought she might have come to speak with you," Alys said. "I didn't know you were sleeping."

For a moment, she wasn't sure her mother had heard her. A moment of fear, brief and bright as a falling star, went through her that something was wrong. That her mother was sick or lost in drink or that age had eaten her while Alys was away. Then the old woman shrugged and turned back to the darkness of the house. She left the door standing open. Alys waited for a moment, uncertain, before following her in.

S he didn't play, you know," Tregarro said. "Andomaka, I mean. She didn't play."

"She may have picked up an interest," it said with her mouth. "I have stepped into lives before this one. Still no sign of Elaine a Sal?"

Tregarro shook his head. They sat in a drawing room that overlooked the courtyard. The carved wood walls glowed with borrowed sunlight, seeming deeper than they were. Outside, birds sang their courting songs, and inside, the board between them was clear. It put the red beads on the starting places on its side, the clear ones before Tregarro. The captain of the Daris Brotherhood's guard and initiate to its secrets waited for it to be done, then made a standard opening move. The thread of Kithamar considered whether to follow the old pattern or risk something new. After a moment, it refused the sacrifice, staying with the old strategies. A change in one thing might tempt it to change something else.

The scarred man was interesting. It had known him when it

was Ausai and Tregarro an initiate from the east with a ready sword and a deep loyalty to the brotherhood. He had no roots in the city, and so his loyalties could be pure. While it had been the Bronze Coast boy, Tregarro had seemed much the same. It was only now that it was Andomaka that the guardsman had begun to seem different. Softer, with a mordant humor that he tried to keep hidden. Tregarro had become a strong and melancholy man. It didn't know whether that was because Andomaka saw things like that more clearly in the same way her tongue changed the taste of salt, or because Tregarro had treated her differently than he had Ausai and the boy and now couldn't change the habit.

"If we must find Elaine, though," Tregarro said, "I know how to bring her out. She'll have to come to her coronation."

Was he showing off? Maybe. People often built dreams of and even love for those forbidden to them. If Tregarro had put a handle on the back of his head, there was no reason that the thing that called itself Kithamar shouldn't use it. It canted its head forward, flirting with him, and looked up at him now with a half-smile. "You're thinking the next step is to unmake Byrn a Sal?"

"Hear me out," Tregarro said, pushing a bead. "I know you counsel patience. I understand it. But the Longhill girl was in here. She was at the altar. You held her by the hand, and she held yours. The boy's mother was in the city, and there's no reason to think she's gone."

"I have enemies. I've always had enemies."

"And you've had the city to protect you. Now you only have me and mine. And if that is not enough, I will have failed in my sacred duty. If Byrn a Sal dies, Elaine will walk at his funeral and sit her coronation and we will know where she is, or else when he dies she'll have vanished and you will be in the palace where you should be."

There was something in its new-acquired breast that leapt at the idea. It let the smile widen a degree. Enough to show amusement, but not permission. It pushed a bead to block. "That's blowing hot and cold out of the same mouth. The palace keeps its prince safe or else it doesn't. Byrn has all the protections you're offering me. Why do you think taking action is a better strategy than waiting for him to make a mistake?"

"I have a . . . thought. A plan. And even if it fails, it will only cost my life. Not yours."

"Tell me."

As they played, he spoke and it listened. Its mind shifted between the layers of what it heard: the plan itself and also how it was presented, the way its servant leaned forward as he spoke and the words he chose, the play of violence and politics as inevitable as the grooves in the board where the glass beads shifted. It might have been the lingering intoxication of danger or the impatience that came from feeling exposed or the echo of the trust Andomaka had had for this man, but it found itself being persuaded.

It shifted a crimson bead, closing the trap against the last clear piece, as Tregarro's proposal reached its ending. The coincidence felt like an omen, and it caught a stray memory—a scrap of Andomaka that still remained in the labyrinth of her flesh. Shau the twice-born, walking the streets of the city in two girls. A bit of dream that hadn't faded with daylight, meaningless.

It leaned back in the chair, the wood creaking under it, and for a long, quiet time it thought. Tregarro pressed his lips tight at first, anxious and uncertain, but with time the man's emotions settled and the city's did as well. It waited to see what it thought. It was safer now that it was in Andomaka's flesh, but that didn't mean it was safe. If the line of a Sal could be ended, and ended before Elaine found herself carrying some new babe it would have to kill along with her...It rubbed its new lips with the back of its new hand.

"There is some virtue in that," it said. "But if you are captured, a Sal and his men will look to the brotherhood."

"If I'm captured, I won't be questioned," Tregarro said. He meant he would die before he betrayed the brotherhood. It believed him.

It went through the connections of court like it was recalling the players in its favorite poem. Which of them would suspect that the sudden deaths of the prince and his daughter were more than mischance, and of those what fraction would care. It carried generations of intrigue in its mind. There would be ripples, complications, changes that it would need to make. It all would have been so much simpler if it had been able to take Byrn a Sal's flesh instead of this.

It wondered now, looking back, at all the trouble it had had fathering a child when it had been Ausai. Apart from his secret bastard in the Bronze Coast, none of the women it had cultivated had managed a child. Had that been planned too?

"Ah, Tallis," it said to its dead son and brother, "what did you think to win?"

It reached out and started putting the beads back in their starting places. The glass made soft, soothing ticks against the wood.

"Another game?" Tregarro asked.

"No, not now," it said. "After the prince is dead."

A dric had a long, horsey face for an Inlisc. His hair was black and curled, and he wore it pulled back in a way that he probably thought made him look dashing. He was also older than Sammish by a couple of years, which didn't matter much now except that he might still think of her as too young and inexperienced to set her own pulls. At least, that was her fear.

She was on the street when she caught sight of him in the shadows under the canal bridge in the heart of Seepwater where the stoneworks met the water. Flatboats passed, poled by men without shirts who shouted casual obscenities at each other as they negotiated rights of way. On the bridge above him, a prison cart was preparing a load of shit, debris, and dead animals to toss into the water as they did every week. A few people braved the stink in hopes of seeing a boatman drenched in it. It happened sometimes. A pair of ruined leather shoes were nailed to a pole at canal's edge, taken from a drowned corpse and left there in case anyone could recognize them and identify the dead. Sammish didn't know them, though they looked well made. Kithamar might be up to its tits in thieves and corruption, but no one stole clothes from the drowned. There were limits.

As she made her way along the quay, Adric watched her come. He had a long-stemmed pipe and puffed bluish smoke that smelled better than she expected. She sat down beside him and looked out over the water: dark in the shadow and blinding in the light.

"Thanks for coming," she said.

"Nowhere particular to be."

"Still."

"Welcome." He drew on the pipe and puffed out smoke. "Work, is it?"

Sammish felt the knot in her stomach tighten. When she'd rehearsed the plan to herself, it all sounded plausible. Now that she was speaking aloud, she worried it would seem ridiculous.

"It's a safe-cache pull," she said. "In Green Hill."

He shifted to look at her, curiosity in his expression. "Which family?"

"No family. One of the religious brotherhoods. I won't say which yet. You understand."

"I do. What's the take?"

Sammish shrugged. "Depends on what's in the cache. It's Green Hill, though. One of their dinner plates is worth a week's food in Longhill." She chuckled, but it sounded forced even to her. A scowl touched the corner of Adric's mouth, and she felt herself losing him. "I'm looking for something in particular. It's my cut. Anything outside it, that's the payout."

"What is it you're wanting?"

"Last harvest, I had a knife I was looking into. Finding where it was from. Who wanted it. They have it, and I want it back."

Adric nodded. That, at least, was a scenario he understood. "Who's the buyer?"

"Me. Just me."

"No one else behind it?"

"Someone else with me. Not behind me, though. This one's mine."

One of the boatmen shouted and lifted his pole, dripping and green, from the canal to swing at another boat. Adric sighed. "You have someone inside?"

"No, but I've been in before. Not a whole map, but enough to start, and their guard captain will show us the rest of the way."

"How does that happen?"

"We start a fire and come in with the sand-and-water crew. The captain's been burned before. Badly. Wading into the flame won't come easy for him, and getting the blade out safely will be what he needs to do."

"This thing's more important than keeping his people alive?"

"It is. We raise the alarm and start the smoke when he's some-place we can see him, and then follow him back. He'll lead us straight to it. We take what's ours in the chaos, and get out before the ashes drown."

"Did something like that at a warehouse three years back," Adric said. "House man got so scared, he grabbed the payroll and ran out the back. We took him in the alley."

"I know. It's why I wanted you on it."

"Yours has more risk."

"Mine has a bigger payout, and I'm not taking a cut except the knife."

"What are you going to do with it?"

"Sink it in the river and let the fish shit on it forever," Sam-mish said with more heat than she'd intended. Adric nodded, leaned forward, and tapped the ash from his pipe into the canal; the grey flecks darkened and vanished as soon as they touched water.

"Interested, then?" Sammish asked.

"No."

"Oh," she said, and looked out at the canal. She tried not to speak. "Why not?"

"Too many holes in it." He might have been talking about the weather or the odds of a fight he didn't have money on. "You have to find this captain before you start the fire so you can follow him. He has to go for the safe cache instead of any of the other thousand things. If someone else is assigned to grab the payroll, you'll be following the wrong man. You don't have anyone inside, so you have to get in while he's already reacting. Walking through a Green Hill compound's a hard pull. Aunt Thorn wouldn't do it. It's the kind of thing someone would do at the top of their arc, to show they could, and most of them would fail. It's an amateur plan. No offense. We all start amateurs. But pick a tailor's house or a farm cart first. Spend a few years getting good at it. Then you'll know enough to see why this one's too hard. And anyway..."

He tucked his pipe up his sleeve, shaking his head gently from side to side. His hair looked stupid.

"Anyway?" she said, the way she knew he'd meant her to.

"It's not really a pull, is it? We work pulls to get coin, and there's no coin in this. It's revenge, maybe. Or pride. I don't know, and it doesn't matter to me much. But you're leading this one with your heart, not your head. I don't do passion work. It's a rule of mine."

"All right. I respect that. You know anyone looking for work that doesn't have your scruples?"

"Anyone that would take the job, I'd be doing you a favor by not naming them." Adric shifted, stood, and stretched. "You shouldn't do this unless you have to."

Sammish nodded. Then, when he didn't walk away, "I have to."

"Pray first." Adric turned to the north, walking toward Newmarket and whatever business or whim called him there. Sammish pulled her knees up and hugged them. She was going to have to make her way back to Saffa without good news. And worse, everything Adric said felt true. The plan wasn't right yet, and she wasn't ready. She'd never even been a cutter, just a walkaway. This was beyond her, and she needed it anyway and couldn't quite explain why except that she did. If she couldn't give Saffa hope that the pull would work, the older woman might go back to the Bronze Coast to heal from her wounds or else only live with them. Sammish would be on her own.

And even then, she'd get that fucking knife back.

She watched the flatboats for a time, hoping for some inspiration that didn't come. A boat heavy with tuns from a brewer's house poled its sluggish way north, and the boys on the bridge shouted down, begging the boatman to drop one over the side for them. The boatman made a friendly obscene gesture. Across the canal two older men walked together, hand in hand, their grey heads canted in toward each other as they talked. The sun shifted the shadows around her, but no new wisdom came to her. When she rose, her legs ached.

As she hauled herself along the quay, she heard her name called from the bridge. She squinted up, hand blocking the sun, and saw Little Coop waving down at her. She lifted her chin, acknowledging him, and started walking away, but he motioned for her to wait. He clambered down to the quay. She stood by the water's edge. The sunlight against her neck felt good. Little pleasures, even in evil times.

"Was looking for you," Little Coop said, catching his breath.

"Here I am."

"Alys was at the Pit. Paid me to tell her how to find you."

This day just keeps getting better, Sammish thought, and spat into the water. "You can tell her I was here."

"Would I do that for? She's made it pretty fucking clear from how she dresses and throws her coin around that she's too good for Longhill. I just thought you should know she was looking. In case you don't want to get found."

"Thanks for that."

"What happened to her anyway?"

Sammish shook her head. "She lost someone," she said.

Alys waited for a moment, uncertain, before following her mother into the gloom of her house.

The stink of wine was stronger inside, and with it the smell of dust and sweat. Her mother seemed to sink into the dimness like a fish swimming down in murky water. Before Alys's eyes could adapt to the darkness, there was a clatter of wood against wood, and her mother opened a thin set of shutters. Daylight spilled in, thin as milk water. The room was small and narrow, and the wood it was made from was dark with age and old smoke. There were two cots, one against either wall. One was clean, with a wool blanket folded neatly at its foot. Her mother sat on the other one. The floor was old earth, doused with steer's blood and pounded until it was nearly hard as stone. A handful of rushes were strewn on it, but they didn't look fresh. The only decoration was a length of yellow cloth nailed to the wall with a prayer written on it that Alys didn't recognize.

Her mother saw her looking at it. "It's not mine."

"No?"

Her mother yawned and shook her wide head. "Thin Maddie prayed to the Faceless, and apparently it came through, because she's gone all pious. I share the place with her and Coul. Rennie's Coul, not Big Coul."

"You're a bed short."

"They've got work in the days," her mother said. "Thin Maddie's cleaning for a couple families in Seepwater. Coul's got a place on a flatboat, if he doesn't show up late again. The pole man's Hansch, and he don't like Inlisc on his water. But the coin's good."

"What about you?"

Her mother heaved a great sigh. Her smile was joyless. "I'm hauling piss from the open troughs to a launderer's yard in the Smoke. Half a bronze for every jug of it. They use it to keep the white cloth brighter. When that's not work, there's a butcher that lets me pull feathers off the birds. The piss money's better, though. Things are harder since Timor went back south to the river villages. He could pull in enough coin we didn't need anyone but us." Timor. The thin man Alys had shouted down the day that Darro died.

"Why didn't you go with him?" Alys asked, and it didn't come out as harshly as she'd meant it to. It sounded almost like she cared. The thickness in her mind was still loud.

"I'm Longhill," was all her mother said.

A silence fell between them. Alys felt it like a hand on her shoulder, pressing down. She crossed her arms and squared herself. Her mother's glance down and up along her felt like a joke she wasn't in on. "I'm looking for Sammish."

"You said."

"Have you seen her? Did she come talk with you?"

"What do you want her for?"

"She betrayed me." She hadn't said the words to anyone until now, and they were like opening a door. She clenched her fists until they ached, trying to steady herself, but the fog and confusion that had been spinning her around like a dancer at a masquerade had lifted its mask. Now that she knew it was sorrow, she could no more stop feeling it than will her skin numb. Fat tears dropped from her eyes. She tried to put rage in her voice, but what came out was the wail of a child. "She said she was helping me, but she found Orrel weeks ago. Months ago. And she didn't tell me. I did everything. I almost killed a girl because they told me to, and all this time, Sammish knew. She knew what happened to Darro. She probably knows who killed him and she..."

Didn't tell me was lost in a cough and a sob. Alys's club dropped to the ground with a soft clatter, and she closed her eyes, willing her body to stop. Demanding that the vast sadness tearing through her go back to its cage where she could forget it again.

Everything seemed to bleed together. Darro's pale body on the altar and Ullin's blood-soaked face, Sammish's unexpected contempt, and Nimal talking of Orrel and the girl Alys had been meant to kill but didn't. Everything stood on everything else, until she didn't know what she was mourning for except all of it. She was overwhelmed by a storm she couldn't see, but felt it beating at her from every direction.

She turned her back on her mother, wrapped her arms tightly around her belly, and stood as still as her weeping would allow. The tears felt like she was vomiting out a black river that would never end. Her face was hot. The corners of her mouth pulled down fish-like and hurting. Her nose was running like she was sick, and she ached at the core from belly to heart.

Some timeless hour later—a minute or a day—she heard her mother shift, and expected to feel soft, enfolding arms pulling her into an embrace like she was still small, but when she looked over, her mother had only pulled one foot up onto the cot and leaned against the wall. Sad Linly watched her with the same impassive calm a butcher might have for a pig being led into the slaughterhouse.

"What?" Alys spat.

"Darro killed Darro. Anyone holding the blade was coincidence."

Alys felt her jaw slide forward. Her body felt raw, like her skin had been stripped away and even a breath of air could sting her like salt on a wound.

Her mother shrugged. "It's truth. I loved my boy to the stars and down again. It broke me, him dying. But it wasn't a surprise. He was too much of his own. He thought he was cleverer than everyone else put together. As soon as he moved away from me, I saw how it would be. I hoped I was wrong, but I wasn't."

"Take that back," Alys said.

"Or what? You'll beat me?" Her mother leaned forward, elbows on her knees, and shook her head. "I loved my boy, and I mourned him. I won't be done mourning him 'til it's my turn on the pyre. But I know what he was. Thought he was better than everyone else, that his shit didn't stink. It got him in trouble, and not just this last time."

"He was…" Alys began, and then realized she didn't know how to end.

"He looked out for you," her mother said. "And he dreamed big. Give him that. If he'd stolen the moon one night, he'd have been scheming against the sun come morning."

"He was helping to save the city," Alys said. "Not just Longhill. Everything."

"Did he tell you that? Or was it his puppeteers up in Green Hill?"

Alys reached for an answer and came back with silence.

Her mother pointed at her with a rueful smile, taking the silence for a reply. "He sang the song for them, but all he wanted was the coin and the chance at something bigger. Broader. Grander. He was never going to make it there. He was their hired knife, and they were never going to let him be more."

"His rooms were better than this," Alys said, gesturing at the hovel around them, and her mother laughed.

"How do you think he paid for them? The sweat of his honest brow? His cunning and stealth?" Her laughter was serrated. "Every few weeks he came by with that sad smile of his and a story and promise that he'd get it all back to me. I should have cut him off. Should have told him that if he wanted help, he could bring a bedroll and take a spot on my floor. Save up his coins until he could do whatever it was this time. But he was my boy, and it would have humiliated him, so I gave in. When he died, he owed me eighteen in silver. You know what I could do with eighteen in silver? Not share a cot with Thin Maddie for one thing."

"You paid for his rooms?"

"And his jaunty clothes and his boots. And probably his whores and pork bowls and beer. What's worse? I borrowed sometimes to do it. I thought it would be better. Someone gets a young man like that in debt, and they can make him do things to come even. The kind of things that puts a magistrate's rope around your neck. If there was going to be a burden carried, better it be mine than my babies'." She shook her head in disgust. "Go ahead and laugh. I'm funny."

"That's not truth. He worked. He made his own pulls."

"He was better at spending than working. He was looking for the one grand gesture that squared everything. Only when he found it, he died and gave it all to you, didn't he?"

"I was doing what he did," Alys said.

"If you had been, you'd have been begging me for money, not shaming me to everyone on the street. Not attacking me at my son's wake. Not turning away from me every time I saw you like I smelled like someone fresh from the shit carts."

Alys didn't know she was going to shout until she was already shouting. "I was keeping him alive!"

For once her mother didn't flinch or even turn away. "How did that go? Is he living?"

"There's more of him here than if you'd been left to it alone," she said, but the words had no weight. She sounded petulant and young, even to herself.

"Some days, I think Caria was the best child I had," her mother said. "She didn't live long enough to treat me like you two did."

"That's not fair."

"Who gives a shit? Who promised you fair? I didn't. Fair is good people get treated good, and bad people get the bad. That sound like anyplace you know? I've never been there."

Her mother's cheeks were shining in the dim light, wet with tears Alys hadn't seen falling until now. There was no thickness in her voice to announce her sorrow, just the vast weariness of rage pithed by hopelessness.

Alys sat on the other cot, old wood creaking under her weight. The noise and storm had gone from her mind, and what was left was calm and empty and exhausted. She felt still—really still— for the first time she could recall. "I want him back."

"I do too. But we can't have him. So we have to let him go."

"I don't want to. I'm not sure I can."

Her mother shook her head slowly. "Then he'll drag you with him."

Alys leaned over and put her cheek on the folded blanket. The roughness of the wool should have itched, but giving her weight over to it felt so comfortable she could ignore that little part. Across the room, her mother tilted her head and lay down too, looking across the little gap, eye to eye with Alys, like they were still upright and the whole world had turned around them. Alys felt other words rising at the back of her mind: *I'm sorry* and *I've made a mistake* and *I'm so tired of being myself.* None of them seemed urgent enough to say. Her mother's gaze was steady and passionless, but the judgment was gone from it. She reminded Alys of an old frog sitting in the spray of a fountain. She reminded Alys of the woman who'd been her mother when she had been a child—someone who'd looked like this, but with darker hair and smoother skin and less weathering around her eyes.

She didn't feel herself falling asleep, but she must have, because a moment later the room was dark and her mouth tasted stale, and her mother was opening a little safe cache and lighting a candle. Andomaka and Tregarro and Ullin and the girl in the garden all seemed like something from a play she'd seen down in Seepwater. Not real people, not the things she'd shaped her life around for months. They were all Green Hill and Stonemarket. She was Longhill.

"Got to work," her mother said. "Coul and Thin Maddie should be here quick. They'll want to sleep."

Alys nodded, rose, and took up her club. In the candlelight, it looked gaudy. Too expensive for a stick and a lump of lead. Her mother stepped out to the street, and she followed. They walked together through dark streets and alleys, their steps finding each other's rhythm. They didn't speak. If her mother was surprised by the company, she didn't say it. They stopped at the common trough outside a taproom where a tin pail overflowing with old piss was waiting. Her mother took it by its handle, and they walked on. Another trough in a square, another pail, and

Alys took this one. It was heavier than she'd expected, but she didn't complain. They stopped at two more places as they passed through Seepwater to the bridge. The night was full dark, and almost moonless by the time they reached it. The Khahon flowed black under the southernmost bridge. The yellow stone and black mortar were only different values of shadow. Cold piss spilled over the lips of the pails. Alys got it down the side of one ankle bad enough that her boot squeaked, but she didn't complain. It was the work. If it wasn't filthy, degrading, disgusting, then it wouldn't pay.

The launderer's yard was at the edge of the Smoke, and bright with lanterns. The air stank of the forge, and the fat, squat man at the side door greeted Alys's mother with a nod that wasn't unfriendly. He sniffed at the pails to make sure they weren't just river water being passed off as the real thing, then waved them in. Her mother poured the buckets into a tank, and Alys did the same. As they carried their empty pails back out, the squat man handed them each a bronze coin old enough that the face of Prince Ausai had started going a little green with verdigris. Alys passed hers to her mother.

"Against the eighteen silver," she said. They were the first words they'd spoken since they left her mother's room. They walked back across the bridge, the empty pails clanking, and headed to other places where men and women drank and ate and shouted and slept and begged and threatened, seeking out the ones whose keepers and guardsmen cared enough to leave a pail out for the rats of Longhill to carry away. It left the streets of Seepwater smelling a little better, and it was a charity to let the poor Inlisc bastards scrape up a little coin. Twice more, Alys and her mother crossed the bridge and came back. The stars shifted above them like a vast audience of gods and spirits, looking down at the show.

The third time, Alys kept the squat man's coin. As they reached the Seepwater side of the bridge, she leaned over and kissed the side of her mother's head. The older woman patted her shoulder. Alys turned a corner by herself, and her mother was only the sound of soft footsteps moving away in the night.

She made her way up the steep black stairway and into her room—Darro's room—in the blind darkness. She remembered leaving there in the morning, possessed by confusion and shame. It seemed like longer. It seemed like someone else's memory.

She stripped off her fouled clothes and found something cleaner. By the time she pulled her boots back on, the sound of birdsong was shouting through the still-dark streets. She opened her shutters and looked east, but whatever light the finches and sparrows and pigeons were celebrating was still too dim for her eyes. She stopped at Darro's box and ran her fingertips over the wax-filled cuts of his deathmark. Sorrow still flooded her heart, but it came up slowly, like the river rising inch by inch, and not the crushing impact of a wave. She didn't know what it signified, except that something had changed. And since Darro couldn't change anymore, that meant she had.

The eastern stars were fading into grey by the time she reached the baker's. He had been up for hours, apparently, because the oven was hot and the air smelled like butter and flour and hot fruit. She knocked at Sammish's door, and when there wasn't an answer, she sat by it, legs folded. The baker came out to pull a batch of plum tarts from the oven and put the next batch in. Alys used her one bronze piss-coin to buy three of them unglazed and hot from the oven, then sat with them on her thigh until they cooled enough to eat. She didn't know when Sammish would come back to the little room, but it seemed likely that sooner or later, she would. Instead of rushing through Kithamar flinging coins and making threats like some private guardsman, Alys could just wait here and be patient. It was interesting to see how much of the urgency and panic had been Andomaka's and Tregarro's, and how little Alys missed it now that she'd put it down.

She ate one of the tarts as the sun rose, casting gold and rose across the rooftops. The noise of Kithamar—of Longhill— surrounded her: voices in laughter and contention, the paired clatter of hooves and cartwheels, the bark of street dogs joyful and threatening and bored. The plum was sweet and sour, and even with the pastry cool enough to rip off bits with her bare fingers, the center of the tart would still burn an unwary tongue. She ate slowly, noticing the way the sweet and the salt matched each other, the way the flavors changed as it dissolved in her mouth.

She saw Sammish as soon as the nondescript brown girl turned the corner, and she was almost shocked to see how thin she'd become. The mouse-brown hair was pulled back from a sterner face than the one Alys remembered her having, and the dark brown eyes were hard and bright as stones in the river.

Sammish's steps faltered when she saw Alys, but they didn't fail. Sammish came forward, mouth pinched, chin high. Alys didn't stand up, and she noticed that Sammish stopped far enough away that she couldn't get grabbed.

"Heard you were looking for me?"

"I was," Alys said.

"What for?"

"Well. It was because Andomaka wanted me to track you down for that stunt you pulled at the brotherhood's house. Going in after the boy. Job was to find you and bring you to her."

"So you're her hunting dog."

"Was. Don't seem to be now."

Sammish crossed her arms, but her expression softened. Not

all the way back to the girl Alys had known, but to someone less clearly on the edge of flight. "Why are you here, then?"

Alys considered the question like it was a riddle. When she spoke, she spoke slowly, picking the words with care. "To say that I'm sorry, I think."

"For what?"

She picked one of the two remaining tarts off her leg and held it out. "All of it."

W hat did you tell her?" Saffa asked. There was no judgment in her voice.

Sammish leaned back, crossed arms on her chest like she was
protecting herself. "Didn't tell her about the pull. Or where to
find you. Where to find us, I mean."

"But the rest."

"Yeah. The rest. What Orrel said about how Darro died. And
about you, and about Timu. What Prince Ausai was. What the
knife was for. Everything."

"What did she say?"

"Nothing worth passing on. She listened. I'm not sure she
cared about anything that wasn't about Darro, not really," Sammish said. She shifted her weight, her eyes on the open door
and the empty, sun-washed street beyond it. Saffa gave her the
silence like a gift. "She didn't seem surprised, though. I mean,
not like she already knew about Andomaka and Ausai, but not
like she didn't believe it. She just accepted it as true and we
moved forward."

"And do you believe her?"

"About what?"

"Her change of heart."

Sammish leaned forward and closed her eyes. The hollowness in her chest ached, and she didn't understand why. Or she did, but she didn't want to. "Why not? People see through their own bullshit sometimes. It can happen."

"Or they can pretend as a way to set a trap."

"She's not that good a liar."

Sammish opened her eyes and stood. Staying still wasn't comfortable. Moving wasn't either. Ever since she'd found Alys at the door of her rooms, the best she'd been able to find was shifting between the two. Three steps got her to the doorway. Saffa had let the illness she brought to the street fade for fear that it would bring more attention by lasting longer than the protection was worth. It meant no more ropes at the mouths of the alleys and streets. The only thing that kept Saffa safe now was not being noticed. That was a thin and brittle armor.

At the end of the street, people were walking. Mostly Hansch, but enough Inlisc that Sammish didn't stand out. Not that Sammish ever stood out. "You're dead calm about all this."

Saffa's smile was weary. "I am sworn of the spirit house. I'm well practiced in grief."

"Well, I'm still a beginner," Sammish said acidly. "Adric won't join us. I talked him through the pull, and he thought there were too many holes in it."

"Why?" Saffa asked.

"Because there's too many holes in it. He's right. We have to be in the compound and have the guard captain in sight before the fire warning comes. And Andomaka too. Once they show us where the knife's kept, we'll know how to get it."

"Then we kill them and take it?"

"Was the thought, yes."

"You seem sure that we can beat a professional swordsman. Or the beast at the heart of Kithamar in its own lair. Or both."

"I was more sure when I saw Adric doing the fighting. So maybe we find the place, then hide in the compound. They put it back when the warning's over, and we take it in the night, leave under cover of dark, and no one the wiser."

Saffa tilted her head.

"Holes," Sammish said. "I know."

"We ought not do this." When Sammish shook her head, Saffa scowled. "I haven't asked it of you, and if I had, I would release you from your promise."

The hollowness grew—dread and sorrow and confusion. "I started all this for her. For Alys. And they took her. Or gave her a way for her to take herself."

"And that mattered?"

The hollowness changed at the words, collapsing into something exquisitely painful and vast. "It did."

"But if she's back now, why?"

"Because I'm not back. I knew what I was. Now I don't. They took my home from me. Everything's still here. Everyone's still here. But I don't fit it. That's what they took from me."

"This won't win it back, you know."

"I do."

The older woman came to her, laced her dry, thin fingers with Sammish's own, held her for a moment, then released her and wiped the tears off her cheek. "And your friend whose brother I killed. Are you thinking of asking her to help us?"

Sammish looked out the door again.

Tregarro's quarters in the brotherhood were the same ones he'd taken when he first came there years and years before. Thousands of nights, he'd dreamed on that same bed, woken to the light spilling through those same shutters. He pulled on his leathers now. They didn't have the crest of the brotherhood or of his family. Not that his family would have meant anything here. They were good, solid huntsman's clothes, these. Worn, if not by him, at least by a man near his build. His blade was not his usual, but a plain length of steel with a good edge. Anything more would have been too much. His scars marked him, as they always had, but there were other men who had been burned young. If he took himself far enough away from the city, he could be anyone. It was the price of his plan.

And it was the draw of it.

The poison, he had in a small stitched leather bag no larger than his thumbnail. Grains like salt, but with a thin greenish cast. He tucked it between his belt and his hip, easy to retrieve and easy to overlook. The last thing was a grey cloak with a deep hood to help hide his face. Once it was on, he could go. Instead, he sat for a moment on the edge of the little bed and rested his head in his hands. It took more time to gather himself than he would have liked.

In the halls, he wore his hood up and kept his eyes down. He didn't know whether the people he passed would recognize him from his stride. If any did, they would know better than to ask questions now or tell tales later. He gave himself credit enough for keeping discipline that well, anyway. He passed through the public temple, past the guest houses, and in through the kitchens where a brace of pheasant hung on a string. Their tiny feet were bound, their black eyes sightless. He took them over his shoulder, paused, and put them down. There was time enough to see her one last time.

Andomaka, the transformed Andomaka, was in the private temple, sitting on the altar in the same pose the Bronze Coast boy had sat. The board in play before her. She didn't look up, but she knew he was there. Neither spoke for a time as he considered the well-known contours of her face. No one thing had changed in her, but the way all of her features came together was like seeing a different woman. Which she was.

"I'm off," he said. "I won't be back . . . for some time. Perhaps weeks."

"No," she said, and she turned to look at him. Her smile was knowing. The sense of seeing Ausai wearing her body like a cloak had been eerie at first. But it had grown harder and harder to see the old prince in her expressions. The thread of Kithamar passed through them both like they were beads on a necklace, but they weren't the same person. That, surely, was what he had come here to see.

"No?" he asked.

"When you have done this," Andomaka said, "your duty to

me will be complete. You have done well, Tregarro. You don't have to come back."

"But the girl—"

Andomaka stepped toward him, and without realizing it, he took a step toward her. "Elaine a Sal will be my problem, and I will solve her. Don't concern yourself."

"Have I given reason for your displeasure?" His voice came out as a whisper.

"Quite the opposite. You have dedicated yourself to the brotherhood and all that it serves. And to Andomaka Chaalat, who will be the prince of the city. But I have done this before enough to recognize...patterns. Your work here was good. And your work here is finished."

The tears in his eyes humiliated him. "If...if this is your will...then I...of course, I will..."

She pushed back his hood, considering him in the candlelight. Her eyes were unforgiving, but not wholly unkind. He chuckled once, like a cough. "I have endeavored not to let any feelings on my part interfere with my duties. I...I tried to be discreet."

"She didn't know," Kithamar said. "I wouldn't have, except that I've seen it all before. Generation upon generation. It doesn't change. And doesn't get easier. When you have found yourself a new place in the world, send to me on my throne. No matter what flesh I inhabit, I will see that you are cared for. You will be a powerful man, wherever you choose to make your home. And you will have any woman you wish at your side."

"Except the one I want."

"Yes," she said. "Except that one."

She kissed him then, her pale, soft lips on his scarred, half-numb mouth. Once, and then she turned and walked into the shadows, leaving him alone in the temple.

Trembling.

Alys stepped out of the heat and sunlight into the shadows of the Stonemarket taproom. The keep was a Hansch man with white hair and a thin beard. He scowled at her and shook his head, but he didn't tell her to leave. She'd been here once or twice with Ullin and his friends, it seemed like a lifetime before.

She went toward the back. Beside an empty fire grate, Sammish and an older woman sat with mugs of beer and bowls of barley and fish. Alys waited for her heart to race or her jaw to clench. It was a moment that deserved some overwhelming emotion. Instead, there was a little sorrow, a little shame, and the sense that the great drama she'd constructed in her head and her heart—her noble brother and his allies defending the city from treachery—must be happening someplace else. This was just three people talking about a pull.

She sat down across the table from the woman. She was clearly foreign. There were threads of white shot through the dark of her hair, and a mole on her cheek. She'd have been a good mark in a crowd because she wasn't from around here, but other than that, she could have been anyone.

You killed my brother, Alys thought, and then waited for the rage and hatred. *You killed my brother while he was trying to kill you after he cheated you out of the money I've been living off for months. And he did that so his patrons at the Daris Brotherhood wouldn't know that he'd been playing his own games on them. And I delivered your son to them for them to murder in their rites.*

It was too much for anything simple. She couldn't forgive this woman. She couldn't condemn her. With her, Alys had reached a place beyond judgment, and they'd only just met.

"I'm sorry for what happened to your son," Alys said.

The woman nodded. "I am sorry for your grief at losing your brother."

They sat in silence for a few heartbeats as Alys reached for something more to say. She couldn't find it. Sammish shifted impatiently and leaned forward on her elbows.

"All that's past," she said. "We need to talk about what's coming next."

"The pull," Alys said.

"It's a safe-cache pull. Not quite the usual shape, but close. I'd thought we could start a little fire and go in with the sand and water, follow the scarred man—Tregarro—when he went for the knife."

"That'd be a run," Alys said. "I mean, yeah. The knife's important. They'd save it if things went bad, but finding and following him? That's a trick."

"I know."

"Easier if you're already inside when the fire starts," Alys said.

"I snuck in once, but that hole's been filled. I'd need a new way. Making it is where you can help."

"Why not walk in the front door?" Alys looked from

Sammish to the woman, then shrugged. "My job right now is to find you and take you to Andomaka. And likely Tregarro. Loop a little loose rope around your wrists so you look tied. I'll carry a spare blade for you in case they search. The timing will be a trick, but not too hard a one. If this one"—she nodded at the Bronze Coast woman—"can count to five hundred from the time we go in, that'll give us some time to find them and not so much I can't keep them talking before they try taking you away. When the call goes up, I say that I'll keep an eye on you, and when they go, we follow. Plus if they go two ways, there's one of us for each."

Sammish licked her lips, thinking. After a moment, she nodded, more to herself than to them. "That could work."

"How would I raise this alarm?" the woman asked.

"Just shout," Alys said.

"We need flame, though. Smoke," Sammish said.

"You're sure? Live flame can be tricky."

"We're not just spooking a storehouse overseer. It has to be true enough that they think there's real danger. We can get a cheap tin lantern and some good fish oil, light it and chuck it over the wall. The oil spills, catches. Smokes a lot and stinks to the clouds. Then just shout fire until someone notices. It won't take long. After that, Saffa can fade back and wait for us."

The Bronze Coast woman nodded once. Her lips made a thin, angry smile.

Alys tapped the table. "There's a thing, though. They lead us to the blade, all well and good. But then there's getting it from them."

"If we do it right, they won't know we're there with them," Sammish said. "Take them by surprise, and we can do it."

"I can't, though," Alys said. "I wanted to be someone who could. I wanted to think I could kill someone, but I've been in that moment, and I can't. I wanted to, and badly. I couldn't then, and we shouldn't expect that I can now. I'm sorry about that."

The woman's smile warmed, softened. "Killing and dying are deep work. Taking them lightly costs. The wise and the fortunate know that."

"Still fucking inconvenient for me," Sammish said. "But... all right. I hear you. If it comes to killing someone, I'll do it."

The thing that called itself Kithamar sat in one of the little gardens, sipping apple cider from a silver cup. The sun filtered through leaves that had lost the brightness of spring, and it listened to birdsong and the whirring of insects' wings with its new ears. Living as it did in body after body after body had made it into a sensualist, savoring the ways each perception was different. And also a strategist, wise in the management of its own peculiar cycle.

It missed Tregarro, though how much was its own fondness for the man and how much Andomaka's residual emotions still held in her flesh was hard to say. If she had not been needed—if Irana and Tallis hadn't put a bastard and a cuckoo on the throne—Andomaka and her captain might have become lovers in the next few years. But one of the first things it did when the cycle began again was break with those people its new body had been close with. Too often, those who knew the person it displaced found the transition unnerving.

Ausai had spent days with a beloved teacher whom it had sent away when it took his flesh. It had made plans to remove Halev Karsen from the court once it was in Byrn a Sal. In ancient days, it had only narrowly escaped death at the hands of children and lovers convinced it was an impostor. Tregarro's connection with Andomaka should have been broken weeks earlier, except that Tregarro was an initiate of the brotherhood. He knew what it was, and had been. And the struggle to reclaim its place had made keeping him seem wise. With luck, the scarred man would complete his task and go on to live a full and happy life someplace that being near Andomaka's flesh wasn't eerie for him. Sending him away wasn't only good strategy, it was also a kindness.

It lifted the cup to its lips and drank. A tiny insect had fallen into the cider and died there. It was almost invisible, except as an irregularity on the liquid's skin. It drank that too.

An Inlisc servant girl scratched at the archway from the house, bent almost double with distress and apology. It put down its cup.

"I am so sorry, lady," the girl said. "But there's a man from the palace. He said it would be all right."

"Who is he, and what did he say would be all right?"

"It's young Karsen, lady. The prince's second. He said he'd known you since you were children, and that you wouldn't mind."

It rose, leaving the cup forgotten. "Wouldn't mind what?"

The servant girl flapped an arm in distress. "He's in the private temple, lady. We know no one's supposed to go there, but there's no doors and he insisted and no one was going to draw a blade on him—"

The thread of Kithamar brushed past her. Its heart was beating fast. Perhaps Tregarro had already succeeded. Or perhaps he had failed. Or this was bare coincidence, and the gods had brought the Karsen boy there because it had been musing on him.

It stepped into the private temple, hands behind its back. Fear and anticipation and mistrust made the room seem brighter. The lanterns burned at their positions, echoing the geometry of the stars and the language of the gods. The ancient tapestries stood still against the walls, and the game board sat on the altar with its beads laid out in the middle of an unfinished game. And as out of place as the gnat in a drinking cup, Halev Karsen paced through the room, hands behind his own back, and faint interest in his expression. Like a man appreciating art he didn't particularly like.

"Karsen," it said, careful to keep its voice neutral. "There are more comfortable rooms, you know. And ones that aren't sacred to the rites here."

"I know, I shouldn't be in here. But the curiosity's hard to overcome. I apologize."

He turned to consider her. In the steady, soft light of the lanterns, he seemed older than it remembered him. Crueler too, somehow. "What brings you from the palace?"

"My sister, actually. She's having one of her religious moments, and I was hoping Daris might be a rite she could engage with and not risk embarrassing the family. You know how she gets when she's in the heat of a new enthusiasm."

The thing that called itself Kithamar smiled indulgently and casually maneuvered itself between Karsen and the altar. Something about this felt very wrong, but it wasn't certain what.

"She's welcome to present herself," it said. "I'd be happy if she did. But I couldn't promote her without putting her through the same forms as everyone else. Even priests are constrained by the gods."

"Especially priests, I'd think," Karsen said. "I'd appreciate it if you kept an eye on her, is all. Her piety doesn't last long but it burns bright. Chanters and all."

It didn't know what he meant, so it smiled. "Yes, of course. Chanters."

"You remember that time she decided that the Longest Night chanters were heretics and started whipping that poor old man in the street?"

"I think I do," it said. "It was a long time ago."

Karsen's smile widened. "It was. The family went through a lot to keep it quiet. We're just trying to keep history from repeating."

It spread its arms. "Anything I can do."

"Thank you," he said. "I should get back to the palace. I do appreciate this. I'll pay you back, somehow. I promise."

"I'm happy to help," it said. "It's always good to see you."

Karsen bowed, and if there was a little mockery in the gesture, it wasn't more than old friends might allow each other. Karsen left the temple, walking lightly. As soon as he'd gone, it checked the locked safe cache hidden under the altar, ready to raise the alarm, but the silver blade was still there.

The thing that called itself Kithamar sat on the ancient stone, rubbing its chin the way it had when it was Ausai. Had there been a strangeness to Halev, or was it only that the murder of Byrn a Sal was underway and so anything that touched on the false prince took on a significance it didn't deserve? Something about the visit left it unsettled, but it couldn't say what or why. It rubbed its fingertips together, a dry, fast hiss. Something was wrong.

When from habit it sat on the altar and reset the game board, one of the red beads was missing.

With morning came the wind. It drove from the east, raising dust as it came. It muttered and it howled. Somewhere in the secret depths of Longhill, Inlisc priests who kept the old ways drank their holy teas and listened for the voice of God in it. The serpent-curved streets broke the air or pushed it back up and away from the ground. In the Hansch quarters, shutters banged like hammers. The proud tower of the Temple stood against it like the prow of a great ship cutting through troubled waters, and the face of Oldgate was the city's mast and sails. There was a story that a kerchief dropped between the center two of the four bridges of Oldgate would land on the palace, blown up the face of the hill faster than a horse could run. That was only a story, though.

Green Hill was, as they walked along its wide and well-kept streets, almost calm. The great promontory of Palace Hill sheltered the western edge of the city from all but the eddies, protecting the noble compounds from the weather like a mother pushing a child behind her. The trees around the brotherhoods and compounds of the high families shimmered their leaves, but they didn't twist or bend.

Alys wore her leather, even though it was a little too hot to be comfortable. Her body felt tight and a little ill, like she was in the first part of a fever, but once they were doing the thing, she knew she'd be fine. It was only the nerves before. Sammish wore a brown tunic, a skirt, and a cutter's knife—thin, sharp, and easily concealed—bound against her arm at the elbow. Only Saffa had what might be called a disguise, and it was so intentionally nondescript, she could have been a low servant from any number of houses. The only thing odd about her at all was the woven sack across her body where the unlit lantern plinked and sloshed as she walked.

"The stables are at the back," Sammish said. "You remember? By the gate?"

"I remember," Saffa said. She sounded calmer than Sammish did. Alys didn't know if it was that she, unlike them, was staying outside the compound or if her work as a priest just made her more sanguine about dying or being captured.

They rounded a corner, and the Daris Brotherhood stood before them. It wasn't even a particularly large compound. It was only her focus on it that made it intimidating.

"Count to a thousand," Sammish said. "But only once we're inside."

"I know," Saffa said.

Alys pulled the leather thong from her wallet and tapped Sammish's shoulder. "Wrists," she said.

Sammish put her hands behind her. Alys looped the binding around the base of Sammish's hands where the thin bones of her wrists began to delta up into palm and thumb. The knot was an old trick Darro had taught her. It looked and felt solid, but a twist from Sammish would undo it.

"Wish us luck," Alys said.

The Bronze Coast woman nodded once and said, "Luck." Alys prodded Sammish forward with the lead-dipped head of her club just as if she were a prisoner. They crossed the wide square, Sammish taking deep, sighing breaths. "I'm trusting you."

"I know," Alys said. "Try to look nervous."

Sammish laughed, and Alys smiled. But then they were at the wooden gate, and two guards with swords at their hips stepped out to meet them. Both were Hansch, both wore the colors of the Daris Brotherhood. One was a half-head taller than the other, but beyond that, they could almost have been the same man.

"What's this?" the taller one asked.

"Delivering what was asked for," Alys said. The swagger in her voice was the same that she'd been cultivating for months, but this time it felt like a performance. "Tregarro knows what it's about."

The guards exchanged a glance. Alys saw herself through their eyes: a Longhill rat hauling another one like herself to the master for a little coin and a pat on the head. Their contempt wasn't even a sneer, but a smile. "All right, we'll take it from here," the taller one said, reaching out for Sammish.

Alys yanked her back. "No. Straight to him. That's the agreement."

"Whatever it was or wasn't, he's not here anymore. You can give this one over or you can take her home and feed her table scraps."

The words washed over Alys like a cold wind. She saw Sammish stiffen. If Tregarro had gone, what else had changed? She didn't know what they were walking into, except that it wasn't what they'd thought.

She wanted to talk to Sammish, wanted to ask her what they should do. She couldn't. This was her decision to make, so she made it.

"I need to talk to her, then," Alys said.

"Her?"

She fixed the guard with contempt of her own. "You know who I mean. If he's not here, I'll talk with his master. Tell her the wolf girl is here, and I've done what she asked me to do."

The men seemed less certain now, wondering, she guessed, whether Andomaka really lowered herself to speak directly to someone like Alys. She lifted her chin in defiance. One of them shifted his weight, stepping back from her without quite meaning to, and she knew they were in. The taller one put a hand on the pommel of his blade and nodded her forward. Alys pushed Sammish, who stumbled a little too theatrically. The guards didn't notice anything false, though. They walked to the wooden gate, opened it, and escorted them through.

Alys expected them to take her and Sammish to the little cell where Tregarro had hauled her a lifetime ago when she'd brought them the silver knife. Instead, they moved toward the main building of the compound, near the entrance to the public temple. Servants and guards seemed to be everywhere, but it was likely no more than the usual. It was her anxiety that made them seem like ants on a dead rat.

They led her to the side of the building and down a set of old wooden steps to a basement servants' entrance, and then to a thin, bare, high-ceilinged room. It was the sort of place where a merchant's factor might meet with a head cook or houseman. The furnishings were threadbare chairs and a rough wood table. The only light came from a narrow window at the top of the wall. Thick wooden rafters shifted with the shadows of ankles passing by. Alys had the sudden, visceral memory of staying in

Aunt Thorn's underground halls, hiding from bluecloaks while Darro got himself killed. She wanted to leave, to go back up the stairs and into someplace with more ways to flee.

"Wait here," the taller guard said, then left. Their footsteps, muffled by the closed door, faded quickly. Alys sat, then stood, then paced.

"He isn't here?" Sammish said, her voice soft and low as if they might be overheard.

"I don't know," Alys said. "He always has been before."

From the window above them, someone called out, and Alys's blood went bright and fast. But no one took it up. It wasn't the fire. How long had it been since they'd passed through the gate? She'd meant to start counting when they lost sight of Saffa, but she'd forgotten to do it.

"Maybe it's better like this," Sammish said. "If he's not here, that's one less person to follow. More likely that Andomaka will go after the knife."

"If she comes. What if she's doing something and doesn't mind letting us wait here for an hour or two? We're not that important to her."

"Saffa is," Sammish said with a certainty Alys didn't share. "She'll come as soon as she knows we're here."

"And if she doesn't reach us before the call goes up?"

Sammish, her arms still tied behind her back, shrugged. "Then we'll go find her."

Outside, in the clean, washed streets of Green Hill, a woman with a woven sack on her hip and a mole on her cheek walked with calm purpose. She certainly wasn't Hansch, though she didn't quite look Inlisc either, but she carried herself with purpose and grace. If anyone noticed her, it was as a mild curiosity. Not as a threat.

She turned down one of the less beautiful paths meant to let servants come and go without being seen. Her head shifted from side to side as if she were reciting something silently. She paused at the wall of the Daris Brotherhood. The wall there was pale stucco ten feet high, with a thick layer of ivy—green leaves covering old brown stems. The wide wooden carriage gate was farther ahead, and closed. The smell of manure and the sound of horses said that the brotherhood's stables were on the wall's far side. The woman stopped, stretched, and put her sack down gently on the paving stones. When she leaned over, rooting through it, she seemed very much at ease.

The lantern she took out was no bigger than two balled fists together. Its tin belly clinked and sloshed with oil, and the little glass flue that would protect the flame from draughts was greasy and cheap. Her head still shifting almost imperceptibly, she rolled out far too much wick. Used like that, it would smoke the glass, but she didn't seem concerned. A little striker held a chip of flint almost too small to be useful. She flicked it with her thumb half a dozen times before the flame took. She put the glass flue back in place and stood, looking at it.

Her head went still.

Tossing the lantern over the wall was almost effortless, more like releasing a bird than throwing a missile. The lantern rose up in a slow arc and almost seemed to pause above the wall before deciding to plummet to the ground on the far side.

It landed awkwardly, the glass flue splitting into shards and the little tin belly popping its seams, rolling and leaking. The oil spread, darkening the paving stones. The little wick lay down, and the small flame became a wider one. A puff of smoke rose and was whipped into nothingness.

On the street side of the wall, the woman shrugged her bag back over her shoulder and walked on as calmly as if she had done nothing odd. No one took notice of her as she reached the corner and rested there in the shade of an old stone statue of a Hansch god standing at a gate. She peered back the way she came, scratching her cheek in what might have been anxiety, looking for some sign of reaction to her vandalism.

The stables of the Daris Brotherhood were busy. The wind lifted grit and bits of dry hay and dried manure into the air, and left the groomsmen and carriage driver squinting. Near the wall, the pool of oil flowed under the bright green of the ivy, and the fire followed with it. The leaves were thick and waxy. They defied the fire. The old leaves and stems beneath them, evidence of many years' growth that no one had taken the trouble of clearing away, were drier, more brittle, and ready to burn. If anyone had been there to see it, it would have been beautiful, the warm orange light glimmering through the broad green, but it was an unpleasant day, and no one saw.

Hidden, the flames grew and spread until the heat was enough to shrivel the green, and a thread of dark smoke rose. The horses sensed the danger first, but the boy minding the stables didn't know why they were agitated. The flames reached the wide wooden carriage house, but the sides were old, hard wood. They might char, but it would take more than the wet tinder of ivy to set them alight.

The smoke was thicker now, a shadow against the sky. The woman sitting by the god saw it, but only because she knew to look. She leaned forward, anxious and wondering whether to sound the alarm herself.

Beneath the ivy, the fire began to die, its easy fuel exhausted. The green leaves slumped a little, but the brightness behind them dimmed to a vague orange. The gate opened, and a carriage rolled in, a thick-bodied coachman handling the two-horse team. He paused at the gate, lifted his eyes to the sky, caught by a scent he couldn't quite identify.

Please, the woman said. *Please*. Less than a prayer, but with the same intensity.

The wind, as fickle as wind, shifted to flow down across the city from the north like a bellows blowing in a forge. The green leaves shuddered and danced. The orange brightened to gold. Embers and smut blew out from the hidden fire like a swarm of glowing insects. The movement caught the carriage driver's eye, but by then a new little flame had found its home in the hay. Another, in a pile of old rags the boy had meant to clear away but had forgotten. Another drifted through an unshuttered window in the brotherhood's main house.

The coachman shouted. The horses screamed. The wind muttered, and then it howled.

The door opened, and a guard Alys didn't recognize stepped in. He looked around the room like he was checking for something, but she couldn't guess what. Then, apparently satisfied, he stood at the side of the door without acknowledging her, and Andomaka stepped in. Now that she knew to look for it, she could see changes in the pale woman. She held herself differently. Not straighter, exactly, but more stiffly. The Andomaka who had appeared in the smoke of Alys's Oldgate cell in the fall had flowed through the world like smoke. This one was harder, harsher, and crueler somehow.

The pale eyes clicked between Alys and Sammish, then lingered on Sammish. A small, satisfied smile touched the corner of her mouth. Sammish, hands behind her back, stared at the ground by Andomaka's feet like she was trying to disappear. Alys felt the knot of fear in her gut tighten.

"Is this the one, then?" Alys said, needing to break the silence.

"It might be," Andomaka said. She reached out a hand to

Sammish's chin and lifted it until they were facing each other. "Well? What do you think, little one? Have we met before?"

Sammish swallowed and shook her head. *No.*

Andomaka's smile was pure cruelty. "Are you sure about that?"

Sammish shook her head again, maybe meaning no, they hadn't met, or no, she wasn't sure.

Andomaka's smile widened. "Is she still here? Is she still in the city?"

"Who?" Sammish asked, and Andomaka punched her hard on the bridge of her nose. Sammish yelped and fell back, blood pouring down her face. Andomaka turned and put her hand out. The guard at the door drew a short-bladed knife from his side and put its handle in her palm. Sammish mewled in pain and fear.

"Hey!" Alys said, putting herself between them. Her heart was bright and racing.

Andomaka scowled. "You should stand aside."

"I haven't been paid," Alys said. "You want to put her in ribbons, that's your choice. But where I'm from, you pay the butcher before you eat the sausage."

"You'll get your reward," Andomaka said, and moved forward as if Alys would get out of her way. The impulse to step back was powerful, but she stood her ground.

"I'll take it while there's still some blood on her insides. No offense meant, but it's how I work. Until I'm paid, this one's still mine, and I'd appreciate you not bruising my goods."

Andomaka's laugh was as short and sharp as the blade in her hand. "Don't think you have power here. This is my house. And my city."

"It is," Alys said, crossing her arms. "But it's my work, and I get paid for it."

Annoyance and amusement warred in the pale eyes. Alys steeled herself, feet planted like she'd put roots into the stone floor. The shadows high on the wall flickered, and for a moment, the only sound was the patter of feet outside the high window. And then, faint but unmistakable, a man's voice shouting *Fire!*

Andomaka looked up, her eyes narrow. The call came again, and then other voices took it up. *Fire, fire, fire.* The pale woman grew paler.

"Stay here," she said to Alys. "Guard her. I'll be back."

Andomaka turned and strode out of the room, the guard at her heels. When the door closed, Alys sank to the ground. Sammish, arms still bound behind her and blood sheeting her mouth and chin, met her eyes. "She was going to kill me."

"Yeah."

"What a shithead." Sammish shifted, twisting at the shoulder, and her hands came loose. She wiped the blood on her sleeve. "We've got to get after her."

"Can I wait until my heart stops trying to crawl up my throat?"

Sammish's grin showed blood on her teeth. "No."

Alys, to her own surprise, laughed. Sammish stood first and helped haul her up. Outside the window, the traffic of ankles was thicker, and the clatter of horses freed from their stalls joined the chaos of voices raised in alarm.

"Let me take lead on this," Sammish said. "I've been through this place before a little. I have an idea where she may be going."

"Fine," Alys said, and pushed the door. It didn't open. She pressed at it, but it wouldn't budge. Squinting at the crack where it met the frame, she saw the shadow of a bar. "They shut us in."

Sammish took the thin knife from her sleeve and held it out to her. "Lift the bar."

"There's not enough room."

"Then we have to break it," Sammish said, desperation in her voice. "She's going to get where we can't find her."

Alys looked at the bare, sad room. The weary chairs and spindly table. The wooden rafters, still dancing with shadows.

"Can you fit that window?" Alys asked.

"How would I get there?"

"Come on," Alys said, moving to the table. Together, they shifted it to the wall under the narrow, high window. The calls of fire were louder now, and the wind stank of smoke. Alys took one of the chairs and put it on the table, then clambered onto it. "All right. I'll boost you."

"What about you?"

"Come back for me," Alys said, lacing her fingers together. "When it's done."

Sammish looked at her. They both knew how thin that sounded; how much more likely the other outcomes were and how terrible they would be. Sammish put the ball of her foot in Alys's hands, and Alys strained to lift her. The chair trembled under their combined weight, its legs unsteady and old. Sammish rose, caught the window in her hands, and pulled. Alys felt the burden of her weight lift and pushed her up and out. Sammish writhed, squeezing through the window. It was almost too narrow to pass, but only almost. When she slipped out, Alys grinned.

Sammish's head poked back in. Her distress was nearly hidden by the shadows. "I will be back."

"I know," Alys said. "I trust you."

And then Sammish was gone, and Alys stepped back down to the floor. The wind that blew through the little window stank of smoke.

A man's rough cry was first, and then horses. The woman sitting by the statue of the god stood up. The smoke was thicker now, and impossible to miss, even with the wind whipping it away. Great blossoms of it rose, black and greasy, from behind the wall. The carriage gate opened again, though at first no one came out from it. And then, a moment later, a young mare bolted out at full gallop, her eyes starting and wide, scattering the surprised people in the street.

"Fire!" the woman cried, and pointed at the Daris Brotherhood. "There's a fire!"

The call moved through Green Hill like the ripple on a still pond where a stone has fallen, and panic followed behind it. The woman hid her relief. The plan hadn't failed. Not yet, anyway.

Far down the street, she saw a group of men in the blue cloaks of the city guard running toward the fire, shoving people aside. Servants and merchants and the litters carrying those of noble blood paused to look, making a barrier of curiosity and flesh around the brotherhood that the guard had to fight to make paths.

At first, the sand-and-water effort was only the servants of the Daris Brotherhood, buckets and bowls in hand, running west to the canal and then back toward their burning stables, but in no more than minutes, others joined in. There were servants wearing the colors of half a dozen families and brotherhoods forming a line like ants to pass buckets up and down the street. Young men with spades and buckets of sand appeared, wet cloth over their faces.

A coachman staggered out of the carriage gate, his flesh bright with blood or burn, and sat in the middle of the road, stunned or dying. The woman stepped forward, heading in toward the open gate. No one stopped her. She reached the line of buckets, bowls, and water, took one that was offered to her, and walked into her enemy's home as if she were saving it.

The stables, the carriage house and carriages, the feed store—all of it was in flame. The wall where she had thrown her little lantern was a blackness. A solid stretch of char. The heat was assaulting. The wind whipped around her, pushing acrid smoke in her mouth and nose, leaving her choking a little.

It was everything they'd needed and hoped. All eyes were turned to the conflagration. She took her bucket of water, chose a place in the flames, and threw a bright and powerless spray onto it like she was spitting. The fire didn't lessen.

A man shouted words she couldn't make out, and the line of water buckets shifted, leaving her alone by a burning carriage. For a moment, she was confused. That all those men and women struggling to tame the fire should leave in the same moment was like something from a dream. But no, they hadn't left, only shifted toward the main building. She thought, still confused, that there must be a cistern in the house, that they were pulling from it instead of the canal.

Then she looked up through the smoke and sunlight. High above her, two windows fluttered brightly. And then a floor below them, a third.

The fire had spread.

Sammish ran, but that didn't matter. Everybody was running.

When she'd planned it, she'd imagined herself ghosting along behind Tregarro, who would have seen her for the first time in that moment. She meant to blend in with the servants the way she had before. And she'd imagined Adric at her back. Or Alys. Or someone, anyway. Instead, she was wiping her own blood on her sleeves and chasing alone after the thing that had seen her through Timu's eyes. And as much as she tried to tell herself she was just looking for her pan or trying to find her cousin or any of the other thousand lies that could have cloaked her, the only thing that would fit in her brain was: *I have to find Andomaka.*

The private temple was the obvious place for her to go, and it wasn't that far from where Sammish was now. From where she and Alys had been taken. She crossed a courtyard of flagstone where an apple tree's branches were studded with tiny green fruit no larger than her thumb. The light was wrong—yellow and filthy. Sunlight through smoke.

A thin-faced girl—Hansch, but a servant—ran through a wooden colonnade to her right, and Sammish ran after her, shouting. The girl stopped and turned back. Her eyes were wide with panic.

"Lady Andomaka," Sammish said.

"What?"

"Andomaka. The pale one who's in charge of everything. Have you seen her?"

"What?"

"Have you seen her?"

The girl flinched like Sammish had struck her, and shook her head. When she ran again, Sammish didn't try to stop her. The hallways looked different than when she'd snuck in before. Either they weren't the same places as the map in her mind, or she wasn't the same girl who'd seen them. Both seemed possible. The private temple would be to the west. She was sure of that. She put the morning sun behind her and went as fast as she could.

People were everywhere. Some were carrying armloads of cloth or embroidered chairs. Some were weeping. A few were carrying buckets of water and sloshing so much out as they went that there'd be nothing left by the time they found a fire. Sammish scanned the pandemonium. There was only one thing she needed to find.

She stumbled into a hall that she was sure she knew. Yes, there was the path leading to the window she'd jumped through. The private temple was ahead.

And, brief as lightning, a pale face and hair that passed through a doorway at the end of the corridor. Sammish caught her breath. Her body was rushing like a river at flood, even standing still. She walked down toward where Andomaka had been, telling herself that she was only looking for her cousin at the same time she pictured what she knew of the maze of wooden passages that led to the stone altar at its heart. If she was right, if her memory held, that was the direction Andomaka was going.

She held the little cutter's blade in her hand. It seemed inadequate now, but it was sharp as a razor. She pictured herself pushing it between the pale woman's ribs. Or drawing it across her throat. She was almost certain she could do it. She reached the passage where Andomaka had been, turned down it.

Andomaka was no more than a dozen feet ahead, her back to Sammish. A guard in the uniform of the brotherhood was talking with her. Sammish didn't wait to hear what they were saying. She turned back around the corner and pressed herself to the wall. It was a struggle to hear anything over her heartbeat, but the sound came. Footsteps. Someone was moving. She risked a glance around the corner in time to see Andomaka vanish. She followed, but the guard was in her way, grabbing her by the shoulder.

"You have to go," he said. "Get out now."

"I will. I just have to get something."

"You don't understand. They're giving up the house. We can't save it. The sand-and-water crew is just trying to keep it from spreading. We have to get everyone out."

"All right," she said, and the guard turned and left her, believing that she'd go. It was going to work. She'd only meant to put a little fear into the captain, but this was best. If the house was coming down, they *had* to save the knife.

But she wasn't moving forward. She wasn't chasing her prey, and she didn't know why she wasn't. All she could see was Alys. Alys, in the barred room. Alys, saying *I trust you.*

"There's enough time," Sammish said aloud, as if hearing her own voice would convince her. "You can do both. But you have to *move.*"

Caught between impulses she could not master, Sammish didn't move.

The private temple was empty when the thing that called itself Kithamar entered it for the last time. The tapestries hung as they always had, still and solemn against the walls. The stone altar squatted, the game board on it unplayed. The lanterns marked their sacred geometry. It was all fated for the fire. There was no stopping that now. But it didn't matter. Everything would be fine in the end.

As it strode to the altar, it pushed away the memory of being Ausai in this same place. Of reaching for the sacred blade and finding the locked safe cache empty. Whatever this was, it wasn't that. The blade would be there this time. The dangers of the present weren't the dangers of the past. At the altar, it pushed the game board away. The carved wood crashed to the ground. Glass beads hissed and skittered. It knelt and undid the lock with trembling hands. The thief girl had been here once before. Been at this same altar when it had worn the Bronze Coast boy. But it had been careful since. Karsen, the friend of its enemy, had come and left the knife untaken. Had he only been getting the lay of the land? Was he behind this? No one could have snuck in and taken the knife.

Except that someone had before.

The mechanism turned, revealing the sacred cavity beneath

the altar. With trembling hands, it reached in and clutched at the darkness. It felt the leather sheath and pulled it out. The knife was there, but the thing that called itself Kithamar drew it. It had to see the marks on the blade itself to be sure. It had to feel the subtle hum of its power. And when all was as it should have been, it let out a soft cry in relief and bowed its head.

Everything else could be redone. The altar would have to be retrieved, but no fire could break it. Even if the brotherhood burned to the ground, the stone would wait beneath. Once it took its rightful place as prince, there would be laborers and mules and ropes enough to dig down to the bones of the world if it needed to.

It rose, collecting itself. The panic it had felt only moments before seemed shameful now. It fastened the blade to its belt, tying it in place with leather thongs and knots that would not slip.

It had faced a hundred moments of crisis before. Sometimes, it had died in them. As long as there was an initiate who knew how to call it back and the tools to accomplish the rite, it feared nothing. Its mind grew more focused and clear. The way forward was the palace. Even if Byrn a Sal and Halev Karsen had lit this fire, Tregarro would still be there. It had drawn itself up from nothing before, and it had much more than nothing now.

Something roared in the distance and a wave of human voices cried out in alarm. A wall collapsing, perhaps. The air in the private temple had grown murky with smoke. It was time to leave.

It strode toward the corridors, the courtyard beyond them, and then the city.

Slowly, over the long and terrible minutes, Alys came to understand exactly how much trouble she was in.

At first, she paced in the dim light from the window, her throat thick with excitement and fear. She imagined all the things that might be happening with Sammish and Andomaka—Sammish captured, Andomaka killed, the fire put out too soon and guards returning to open the barred door and demand to know how Alys's prisoner had escaped.

The sounds from outside grew louder. Voices raised in alarm. For a time, she took comfort in them. As long as there were calls of alarm, the attention of the compound would be on that and not her. The wind pushed the scent of smoke in, and the shadows of ankles and carts and heavy buckets flickered above her.

A sound came. A steady rumble, like wooden wheels on cobblestone, only constant. Alys listened to it growing under the voices, not sure what could be making it. A carriage, maybe, but a carriage that didn't fade with distance. The wind, maybe, catching some niche in the architecture and playing the house like blowing across a bottle. Only, when the wind shifted, the rumble didn't shift with it.

Fewer shadows came. Fewer buckets of water. And the rumble grew louder. It was almost a roar when she understood. It was the voice of the fire, and then all other thoughts were blown from her mind.

Alys started screaming. She clambered up the table and chair, cupped her hands around her mouth like a horn, and shouted. *I'm down here! I'm locked in! Let me out!* If anyone heard her, they didn't reply. A thousand childhood nightmares flowed into her. Stories of the times the wooden houses of Longhill had fallen, of the bones in the ash. But this was Green Hill. They built with stone. But the heavy wood above her would burn. The carpets. The shutters. The stones would fall, and she'd be trapped in them like a cat.

Her voice grew hoarse, and the shadows of running legs vanished. Another kind of flickering took their place, and the air began to grow thick and choking. Wisps of pale smoke began shifting along the dark ceiling above her like ripples on water, and she found herself gasping, fighting for air that the fire wanted.

When a scraping sound came from the door, she didn't know what it was. The frame shifting, maybe. Wedging itself further in place or preparing to collapse. Then it came again, and the clatter of a bar falling to the floor on the other side. Sammish pulled the door open and stepped in. The blood was mostly gone from her face, though her nose looked thick and bruised. Her forehead and cheek were smudged with soot.

"Did you get it?" Alys said. "Where's Andomaka?"

"I didn't, and I don't know. We need to get out of here."

Too close by, something large collapsed, the cacophony of stone followed by a wave of voices calling out in alarm. Sammish took Alys's hand, turned back to the smoke-filled corridor, and together, they ran.

Alys didn't know the way. By herself, she would have been lost in the wide, dark halls. Sammish tugged her forward, and the only choices were follow her or die here. The roar of the fire seemed to come from just overhead, and her chest was working like a forge bellows. When they tried to run, she grew lightheaded and began to lose herself. The world became Sammish's hand in hers, and the next step forward, and nothing else.

She tripped on the stairway before she knew they had found stairs. It wasn't the way they'd come down. These were thin and wooden, crawling up inside the walls of the brotherhood like a secret. Servants' stairs. The top of the flight was lost in thick grey smoke, like an inverted river.

Her panicked mind tried to find the words *If we go up there, we'll drown*, but her tongue didn't work. Sammish dragged her up. Expecting death, she followed, and the smoke took them in. It was hot and choking. She thought she heard Sammish weeping, but she wasn't sure.

And then Sammish kicked open a door, and they stumbled forward into fresh air, and collapsed.

Alys retched, crawled a little forward, and rolled onto her back. Above her, the Daris Brotherhood bled fire from every window. Smoke rose up into the wind and made the blue sky a filthy grey.

"Where are they?" Alys said, her voice thick and gravelled. "Why aren't they putting it out?"

"It's gone too far," Sammish said. "They're just stopping the spread of it. If they can." She sat up, levered herself to her feet. "We have to get to the street."

Alys forced herself up and followed. With every clean breath, she felt her mind returning, and each bit of coming back to herself was a shock at seeing how far down she'd been. Another few smoke-poisoned breaths, and she and Sammish would have died in the darkness. Or worse, the light.

A line of bluecloaks stood in the street, keeping a crowd of onlookers from approaching the spectacle. And there was red among the blue. The palace guard. They let Alys and Sammish pass, and as soon as they had, a familiar face swam up. Saffa took Sammish's shoulder and pulled her into a tight embrace. Alys stepped back.

"We didn't get it," Sammish said. "There wasn't time."

"It's all right," the Bronze Coast woman said. "It wasn't worth dying for."

"I was so close," Sammish said, and the grief in her voice hit Alys like a blow. She looked away, back to the fire. The street was slow with people pausing to stare. Hundreds of eyes turned toward the burning brotherhood.

And one pale head, turned away.

Alys hauled Sammish out of the crowd, pointing. "That's her. Andomaka. She's right there."

Andomaka walked alone, heading south and up toward the palace. Her stride was deliberate, neither running nor spent. She wove her way among the spectators, not looking back, her whole mind on something that was still before her.

"What do we do?" Alys said.

Sammish shook her head, then looked down. In her hand, she held her little knife.

"If you kill her in the street, you die with her. The guard will cut you down," Saffa said, but Sammish didn't seem to hear her. Sammish's lips moved as if she were speaking to herself. Talking something through. When she smiled, it was tight and hard.

"Saffa, you stop her," Sammish said. "Make her turn back. At least make her pause. Do it now!"

Alys saw *Why?* in the older woman's eyes, but it didn't reach her lips. Instead, Saffa nodded, turned, and trotted away quickly after Andomaka. Sammish covered the blade with her hand and turned to Alys.

"You go right. I take left," Sammish said. "Keep eyes on me. I call the go."

It walked calmly and steadily, but its mind was stretching four moves ahead.

Tregarro would have heard. He would still be in the palace kitchens. It would find him there. Or if not, there would be other guards from the brotherhood. Or if not that, Andomaka was still a child of Chaalat. The family had its own places in the palace and without. There was little pleasure in going begging for shelter in its own city, but it would find a place that could be protected.

The voice that called its attention back to the world was a woman's. Loud, even above the catastrophe, and buzzing like a hive with rage. The name she shouted was Ausai.

It turned, and there she stood. Saffa Rej, of the Bronze Coast, not twenty feet from her. She wore a servant's robe and belt as plain as a mendicant's, but she wore it like battle armor. She carried no weapon, but her chin was high, proud and arrogant. The brightness of the flames behind her made her seem darker by contrast.

"There is no Ausai here," it said, in the tongue of the Bronze Coast. "He was a man, and as all men, he died."

"As did our son," Saffa said.

It felt a passing melancholy. The memory of getting that boy-child on her was still fresh, even in this new body. It remembered Saffa as she had been when they had been lovers. The touch of her skin. The pleasure they had shared. If it hadn't been for the plot against it, that would have been all they were to each other. A few intimate moments. Her son would be alive and swimming in the warm waves far to the south. Whoever put Byrn a Sal on the throne, they couldn't have known how far the price for their crime would carry. How many innocent lives they would scar by trying to cut the thread.

"As did yours," it said, and gestured back toward the fire. "This was you, then?"

"You will die for what you have done." She did not approach.

A man with a mule rushed past them, oblivious. Someone cried out that the fire was spreading, someone else shouted back that it wasn't. The thing that called itself Kithamar spread stolen fingers, palms facing the sun. The wind whipped its robe and hers. "I will never die," it said, still in the tongue of the Bronze Coast. "And if you dreamed to break my power, you should have woken before this. Now, it's too late."

It reached past its flesh, deep into the secret depths of the city. Its breath rooted it in place. A servant girl blundered into it and away like a blind fish bumping against a boulder large enough to split a river. With each breath, it drew its power in. Saffa was doing the same. It could see the invisible tendrils, soft as skin, that the woman summoned up. It would have been fearsome magic anyplace else. But this was Kithamar, and it was Kithamar, and for all her power and rage and the profundity of her mysteries, Saffa was a candle flame. It could snuff her out and not blister its thumb.

Behind her, a loud rumble as the floors of the brotherhood's house collapsed. The crowd gasped at the rolling black smoke that rose up and was ripped apart by the wind. Embers glittered in the air like stars going out. The late morning sun turned a bloody orange.

Saffa raised her hands, as if to strike. Then, without warning, turned her back, lowered her head, and sprinted.

The thing that called itself Kithamar waited, ready for some new and unexpected assault, but nothing came. Saffa's dark hair vanished into the press of bodies. Another shout, and a stream of men in red cloaks. More of the palace guard arriving at last with spades and sand to hunt embers and bury them. With a long, shuddering breath, it let its magic fade, seeping back into the city that it came from. It stood for a moment, unsure whether to laugh or rage. Saffa Rej, its old lover and, it supposed, its victim, had come so far and dared so much. It felt a cold, ice-bound pity for her. And a frustration to have come so near the climactic act of violence, only to turn away.

In someplace that wasn't the world, it ground sharp and inhuman teeth. But in the street, it only turned back the way it had been going. Tregarro and kitchens. That was next. And at least it knew now where the fire had come from. It hadn't been young Karsen's hand. If a Sal and his allies had been ready to move against it now, that would have been inconvenient. There would be time to rebuild...

It walked toward the red gates. They stood open now as the guards and servants poured forth to aid in the redemption of Green Hill from the fire. As it reached them, its robe caught the wind and billowed out behind it like a bedsheet. Something about that seemed wrong. It put its hand to its waist just where the swell of its hips began. To the place where its braided leather belt should have rested and didn't.

In that moment, it realized that something precious was gone.

Alys counted under her breath. *Twenty-eight. Twenty-nine. Thirty.* One with each step, her eyes forward and down. Her ears strained for running footsteps behind her, and the fear was like a hand on her chin, wrenching her neck to look back. Just a glimpse. Just enough to know if she'd been seen. Just enough to know whether to run.

She kept her pace slow. Her steps even. *Thirty-nine. Forty. Forty-one.*

Before her, Green Hill sloped down to the bridge at the palace's southmost corner. The one that crossed the canal. She didn't want to go there. Half her mind said it would be safer to swim across the canal. The bridge was a choke point. It was where Andomaka, the thing that lived in Andomaka now, could catch her. A sprint through the trees, a dive into the water, and a fast swim across into the streets of Stonemarket.

She kept her eyes down and forward, holding the cut belt wadded close against her belly. The belt. And the sheath. And the blade. *Forty-nine. Fifty.* She'd made it this far. The impulse to look back had faded. Alys kept going as if she were innocent. She even let herself smile.

Sammish was gone. Like any good cutter, she'd done her part, handed off the take, and vanished into the crowd like a stranger. Saffa was gone. Like any good flea, Saffa had held the touch's attention just long enough, and then dissolved. It was all on the walk-away now.

It was all on her.

The bridge to Stonemarket was crowded, but not blocked. Carts were stopped while the carters gossiped and pointed back at the plume of smoke that had been a brotherhood. The gabble of voices was like listening to geese flying low overhead. The words meant nothing to her. She reached the edge of the bridge, set out across it. Reached the far side. No one shouted to stop her. No one grabbed her arm or her neck.

At the confluence where four streets came together—the easternmost corner of Stonemarket and the northernmost part of the Smoke—she paused to slip the snaky mess of leather and silver under the cloth and next to her skin. Only then, she looked back. Whatever she had hoped or feared to see, it wasn't there. She felt something loosen in her chest. Relief flowed into her, so profound it could have been sorrow.

She turned south, and then west. It wasn't midday yet, and she knew her way through this part of the city better than she once had. She'd be back in Longhill before the sun ducked behind the vast hill that was the Palace and Oldgate.

She'd be home.

Through all the long hours of the morning and into the afternoon, there was no other news in Kithamar than the burning of the Daris Brotherhood. The compound, they said, was still smoking. It was a ruin. The magistrates were going to have the canal redirected, flood the buildings so that no coals could come to life and start the fire again. It had started from a careless maid dropping a candle. Or the oven that cracked and spilled its fire. Or a lightning strike from the clean, wind-driven sky, a clear sign that the brotherhood had offended a god.

In the taprooms of Stonemarket, they found whatever servants had worked there and bought them beer for solace and to loosen their tongues. Old men shook their heads and made sounds of disapproval or sympathy. In Riverport, a half dozen merchant houses called emergency meetings to consider how the fire changed the delicate balances of patronage and allegiance. In Longhill and Seepwater, people said that a fire that took down a compound in Green Hill would have killed hundreds in Longhill and left hundreds more to sleep in ashes, and no one west of the river would have cared. They took a quiet pleasure in the rich and powerful suffering for once, and then went on with their days.

With the afternoon, the wind died down—not ending but growing less vicious. And before the first reddening of sunset, the fire and the brotherhood and all of Green Hill were forgotten. Runners came from the palace, shouting at the tops of their voices, announcing the terrible news.

Byrn a Sal, prince of the city, was dead.

W here's the blade?" Sammish asked, leaning across the table.

"Sunk in the middle of the river," Alys said, only partly lying. "Anyone that wants that thing back had better be a fish."

"And Andomaka?"

"No sign, no word, nothing."

The Pit was open for business in that the door wasn't locked and an ancient, one-eyed man had been paid to take the usual keep's place giving out cider and beer and bowls of stew from the common pot. Alys and Sammish were the only two at the tables, though. Longhill, like all the other quarters, was out, lining the streets for the funeral procession. Some would watch the recent dead pass by and talk in low, worried tones about whether the omen was good or bad—whether losing a new prince so quickly was a doom upon the city or a happy escape from a terrible rule. Others, including most of the regulars of the Pit, were running pulls in the crowd, or preparing them for the celebrations that would come with the next day's coronation. In any other situation, Alys would have been out there with them.

Sammish was wearing a heavy cloak, and her hair was tied back. There were dark patches under her eyes that spoke of sleeplessness, and an urgent, nervous energy around her. Possibly fear, possibly excitement. Her leg drummed a fast tattoo, shaking the table between them. "With any luck, Andomaka and Tregarro and the whole brotherhood'll think we're bones and ash. The only one they know to look for is Saffa."

"Where is she?"

"Leaving. Going back south," Sammish said with a harsh laugh. She sobered. "I'm going too."

Alys sat back. Of the thousands of things Sammish might have said, this wasn't one she'd imagined.

"You're leaving the city?"

"I wanted to find you first. Make sure the knife was done with. And say goodbye." When Alys didn't answer, she shrugged. "I wasn't really thinking past the pull. Everything was toward that, and now it's done. When Saffa and I met up, we started talking about how to get her out. And I was just planning like it was both of us. Me and her. It just made sense."

Alys didn't understand the sting she felt at the apology in Sammish's voice. She shook her head like she was trying to come back from a hard thought. "Where are you going?"

"Bronze Coast, I'm thinking. Back home for her. Someplace no one will be looking for me."

Alys coughed out a laugh. "It is harder to seem like you're under the ruins in Green Hill when you're walking around in the Seepwater streets, isn't it?"

"That's a reason."

Alys looked away, and the one-eyed man lifted his chin in query. She motioned him back. She didn't need more food or drink.

"How long until you come back?" Alys asked.

"I don't know," Sammish said, but the way she said it meant *never*. "The things she talks about there? The spirit house? It might be something to look at once I'm there."

"Following gods? So a religious pull?"

"Maybe not a pull. Maybe just something. I don't know. Can't know until I get there. But the way she talks about it, it sounds...they understand grief there. I'd like to do that too."

"Grief?" Alys said. "You?"

"Lost someone I loved," Sammish said with a wry smile.

Alys tried to hide her surprise, but Sammish saw it anyway. "I'm sorry for that," Alys said. "I didn't know."

"I didn't talk about it," Sammish said.

"All right, then. Give me a day to get ready, and I'll come too."

"No," Sammish said, like she was closing a book. When she spoke again, she was gentler, but the effort to be gentle was obvious. "Better we don't travel together. Two of us is a risk enough. All three, and word could get back. You should stay here and keep your head down, or go west. Someplace where an Inlisc girl won't stand out."

"You're Inlisc."

"I never stand out."

"You do sometimes."

Sammish took her cup and drank her cider to the pulp and grit at the bottom, then put it back on the table gently. As if it were delicate and might break. She stood up, and Alys stood too.

"You did good work," Sammish said.

"You too. Be careful out there."

Alys stepped in and embraced her. Sammish stiffened and started to pull back, but then paused, seemed to make a decision, and softened. They stood for a long, warm moment, and Sammish rested her head on Alys's shoulder as gentle as a cat curling up to sleep. She murmured something like *It would have been good* but Alys didn't want to break the moment to ask what she meant.

After a few long breaths together, Sammish pushed her away and stepped back. They looked at each other for another moment before Sammish turned and walked to the door and the street and the world. Alys sat back down.

The old man trundled forward, and Alys gave him Sammish's empty cup. She sat alone for a time. She still had a little money left. She felt a little bad that she hadn't given it back to Saffa, after all the Bronze Coast woman had been through. But Longhill was hard for a girl with no coin, and Alys still had to eat. The common pot had barley and pork and something that had probably been trout, and it tasted fine. She ate slowly, and she ate alone.

She could tell when the funeral had passed from the sounds on the street. The eerie silence gave way to footsteps and hooves, the clatter of wagons and carts. Some laughter. A man berating a woman for flirting with someone that wasn't him. Alys waited.

The first crew to come to the Pit was Nimal, Little Coop, and two others. Alys nodded to them, but they were older than she liked, skilled at what they did, and too likely to use any opportunity she gave them to their own advantage. She waited, pointedly ignoring them while they split their morning's take. The regular keep came in next with a sprig of funeral flowers behind one ear and a dolorous expression. The one-eyed man left, and Alys wasn't sorry to see him go. The next crew that came was younger. Dark Aman was among them. It had to be one of the girl's first pulls, and her cheeks were dark and flushed with the pleasure. Alys waited until the younger crew had done their cut, then waved the girl over.

"Good day?" Alys asked.

"Did all right," Dark Aman said, wanting to brag and not wanting to announce that she was carrying coin. Smart girl.

"Want to get an extra bronze?"

"For what?"

"An errand for me. I need some things from my old room. Someone might be looking for me and I don't want to get found. Since you're not me, you could get in, get out, and bring my things to me here."

"For a bronze?"

"Two if you hurry."

The girl licked her lips, caution warring with avarice. "What do you want me to get?"

"A couple robes. A satchel. A wallet, and I know how much is in it, so don't think to help yourself. And a box."

"What's in the box?"

"Ashes," Alys said. "Just ashes."

There was a name for that night. *Gautanna*. It was an old word, from back before the Hansch had come. It meant the moment of hollowness, or the turn from effort to release. From fighting for air to letting a breath flow back out into the sky. Kithamar, that night, had no prince, and things that were impossible at other times became possible then.

Or that was the story people told. Maybe it was only a way to paint over the unsettling times that came when a prince died. Maybe playing at there being gods in the streets was enjoyable. An easy thrill that no one had to pay for. The last time hadn't quite been a year ago, and Alys had spent the dark hours with Orrel and Sammish, planning for morning and the drunkenness and joy that followed the coronation. She hadn't felt anything then but the bright anticipation of a good day's take. Now Orrel was dead and Sammish was gone, and the idea of the world growing thin and gods on the streets, of cold and deep magics stirring in uneasy sleep, seemed too plausible.

Her mother was waiting for her. The old woman was on a stool outside her door, smoking a pipe and looking up at the clouds as the sunset turned them to gold and blood. She smiled when Alys squatted down beside her.

"All well?" her mother asked.

"Well enough. Did anyone come asking for me?"

"No one."

"And you still have it?"

Her mother took a long, thoughtful puff of her pipe. "I do."

"Did you look at it?"

"I didn't. You told me not to, and so I didn't."

"Are you lying?"

"Oh my, yes. But only about looking. All the rest's true." She grinned, shifted her weight, and took a grey rag out from under her thigh. Alys unwrapped it to see the leather sheath, and drew the blade to check the markings along the silver. It wasn't that she didn't trust her mother. It was that she knew her mother was Longhill. If the old woman took offense, she didn't say it.

"Bring that back, and we could find a buyer for it."

"Some money isn't worth the trouble it brings."

"Now that's wisdom," her mother said. "No, I mean it. Took me more years than you've got to see that for truth."

"You can't tell anyone you had this."

Her mother mussed her hair affectionately. "I don't know what the fuck you're talking about."

Alys shoved rag and blade together into the cloth satchel at her side. When she stood, the high clouds were already fading to grey. The first stars flickered in the east. There would be many more soon.

"You'll come back to see me?"

"I will if I can," Alys said, and turned her back to the stars.

The Khahon was black and as smooth as glass that night. If she paid attention, the sound of the water had tones in it like a musician giving their instrument free rein and hoping it would lead them to some new melody. Alys crossed the southernmost of the four bridges that led to the base of Oldgate. The switchback road rose above her, climbing to Palace Hill and whatever was happening there that night. Torches and lanterns marked the way up, but that wasn't where Alys was going.

She walked along the river's western edge. Two bluecloaks passed the other way, watching her with suspicion, but they didn't stop her. She didn't look like trouble, and she didn't look like fun. They passed along their way, and she passed along hers.

A path snaked under the northernmost of the four bridges. In sunlight, the stones were green with algae. At night, they were the same black as the river. Alys went down the old, well-worn stairs and then along the path, feeling the slick under her feet, slippery as ice. Where the river hit the stone pylons, it threw up a pale foam. She waited, listening. Sometimes the streetbound took shelter there in the shadows, but not tonight. Tonight, she was alone. She wasn't sure whether to feel pleasure or regret for that.

She didn't know when she'd decided on her plan. Maybe when Sammish had told her about the rite and she understood what she'd seen in that slaver's room on the night they'd taken Timu. Maybe when she was walking away with the blade in her hand. It hadn't felt like making a choice so much as becoming aware of one that had already been made. She was sorry not to tell Sammish. It felt wrong to leave that friendship on a lie, but the girl wouldn't have understood. She might have stopped her. And as good a friend as she was to her, Sammish wasn't blood.

She wasn't her brother.

She sat at the water's edge. If she'd wanted to, she could have taken off her boots and cooled her feet in the river, but instead she pulled off her satchel and put it beside her. It was darker than she'd expected, and unbuckling the straps took a while. She took out the blade first, unwrapping the rag and then taking the silver from the sheath. It seemed brighter than it should have been, as if it were in a shaft of moonlight that nothing around it shared.

Next was the box. Darro's box. Darro. She ran her finger over the grooves of his deathmark. She'd brought it in case her memory failed, but now that the time had come, she knew every line and curve. She'd spent too many nights in the last year with Darro as her best company to forget it. A tightness took her throat, and tears rose in her eyes. She didn't sob, only let the sorrow come.

There were times now she didn't feel it. Or at least forgot to feel it. Sometimes for days in a row. She felt it now, and deeply.

With the rag, she rubbed a bit of paving stone clean. Or as clean as it could be. When that was done, she took the silver blade and pressed it to her arm. It was sharp. It bit her easily. Eagerly. Blood welled up, black in the darkness, and then she drew the tip of the blade through it like it was ink.

The impulse to hurry was profound, and she pushed against it. She didn't know what would happen if she got it wrong, so she kept her eyes open and wide to catch any bit of light. Slowly, carefully, she drew the deathmark just the way she'd seen a thug dressed as a coachman do, back in some other lifetime. Only this mark was Darro's. The thinness of the world around her seemed to ripple like a curtain.

When she was done, she sat back, knife in her clenched fist. She hoped nothing would happen. She would have tried and failed, but that would be enough. The thing she couldn't bear was not to try at all. She waited, caught between longing and dread.

It was too dark to see the blood beginning to smoke. She smelled it instead, like overheated iron. The murmur of the river fell away into some deeper silence. Something like mist or smoke seemed to rise from the water. Or not from it. *Through* it, as if all the world were insubstantial and the shadowy mist was the only real thing. She heard her own breath catching and stuttering. It was how she knew she was on the edge of panic.

All around her, the shadows grew thicker, darker, more solid. A sensation like insects crawling over her skin raised gooseflesh. The attention of the dead was on her, and it was heavy, cold, and unsympathetic.

She tried to speak, but all that came out was a thin whine. She balled her fists until her fingers ached, swallowed, and tried again. She'd come too far to stop. Not until she was sure.

"Darro?" she said to the roiling dark around her. "Darro, are you there?"

For a long moment, nothing seemed to change. But then, slowly, the darkness gathered, condensing into a solid shape. A man's body, dark within the darkness.

"Is that you?" she whispered. The figure didn't move at first, but then slowly lifted a hand, as if in greeting. Alys rose to her feet.

"I wanted to see you. I wanted to know that you're all right. Are you all right?"

The figure made no response. She tried to see its face, to see Darro's face in it. The emptiness was too profound.

"I miss you," she said. "I tried so hard to have you still be here, but... I miss you. I love you. I think there's a way I could bring you back, but then I wouldn't be here anymore, and that's too much. I already tried it, in a way. It's too high a price, and I'm so sorry it is. I'd save you if I could, but not like this."

She waited. The darkness waited too.

"I didn't get to say goodbye." There were tears on her cheeks, thick and warm and flowing, but her voice didn't waver. "I had to tell you how much I miss you. And goodbye."

The figure didn't move. The formlessness that was its head and body remained as blank and featureless as before, but she had the impression that she was looking at its back now. That it had turned away. Maybe that was all it could do.

She waited a moment more, savoring it and hating it and carrying the knowledge of what came next like stone in her belly. She slid her foot forward, putting it over the deathmark, and twisted at the ankle, smudging the mark out. Instantly, the figure was gone, and with it the unreal mist and the abrading attention of the dead. Alys bowed her head, noticing the tightness in her chest and her throat. She tried to love the sorrow, because it was all that was left of her brother. And because she knew now that even it would fade.

Across the water, a carriage barreled through the darkness, torches bright on its roof. The river murmured as it had before. The city all around her shifted and muttered and slept, a vast beast with tens of thousands of eyes. She had to force her hand to relax, then stretch out her fingers, working the joints until the stiffness and ache were gone. She took the blade by its point, cocked her arm back like a knife thrower at a carnival, and aimed halfway between the horizon and the top of the sky. She put her hip and shoulder into the throw, and two long, breathless seconds later, she thought she heard a splash in the voice of the water, but it might only have been her imagination. She sat alone in the darkness for a time, feeling something that wasn't peace—not yet—but that was near to it.

W e have a problem, you and me," the boatman said, lifting a lantern so that the light was in her eyes.

Sammish squinted up at him. Her body was sore, and her sleep so fueled by exhaustion that it was hard to tell the thick-bodied man from a dream. She sat up, willing herself back to consciousness.

They were five days south of Kithamar now. Saffa had negotiated passage on one of the flat-bottomed boats that floated down from the northern city to river villages in exchange for loading and unloading at the docks along the way. The food was little more than starvation flavored with fish, the sleeping cots were piled so close over each other that Sammish had opted to brave the flies and mosquitoes on the open deck, and the work would have been punishing for a man twice her size.

They'd reached the second village of the trip near sundown, tying up to an old, waterlogged dock. The plan had been that Sammish and one of the other hired hands—Hansch, with what had been a neatly kept beard that was quickly becoming less so—would unload the cargo before they slept, and Saffa and the boatman would load what was waiting onto the boat in the dark of morning so that they could leave with the light.

The light hadn't come, but the birds were loud with the threat of it.

"What's the matter?" Sammish managed at last.

"She's not working is the matter," the boatman said. "We have to be off the ties before the next boat comes, and at this rate, we won't be."

Sammish cursed under her breath and pushed herself up. The boatman stepped back toward the dock. The river hushed and spat around them as she followed him to the dock. The darkness smelled like the green of summer. Saffa was there, a sack across her shoulders, her eyes cast down as she walked. The boatman went past her like she wasn't there, making his way to the hand-cart and the looming darkness of the village warehouse beyond it. Sammish fell into step beside the Bronze Coast woman.

"All well?" Sammish asked. "Big man said you were struggling."

"I'm fine. I'm sorry. It's only that I was thinking too much."

Sammish took the sack from her and slung it across her own shoulders. Saffa walked faster when she wasn't burdened. "What's on your mind?"

"It's almost my son's nameday," Saffa said. "And I hear him in the water. He is very much with me. Or his absence is. I'm sorry. I should be able to work."

Sammish dropped the sack beside half a dozen others like it. Barley left over from the winter promised to a place downstream where the crops had failed. Sammish's back hurt. "It's all right. You put off feeling too much about him all while we were in the thick of things. Now you're safe, it's time you did."

"I'm not doing my part."

"Sure you are," Sammish said. "Just your part's for Timu right now. Go get some rest. I'll take care of this."

"I'm sorry," Saffa said again, but at least she headed back toward the cots and didn't try to keep working. Sammish stretched, spat into the river, and started back along the dock. The boatman had pushed the rest of the sacks off the handcart and gone back into the darkness for another load. Sammish picked up one, balanced it on her shoulder, and then took a second one on her hip like it was a dense, limp, oversized baby. She tried to be careful going back to the boat. The water made the wood of the dock slick in places, and if she slipped and dropped one of the sacks into the river, they'd be walking to the Bronze Coast.

She'd thought that leaving Kithamar would mean a change to everything. She had put the city of her birth—of her full life—behind her. She'd thought that leaving the streets she'd known would mean leaving the girl she'd known too, but here she was, carrying someone else's weight. Or maybe it was just that all of life everywhere was just the next set of problems, one after the other, until she could sleep in pyre flames.

And in truth, she almost hoped it was.

To leave everything and begin again was a frightening thing. The night when they'd burned the brotherhood and stolen back the knife, she'd found Saffa in the streets of Riverport. When Sammish realized that she was planning to go with her when she left, it had felt like looking over a cliffside. Now that it had happened, it was just more work, more hunger, more inter-rupted sleep. She knew how to do that.

Another two sacks, and when she went back again, boatman and cart had returned. He didn't say any words, but his grunt seemed generally approving. He carried a sack with him, Sam-mish behind, and then stayed on the boat, rebalancing the load. The rest of the carrying looked to be on her.

Sweat trickled down her back and sides. Her muscles hurt. She found herself struggling to get enough air into her lungs and out again. But with each trip to the shore and back, the pile grew less. The birds were louder now, and the star-sown sky to the east was fading from black to charcoal. What had only been blackness had the hard lines of rooftops, the softer curves of trees. The pile of sacks on the ground grew smaller. The one on the boat increased. Sammish suffered, and found to her surprise that she was also enjoying herself.

As she carried another pair of sacks in toward the boat, the other hand came out toward her, and they danced a little, side to side, as they silently worked out how to pass each other. On the boat, she waited for him. He was only carrying one sack.

"We should go together," she said. "That way we don't accidentally knock each other over the edge."

The Hansch scowled at her, as if he were unaccustomed to taking orders from some forgettable wisp of an Inlisc girl, but then he shrugged. "Fair point," he said.

With him helping, they had the sacks cleared from the dock and secured on the boat before the sun came up, but it was a near thing. The stars were all gone and the clouds the pink of roses when the boatman and the village taxman threw off the ties and pushed the flatboat out into the wide, lazy current of the Khahon. The boatman went into his cabin—a tiny room hardly wider than his shoulders and still bigger than the one his three hired hands shared—and came back out with a brass horn that he blew on. Three long notes, and one short that echoed away down the river. A moment later, she heard an answering call with two short and two long from upriver.

"Cut that one too fucking close," the boatman said, but there was satisfaction in his voice. "You can make yourselves food if you like. I'll watch the water."

The bearded man nodded, and Sammish followed him back to the little crate of rice, dried apples, and salt pork. She started a little cookfire on the stone and he put a mash of rice and apple and river water in a tin pan hardly larger than a fist. It was supposed to be for all three of them.

"What do you think he's watching for?" the man asked, nodding toward the front of the boat. It was more than he'd said to her since they'd left the little docks by the hospital outside Kithamar.

"Logs, maybe," Sammish said. "Sandbars."

He grunted his agreement.

"First time on the river?" she asked.

"Yes."

"Mine too."

"I took that from what your friend said. Will she be all right?"

"She needs some time is all," Sammish said, and hoped she was speaking the truth. She thought she was.

The water started boiling, and the steam from it smelled of old apple and salt. The man started to stir it, and she stopped him. *You'll make it gummy. Just let it boil.* He took her advice, and she liked him better for taking it.

The sun rose and burned off what little fog there was on the river. The apple rice cooked through, and the bearded man took a little bowl of it off for Saffa while Sammish ate her share slowly. That was one of the tricks to being hungry. Wolf it all at once, and her body forgot it had been fed. Go slowly, notice the taste of it, and even too little food left her close to sated.

When she was done, she lay back, stretching out in the heat of the sun and the humidity of the river, and listened to the buzz of the insects, the distant call of boats working the river, and the soft murmur of the Khahon.

Good enough, she thought on the edge of sleep. It wasn't the life she'd dreamed of. It wasn't a place at the brewer's window. It wasn't a room in Seepwater. It wasn't Alys, or the girl she'd dreamed Alys to be.

But it was enough.

Alys woke in the morning to the sound of the baker singing to himself as he tended the oven fire and put his day's buns and loaves in. Alys shifted as she woke, and the cat at her knees got up petulantly, walked to the door, scratched it, and looked back at her with an expression of unmasked disappointment. Alys had assumed the animal was dead, but then it had appeared a week after she'd taken Sammish's room with a new notch in its ear and no apparent notice that the girl sleeping in its bed had changed to someone else.

It was five weeks now since the brotherhood had burned and Byrn a Sal had died. For the first week, Alys had kept to the deepest shadows of Longhill that didn't belong to Aunt Thorn. She'd even sent her mother to the taprooms to listen for word of Andomaka Chaalat, and whether anyone from Green Hill had been asking after someone who looked like her. No word came, and day by slow day, Alys came to believe she'd escaped. The Alys that Andomaka had called wolf girl was dead in the rubble of Green Hill, and there was a sense in which that was true. Still, she'd cut her hair short and sold all her old clothes and the wooden club too. Just in case.

She washed with a cloth and water that she'd taken in with her the night before, then dressed in a simple tunic and workman's leggings of canvas. They'd be warm for the weather, but she expected the day's work to be rough, and she preferred heat to skinning her knees and ankles.

When she opened her door, the east sides of the rooftops were glowing gold, like the sun was sitting on the top of the Temple and looking out over the city. The smell of molasses bread and baked raisins came from the oven, and Nimal was sitting by the door, a smile on his lips.

"No," Alys said as she walked south.

"You haven't even heard it," Nimal said, skipping along to catch up with her. "It's safer than washing clothes. Practically legal."

"Would the bluecloaks say that too?"

"Since when do they need us to be guilty of something to crack our heads?" Nimal said.

"No. If it's a pull and it goes wrong, it could come to violence, and I'm done with that if I can be. I'm not good at it."

"Come on, Alys. Please. I've got most of the crew together. I just need one more who I trust. You can't be out of the life. Not really. Can you?" His wheedling sounded like a little boy begging his mother.

Alys stopped and turned to face him. She wasn't angry. She was barely annoyed. Nimal lifted his eyebrows and pulled a face he thought was charming. "Have you ever killed someone?" she asked.

"I've been in my fair share of fights. I carry myself fine."

"No, I mean have you killed someone. Looked at them, known you meant to do it, and then done it? You have or you haven't. Which?"

His smile faded. "I get safe. I'm too slippery for that kind of thing."

"I'm not. I've been there, and I'm not going back. That's the end of the talk, yeah?"

He looked sober now. "Shit, Alys. Did you kill somebody?"

"Good to see you," she said. "Best of luck with the pull."

She walked away, and this time he didn't follow. She made

her way along the route she had before, passing her houses in turn. Black Nel's uncle was hauling shit off the streets for the magistrates, and so she had his daughter, her cousin, Ullya. Big Salla and Little Salla who lived across the street from each other. Gibby, Tall Janna's son, was almost too young to be useful, but keeping him out of the house for the day was a kindness to his mother since it let her do her sewing work uninterrupted. That was worth a bronze in itself, when Tall Janna had it to spare, and a favor for later when she didn't. She passed her mother's house, but didn't stop there. Nicayl, who'd been an apprentice at the Seepwater butcher until the bluecloaks took the butcher away for hiding his tax money and passing off dogmeat for pork. Pale Elbrith, as thin as ever, but half a head taller than he'd been in winter. All Linnet's old crew, less Dark Aman, who'd decided she was too old and dignified for the work.

Alys gathered them and marched them along the streets, leaving Longhill, but leaving it together. They sang the same songs that Grey Linnet had taught them. That she'd taught Alys, when Alys had been young. And while Alys pretended to enjoy the song about the tiny shiny eel and the big black toad, there was actually a part of her that did. The children gave her an excuse to dance along the street and caper, and even if she rolled her eyes when she caught an older person's gaze, not all of her pleasure was feigned.

It wasn't even midmorning when they reached the southernmost bridge with its yellow stone and black mortar, and when they walked along it, she had to pull Elbrith off from the stone rail. He wanted to walk along it with nothing between him and the fast, dark water but air. She had the sense he was showing off for Little Salla.

At the far end of the bridge, they clambered down the stones and onto the thin, bare strip of the Silt nearest the water where the land was too new for trees to have grown. The children all walked together, hand in hand, along the side of the river. The Khahon slid past them, seeming to go faster now that they moved against the flow. At the edge of the trees, an old man sat on a white wooden stool. He had filthy grey hair and hooded eyes, but he hadn't approached her or the children yet. Alys kept an eye on him all the same. No one who actually lived on the Silt could be trusted.

She also watched the water—where it broke against the sand and where it lapped over it, where it pooled and where it leapt, how it had changed the shape of the land from the day before and where it had left it alone. When they came to a likely-looking stretch, she stopped and lifted her arms to the sky. The children of Longhill all circled her and lifted their own hands too.

"Now," she said, and paused, letting the little ones fill with anticipation, except for Big Salla, who was getting a little old for the game. "Get a digging stick!"

They scattered like puppies, pulling branches off of saplings or hauling driftwood from the water's edge. She watched them, aware as a mother wolf. When she whistled, they circled back. Elbrith was talking to Little Salla and wouldn't be quiet until Alys made them sit apart. Then he sulked, but at least he sulked quietly.

She could remember clearly being in the circle herself. She stood now as she remembered Linnet standing, smiling the way Linnet had smiled. Only not quite, because she wasn't Linnet. She was Alys, who had been Linly's Alys, and Darro's. Who had been a flea for Orrel when he was cutting and a lookout for Korrim when he'd been breaking into merchant stalls in Riverport. And now she was this, and maybe would be for the rest of her life. Or maybe not.

"We all do the rules," she said, as Linnet had done. "What's the first rule?"

They all spoke together, a little chorus of voices above the rush of the water. "Don't go into the river."

"That's right. Water's hungry. Everybody knows that. What's the second rule?"

"Don't go into the trees."

"There's nothing there that's our business, and too much that isn't. Third?"

Little Salla looked over at Elbrith and grinned. He grinned back. So at least the flirting went both ways. "Always stay together."

"And what do we do with the things we find?"

"Bring them to Alys."

"Yes. Everything comes to me, and I'll make sure it's shared out fair. Anyone who holds out is a cheat. We don't let cheats come with us."

We drown them in the river, Elbrith shouted, gleeful at the prospect. Alys let it go. Those were the rules that Linnet had given, every day since forever, it seemed. But there was a new rule.

"And what," Alys said, "do we do if we find a knife?"

"Throw that bastard back," the children shouted together.

From the edge of the trees a sound came that might have been wind or might have been a man's laughter. Or a spirit's. Or a god's.

"All right," Alys told the children of Longhill. "Let's go find some treasures..."

Here ends the first book of the Kithamar Trilogy,
where not even grief endures forever.

The story continues in . . .

BLADE OF DREAM

Book Two of the Kithamar Trilogy

Keep reading for a sneak peek!

ACKNOWLEDGMENTS

I would like to thank Danny Baror and Heather Baror-Shapiro at Baror International for having my back in this tumultuous industry, the team at Orbit who made this possible (particularly my always-patient editor Bradley Englert and publisher Tim Holman, who took the chance of picking up this very odd project), and the small council (Ty Franck, Kameron Hurley, Paolo Bacigalupi, Carrie Vaughn, and Ramez Naam) who helped to keep me sane during the writing. And, as always, thanks to my family for supporting me all the nights I spent wandering the streets of Kithamar.

Any failures and infelicities in the story are exclusively my own.

extras

orbit

meet the author

Kyle Zimmerman

DANIEL ABRAHAM is the author of the critically acclaimed Long Price Quartet and the Dagger and the Coin series. He has been nominated for the Nebula and World Fantasy Awards, and he won the Hugo Award and the International Horror Guild Award. He also writes as James S. A. Corey (with Ty Franck) and M. L. N. Hanover. He lives in New Mexico.

Find out more about Daniel Abraham and other Orbit authors by registering for the free monthly newsletter at orbitbooks.net.

if you enjoyed
AGE OF ASH

look out for

BLADE OF DREAM

Book Two of
The Kithamar Trilogy

by

Daniel Abraham

*Kithamar is a center of trade and wealth, an ancient
city with a long and bloody history where countless
thousands live and their stories endure.*

This is Garreth's.

*Garreth Left is heir to one of Kithamar's most prominent
merchant families. The path of his life was paved long before he was
born. Learn the family trade, marry to secure wealthy in-laws,
and inherit the business when the time is right. But to Garreth,
a life chosen for him is no life at all.*

*In one night, a chance meeting with an enigmatic stranger changes
everything. He falls in love with a woman whose name he doesn't
even know, and he will do anything to find her again. His search*

*leads him down corridors and alleys that are best left unexplored,
where ancient gods hide in the shadows and every deal
made has a dangerous edge.*

*The path that Garreth chooses will change the entire future of not
only those he loves but also all of Kithamar's citizens.*

**In Kithamar, every story matters—and the fate of the city is
woven from them all.**

Ivy grew up the courtyard's northern wall, broad leaves a green so
rich and dark they seemed almost black in lantern light. The day's
heat radiated up from the stones, and the thick breeze was what
passed for coolness in midsummer. It smelled like the river.

"Then five more came out," Kannish's uncle Marsen continued,
holding up his splayed hand. "So there we were, me and Frijjan
Reed and Old Boar with a full dozen Longhill thugs around us,
and no other patrol close enough to hear the whistle."

Maur was leaning forward like a child, not a grown man with
two full decades of life behind him. Garreth swallowed another
mouthful of cider and tried not to lean forward too. Kannish, who
had the blue cloak of the city guard for himself now even though
he wasn't wearing it, crossed his arms and sat back against the wall
as if by joining the guard, he'd made all his uncle's stories partly his
own.

Marsen stretched his arms along the back of the metal bench,
shaking his head at his own memories. He was halfway through his
fifth decade, with grey at his temples and in his beard, and he wore
the uniform with the ease of long familiarity. The uniform was so
much a part of him that going shirtless like the boys never occurred
to him, even in the heat.

"Did you get your ass split the other way, then?" Maur asked.

"No," Marsen said. "We could have, no mistake. These were all

Aunt Thorn's knives, and she's a bloodthirsty piece of Inlisc shit. Our badges of office make us targets for her. But we were in Longhill itself. You boys ever go to Longhill?"

"Just on the way to the university and the theater," Garreth said.

"Well, don't. If you're going to Seepwater, stay by the river to get there. It's a maze, Longhill. The way the Inlisc rot out their houses and throw up new ones, the streets shift from week to week, and the new places are built from the same wood that the old ones were. That was what saved us." He nodded, and Kannish nodded with him like he knew what was coming next. "One of them had an oil lamp. Crap little tin-and-glass thing. So that's what I went for. He dodged out of my way, but I wasn't aiming for the meat of him. Oh no. I caught the glass and the tin. Shattered the fucking thing and got oil everywhere. Up and down my blade too. Looked like something out of a priest's story for a little bit. Gods with flaming swords, but it was just me and a bit of cheap oil." He held his right hand out, palm down, and pointed at his thumb. "You can see the burn scar from where it dripped right there."

Maur whistled low. The knot of scar was pale and ugly, and the pain of getting it seemed like nothing to the man who wore it.

"Point was, Aunt Thorn's boys saw the flame, and they panicked. Damn near forgot we were there. Started running for water. We had half of them dead or roped before they knew what was happening, and the rest scattered. They're dangerous, but they spook easy when you stand up to them. That's truth."

"What about the fire?" Garreth asked.

"The locals had it out before we had to turn to it. Longhill knows that if it starts burning, it won't stop. They've got hidden wells in some of those houses. There wasn't any real danger. But distraction? That's half of what fighting is."

"Outthinking the enemy's as deadly as speed or strength," Kannish said. "More, likely. That's what Captain Senit always says."

His uncle's eyes narrowed and he looked to his left. "He does say that."

A woman's voice called from inside. Kannish's mother, the host of the night's meal saying a wide, loud good night to some of the other guests. Garreth had spent time in Kannish's home since he and Kannish and Maur were all pot-bellied, unsteady boys playing swordfight with loose sticks, and he knew a hint when he heard one. The others did too. He and Maur pulled their tunics back on over their heads, and Kannish shrugged his blue cloak back into place. Kannish wasn't on patrol any more than his uncle was, but the uniform was a boast. A statement of who Kannish had become and his place in the city.

"Could head for the tap house," Maur suggested.

"It's a pretty thought," Marsen said, "but it's back to the barracks for us."

"I have patrol in the morning," Kannish said, "and Uncle's pulling tolls at the Seepwater gate."

Maur tried on a smile. "Another night, then."

Together, the four of them passed under the stone archway and into the house proper. The servants had cleared away the remains of the meal, and Kannish's mother and father were standing in the front hall along with their two eldest daughters. It was hard for Garreth to think of his friend's older sisters as anything but the agents of torment and objects of adolescent curiosity that they had been for him when he was younger, but they were women now, full grown and ready to take their places in the family and business. The elder had just announced her engagement to the son of a magistrate, and the night's meal had been one of several meant to celebrate the coming union.

Garreth thanked Kannish's father and mother for their hospitality, as form required, and they laughed and hugged him. The merchant houses of Kithamar were at constant war with each other, but it was a war fought with favors and alliances and a firm eye on how to wring advantage out of every situation without quite crossing the law. That it was usually bloodless made it no less intense. The decision, made almost all of Garreth's lifetime ago, to have the three boys play together in the family courtyards had meant something, as did the choice to invite Kannish's friends to the meal tonight. That was the way in Riverport. Everything was something more than it appeared.

Kannish and his uncle turned south, heading toward their barracks. Maur and Garreth made their way west. It was the height of summer, and the long slow hours left a touch of indigo on the horizon. Palace Hill was off to the southwest from them, Oldgate glittering with lamps and lanterns all down the left side, like the hill was a head seen almost in profile with the palace of Prince Ausai atop it like a crown. Kannish had been in the guard for almost half a year already, but it still felt odd to be walking through the warm, fragrant night without him. Like someone was missing.

At first, they didn't talk, just moved through the dark streets with their footsteps falling in and out of rhythm. At the little square by the chandlers' guild, Maur hopped onto the low stone wall and balanced on it like an acrobat with very little skill. When they reached the end, he jumped down and sighed. "You heard about Prince Ausai being sick?"

"I don't believe it. People like telling stories about how things are about to fall apart."

Maur made a little noise that might have been agreement or might have been nothing. He sighed again, more deeply. "I'm going to join too."

"Join what?"

"The city guard. With Kannish and Marsen."

"Oh," Garreth said.

"Don't."

"Don't what?"

"Feel betrayed. It's not about picking him over you."

"I didn't think it was," Garreth said. And then a moment later, "You know those stories the old man tells are more than half bullshit. All that about girls throwing themselves at bluecloaks and how the guard wins every fight? That's him on a stage."

"I know, it's just we're getting to where we need to find a place, you know? It's easy for you. You're the oldest, and only one brother under you. I've got six siblings ahead of me. My father had to make up a new position in the company last year so that Mernin could report to him straight and not to one of the other children. Saved his dignity. They're already spending half the time they should be working at plotting out how to run the business after my parents die."

"The eternal fight."

Maur nodded, squinting up at the moon. He looked like a sorrowful rabbit. "It'll be kindness to them and good for me if I find another path. And the guard's better than the Temple."

They were walking slower now. The corner where their paths divided was coming up, and Garreth found himself dreading it. "You don't want to spend your days praying to the gods and scraping wax out of the candleholders?"

"I'm not the gods-and-spirits type," Maur said. "At least the guard has some adventure to it. And it's not as humiliating as taking hind tit in the family trade. Anyway, Kannish said there's an opening in his watch. One of the old-timers caught a knife in his gut, and it went septic."

"Lucky for you."

"Don't be bitter."

"I'm not," Garreth said. "I'm just... it's late and I'm tired."

The corner came, and they paused. Maur was shorter than Garreth by almost a head, thin across the shoulders, and with wide brown eyes with one a little higher than the other. They were the same age, except Garreth was born in the spring and Maur the autumn. How had it come that they weren't still boys digging in the mud and daring each other to climb the tile rooftops?

"Well," Maur said.

"Yeah," Garreth replied.

Maur turned north. His family lived almost against the city wall. Garreth went south, walking alone in dark streets. In Seepwater or Newmarket, a man walking alone at night could attract the wrong kind of attention, and he wouldn't have gone to Longhill even with friends and weapons. He'd only been across the river to Stonemarket and the Smoke after dark a few times, and then with company who knew the streets. But Riverport was home almost as much as his own family's compound, and its streets were as much a part of his place in the world as his own kitchen garden.

House Left had been part of Kithamar since before Kithamar had been a city, or so the story went. Back in the dim past when the Khahon had been a river border between the cities of the Hansch to the west and Inlisc hunting tribes to the east, a Hansch general had taken a merchant woman as lover. Their child, noble by blood but embarrassing to the general's wife, had been given favors of trade and custom under the mother's name. And so House Left was half merchant class, half secret nobility, and one of the founding trade families that had made Kithamar independent of the cities around it. Maybe it was even true.

Riverport was the northernmost navigable port on the Khahon, and the link between the farms and ocean cities to the south and the harder, wilder lands to the north and east. It was a key stop on the snow roads that went across the frozen deserts from Far Kethil to the Bronze Coast in the sun-drunk south. It was the first place that the cedar and hard oak floated down to from the logging camps in the north.

If you want to make steady coin, his father always said, *put yourself between something and the people who want it.* As wisdom went, that sounded less noble than stories of glorious war and forbidden love, but it had kept House Left in respectable buttons and warm houses for generations. And if Garreth's grandfather had maybe taken a few too many speculative shipments that hadn't paid out, if his father's plan to accept discretionary deposits had been foiled by the bankers' guild, if his mother's bid to regain the losses by shifting the family trade from wood and wool into more expensive goods like sugar and dye and alum hadn't made the returns they'd hoped, if she'd in fact been gone on secret business since late spring...

Well, no one knew that who didn't see the family's private books. At any time, a third of the merchant houses of Kithamar could be on the edge of collapse and keeping their plumage bright as a songbird so that no one could tell. House Left had weathered private storms before this, and they would again. That was what Garreth's father said, and he said it with conviction.

The compound they had lived in for the last three generations was large enough to be a little boastful. It didn't dominate the street the way the Dimnas or Embril families did theirs, but it had four white stories with shutters in the pale blue peculiar to House Left. The ground floor was for business and the entertainment of guests, the second for the family, the third for the handful of servants under the watchful eye of their head of house, and the fourth was storage for old furniture and generations of the family records and the unending battle against mice and pigeons who wanted to make it home.

Garreth walked down the moon-soaked street toward bed, his thumbs hooked in his belt and his mind lost in itself. He didn't notice anything odd until he was almost at the door.

The shutters were open, inviting in the cooler night air, but not only on the upper floors. The ground floor windows were bright with candles. Garreth's steps faltered. As late as it was, he'd have expected nothing more than a flicker in his brother's room or one of the servants' windows. The light spilling out to the street meant that something had happened. He told himself that the tightness in his throat was excitement, that whatever it was would be something good and not another setback.

The front door was latched but not barred. Voices came from the back. First, his father's low, measured voice, capable of cutting sarcasm with almost no change of tone and spoken too gently to hear the words. Then Uncle Robbson, sharp and barking: *Well, the old direction isn't working, is it?* Then his father again. Garreth closed the front door behind him quietly. The third voice was as unexpected as a snowstorm in summer.

"Mother?" Garreth said, already walking toward the lesser hall.

She sat beside the empty fire grate, still in a traveler's robe of leather and rough cotton, her hair pulled back in a severe bun that showed the grey at her temples. Garreth's father leaned against the front wall, his arms crossed over his chest, and Uncle

450

Robbson—chin forward and chest puffed out like a rooster— stood in the middle of the room facing Father with anger darkening his cheeks. Mother ignored Uncle Robbson's tantrum with a calm she'd been practicing since she'd been old enough to change her little brother's diapers, turning her attention instead to Garreth.

"Where have you been?"

"Kannish. His parents had a dinner. I didn't know you were coming back."

Mother tapped Uncle Robbson on the leg and nodded for him to sit. He obeyed. Father remained where he was, expression placid as always. "I'm not back. Not exactly," Mother said. "Hopefully no one knows I'm in the city, and I'll be out again come morning."

"Why?" Garreth said, a little ashamed to hear the ghost of a whine in his voice. He was a grown man, not a child running after his mother.

"You know the policy on things like this," his mother said, and Garreth looked at his toes. For the family, policy was there to keep anyone from error. If the policy was to take debts to the magistrate after fifty days, it meant that even the closest friends didn't get a fifty-first. If it was policy to write family matters in cipher, even the most trivial house matter went into code. If the policy was that the secret business of the house was known only to those who had to know it, then the number of people who might let something slip was never more than it had to be. Judgment could be swayed by drink or desire, but policy was implacable.

Which was why his father's gentle, amiable words were more shocking than a shout. "Now then, Genna. I think we owe the boy something, don't you?"

The emotions on his mother's face were too fast and complicated to read. She looked into the empty grate as if there were a fire there to gaze into. "The business...is worse than we let on. Over the last five years, we have lost a great deal of capital. More than we can afford."

"All right," Garreth said.

"There is a plan to put things right," she went on. "There's risk, but if it goes well, it will more than make up for our losses."

Garreth felt his heart tapping against his chest like it urgently wanted his attention. His parents had always been very careful to explain the workings of the house once a deal was complete. That was his training. To be told of something that was still uncertain in its outcome... Well, it was the ragged edge of policy, and it made him feel like a child in an adult conversation.

"How bad is it?" he asked.

"If this fails," his father said, "we will need to sell the warehouse."

Uncle Robbson slapped his thigh like he was mad at it. "You can't do that. If you start selling what brings the money in, you've already lost. It's like a farmer grinding his seed for flour."

"Robbson," Mother said. She shifted her eyes back to Garreth's. He didn't understand the hardness he saw there. She rose to her feet, walked to the door, and nodded for him to follow. The two older men stayed where they were, Robbson with his lips pressed thin, Father with a little smile that gave nothing away. Garreth followed his mother.

They went down the short hall to the dining room. He heard the clatter of the plate before they reached the archway. An Inlisc girl sat at the table alone, like a servant playing at being above her station. If someone had made an unflattering caricature of a Longhill street rat, it would have looked like her: plate-round face, curled hair, dark eyes. She didn't jump to her feet, though, or show any sign of embarrassment the way a servant would.

"This is Yrith, daughter of Sau," Mother said, "and you're going to marry her."

452

if you enjoyed
AGE OF ASH

look out for

THE LOST WAR
The Eidyn Saga: Book One

by

Justin Lee Anderson

Justin Lee Anderson's sensational epic fantasy debut follows an emissary for the king as he gathers a group of strangers and embarks on a dangerous quest across a war-torn land.

The war is over, but the beginnings of peace are delicate.

Demons continue to burn farmlands, violent mercenaries roam the wilds, and a plague is spreading. The country of Eidyn is on its knees.

In a society that fears and shuns him, Aranok is the first mage to be named king's envoy. And his latest task is to restore an exiled foreign queen to her throne.

The band of allies he assembles each have their own unique skills. But they are strangers to one another, and at every step across the ravaged land, a new threat emerges, lies are revealed, and distrust threatens to

453

destroy everything they are working for. Somehow, Aranok must bring his companions together and uncover the conspiracy that threatens the kingdom—before war returns to the realms again.

CHAPTER 1

Fuck.

The boy was going to get himself killed.

"Back off!"

Aranok put down his drink, leaned back and rubbed his dusty, mottled brown hands across his face and behind his neck. He was tired and sore. He wanted to sit here with Allandria, drink beer, take a hot bath, collapse into a soft, clean bed and feel her skin against his. The last thing he wanted was a fight. Not here.

They'd made it back to Haven. This was their territory, the new capital of Eidyn, the safest place in the kingdom—for what that was worth. He'd done enough fighting, enough killing. His shoulders ached and his back was stiff. He looked up at the darkening sky, spectacularly lit with pinks and oranges.

The wooden balcony of the Chain Pier Tavern jutted out over the main door along the front length of the building. Aranok had thought it an optimistic idea by the landlord, considering Eidyn's usual weather, but there were about thirty patrons overlooking the main square with their beers, wines and whiskies.

Allandria looked at him from across the table, chin resting on her hand. He met her deep brown eyes, pleading with her to give him another option. She looked down at the boy arguing with the two thugs in front of the blacksmith's forge, then back at him. She shrugged, resigned, and tied back her hair.

Bollocks.

Aranok knocked back the last of his beer and clunked the empty tankard back on the table. As Allandria reached for her bow, he signalled to the serving girl.

"Two more." He gestured to their drinks. "I'll be back in a minute."

The girl furrowed her brow, confused.

He stood abruptly to overcome the stiffness of his muscles. The chair clattered against the wooden deck, drawing some attention. Aranok was used to being eyed with suspicion, but it still rankled. If they knew what they owed him—owed both of them . . .

He leaned on the banister, feeling the splintered, weather-beaten wood under his palms; breathing in the smoky, sweaty smell of the bar. Funny how welcome those odours were; he'd been away for so long. With a sigh, Aranok twisted and turned his hands, making the necessary gestures, vaulted over the banister and said, "*Gaoth*." Air burst from his palms, kicking up a cloud of dirt and cushioning his landing. Drinkers who had spilled out the front of the inn coughed, spluttered and raised hands in defence. A chorus of gasps and grumbles, but nobody dared complain. Instead, they watched.

Anticipating.

Fearing.

Aranok breathed deeply, stretching his arms, steeling himself as he passed the newly constructed stone well—one of many, he assumed, since the population had probably doubled recently. A lot of eyes were on him now. Maybe that was a good thing. Maybe they needed to see this.

As he approached the forge, Aranok sized up his task. One of the men was big, carrying a large, well-used sword. A club hung from his belt, but he looked slow and cumbersome; more a butcher than a soldier. The other was sleek, though—wiry. There was something rat-like about him. He stood well-balanced on the balls of his feet, dagger twitching eagerly. A thief most likely. Released from prison and pressed into the king's service? Surely not. Hells. Were they really this short of men? Was this what they'd bought with their blood?

"You've got the count of three to drop your weapons and move," the fat one wheezed. "King's orders."

"Go to Hell!" The boy's voice cracked. He backed a few steps toward the door. He couldn't be more than fifteen, defending his father's business with a pair of swords he'd probably made himself. His stance was clumsy, but he knew how to hold them. He'd had some training, if not any actual experience. Enough to make him think he could fight, not enough to win.

The rat rocked on his feet, the fingertips of his right hand frantically rubbing together. Any town guard could resolve this without blood. If it was just the fat one, he might manage it. But this man was dangerous.

Now or never.

"Can I help?" Aranok asked loudly enough for the whole square to hear.

All three swung to look at him. The thief's eyes ran him up and down. Aranok watched him instinctively look for pockets, coin purses, weapons—assess how quickly Aranok would move. He trusted the rat would underestimate him.

"Back away, *draoidh*!" snarled the butcher. The runes inscribed in Aranok's leather armour made it clear to anyone with even a passing awareness of magic what he was. *Draoidh* was generally spat as an insult, rarely welcoming. He understood the fear. People weren't comfortable with someone who could do things they couldn't. He only wore the armour when he knew it might be necessary. He couldn't remember the last day he'd gone without it.

"This is king's business. We've got a warrant," grunted the big man.

"May I see it?" Aranok asked calmly.

"I said piss off." He was getting tetchy now. Aranok began to wonder if he might have made things worse. It wouldn't be the first time.

He took a gentle step toward the man, palms open in a gesture of peace.

The rat smiled a confident grin, showing him the curved blade as if it were a jewel for sale. Aranok smiled pleasantly back at him and gestured to the balcony. The thief's face confirmed he was looking at the point of Allandria's arrow.

"Shit," the rat hissed. "Cargill. Cargill!"

"What?" Cargill barked grumpily back at him. The thief mimicked Aranok's gesture and the fat man also looked up. He spun around to face Aranok, raising his sword—half in threat, half in defence. Nobody likes an arrow trained on them. The boy took another step back—probably unsure who was on his side, if anyone.

"You'll swing for this," Cargill growled. "We've got orders from the king. Confiscate the stock of any business that can't pay taxes. The boy owes!"

"Surely his father owes?" Aranok asked.

"No, sir," the boy said quietly. "Father's dead. The war."

Aranok felt the words in his chest. "Your mother?"

The boy shook his head. His lips trembled until he pressed them together.

Damn it.

Aranok had seen a lot of death. He'd held friends as they bled out, watching their eyes turn dark; he'd stumbled over their mangled bodies, fighting for his life. Sometimes they cried out, or whimpered as he passed—clinging desperately to the notion they could still see tomorrow.

Bile rose in his gullet. He turned back to Cargill. Now it was a fight.

"If you close his business, how do you propose he pays his taxes?" Aranok struggled to maintain an even tone.

"I don't know," the thug answered. "Ask the king."

Aranok looked up the rocky crag toward Greytoun Castle. Rising out of the middle of Haven, it cast a shadow over half the town. "I will."

There was a hiss of air and a thud to Aranok's right. He turned to see an arrow embedded in the ground at the thief's feet. He must have crept a little closer than Allandria liked. The rat was lucky she'd given him a warning shot. Many didn't know she was there until they were dead. Eyes wide, he sidled back under the small canopy at the front of the forge.

Cargill fired into life, brandishing his sword high. "I'll cut your fucking head off right now if you don't walk away!" His bravado was fragile, though. He didn't know what Aranok could do—what his *draoidh* skill was. Aranok enjoyed the thought that, if he did, he'd only be more scared.

"Allandria!" he called over his shoulder.

"Aranok?"

"This gentleman says he's going to cut my head off."

"Already?" She laughed. "We just got here."

All eyes were on them now. The tavern was silent, the crowd an audience. People were flooding out into the square, drinks still in hand. Others stood in shop doors, careful not to stray too far from safety. Windows filled with shadows.

Cargill's bravado disappeared in the half-light. "You...you're... we're on the same side!"

"Can't say I'm on the side of stealing from orphans." Aranok stared hard into his eyes. Fear had taken the man.

"We've got a warrant." Cargill pulled a crumpled mess from his belt and waved it like a flag of surrender. Now he was keen to do the paperwork.

Perhaps they'd get out of this without a fight after all. Unusually, he was grateful for the embellishments of legend. He'd once heard a story about himself, in a Leet tavern, in which he killed three demons on his own. The downside was that every braggart and mercenary in the kingdom fancied a shot at him, which was why he tended to travel quietly—and anonymously. But now and again...

"How much does he owe?" Aranok asked.

"Eight crowns." Cargill proffered the warrant in evidence. Aranok took it, glancing up to see where the rat had got to. He was too near the wall for Aranok's liking. The boy was vulnerable.

"Out here," Aranok ordered. "Now."

"With that crazy bitch shooting at me?" he whined.

"Thül!" Cargill snapped.

Thül slunk back out into the open, watching the balcony. Sensible boy. Though if this went on much longer, Allandria might struggle to see clearly across the square. He needed to wrap it up.

The warrant was clear. The business owed eight crowns in unpaid taxes and was to be closed unless payment was made in full. Eight bloody crowns. Hardly a king's ransom—except it was.

Aranok looked up at the boy. "What can you pay?"

"I've got three..." he answered.

"You've got three or you can pay three?"

"I've got three, sir."

"And food?"

The boy shrugged.

"A bit."

"Why do you care?" Thül sneered. "Is he yours?"

Aranok closed the ground between them in two steps, grabbed the thief by the throat and squeezed—enough to hurt, not enough to suffocate him. He pulled the angular, dirty face toward his own. Rank breath escaping yellow teeth made Aranok recoil momentarily.

"Why do I care?" he growled.

The thief trembled. He'd definitely underestimated Aranok's speed.

"I care because I've spent a year fighting to protect him. I care because I've watched others die to protect him." He stabbed a finger toward the young blacksmith. "And his parents died protecting you, you piece of shit!"

There were smatterings of applause from somewhere. He released the rat, who dropped to his knees, dramatically gasping for air. Digging some coins out of his purse, Aranok turned to the boy.

"Here. Ten crowns as a deposit against future work for me. Deal?"

The boy looked at the coins, up at Aranok's face and back down again. "Really?"

"You any good?"

"Yes, sir." The boy nodded. "Did a lot of Father's work. Ran the business since he went away."

"How is business?"

"Slow," the boy answered quietly.

Aranok nodded. "So do we have a deal?" He thrust his hand toward the boy again.

Nervously, the boy put down one sword and took the coins from Aranok's hand, tentatively, as though they might burn. He put the other sword down to take two coins from the pile in his left hand, looking to Aranok for reassurance. He clearly didn't like being defenceless. Aranok nodded. The boy turned to Cargill and slowly offered the hand with the bulk of the coins. Pleasingly, the thug looked to Aranok for approval. He nodded permission gravely. Cargill took the coins and gestured to Thül. They walked quickly back toward the castle, the thief looking up at Allandria as they passed underneath. She smiled and waved him off like an old friend.

Aranok clapped the boy on the shoulder and walked back toward the tavern, now very aware of being watched. It had cost him ten crowns to avoid a fight...and probably a lecture from the king. It was worth it. He really was tired. The crowd returned to life—most likely chattering in hushed tones about what they'd just seen. One man even offered a hand to shake as Aranok walked past; quite a gesture—to a *draoidh*. Aranok smiled and nodded politely but didn't take the hand. He shouldn't have to perform a grand, charitable act before people engaged with him.

The man looked surprised, smiled nervously and ran his hand through his hair, as if that had always been his intention.

Aranok felt a hand on his elbow. He turned to find the boy looking up at him, eyes glistening. "Thank you," he said. "I...thank you."

"What's your name?" Aranok asked. He tried to look comforting, but he could feel the heavy dark bags under his eyes.

"Vastin," the boy answered.

Aranok shook his hand.

"Congratulations, Vastin. You're the official blacksmith to the king's envoy."

Aranok righted his chair and dramatically slumped down opposite Allandria. The idiot was playing up the grumpy misanthrope, because every eye on the top floor was watching him. He looked uncomfortable. Secretly, she was certain he enjoyed it.

Allandria raised an eyebrow. "Was that our drinking money, by any chance?"

"Some of it..." he answered, more wearily than necessary.

Despite his reluctance, Allandria knew part of him had enjoyed the confrontation—especially since it ended bloodless. The man loved a good argument, if not a good fight—particularly one where he outsmarted his opponent. Not that she'd had any desire to kill the two thugs, but she would have, to save the boy. It was better that Aranok had been able to talk them down and pay them off.

"You could have brought my arrow back," she teased.

He looked down to where the arrow still stood, proudly embedded in the dirt. It was a powerful little memento of what had happened. Interesting that the boy had left it there too...maybe to remind people he had a new patron.

"Sorry." He smiled. "Forgot."

She returned the smile. "No you didn't."

"You missed, by the way."

Allandria stuck out her tongue. "I couldn't decide who I wanted to shoot more, the greasy little one or the big head in the fancy armour." The infuriating bugger had an answer to everything. But for all his arrogance, she loved him. He'd looked better, certainly. The war had been kind to no one. His unkempt brown hair was flecked with grey now—even more so the straggly beard he'd grown in the wild. Leathery skin hid under a layer of road dust; green eyes were hooded and dark. But they still glinted with devilment when the two sparred.

"Excuse me..." The serving girl arrived with their drinks. She was a slight, blonde thing, hardly in her teens if Allandria guessed right. Were there any adults left? Aranok reached for his coin purse.

"No, sir." The girl stopped him, nervously putting the drinks on the table. "Pa says your money's no good here."

Aranok looked up at Allandria, incredulous. When they'd come in, he wasn't even certain they'd be served. *Draoidhs* sometimes weren't. Innkeepers worried they would put off other customers. She'd seen it more than once.

Aranok tossed a coin on the table. "Thank you, but tell your pa he'll get no special treatment from the king on my say-so, or anyone else's."

It was harsh to assume they were trying to curry favour with the king now they knew who he was. Allandria hoped that wasn't it. She still had faith in people, in human kindness. She'd seen enough of it in the last year. Still, she understood his bitterness.

"No, sir," the girl said. "Vastin's my friend. His folks were good people. We need more people like you. Pa says so."

"Doesn't seem many places want people like me..."

"Hey..." Allandria frowned at him. He was punishing the girl for other people's sins now. He looked back at her, his eyes tired, resentful. But he knew he was wrong.

"Way I see it"—the girl shifted from foot to foot, holding one elbow protectively in her other hand—"you've no need of a blacksmith. A fletcher, maybe"—she glanced at Allandria—"but not a blacksmith. So I want more people like you."

Good for you, girl.

Allandria smiled at her. Aranok finally succumbed too.

"Thank you." He picked up the coin and held it out to her. "What's your name?"

"Amollari," she said quietly.

"Take it for yourself, Amollari, if not for your pa. Take it as an apology from a grumpy old man."

Grumpy was fair; *old* was harsh. He was barely forty—two years younger than Allandria.

Amollari lowered her head. "Pa'll be angry."

"I won't tell him if you don't," said Aranok.

Tentatively, the girl took the coin, slipping it into an apron pocket. She gave a rough little curtsy with a low "thank you" and turned to clear the empty mugs from a table back inside the tavern.

The girl was right. Aranok carried no weapons and his armour was well beyond the abilities of any common blacksmith to replicate or repair. He probably had no idea what he'd use the boy for.

Allandria raised the mug to her lips and felt beer wash over her tongue. It tasted of home and comfort, of warm fires and restful sleep. It really was good to be here.

"Balls." A crack resonated from Aranok's neck as he tilted his head first one way, then the other.

"What?" Allandria leaned back in her chair.

"I really wanted a night off."

"Isn't that what we're having?" She brandished her drink as evidence. "With our free beer?" She hoped the smile would cheer him. He was being pointlessly miserable.

Aranok rubbed his neck. "We have to see the king. He's being an arsehole."

A few ears pricked up at the nearest tables, but he hadn't said it loudly.

"It can't wait until tomorrow?" Allandria may have phrased it as a question, but she knew he'd be up all night thinking about it if they waited. "Of course it can't," she answered when he didn't. "Shall we go then?"

"Let's finish these first," Aranok said, lifting his own mug.

"Well, rude not to, really."

Her warm bed seemed a lot further away than it had a few minutes ago.